DEATH WITHOUT A FACE

Gripping the pistol in his right hand and fumbling for the switch with his left, Rabat struck the door with his shoulder. But before he could find the light, a heavy force slammed against him from the opposite side, knocking him backward. Excruciating pain wracked through his body as his quarry grabbed his hand and twisted crudely, snapping the wrist like a twig.

Rabat fired at chest-height, no longer caring whether anyone heard. He needed help and was — for the first time in his life — on the verge of calling for it. He pushed himself to his feet and retreated toward the partially open doorway. His hand shook; his knees quivered uncontrollably.

All was dark in the room and there was no sound now from the enemy. Suddenly Rabat sensed body heat by his arm. Shrieking wildly, he swung the gun around, but the knife-like edge of a hand collapsed his larynx before he could pull the trigger. Goggle-eyed, dropping his weapon and grasping his throat, he sank to his knees — never seeing the foot that fractured his skull — and killed him!

THE DEAD SURVIVOR

ZEBRA BOOKS
KENSINGTON PUBLISHING CORP.

ZEBRA BOOKS
are published by
KENSINGTON PUBLISHING CORP.
21 East 40th Street
New York, N.Y. 10016

Copyright © 1979 by Kensington Publishing Corp.

All rights reserved. No part of this book may be reproduced in any form or by any means without the prior written consent of the Publisher, excepting brief quotes used in reviews.

First Printing: April, 1979

Printed in the United States of America

PART ONE

Rage supplies arms.
—Virgil, *Aeneid*, I, 150

CHAPTER ONE

He zipped his reversible windbreaker to the neck, then felt for the elastic band of the nylon stocking beneath his black woolen cap. Yes, it was there. Everything was ready.

Fifty yards ahead the thin man disappeared around a corner and Henri Blanche quickened his step. He had noticed immediately how the fellow limped, how even the gentle tug of his leashed dachshund momentarily set him off balance. The man would be easy prey, easy. Trap him, shut up his hound with a swift kick, shove the knife against the cripple's neck. From the look of his clothes, he must be carrying several hundred francs on him. And then vanish, unidentifiable beneath the stocking mask.

As Blanche expected, the thin man was taking a shortcut—probably back to one of the hotels on the Avenue de Clichy. That was why Blanche picked this spot to lurk: the maze-like complexity of the Parisian streets forced walkers to take the narrow alleyways if they wanted to save themselves blocks of needless effort. And that was when Blanche went to work.

To his great surprise—and before he could pull down his disguise—he reached the entrance of the narrow pedestrian alley only to find the thin man coming out. But tonight he was not accepting failure; and with that inspired imagination so common among habitual liars, he said, *"Quelle heure est-il, m'sieu?"*

Now he had a good chance to look at his victim's face, to judge how much resistance could be expected, what sort of threats would be necessary to instill paralyzing fear. Didn't Le Beau once tell him that he was a dangerous man to know because no one could keep a secret from his huge round eyes?

The cripple, poised on his wooden cane as his dog sniffed at Blanche's trouser cuff, wore dark glasses, however; they hid his expression.

Blanche smiled elatedly, thinking the man blind.

But the thin man pulled up his jacket sleeve and said— in French heavily accented with German glottals—"Five minutes until one."

"Do you need some directions, m'sieu?" Concerned: "You seem a bit lost, if I might say so . . . and I know this section of Montmartre like I know my own mother."

"I am trying to get back to my hotel—the Concorde."

"Ah, yes. But you are a long way from there. You could take a taxi . . . but the dog." Blanche paused, laying a pulpy hand on the man's shoulder. "And it is rather late for the Metro. Here, I am going in that direction. Would you be kind enough to let me show you the way?"

The man nodded, smiling.

"This way, m'sieu," Blanche said, starting up the dark alley.

"Are you sure?"

Sure, Blanche was sure. Sure that the Hotel Concorde lay in the opposite direction.

"I was born within a mile of the hotel, m'sieu," he stated indignantly, as though to doubt his word was equivalent to casting aspersions on his manhood.

The alley was sheltered by tall office buildings dead for the weekend. They loomed above the walkway, almost blotting out the orange sky, crusty with banks of rain clouds. The only lights were dim shaded lamps above service exits, and their illumination actually seemed to darken the surrounding shadows. The alley was L-shaped; and at the apex, where one could watch traffic along two different streets, there was no light at all. Blanche could not have had a more effective work-area if he built it himself.

The man trailed behind Blanche, led on by his inquisitive dachshund who seemed enamored with Blanche's scent. Their footsteps rang hollowly down the blackened canyon, punctuated by the tapping of the wooden cane.

As they neared the turn, Blanche pulled back and took a position beside the cripple.

"Are you well, m'sieu? If I might say so, your leg must—"

"A bit tired, my friend," came the quick reply.

A dirty German, Blanche thought. A stupid Nazi pig who has returned to the scene of his crimes. I should kill him.

The thin man suddenly stumbled on the uneven paving stones and dropped to one hand and knee, yelling in pain. His dog immediately began barking, but stopped when Blanche jumped on its back, breaking the spine.

Inspector Layat stood in the alley, trying to light a Citane under the brim of his sporty chapeau—wrapped in clear plastic to save it from the steady March rain funneled down the passageway by the sheer walls of encroaching buildings—and failing miserably. He couldn't decide whether his matches or the tobacco were too wet, but the situation flustered him more than the sight of the two bodies starkly etched by emergency lamps.

He snapped the cigarette away and strolled into the merged twin pools of light, kneeling again beside the first inert form as a police photographer bustled around its companion. For the third time he lifted the brass tag at its throat and read: GRETCHEN DUMPLING SHMITZER VON HEINHEIM 2-23-73. A pedigreed dog, doubtlessly; that might prove very useful. People who could afford the nobility of the the canine world would certainly register the animal, either as a protection against theft, loss, or for its snob value; which meant the owner could be traced.

Layat traded places with the photographer and once more examined the human victim while the ambulance attendants impatiently stamped their cold feet, anxious to get in out of the weather and back to their canasta game at the hospital. The body was that of a broad-shouldered young man, apparently in good health at the time of his death. The cause of his untimely demise was only obvious when one lifted his windbreaker and saw the small bloody hole in his navel; and even that hardly seemed capable of reducing such a vigorous-looking man to a hunk of sprawling dead flesh.

"What's the story?" he asked, staring up at the coroner who stood just outside the circle of light.

Coroner Bontemp shrugged; then realizing that Layat probably could not see the gesture, he said, "I need more time with him. The puncture wound alone might do it. But since he has been dead, I would say, less than an hour, internal bleeding seems a weak case. Especially since he died on the spot—there being no signs of movement after the wound was inflicted. Do you know him?" His hand stabbed out of the darkness, pointing accusingly at the body.

"Yes. A small-time crook who called himself Berry du Lac, real name Henri Blanche. Ran for a while with a group calling itself Pomme Rouge, a bunch of misfits who started up a homosexual prostitution and blackmail racket."

"Do you think they were sweeping their cellar?"

Layat remained silent. He could easily have said no, but he didn't want to prejudice his honored objectivity. Several reasons told him that none of Blanche's former comrades were responsible for his death: first, the Pomme Rouge had eventually graduated into border-line legitimacy, led by a crafty lawyer named Pierre Le Beau. The gang was disbanded, its senior members forming a business conglomerate that bought into Mediterranean casinos and Parisian bordellos, Normandy fish-processing plants and French Alpine ski resorts. Junior members such as Blanche were given the boot unless they were willing to take jobs as croupiers, bodyguards, couriers or waiters. Blanche refused this less-adventurous life even though Le Beau had taken a personal liking to him. Perhaps the liking proved too physical for Blanche's taste. In any case, he decided to go solo—a decision which cost him two years in prison when he was caught attempting to mug a Swiss tourist just off the rue de Londres in August, 1972. Since his release he had been run up for charges ranging from illegal entry to—of course—mugging, but he escaped conviction in each instance. And Layat remembered that it was Le Beau who always turned up with bail money for his old friend.

The second reason which prompted Layat to doubt an internecine wrangle among crooks was the nylon stocking atop Blanche's head. He had evidently been planning a mugging tonight, only something went wrong. Certainly he would have known better than to play his game with an old acquaintance, someone from his Pomme Rouge days.

Reinforcing this notion was a third reason: the presence of the dachshund. Blanche would have had no use for it, so it obviously belonged to his intended victim. But if a gangster liked dogs, he chose one more defensively appropriate: a German shepherd, for example. (The word "German" momentarily clicked in Layat's mind, bringing to the foreground the animal's name-tag, its German connotations. The Inspector made a mental note to follow the lead.)

No, however one considered a reconstruction of the murder and delved for a motive, it did not point to a falling-out between fellow tradesmen.

"Can they take him?"

"What?" Layat felt the sudden rush of cold water down his back as he tilted his head. "God, what damned weather! Sure, take it and send me the autopsy results as soon as you have them."

"And the dog?"

"What about it?"

"Are you not interested in how it died?"

Layat puffed out his hollow cheeks, the urge for a cigarette growing stronger. "Broken back, I should think."

If Layat could have seen through the darkness streaked with rain pellets, he would have been surprised by the coroner's smile.

"No. It back was broken, yes. But someone snapped its neck too, apparently after."

"After what?"

"My guess is that this character here broke the animal's back, was killed in retribution—or whatever, and the owner then put his pet out of its misery by a quick twist." The coroner snapped his fingers. "Painless. Or so I am told."

By whom? Layat wondered. Who ever survives to bear witness to the experience? Does God have a long white beard? Did Lazarus ever say?

But he said, "Go haunt the morgue, Bontemp."

Pierre Le Beau was once an honest man. Years of dealing with the criminally-inclined, however, convinced him that great wealth comes only to those born to it or those willing to take advantage of others' weaknesses. Since his father had been a poor shopkeeper in Ambert and his mother belonged to an undistinguished family from Reims, Pierre and his three younger brothers inherited no more than their parents' combined genes. Still, he persevered in his search for fame and fortune, worked his way through college and law school, and entered into practice with the one brother who managed to both emulate him and survive the French catastrophe in Algeria.

By the mid-1960s the two Le Beaus were enjoying

substantial notoriety for their aggressive defense of hardened criminals, and few months passed without one of their cases being mentioned in the leading Paris newspapers. Though frequently making spectacles of themselves by their insistent, derogatory manner before the Court, the Le Beaus too often won their client's case, indulging in free-floating repartee with magistrates until a minor technicality broke the prosecution's case, appearing unduly prejudicial to the defendant.

This blatant strategy of intimidating the French system of justice, of bringing in ancillary matters which might or might not have a bearing on the case at hand but which implied that French law was a travesty of human rights, of haranguing prosecution witnesses—to the point of indecency—as to their qualifications for casting the first stone, earned the brothers the eternal damnation of their peers. Outcasts from the society of fellow attorneys, they graduated by necessity to the company of their clients, the mercenary relationship at last evolving into a symbiotic need.

When his brother Charles was killed near Trappes by a drunken motorist in 1969, Pierre renounced law for a more lucrative career in crime, overseeing the dissolution of the Pomme Rouge and organization of a financial combine that effectively siphoned ill-gotten gains into legitimate enterprises. His superior administrative ability made him a natural choice for Chairman of the Board, so that by 1975 he was undisputed head of a syndicate spanning the length and breadth of France and rivaling the Union Corse in its influence.

Because his new role demanded a low profile and because he did not care to involve his organization with the more brutal Corsican *mafiosi* based in France, Le

Beau prohibited the further use of violence by his men; when renewal of capital was necessary, he opened his contacts with the placid criminal arts: forgery, blackmail, burglary, and smuggling. Thus the police, already wary of his specialized knowledge of the law's intricacies and how they may be used to divert the course of justice, were extremely cautious in approaching him. Unless a dead body turned up on the premises of one of his syndicate holdings, Le Beau could be reasonably assured the *gendarmerie* would leave him in peace. He certainly paid them enough to keep their distance.

Tonight, alas, he wished the police had been bold and arrived for a *tête-à-tête*, a contribution, even for a few indelicate questions. Their appearance might have prevented this unsavory business.

He stared past the lattice-work on his bay windows, past the sheets of rain drenching the panes, and across the fields rolling endlessly away from his country-home outside Moret. Seen by cracking bolts of lightning, the gray and blue undulations seemed horribly Gothic—gangrenous pustules ready to explode. He realized with a twinge of alarm that he had never before thought of these beloved hills of Fontainebleau in quite this way, and wondered whether it was because the man behind him emanated a sense of sulphurous evil.

Turning, Le Beau tried to locate the man in the darkened study, letting his eyes adjust slowly to the change in light intensity; but all he saw amidst the dark leather pieces of furniture was the shape of his bodyguard in an easy-chair: motionless, head between his legs, a pool of vomit against the plush maroon carpet beneath him.

How had the man gotten inside the grounds? Le Beau

puzzled over the problem yet again; which—because the mystery appeared unsolvable—made him increasingly nervous. The grounds surrounding the small chateau were enclosed by low brick walls surmounted by wire sensors. True, the monitor was off for the holiday weekend and Le Beau was unable to find an immediate replacement, but an automatic alarm should have sounded just the same if the stranger came over a wall. The single gate at the northeast corner of the house was locked at sundown and a sentry posted inside with an adjoining kennel of guard-dogs. So why had the stupid curs not howled their fool heads off—as they did every other night, whether with reason or not—when they scented the stranger? And now Jean, his personal bodyguard, a victim of one of the oldest tricks in the book: the houselights went out, Jean started to investigate and had been chopped on the head. The stranger dragged him into the study and propped him up until he began vomiting and lost consciousness again. Le Beau had good reason to wonder about the value of his protection.

Then the demands the stranger had made. What was he planning? Something Le Beau and the Corporation might want a piece of? Of was it all perhaps an elaborate police trap? How could the stranger convince him of his sincerity? Did, in fact, he really want to be convinced? More importantly (since the protection Le Beau hired to fend off unwanted guests appeared to be sleeping through the storm), did he dare refuse the stranger? The syndicate head had a horror of dying; he could philosophically accept the giving up of one's spirit because he was Catholic, but the thought of physical suffering before final release terrorized him.

He spoke into the turgid darkness, hoping the man would betray himself by answering. "Is the weather as bad in Paris?"

"Stick to the point," a voice whispered in his ear, shocking him. The stranger had been hidden by the window curtains and now stood behind Le Beau.

Le Beau wondered whether he had invited anyone to the chateau tonight, whether he could expect company— and rescue—from a business associate, one of his mistresses with her bi-sexual escort, an operator from his underground network who wanted advice that could not be given over the phone, perhaps a junior executive who hadn't gotten into the swing of things yet and needed instruction. There was little chance of the latter, though, for he made a pact with himself years before not to let the tribulations of running the Corporation interfere with his weekends here in the country. His secretary—who doubled as his bodyguard—would have mentioned any appointments if they existed.

"Very well, m'sieu, I will stick to the point—as you put it," he added forcibly, condescending to the man's Norman accent. Then raising himself to his best oratorical manner, he went on: "But what is the meaning of your illegal entry into my home? If you are indeed a good friend of my own good friend Henri Blanche, I would be only too pleased to give you my attention at any reasonable hour. There is no necessity in these intrigues. Let me switch on the light and—"

"No. The electricity has been switched off at the mains. Just tell me how soon I can collect what I want."

"You break into my house and expect—"

"How soon?"

Le Beau paused. Since the man was obviously an

educated compatriot from Normandy despite his crude attempts at low French, he would be relatively easy to trace and negate—if that became necessary. If he was a policeman trying to gather evidence against Le Beau and the Corporation, his forcible entry and bludgeoning of the bodyguard would destroy the prosecution's case.

"It is very dangerous, m'sieu. And it costs money."

"How much?"

"Two thousand francs for an unmarked, unregistered gun. The passports will demand great skill, more time. Three thousand francs apiece."

Le Beau felt certain the prices would discourage the man. After all, he was dressed in shabby clothes—a point which the former attorney, whose tailor-made suits came from London's Savile Row—noticed immediately. For that reason he had first thought the stranger a thief. Yet the man gave no indication that the prices were beyond his expectations—or that he was unwilling to pay them.

"How soon?"

"The money must be paid in advance," Le Beau said irritatedly.

"I understand. Now how soon can I have them?"

"Two weeks. Say, within two weeks. Before the passports can be completed, however, you will have to provide the designer with particulars."

A large folded envelope suddenly materialized under Le Beau's aquiline nose. He accepted it and began to break the seal, but the man told him to wait until he had gone.

"Inside, you will find a detailed description of each passport holder as well as a corresponding photograph to be stamped. Also included are the weapon requirements: a Beretta Model 195 with sound-moderator, plenty of ammunition, and a shoulder-holster. I will also need a Browning P-35 with the same auxiliaries."

"But the money, m'sieu," Le Beau insisted.

"With the instructions are three 5000-franc notes. This more than covers your projected production costs. But to guarantee delivery I will pay the same amount to the bearer upon receipt of said items. Is that fair?"

Le Beau stood speechless.

"A final point: the delivery spot. Do you know Rouen?"

"I have been there, yes."

"There is a viewing area that overlooks the city from the east. It is just off the Route de la Corniche. On the Twenty-eighth of this month at 10:30 p.m. a white Fiat 134 will be parked next to the enclosure ramp. The right rear door will be unlocked. The items are to be placed on the floor between the front and rear seats. On the dashboard above the steering column will be an envelope such as this, and it will belong to you. Understood?"

"Certainly."

"In the unlikely event you fail to comply with these instructions or attempt to enjoin the police to seek me, I suggest you remind yourself of tomorrow's obituary."

"Tomorrow? Whose?" Le Beau asked, frightened.

"Don't you wonder how I found you? How . . ." The sepulchrous voice trailed into silence, a silence more meaningful than anything the stranger could have said.

"We have a bargain then?"

"Yes, yes, a bargain." Le Beau was already calculating his profits and choosing which counterfeiter he would employ for the passport job.

The sword-cane which the stranger had used to menace Le Beau slid quietly into its wooden sheath, and the man turned to the bay windows. Before Le Beau could say anything else, a window had been flung open and the stranger disappeared through it.

The head of the Corporation stared out for five minutes, but his visitor had been swallowed by the night.

And still the storm raged on, thunder shook the Business Achievement Awards on the walls of the study, and lightning crackled above the distant hills.

Inspector Layat got the call at almost the same moment the stranger passed Le Beau's kennel of drugged Doberman pinschers and the guard slumping unconscious against a wall of the tiny gatehouse.

"Inspector? Bontemp. Said you wanted a rush on the Blanche murder."

"Go ahead."

"Blanche died of massive internal hemorrhaging. We missed a lot of it because the heavy rains washed most of the external bleeding from the body. Or so I suspect. Blanche must have been stuck with a corkscrew. Insides all ripped up. I'll send a full report later in the morning. Get any sleep yet?"

Layat ignored the question. His wife had called him ten minutes before and asked the same question—though with more peevishness. Could he help it if some small-time loser decided to croak just before he went off duty?

"So he was finished with a corkscrew. Is *that* your conclusion? Might it not have been a can-opener—or possibly a cheese-grater? Give me more, Bontemp, before we both lose our jobs."

The coroner sighed deeply into the telephone as if tonight had been just too much for him.

"A sharp instrument, straight like an ice-pick but thicker and longer. The killer thrusted it in and twisted, ripping major arteries, the left kidney, liver, and upper intestines. Adrenal shock set in and Blanche was as good as dead when the weapon came out."

"Rounded blade?"

"Rectangular. The type you find on fencing foils, only it must have been stiff—no flex. By the way, you trace that dog-tag yet? Never mind. I should have realized that nobody but us zombies are awake at this hour."

"Actually, I have traced the dog's owner—a certain Fraulein Ingrid von Heinheim from Cologne, presently staying at the Hotel Commodore on the Boulevard Haussmann."

"Did you check out her whereabouts tonight?"

"It wasn't necessary. She reported her dachshund stolen nearly four hours before Blanche's body was found by the Moulin Rouge dancers." Layat had already surmised the dog may have been snatched (would a killer leave his pooch at the crime scene wearing an identification tag?), and so he contacted the police coding center and asked whether any reports on a particular dachshund had come through.

No, Fraulein von Heinheim did not know Henri Blanche and was left cold by news of his death. Her dog's demise, however, crushed her and she viciously cursed Paris until Layat finally grew tired of nodding in agreement and departed back to the station. At least she had been sure of one thing, she said as he was closing the door behind him.

"What is that, mademoiselle?"

The dog-napper was a tall woman with short blonde hair. The German woman had let Gretchen off her leash as they went window-shopping along the Boulevard Hausmann. She hated being near the dog when it pissed

19

on a car-tire or lamp-post or fouled a store entrance. Gretchen had gotten fifty or so feet ahead when suddenly this blonde woman darts from a pedestrian alley, scoops up Gretchen in her arms, and disappears.

"What do you think of her story?" Bontemp asked, resigned to the same routinely curious questions with which he plagued every inspector he had known during his last twenty-three years as police surgeon and coroner.

"I believe it. But what does it all add up to? Do you think a woman could have murdered Blanche?"

"Not that way," came the quick reply. "Not much sign of a struggle, right? It's as though Blanche had several attackers, some holding him down while another perforated his abdomen."

Layat replaced his half-eaten liverwurst sandwich in its cellophane wrapping and sourly looked at the phone.

"Of course, an extremely powerful man could have done the job. But not a woman alone, my good Layat, not a woman."

The Inspector thanked him and hung up, then sat back in his office chair and watched the flow of traffic outside. So far he had gotten nowhere. Still, the case was new and after a good sleep he would doubtlessly see some way of linking the dog theft and homicide.

Yet he remained worried as he drove home to Villeneuve on the N5. Irritated by the presence of the dog in the Montmartre alley, his mind groped vainly for a plausible motive for the murder. Not that Henri Blanche would be missed: his loss actually pleased Layat who knew exactly what kind of man he had been; but killers must be caught and imprisoned or someday they might murder an innocent. And, too, the mystery tantalized his personal curiosity. What kind of killer ruthlessly minced his victim's guts, then mercifully snapped the neck of a dog in agony? Was the female dog-snatcher his partner? Had she witnessed the murder? Then could the killer be traced through an accomplice?

Layat stayed in the outside lane for the Villeneuve exit, while two miles ahead a pale blue Fiat 134 headed in his direction. The car's color was indeed pale blue, though under the reflection of a waxing moon it looked white. It passed the exit for Villeneuve without slowing and continued on toward the heart of Paris.

CHAPTER TWO

The yellow and green puzzle-pieces on the blue foil were at first unappreciated by Mrs. Helen Jacobi. Her eyes were focused on a tiny speck between the thick layers of plasti-glass windows and her thoughts centered on her husband Michael whom she had not seen for two months.

A technical advisor for a British building firm, Michael Jacobi had been sent off to handle one of the firm's largest orders: the construction of a small machinery plant on the island of Gozo. With the children still at school in Chelsea, he had regretfully been forced to leave his wife behind until the summer vacation.

The IRA fixed that, however, by starting an all-out campaign against the English populace, bombing schools as well as banks, government offices, pubs, and department stores. London, as usual, was the terrorists' favorite target, the heart (if not the soul) of the nation. So Helen Jacobi contacted her husband and told him she and the kids would arrive the next Friday afternoon. Not to worry: they'd be a hundred times safer with him than in London.

Both the British Airways and Air Malta flights direct to Luqa were booked solid, so Mrs. Jacobi made reservations with Alitalia. She was desperate to get away from the flat in Carlyle Square even if it meant a stop in Rome and two extra hours of flying time before reaching Malta.

And even then we were held up several more hours in Rome by an air controllers' slowdown, she thought now, irritated by the Italians' indifferent attitude toward time. Would Michael still be waiting for them at the airport?

The possibility that he might have decided they had delayed their trip startled her out of her reverie, and she turned to her two sons, Geoffrey and Terence, who were flinching in their seats while trying to get a better view out the window.

She followed their gaze to the islands below: Malta, 95 square miles of limestone plateau tipping toward the east, a fortress of soft rock that had defied the rage of assaulting invaders for over three thousand years; Gozo, a quarter of Malta's size but just as beautiful; and then a splatter of smaller islands joining the two, chunks of rock that suddenly vanished as the plane swung around to begin its descent to the 2377-meters long asphalt landing-strip at Luqa, five miles from the capital, Valletta.

Checking her children's seatbelts for the third time, Mrs. Jacobi noticed the girl across the aisle. She was removing a double-headed tambourine from her carry-on luggage, and Mrs. Jacobi pleasantly remembered how the girl had been joined by three young men playing a lute, zither and harmonica shortly after take-off from Rome's Leonardo di Vinci Airport. They said they were musicians hired for a week's work at a Valletta nightclub.

Mrs. Jacobi had wondered why anyone would want to listen to such cacophonous music—if it could be called that. At least the quartet played with youthful enthusiasm and had helped calm the nerves of queasy passengers by an obvious desire to please.

Now, however, the girl appeared uninterested in playing again. She took a nail-file from her purse and stabbed the skin of the shallow drum, then slashed it diametrically.

Mrs. Jacobi watched in amazement as the girl removed a metallic-green egg from inside the instrument.

The three male musicians were also active at the front of the aircraft. They had uncased their instruments again, then torn apart the lute and zither to get at pistols. The harmonica player was waving his mouth-organ above his head; a wire now extended from each end, one strand connected to a small transistor battery.

Before anyone could think of reacting, one of the men ran forward with his gun, disappearing behind the fireproof beige curtain that separated First and Tourist Class compartments. The harmonica player confidently strolled to the front of the Tourist section and jerked the curtain aside, while the third man nodded his gun at the girl across from Mrs. Jacobi and she headed toward the stewardesses' station at the rear of the plane.

The passengers sat frozen in their seats, buckled down and disbelieving. It seemed incredible that the plane would be hijacked just as it was making its landing approach. And to be hijacked by such personable young people, darkly handsome and free-spirited! Incredible!

Soon a voice, unnaturally loud, boomed over the plane's intercom system: "Good evening, ladies and gentlemen," it said in Italian. "This is Captain Montani speaking. We will be landing at Luqa Airport in a few minutes, and I would remind all passengers to observe the No Smoking sign and remain seated during our final approach and while we taxi on the runway. The present temperature at Luqa is 74-degrees Fahrenheit, with a cool wind running five knots out of the northeast. The time is currently 7:23 on the Maltese islands. For the entire crew, I would like to thank you for flying Alitalia, and hope we again have the chance of serving you."

That was all. Not a word about a hijacking, not a single warning to stay calm and don't do anything foolish. Smiles broke out among the passengers as the whine of the landing struts disturbed the sudden silent deceleration of the DC-9 and the plane seemed to hang motionless in the air. They felt reassured by the pilot's measured tones.

The feeling of relief did not last long. As the plane touched ground, the armed man at the front of the Tourist section took aim and fired. The bullet wounded a man in the first row and probably would have wedged in the abdomen of the woman behind him if her metal fold-down dinner tray had not spent the force of the projectile so that it rolled harmlessly into the woman's lap. She screamed; then fainted, falling forward.

"You are now under the guidance of the General Command of the Popular Front for the Liberation of Palestine," the young man yelled, lifting the smoking barrel of his revolver. He spoke in English, which was translated into Italian by the girl who stood at the rear holding her grenade. "Nothing will happen to you unless you resist or fail to follow instructions. Your release will depend entirely upon the attitude of the Italian Government, so pray that they care about you in Rome.

"First, you will hand your passports to my comrade when she asks for them.

"Secondly, you will not leave your seat without gaining permission.

"Thirdly, no food will be served to you after dark. All the lights inside the plane will go off except for those above the front and rear exits, and this will make it impossible to serve food until tomorrow morning—by which time you will probably be free anyway and can eat where you want.

"Fourthly, this is no joke. We can and will blow this plane unless certain conditions are met and met quickly."

The harmonica player was again at the doorway separating the compartments. He conferred briefly with the spokesmen, evidently to find out why the young man had wounded a passenger, then he disappeared forward.

Soon a new voice came over the audio-system and repeated what the first spokesman had said, and for the first time some of the passengers began to think that the terrorists were not as coordinated as they might have been. Why was it necessary that the gunman in Tourist Class give his instructions when they were to be repeated for First Class passengers—and when use of the DC-9's sound-system would be more efficient? Why was the passenger shot? He certainly had shown no hostility toward the terrorists. And though they were not responsible for the late arrival of the Alitalia flight, why had the terrorists waited until the last moment to seize control of the plane?

Dom Lucas dressed quickly, trying to decide whether he should tell his wife the true reason for his forced departure in the middle of their love-making. Could she be trusted to keep her mouth shut? Or did it matter, since in a few hours the news of a skyjacking over Malta would be spread across the front page of every Western newspaper?

"Dom?" Eloise came into the bathroom where her husband was hurriedly checking the respectability of his beard stubble and wondering if he had time to shave.

He gave her a sidelong glance in the mirror and knotted his tie.

"You'd better put something on, love. Newsmen may be arriving soon."

"What!"

"Some terrorists seized today's flight from Rome. They want immediate action from a government official. Since the Prime Minister is in London and the President has chosen to take his vacation in Zurich, that leaves me to mind the store."

"Terrorists!" his wife croaked, gathering the flimsy material of her negligee to her throat. "What could they have against our country?"

"Do these types really need motives?" he answered, swinging past her and heading for the hall closet. "Look out and see if my driver is here yet."

Having shot the male passenger, the terrorist was apologetic afterward. He solicitously stood by as a stewardess bandaged the flesh wound, and even ordered his female companion to fetch some medicinal alcohol from the plane's first-aid station.

In the cockpit, Captain Redento Montani, a twenty-eight year veteran who had once flown bombing missions over Malta from Sicily, calmly relayed the instructions given to him by the armed terrorist standing behind his co-pilot. He had taken procedural lessons in how to react to a skyjacker, and so the present experience did not outwardly upset him. Though he held annoying doubts about his government's ability to deal with this situation, he wisely refrained from giving the terrorists an opinion on whether the Italians would render up their prisoners without a challenge.

"Can you guarantee the safty of my passengers if they offer no resistance?" he asked the young man whom the harmonica player had referred to as Raoul.

"No." Raoul grinned, displaying teeth so white that they reflected the DC-9's instrument-panel. "Suppose the plane is attacked. How can we be responsible for what happens then?"

The air-traffic controller's voice again came over the radio, announcing that Malta's Foreign Minister had arrived and would be conducting negotiations.

"Put him on," Raoul said, sneering.

Dom Lucas' deep baritone filled the cramped cockpit. "Captain Montani? My name is Dom Lucas. I am Foreign Minister of Malta and have instructions from my Prime Minister and a senior deputy of your government to negotiate for the release of the passengers and crew of your plane."

"Never mind all that shit!" Raoul screamed into the open microphone. "The General Command has already given its demands to the traffic controller. You have a list. If all the requirements are not filled within two hours, we throw a corpse out of the plane."

"Could you please repeat your demands? I don't seem to be able to find . . ."

"We want spotlights put around the plane—but facing

away from it. And don't tell me you can't find any, because you can rip out some runway lights if nothing else.

"Then we want all air traffic diverted from Malta. No planes land at Luqa or we shoot some hostages. And no helicopters flying over. Understand?

"Also, we want the three freedom-fighters released who are now being held by the Italian fascists. They are Abdullah Habete, Ali Mustafa Eyam, and Fuad al-Kabeem."

"This cannot possibly be accomplished in two hours," the Foreign Minister expostulated.

"We will give the Italians until daybreak to collect their prisoners and fly them here. In the meantime we want the lights put up and the plane refueled."

Sitting in Luqa's Control Tower, Dom Lucas turned to the traffic-controller seated beside him and smiled wryly, then spoke again into the microphone.

"First, it would help if we knew where you intended going—since the pilot will need flight path information—and whether or not you will release your hostages once the three men are brought here."

"Do not worry about that!" came the terrorist's angry reply. "We will tell you in good time."

"Secondly, how can the Italians fly the three men to Luqa if you refuse to allow any planes to land?"

There was a moment's silence. Obviously the sky-jacker had not completed his plans for the political blackmail or he would have avoided contradicting himself.

"We will allow only one plane to land, and it must not arrive before daybreak—carrying our compatriots."

"Anything else?"

No reply.

Suddenly inspired, Dom Lucas argued, "When the news of this event reaches the outside world—and I can assure you that it already has—journalists from many countries will want to come to Malta to learn firsthand what your grievances are and what your organization is trying to accomplish besides the release of the prisoners. How will they get here before you leave, unless you allow planes to bring them?"

"You are trying to trick us! We will not allow fascist commandos to come near this plane! Understand?" After a considerable pause: "If all the other conditions are met, we will allow planes to land for the next two hours. But the spotlights are a priority, Lucas, understand? You will arrange for adequate lighting and have the plane refueled within those two hours or we throw you a body. That is all."

The transmission ended, and Dom Lucas settled back in his chair, somewhat satisfied with himself.

Lucas wanted to leave as many options open as he could for the Italian commandos—and he thought he had done that. He also assumed the commandos were already being briefed on the situation and would not want spotlights keeping them at bay all night. Of course the truck that came to refuel the DC-9 could carry commandos, but they might not arrive before the terrorists' two hour dead-line ran out.

"Where's the telephone?" he demanded.

It was exactly 9:00 p.m.

Italy's Defense Minister, Emilio Napolita, drummed quietly on his desk-top, then impatiently got up and went to the window, staring at the long lines of night traffic inching along the Via Nazionale. Did the drivers know or care what was happening at Malta's Luqa Airport, what would happen to the image of their country if the hijacked plane and its passengers were not freed?

No. They might say their prayers to the Virgin Mary and hope for the hostages' deliverance, but nothing more. *"Che io posso fare?"* they would shout indignantly, lifting beseeching arms till their bodies formed a cross. Stupifying innocence would beam from their eyes. They would wonder why the three *prigionieri* were simply not freed immediately. How easy the solution!

Yes, how easy. A light appeared on his white phone. He picked up the receiver, listened for a moment, then grunted: "Yes, we are ready to send half of them. Twenty-five. Transport jet to Catania then helicopters to Valletta. . . . Because the two hours have expired. It would have been impossible to coordinate the necessary elements, brief the Squadra Anti-Commando, and get everyone on the island before the terrorists stopped all air traffic. They have threatened to kill a passenger if . . . The Maltese were forced to refuel the plane and surround it with protective lights. If the lights should go out—no matter the reason—a passenger dies. We could not take that sort of responsibility. . . . Well, sir, I would have to say not before three this morning. I have to allow some time for the transfer of prisoners and the SAC. The Maltese Foreign Minister has been negotiating since the beginning—as you must know—and perhaps he will have some luck. . . . Thank you, sir."

Napolita hung up even as he grabbed the green phone. Having pressed a coded sequence of buttons, he said immediately: "Proceed as planned. The Premier has given his best wishes. Further instructions, if necessary, will be radioed to you in transit. *Buona fortuna.*"

Mrs. Jacobi wondered what her husband was thinking. He was surely sitting somewhere in the flat, dimly-lit terminal and smoking himself to death. She saw figures, shadows, goblins dancing against the walls of the outer buildings in the distance. Rescuers? Or Michael going crazy with worry?

The terrorists had moved the five passengers in First Class to the rear cabin (to simplify their own security measures), then extinguished all lights inside the craft. A middle-aged woman, who was discovered brazenly trying to send signals with her cigarette-lighter, proved unmanageable until she was beaten and—to everyone's relief—passed out. She was the only passenger who did not blindly obey the skyjackers' orders.

Some kind of negotiations were going on up front. Mrs. Jacobi could hear voices sometimes raised in anger, at other times placating.

If the authorities had succumbed to the terrorists' demands so far, furnishing lights and refueling the plane, wasn't it obvious that *all* the demands would be fulfilled and that release could only be a few hours away?

News of the skyjacking traveled quickly, and major news agencies without correspondents on Malta scrambled to get some of them there before the terrorists' two hour dead-line ran out. Small charter airlines did a raving business, and saw no reason to inform their frantic clients that sea-planes could land anywhere along the coast and at any time.

By 3 a.m. an army of journalists and photographers

were assembled on the ground floor of Luqa's Administration Building, anxiously awaiting the promised press bulletin. Naturally they were barred from the northern end of the airport's shorter runway where the Alitalia DC-9 now sat, invisible behind the glare of scavenged lights. Though understanding the reasons for being forbidden near the area, the reporters were made even more hungry for news by the cloak of mystery that had settled over the skyjacking.

Dom Lucas, his face gaunt and blue with beard stubble, spoke with his public relations officer just out of earshot of the impatient newshawks.

"You know what has happened, John. The terrorists want three specific prisoners released from jail in Italy and brought to Luqa. Once the prisoners are here, the hostages will be released. Or so the skyjackers say. But since they apparently intend to fly away afterward, they will have to keep the pilot and co-pilot.

"Actually, the leader seems a bit confused, and I wonder how much planning went into this operation. Perhaps after a bit more negotiating he will see the futility of his ways. I doubt that, but we can hope for the best.

"The Italian Government has offered its full cooperation in this matter. Malta will be only too grateful for any help, any advice in securing the quick release of the hostages."

"What about the Italians? Do they plan to release their prisoners?"

"I don't know, John. I'm not going to try to second-guess them. And you'll want to steer clear of any questions on that matter. We don't need to ruin relations between Malta and Italy by preaching to

Rome. Understood?"

"Don't you find it rather remarkable that the skyjackers have not demanded more?"

"Yes, I do. But I'm careful not to mention it to them. And don't you mention it to those reporters or I'll brain you."

"What about the hostages? The press is always anxious to know how many liters of blood were spilled. What do I tell them?"

"I believe one man was wounded in the arm during an initial scuffle, but he has received treatment and is in good spirits. The captain tells me the passengers are, generally speaking, controlling their natural anxieties exceptionally well. One woman became hysterical and has been put under some form of sedation. The skyjackers evidently want her off, but refuse to allow an ambulance or ramp near the plane. I hope to convince them to relent."

"How?"

"By promising that the medical personnel who come to take the woman off will not be disguised policemen or use any force whatsoever; that their sole mission will be to get her to a hospital as quickly as possible."

"Can I quote you on that?"

"Heavens, no, John! Are you crazy? Tell them the bare essentials—some copy to make their editors happy—and keep the rest under your hat. These kinds of negotiations cannot be dealt with publicly."

"Mr. Lucas?"

The p.r. officer's press bulletin ended with a general stampede for the rows of phone booths in the Arrivals Terminal, but the stoop-shouldered reporter had come instead to the Foreign Minister who was about to take an elevator up to the air-traffic controllers' station.

"I'm sorry, but I'm not available for comment. And you are not allowed in this part of the building."

The man shrugged and turned as if to go; then he said, almost apologetically, "I know. I only wanted a personal interview with you." He stared sorrowfully through thick-lensed glasses. "I am so sorry to have bothered you," and he began to walk toward the exit.

"Wait." Dom Lucas' curiosity—and vanity—was captured by the reporter's soft, unobtrusive, unassuming manner. "Why would you want a personal interview with me? Because of this?" and he waved his arm in the general direction of the hijacked plane.

The reporter smiled warmly. "I would be lying if I said no. Yet it is more than that. Naturally I am interested in how you are negotiating with the terrorists, how you have been able to handle their dead-lines so adroitly and forced them to give the Italian authorities more time to collect their prisoners. Few of my colleagues seem to realize the value of a skilled negotiator when dealing with fanatics like these."

Dom Lucas protested modestly, then asked the reporter's name.

"Federico Basilia of Madrid's *El Sol*."

"Ah, I thought I recognized your accent. You speak English very well, Señor Basilia."

"I have been posted in New York City for the past seven years, covering the United Nations and regional politics."

"And this interview. I don't understand—"

"You are not as little known as your island country, I assure you, sir. I returned to Madrid a fortnight ago for a vacation with my parents. I am not married, I don't mind telling you. When my editor phoned me tonight and ordered me onto a waiting plane, I would have refused to leave if he had not said that you were handling negotiations with the terrorists. Palestinians, aren't they?"

"We are not yet sure they are Palestinians, only that they claim to represent a splinter group of the PFLP."

"My apologies. Anyway, having read your articles on Malta as part of the Praetorship of Sicily and on the Mycenaen ruins at Hal Saflieni in magazines such as *History Today*, *National Geographic*, and *World Survey*, I very much wanted to meet this man of many faces, this multi-talented diplomat."

"You embarrass me, Señor Basilia." Dom Lucas made no effort to escape these accolades, however. He knew that the Foreign Minister of a nation smaller than the Isle of Wight and with less than 320,000 inhabitants had few if any opportunities to make his presence known to the rest of the world. Perhaps it would be wise to invite Federico Basilia into the Control Tower where he could witness the negotiations.

"May I see your press card, please?" He examined the worn ID at some length, hoping Señor Basilia would not remark on his ability to read Spanish—since he couldn't.

"I do this only as a precaution. One never knows . . ."

"I quite understand, sir, and would be amazed if you were to openly speak with me about your public and private life without first verifying my credentials."

Dom Lucas was convinced they would get along famously.

At 6:30 a.m. the army helicopters carrying twenty-five members of the Squadra Anti-Commando finally arrived at Valletta. By then it was too late to mount a night attack, a circumstance which Italian Defense Minister Emilio Napolita had secretly been hoping for—since he was reluctant to commit his elite force to an operation on foreign soil. He thought the matter should be left to the Maltese—regardless of the nationality of plane or passengers. Why risk the reputation of his men unless absolutely necessary? And by dawn perhaps the situation would have resolved itself one way or the other.

After a last-minute lobbying effort by the Israeli Ambassador to Italy, Rome decided to send the three desired prisoners to Luqa, but to hold them at least until all the Alitalia passengers were freed; and then only if the terrorists could not be overpowered. Since Malta's regular land forces and part-time territorial army were untrained in anti-terrorist operations, any attempt to storm the hijacked plane would necessarily have to be made by the Italians.

By 8:00 a.m. the terrorists had set their dead-line back four times. This was understandable: all their conditions had been met except the transfer of the three prisoners to the DC-9, daylight would remove any surprise advantages a commando group might have, and they were able to speak with their comrades over the plane's radio. They were convinced the Italians would hand over their prisoners as soon as the hostages were released.

Federico Basilia sat beside Malta's Foreign Minister as the latter conducted what he believed to be the final negotiations for the transfer of hostages and prisoners. During the past five hours the two men had developed a common rapport, discovering mutual interests and shared ideals. Dom Lucas was impressed with the intelligence and wit of his new friend and invited him to his home when this ugly affair ended. He regretted that they could not have met under more fortunate circumstances.

"We are waiting," Raoul radioed, using his hackneyed phrase yet again to express his impatience. "Where are our comrades?"

"You have spoken to them, you know they are here. We are presently trying to arrange transportation for them to the plane," Lucas said into his transmitter. "Be patient. Haven't we followed your orders thus far?"

"Transportation! Let them walk to the plane!"

"But we will need buses to remove the passengers from the area. After being cramped in the plane for over twelve hours they won't be in any condition to walk away."

Then came Raoul's clincher: "The General Command has altered its plans. As a humanitarian gesture the women and children will be allowed to leave, but the men must stay—to insure that we are allowed to depart once our three comrades are aboard."

Lucas turned to the Italian commando leader standing behind him and frowned. "How does this change your plans, Lieutenant?"

Meni Vestanzi lifted a bushy eyebrow. His orders had been exact, unequivocating, couched in the negative: Don't do anything that might endanger the lives of the passengers. Don't let the Maltese stall the terrorists until a dead-line becomes a death-notice. Don't be accused of interference in the negotiations unless advice is requested.

"It would help to know when the remaining passengers and crew will be released—and where. Few governments want to handle skyjackers anymore," Vestanzi said.

"Do we have a deal is what I'm asking. I doubt if the terrorists will accept any further delays."

"May I suggest something?"

Everyone looked in astonishment at the hunched reporter from Madrid's *El Sol*, scribbling his notes in short-hand even as he spoke.

"Of course, Federico!" Dom Lucas was anxious to humor the man who would bring his name before the world—but not so foolish as to relinquish credit for any innovative ideas. "What do you think we should do?" he said condescendingly.

When Federico Basilia finished speaking, heads were nodding sagely. His plan was the obvious one, the most likely to satisfy both parties at once. No one suggested, however, that it should have occurred to the negotiating team long before now. The Foreign Minister did not accept criticism light-heartedly and Meni Vestanzi was much too bland to possess an imagination.

"I will contact the Prime Minister," Dom Lucas finally said, breaking a long silence. "Then we can act upon his response."

"One of my men should go."

"Under the circumstances, Lieutenant Vestanzi, perhaps Señor Basilia is correct in arguing that he is the better choice. Your commandos have certain political realities to abide by. Since Señor Basilia is not here as a representative of a specific government, he is immune to these realities. And because of that, the skyjackers are more likely to trust him. In which case," the Honorable Dom Lucas added, "the unlikely is less likely to happen. Señor Basilia will be playing the game straight."

CHAPTER THREE

Another drop of sweat hit the microphone. Dom Lucas leaned back and pulled a damp monogrammed handkerchief from his jacket-pocket and wiped his forehead.

It was 9:07 a.m. and a final agreement had at last been reached with the terrorists. Now all he could do was await developments and pray that none of the Italian commandos botched the deal by staging some last-minute heroics.

The leader of the skyjackers had been surprisingly understanding. Evidently he realized the Maltese were in no mood to make fools of themselves by attacking the plane. Nevertheless, he had warned that anyone approaching the plane without prior approval from him would find heaps of corpses below the exit-door. After these many delays and Raoul's increasingly shrill voice, no one could doubt that he meant what he said; certainly they had no intention of testing his promise of retaliation.

At 9:30 a.m. Federico Basilia left his briefing session, escorted by Lieutenant Vestanzi. The chief commando had instructed him on what to look for when he was inside the aircraft: the number of terrorists, their composition (male, female), number and types of weapons, sabotage preparations if any (plastic explosives near the exits and above the wing joints, smell of gasoline in the aisles), and the state (emotional and physical) of passengers and crew.

"Remember," Vestanzi reiterated, "stay just long enough to get the woman out and not long enough to arouse the terrorists' suspicions. We don't want anything unexpected to happen.

"Personally, I don't think you are the right man. But you look the part, you have a photographic memory, and Foreign Minister Lucas insists that you go. Very well, you have your orders. Do not deviate from them in the slightest. Get the woman out, drive back to Hanger One, and report. The actual exchange of hostages for our prisoners will be handled by us."

Dom Lucas anxiously watched the middle-aged reporter step into the jeep, the Italian commando leader standing beside the man, talking to him.

Lucas wondered whether he had made the right decision in letting Basilia go. Yet the newsman's arguments were so precisely delineated, so sensible, and with just the correct tincture of astuteness, that Lucas had felt obligated to listen. Even the Prime Minister, having arrived by helicopter from Siracusa only an hour before, was swiftly convinced there was no need to endanger a Maltese when the Spaniard qualified voluntarily for the task. And since no extreme danger attended it as long as the reporter kept his wits about him, why not allow him the opportunity?

The terrorist leader sounded relieved when Lucas broached the new plan to him. He even admitted his readiness to get rid of the hysterical woman as soon as possible, and accepted her release as a prior condition for release of one of the three prisoners. After that, all women and children would be allowed to leave the plane, a second prisoner would be brought to the DC-9, the male passengers would leave along with the flight attendants, and the last prisoner would be rendered up to his comrades. Only the pilot, co-pilot, and flight engineer would remain onboard to fly the terrorists wherever they decided to go—a decision which still had either not been made or was purposely being kept a secret.

Because the plan included no monetary ransom, corpses, or persecution of the twelve Jewish passengers on the Alitalia flight, the Italians felt no qualms about liberating the three Palestinian terrorists presently under their custody—though the three had slain an Israeli businessman and his family in Milan. In fact, in many ways they were glad to be rid of their presence, for it was obvious that eventually they would be ransomed; and until they were, Italy's security forces could not rest.

Helen Jacobi was trying to control her rambunctious sons when she first caught sight of the strange vehicle. From a distance it looked like a piece of modern art: a giant ambulatory triangle propelling itself effortlessly across the tarmac. When it drew nearer she recognized the vehicle as a motorized plane ramp.

Were the passengers going to be released now? The thought exhilarated her. She wanted to gather together her carry-on luggage, unbuckle her safety-belt, and dash to the exit-door—though it was still closed and the skyjackers were making no move to open it. They had told the passengers nothing about the progress of negotiations.

The vehicular ramp stopped just beyond the left wing. Appearing from the rear section, the harmonica player strolled to the front of the plane where his female comrade waited, and succeeded in pushing open the thick lozenge-shaped door. He motioned to the driver of the wheeled staircase; and within a minute its rubber fenders bumped gently against the fuselage.

Having completed the first part of his mission, the driver abandoned his machine and walked to a position twenty yards beyond the left wing-tip where he stood with his hands clearly in view of the terrorists.

Later it would be argued that he should have done something besides stand there and look harmless, but no one was in a position to say what that something was.

Dom Lucas wondered whether the terrorists would release the sick woman as they had promised. The gesture would, in a sense, appease their detractors without really costing the terrorists anything, so there was no reason to doubt their sincerity.

He lifted his binoculars again and watched the jeep riding smoothly across the tarmac. Soon it would stop, Basilia would get out and enter the plane. Raoul insisted that the reporter come aboard for the woman: she was unfit to leave by herself, none of the skyjackers cared to leave the plane's sanctuary, and Raoul refused to allow any hostages a chance to escape before his three comrades were released. But he could certainly do without the hysterical Jewess and her maddening wails that kept the other passengers on edge and liable to act stupidly—which might result in a very nasty conclusion for everyone concerned.

When Mrs. Jacobi saw the lone jeep heading for the plane, her spirits dropped to a new low. One jeep could not ferry all the passengers away from this stifling coffin. She had counted eighty-four people aboard; and even if only the children were being freed, they would not all be able to get in the vehicle. Why, it didn't even have a roof for some of them to sit on!

And the shabby man stepping out—was he to be their saviour? A stooping figure with unnaturally thick glasses and a large, circular bald spot at the crown of his head; a shapelessness dressed in baggy trousers and a dirty loose jacket with a fluorescent orange ID pinned above the drooping breast-pocket?

What the hell is going on? she asked herself as the skyjackers motioned the man to mount the ramp and enter. Is *he* the negotiator?

Lucas concentrated on the front exit of the DC-9. For an instant he saw a girl's shoulder and breast, then a hand beckoning.

Federico Basilia had stopped the jeep ten feet from the bottom of the ramp and gotten out. He appeared confused. Lucas shuddered, momentarily believing the reporter was about to break into a run. That would be disastrous—not only because the Foreign Minister had given Basilia the job of retrieving the woman, but because the terrorists might think it was a signal for a commando strike. And then they might begin shooting hostages.

Basilia answered the summons with a wave, however, and started slowly up the ramp as though his knee-joints needed oiling; and Dom Lucas relaxed back into his chair, listening to the voice of the driver of the mechanized staircase, transmitted through a small walkie-talkie taped to the fellow's chest.

Raoul had posted his second lieutenant in the cockpit and gone into the Tourist section, passing the harmonica player, to personally oversee removal of the troublesome Jewish woman. He watched in amusement as the Spaniard struggled up the steps, puffing from exertion.

"Are you the reporter?" he asked in English when the man had finally reached the top platform.

"Yes." Basilia flipped his garish ID tag. "Of *El Sol*. Where is the injured woman?"

Raoul ordered his female comrade to stay in First Class and keep an eye on the driver standing outside. Then backing up, he motioned Basilia to follow.

Helen Jacobi sighed in disappointment as she watched the stranger move to the row directly in front of her and begin examining the recumbent Mrs. Weinbaum of Los Angeles, the back of his hands covered with liver-spots. He felt her arms and legs, evidently searching for broken bones, then looked up at Raoul who had retreated to a position ten feet away.

"A stewardess gave her a shot of novocaine or something to put her to sleep," the terrorist said, answering the unspoken question. "She was getting dangerous."

Basilia again bent over the woman's body, put his finger under her nose and an ear to her chest. Then he lifted her wrist.

"Well? Well?" Raoul was becoming angry. "Get her out of here!"

Without rising, the reporter said, "Why? This woman is dead."

Mrs. Jacobi gasped. Through the crack between the seats she could see Mrs. Weinbaum's chest rising perceptibly, rhythmically. She opened her mouth to argue—a complaint suffered by most American women; but Basilia's ugly face swiveled in her direction, his magnified eyes glowing with a demonic hatred that shocked, repelled, and silenced her.

Raoul lowered his gun in astonishment, visualizing the General Command's victory slipping away once word of the woman's death reached the Italians—or the Israelis. Would the Italians be so willing to give up their prisoners now, let murderers laugh in their faces and fly off?

"That's impossible." He stepped forward, gesturing to his tall comrade at the cabin divider to join him.

The automatic pistol materialized from the baggy interior of Basilia's jacket as though by magic, and Raoul stared dumbly at the grey-blue silencer in the brief instant before the dum-dum bullet entered his upper chest on an ascending trajectory, neatly clipping his sternum then shredding the top half of his heart as the soft-nosed slug disintegrated. The force—diminished only slightly by the bafflers in the long silencer— knocked him violently backward, and he fell on his side, already dead.

Wheeling, the other terrorist made a dive toward the doorway joining the cabin sections, barely escaping the second bullet which bored a tunnel in his frizzy hairdo. He reacted instinctively, aware only that something had gone terribly wrong; his own weapon was forgotten in the mad desire to escape. Absorbing sudden disaster had not been part of his training in Lebanon's Fatahland: only endless physical exercises, introduction to Al Fatah's Soviet-supplied weaponry, and political indoctrination intended to harden each recruit's determination and discipline. But no practical training in how to answer a weapon firing point-blank.

As the man disappeared into the First Class compartment, his female companion took his place in the doorway, nostrils flaring and even white teeth bared in an angry grimace. Having heard the shocked exclamations of passengers and seeing her fellow terrorist fling himself through the curtained portal, she knew only that their plans had for some reason gone awry.

When she confronted the ugly snout of the automatic leveled at her, her jaws opened as though she suddenly needed more oxygen. Her soft brown eyes widened—the eyes of a horse impaled on a spear—and she threw her grenade at the same moment Basilia's third shot slammed through her left breast.

Basilia ignored the grenade, knowing the girl hadn't pulled the detonator-pin. Besides, he would not have had time to do anything about it even if she had primed the small bomb.

Geoffrey and Terence Jacobi watched admiringly as the stooped man walked forward, stepping over the two bodies littering the aisle. They never liked the people with the guns anyway, the dark men who looked at their mother's passport then at them, calling the young boys "Jew bastards" and making their mother cry and argue that they weren't, that Jacobi wasn't "Jewish"— whatever that meant.

The skyjacker who escaped Basilia's second bullet had pulled aside the curtain shielding the cockpit door and was now attempting to get inside, but the terrorist with the explosive harmonica refused at first to unlock it for him. He had heard the shouts and screams of the passengers, and they frightened him. But the thought of being left alone with the two jumpy pilots scared him even more, so he swung the door open.

His eyes first caught sight of Ishmael, his comrade, standing in front of him with a strange expression creasing his face. He staggered forward, trying to speak, but only a torrent of blood escaped his lips before he collapsed.

It was then that the harmonica player saw the man in the loose jacket and heavy, black-rimmed glasses, positioned comfortably in one of the First Class seats, a twisted smile warping his grizzled features.

"Get away or I blow up plane!" the terrorist yelled. His voice quavered, uncertain, searching for the correct words, his hands holding the oversized harmonica by its wires, one end already affixed to a battery terminal.

The two pilots behind him sat transfixed, their eyes leaping from the plastic explosive to the spot of brown thatch above the First Class seats—all they could see of Basilia. Both were convinced that the commandos had somehow stormed the plane; but how they had gotten aboard mystified them. Should they pounce on the terrorist while his back was turned?

"Harbiya! Sakanah!"

The slug penetrated just beneath the terrorist's loose-hanging chin, splaying deadly fragments, severing the jugular vein and demolishing the neural axis where it joined the head. Dead on his feet, the harmonica player shook as if palsied, then bent at the knees and waist, crumbling into a grotesque, blood-gushing heap.

"Non usa la radio per cinque minuti," the man told

Captain Redento Montani, rising slowly from the seat and stuffing the automatic into a custom-made holster sewn to the inside of his jacket. *"Per piacere, Capitano."*

Dom Lucas re-checked his watch and the clock above one of the four windows that encircled the air-traffic controllers' station.

"There he is now," Lieutenant Vestanzi said at his elbow, passing the binoculars. "He's carrying the woman."

"Thank God!" the Foreign Minister sighed. What had Basilia been doing in the plane for the last five minutes? He'd been told to go in, remember what he saw, and get the hell out with the sick passenger. Vestanzi estimated that that would take three minutes at most.

"What's he doing now?"

"The woman appears to be unconscious. He is laying her across the back seat and getting behind the wheel. Xandeen, are you ready?"

The driver of the movable staircase came across statically on the walkie-talkie. Something seemed to be wrong on the plane. Should he take away the ramp as previously ordered?

"What do you mean by 'wrong'?" The policemen, commandos, and diplomats all leaned instinctively forward.

"Well, sir, I can see people moving about inside now. They've raised the window shutters and—and they're waving to me!"

Vestanzi grabbed a pair of binoculars from one of his assistants and concentrated on the DC-9 poised at the northern end of Luqa's shorter runway. Basilia had already departed with his passenger and the green jeep could be seen pulling into the small hangar near the perimeter of the aerodrome. But from the front exit of the Alitalia plane came a sudden flood of passengers eager to get away from it as quickly as possible.

Others had seen the passengers, for now a great shout of relief and delight erupted from around and inside the Terminal Building; the crowd of reporters, relatives of hostages, and curious spectators broke through the police cordon separating them from the flying field and surged across the tarmac.

"*Mamma mia!*" Vestanzi muttered.

Dom Lucas tried in vain to contact the DC-9 and find out why the hostages were being released prematurely, but the pilot did not answer.

Vestanzi jumped from his seat. "I must see what is going on out there."

By the time Vestanzi reached the plane, however, Captain Montani had broken radio silence and was asking if he could leave his station now that the commandos had rescued his passengers.

By noon all those who had flown on the skyjacked Alitalia flight had been interviewed by representatives of Italian and Spanish Intelligence. Most of the questions dealt with the missing Federico Basilia: what he looked like, what he had done aboard the plane, anything he might have said, whether any of the passengers might have met him before.

It soon became apparent that these questions were of little concern to the Spaniards. The Spanish Registration Office reported that the only Federico Basilias holding passports were a sixty-seven year old retired hotel manager from Barcelona and a twenty-year old tennis player from Cartagena. Further study revealed that the Madrid newspaper *El Sol* had never employed anyone called Basilia and certainly had not sent a reporter to cover the Maltese skyjacking. Only two other Federico Basilias were recorded as having been born in Spain or its colonies since 1900: one died in the Spanish Civil War while fighting the Republicans; the other was an orphan in Toledo—aged two.

An examination of passenger manifests from every plane and ship that touched Malta in the past two months proved only that the man calling himself Federico Basilia had been aboard none of them—at least while using that name. Maltese Immigration had never heard of him. Of course he might have been smuggled ashore from a small boat; but that could only mean he had landed on the island for some other purpose than disrupting the skyjacking, since it was impossible he could have known when or even if one would occur—unless he was personally involved in its planning.

The investigators were stumped. None of the recent guests at any of Malta or Gozo's hotels answered the description of Señor Basilia. Obviously the name was false, the man wore a disguise, and he had an accomplice who helped get him onto the island. And then get him off?

Departing travelers were scrutinized at Luqa Airport and all seaports; but after a week this tactic was abandoned as too expensive and unproductive. Why should Malta have to pay for the folly of a foreigner? Why, for that matter, did everyone want to find this man who had done them a service?

The answer to that question came only ten days later.

Members of a radical West German terrorist gang

hijacked a Lufthansa jet bound from Tehran to Hamburg. Making a forced landing in Athens after the Greek government refused them permission to land, they demanded four million dollars in ransom as well as the man responsible for the deaths of the four Palestinian freedom-fighters at Luqa. The passengers would be shot, one each hour, until their demands were met.

Two passengers died before West Germany's expert anti-terrorist squad, Grenzschutzgruppe 9, was in position for launching its rescue mission. Fortunately, GSG 9 succeeded in liberating the remaining hostages and killing the skyjackers, since no one knew who the phantom Basilia really was or where he was hiding.

European governments knew that more skyjackings, kidnappings, and bombings would occur in an attempt to avenge the slaying of the Malta Four—who, as the papers correctly reported, were promised unhindered departure if they freed their passengers, and who had agreed. The Arab states united in urging a fuller investigation of the Maltese affair; and, naturally, the omniscient, omnipresent PLO headlined the story in its Beirut-based newspaper as "ISRAEL'S LATEST SLAUGHTER OF INNOCENTS."

Out of curiosity rather than urgency (for no government would willingly send Basilia to a certain death in order to satisfy terrorists) Interpol stretched its budget to include the creation of a permanent unit to seek this strange killer-saviour. Lack of quick success, though, soon broke up the special unit—permanently.

The only people who expressed their unqualified joy at the fake reporter's disappearing act were Terence and Geoffrey Jacobi. They couldn't understand why others disliked the ugly man. Didn't he help them get away from those mean men with guns who liked to spit on people? Their mother's attitude was even more disturbing. She told them to forget all about the hunched man—that he was a simple murderer like the others, and he should be caught and punished like all murderers.

"But he helped us!" they protested in unison.

"Do as your mother says," their father had said, though agreeing with them when outside his wife's hearing.

"He's a mad killer," Helen Jacobi insisted, remembering the single malevolent glance Basilia had aimed at her.

As for her sons, they continued to revere the strange man in the bulky suit—until time and their short attention-span smudged his image; and school began again, and life went on as usual.

CHAPTER FOUR

He carefully removed his iron-rimmed glasses, set them on the closed file in front of him, and rubbed his tired eyes. It was going to be another one of those days, he could tell, when nothing seemed to go right.

As with his immediate predecessor—and no matter how hard one tried to prevent it—some stupid meddling jerk always picked up a piece of inconsequential detail and followed it through until all hell broke loose. Then the DCI had to take a ride to the White House and apologize for discharging his duty, and continue on to the Senate to explain before the Solons just what he thought he was doing by interfering in the internal affairs of another sovereign state.

Having survived as Director of the CIA for one year hadn't been easy, especially when reports like the one in front of him now were becoming commonplace. In this instance, an operative working in the American Embassy's Economic Mission in Brasilia had been caught buying information from a high-ranking official of Brazil's Coffee Institute. The President wanted to know whether or not the Brazilians were correctly reporting their figures on coffee production and, hence, whether they might be guilty of artificially inflating world prices. An American journalist stationed in Rio de Janeiro happened to be investigating the same matter. He shadowed a Brazilian economic official to a meeting with the CIA agent at a small cafe on the outskirts of the capital; and two days later a story appeared in the *Washington Post* which recounted the supposedly secret conversation between the two men and the transfer of a bulky manila envelope. The Brazilians blew their stacks, the operative was hurriedly recalled, and the President discovered that American consumers were being "ripped off."

The present report had been filed by an independent agent, and it stated that the American journalist paid a goodly amount to the cafe waiter for a play-back of the hushed conversation. Since the waiter had given no indication that he knew English, the agent and his contact had not taken the precaution of dismissing him and then speaking only in abbreviations.

True, the information was disseminated among the major coffee-importing nations to stir up indignation against the monopolistic practices of the South American giant; but putting the U.S. at the end of the fuse hadn't raised Latin opinion of "Yanqui imperialism" either. All in all, the low-level operation was a high-bursting fizzle, best forgotten under a more recent scandal.

"Yes, Miss Henderson?" he said, answering the buzz of the intercom.

"The President is on line three, sir."

"Thanks." He picked up the phone, at first suspecting the President wanted to upbraid him about the Brazilian affair; if that had been the case, however, he would probably have used a secure line.

"Yes, Mr. President?"

"Harry?"

"Yes."

"How soon can you get down to Situations?"

"Half an hour," the Director answered immediately, having made the trip only too often.

"Bring what you have on the skyjacking last Friday."

"Luqa?"

"Yes. Everything, Harry. Clean out the file."

"I understand, Mr. President."

The helicopter brought him from CIA Headquarters near Langley, Virginia to the East Lawn of the White House in exactly twenty-three minutes. A Marine guard met him on the grass and ushered him to the remodeled Situation Room in the second basement of the Presidential mansion.

The President, his National Security Council advisor, the Vice-President, the Chairman of the Joint Chiefs of Staff, and the U.S. Ambassador to Israel were seated in a corner of the large, modernistic room. They all rose to their feet when he entered.

Knowing each of them well—better, in fact, than they probably would have liked—the CIA Director did not need formal introductions; he merely smiled in his noncommittal manner, shook hands, and took a seat in the only extra chair, carefully balancing his attaché-case on edge between his legs.

"Down to business, Harry," the President said. "We have a problem with this affair on Malta. Bill here says I should give the press a policy statement before it's too late to matter what the Administration does. I tend to agree. What's your opinion, Harry?"

"I'm not sure I understand, Mr. President," he replied cautiously.

"The Arab League is going haywire trying to place blame on someone for the killing of the skyjackers. Bonn had none of its nationals on the flight and so had no motive for interfering. The British, Italians, and French have openly deplored the shootings, again for the obvious reason: dependence on Arab oil. I believe them. That doesn't leave many possibilities, Harry. Central Intelligence is on the short-list. At the top, I might add."

Silence fell over the group as they awaited the DCI's reply; but he slowly cleaned his glasses and ignored the stares.

"What the President wants, I think, is a clear assurance that the Company had nothing to do with this," NSC advisor Bill Haberstrasse said, accepting the role of interpreter. "He can't go into a press conference saying one thing when a week later a CIA secretary drops an operations report on some Congressman's lap saying the opposite. It makes the Administration look either dumb or dishonest, ignorant of its own affairs or lying through its teeth. Bad business, bad business."

"You understand our position," the Vice-President argued, leaning forward and folding his hands together in a studied gesture of paternal sagacity. "Everyone is waiting for our answer—hopefully our denial. We've forgone those days when America was the world's policeman."

And had to stick its ass on every toilet seat, you mean, the DCI thought, beginning to feel a surge of anger, an uncoiling of his usual lethargic manner. But he continued to smile—though no longer with his eyes, only his lips. He hated political necessities: the give-and-take of negotiation, conciliation, compromise. They left him cold, feeling somehow tainted, knowing that bonhomie and politeness were anachronisms in the modern world.

"Harry? You with us?"

"Yes, Mr. President. I was only speculating as to why you doubt my word. I oversee operations which the NSC has deemed most desirable for effecting American foreign policy, and then at specified intervals I present them for review by the Council. Mr. Haberstrasse knows full-well that I do not run the CIA as my private army. To rephrase the Vice-President's statement, the CIA has foregone those days when it was democracy's active conscience."

"Come, come, you don't present *all* CIA operations," Haberstrasse mocked, sucking on his long-stemmed pipe as if he were trying to swallow it. "And what you keep to yourself is anybody's guess."

The DCI adjusted his glasses over his slightly crooked nose—broken many years ago by an East German agent in Zermatt just before he killed him—and settled deeper in the cushioned chair. "True. I have no intention of endangering the lives of *all* my agents by giving details of minor or as yet unproductive operations to every committee, sub-committee, council, agency, and knitting class that utilizes the openness of a democracy to satisfy its morbid curiosity about covert operations. The NSC particularly has so many leaks down the line that you could make spaghetti with it. So I *do* keep some operations to myself, though they are not major jobs—certainly nothing on the order of the Bay of Pigs, Chile, or our Berlin penetrations. But even these I discuss with the President."

"Would you consider the Malta affair a minor or major operation?" Haberstrasse persisted, irked by the man's cutting remarks about the lack of security in the NSC.

"I wouldn't consider it an operation at all, Mr. Haberstrasse. It goes against percentages—so much so, in fact, that I'm tempted to believe this Federico Basilia was known to his victims. But I have no proof of that."

"How do you arrive at that conclusion?"

"Only little worries, Mr. President. First, the situation over there was ludicrous. The Italians wanted to wash their hands of it because it took place on foreign soil and because strong Communist elements in their government were more than ready to free the three Palestinian terrorists whom the skyjackers wanted. Army commandos were sent to Luqa but took only an advisory role. The Maltese, however, have no one trained in handling rescue operations of this order. And naturally, if the Italians were willing to free the terrorists without an argument, why should the Maltese police risk botching the job?

"Secondly, it was this Basilia who suggested the systematic trade-off of terrorist prisoners for hostages. The plan was simple but did not necessarily guarantee the skyjackers wouldn't be double-crossed. Yet they readily accepted and made no conditions as to who would pick up Mrs."—he opened his attaché-case and fished out the pertinent document—"Mrs. Sybil Weinbaum, or whether he should be dressed only in his undies when he came aboard.

"Thirdly, passengers say that the skyjackers failed to search Basilia for a weapon when he entered the plane, though they showed no deference toward him in any other way. The Palestinians aren't likely to make mistakes like that. They plan every aspect of an operation—even down to teaching their strike-force aircraft marshalling signals so they can detect a bogus groundcrew."

"Of course, this explains nothing," Haberstrasse grumbled.

"I think Harry is telling us the CIA was uninvolved in these events and that the shootings may have been an internal affair initiated by the Palestinian umbrella organization. Maybe it was a political ploy to arouse its own members and fuel the anger of sympathetic radical groups, who would then intensify their own terrorist activities." The Vice-President took a football scorecard from his jacket and began doodling on it. "Is that the essence, Harry?"

"More or less. The Company had nothing to gain by entering the crisis. We didn't have a man on Malta at the time and saw no purpose in sending one. Our file simply reflects what British Intelligence recovered from its men in Valletta and newspaper reports filed by on-site journalists."

"What does your analysis conclude?"

"No evidence to support the involvement of any West European security services."

"Nor the Russians or their satellites? I understand the Czechs do some fairly weird things."

"I can't imagine the purpose, Mr. President. Even supposing they could dream up a cover if their man was caught, what motive would impel them to send an assassin against their allies?"

"Well, I recall Budapest in '56 and Prague in '68 . . . but you're right of course." The President pursed his lips and looked at the U.S. Ambassador to Israel questioningly.

"No," Philip Atkinson said, speaking for the first time since the group had convened *in toto*.

"I haven't said anything, Phil."

"I know that expression, Mr. President, and the answer is no. The Israelis only act when the mission involves their people directly. The carrier was Alitalia, the plane was hijacked over Malta, and the Italians showed an immediate interest in giving up their prisoners. Jerusalem expressed its opinion to Rome that submitting to political blackmail solves nothing, but obviously Rome had its own ideas. Israel stayed out. I'm sure of it."

"Harry?"

"According to our informants, the Israelis made no attempt to rescue the hostages at Luqa. Mossad's masterminds would be sorely tempted to pull out their large-scale maps of Malta and start taking compass-readings, but they're no fools. Sending in a single man at high noon with a heavy hand-gun is more the style of Texas than Tel Aviv."

General Amos Callendar, Chairman of the Joint Chiefs of Staff and a Dallas native, snorted indignantly—which would be his sole contribution to the discussion.

"Then I can assure the American people we had nothing to do with the deaths of the four skyjackers?"

"The CIA was uninvolved, if that's what you mean, Mr. President."

The President nodded smartly, thanked each man for coming, and stood, a signal that everyone could leave.

The DCI was the last to go, the President holding him back with a friendly but firm grip on his shoulder.

"Harry," he said, "look into this. Find out who this Basilia is, who he works for, how he managed the rescue. And his escape."

"Just curiosity?"

"Yeah, I guess that's it. I'd like the answers before I see them in some second-rate TV drama."

"Everyone else is looking too."

"I know. No one wants to have the Arabs pointing the finger in his direction, so there'll be a mad scramble to find the guilty party before the terrorists begin exacting all-points revenge. The more reason to make this top priority."

"I can't promise results. Unless they're playing a very deep game, the Maltese and Italians honestly swear that Basilia vanished into the ether and they haven't a clue where to pick up his smoke. I can put feelers in most major European police departments and check both their interest and progress, but our agency alone doesn't have enough ground personnel for a manhunt, especially after the cut-backs."

"Do what you can, Harry. We have a lot of Arab students over here who are already driving the FBI batty. Unfortunately, it is not in our interests to ship them home."

"What do we do with Basilia once we've found him?"

"Pay me a visit," the President said too casually.

Nathan Green made the 30-mile trip between Jerusalem and Tel Aviv in less than half an hour, pushing his old Ford Pinto to its limit. Despite the fact Voight hinted at no urgency to the meeting, Green was anxious to get into action again. It had been several weeks since any of the three major security services asked for help from the

Special Flying Squad—and then only for tracking down two terrorist infiltrators who disappeared into the Arab section of Haifa, and putting an emergency tap on the Greek Embassy's phones. Though Green had nothing against his dedicated friends in Mossad, Shabak, and Modiin, he knew they tended to monopolize the action, preventing specialists like Green from exhibiting their talents.

Thirty-eight, dark-complexioned, tall, thin, and so long-armed that his high school teammates had given him a permanent nickname—"Spider"—in deference to his blocking abilities on the basketball court, Green had lived an eventful life. Growing up in Russell, Kansas as the only Jewish boy in town, he came to learn that there were indeed some spots on earth where Jews could live free from persecution. But playing it safe never appealed to young Nathan. He joined the Marines at eighteen, stayed on until he grew bored with his work in Naval Intelligence, emigrated to Rhodesia as a "weapons-specialist," was hired as a security advisor for a South African mining firm, met Shashana Egelman, and quickly moved to Israel with his new wife, a strong-willed and beautiful sabra who worked with the Israeli Embassy in Pretoria.

The Greens might have settled down to a long, happy life on the 80-acre farm near Beersheba which Mr. Egelman gave the couple, a life of hard but fruitful work, children, and the company of true friends. But God had other plans. Or so Nathan reasoned, flinching at the memory.

Appearing at the secret headquarters of Mossad in Tel Aviv after the funeral, Green was hurriedly ushered into a small room where a couple of security agents tried to sweat him, demanding to know how he learned the location of their offices. By the time he finished with them, they were both in need of medical attention.

After spending two nights in jail he was taken to a seaside hotel, left alone, and told to wait by the phone. Two more days passed before the call came through, an interview was arranged, and Green found himself a member of the Special Flying Squad. Obviously Mossad had been unimpressed by his pugilistic talents, Modiin used military personnel exclusively, and Shabak—the service responsible for internal security and counter-intelligence—was overmanned at that time. So he found a home with the Squad, assisting the chief security services as all-purpose roustabout, but principally as coordinator of a para-military group assigned to overseas skyjackings.

Following procedure, when Green arrived in Tel Aviv he phoned Headquarters from a telephone box facing the waterfront. He was surprised when his superior simply told him to phone a second number. A new voice instructed him to appear at the security offices of Ben-Gurion Airport in one hour.

At first, Green felt like laughing, thinking the messages terribly dramatic. Why couldn't old Voight have told him to go to the airport? Then he realized his superior was obviously being kept clear of this matter—whatever it was. Yet the open communication between various services of the Israeli intelligence network had always been a reason for its efficiency. Why the hell change that? A leak somewhere? Did they suspect *him*?

Green headed directly for the airport, then had a quick lunch before his appointment. As with most thin men, he was always hungry, fueling his unregulated metabolism and never gaining an ounce. Shashana jokingly berated him about his luck, for she continually felt obliged to diet.

And she never enjoyed being old and fat, he thought, emptying his coffee cup with a swift, angry motion, then making his way from the cafeteria to the Security Department on the second floor of the Terminal Building. All the things he had planned for them, the American rituals he brought with him to this new but ancient land, were simply mementoes, dying brain cells starved of blood.

The door was locked. He tapped gently and suddenly found himself confronting General Yigael Charon, the Director of Sherut Bitachon Klali, the General Security Service known as Shabak, and sometimes referred to by its Hebraic initials, Shin Beth. The old wizened soldier smiled and beckoned him inside.

Two men were seated in the outer office. Green nodded an acknowledgement to their cold stares, wondering what could possibly have brought Mossad agents to Ben-Gurion Airport. Their operational territory lay beyond Israel's borders. Unless they were catching a plane they had no business here. Neither did Charon, for that matter, who usually conducted his work from a modern complex in Tel Aviv.

The spartan furnishings in the inner office reeked of police work, late nights of frustrating details, false alarms, too real alarms as Japanese terrorists sprayed the terminal with bullets, hijacked planes sat on the tarmac, and shot-up Israeli planes limped onto the runways from the hell in the Sinai, the pilots eager to put down before they bled to death. Two desks filled the room, and both were scarred by forgotten cigarettes and spilled drinks. A map of Israel hung above one, a Middle East map above the other. A bank of file-cabinets crouched against one wall.

The place hasn't changed a bit, Green thought, taking the proferred seat by the window that looked onto a long line of hangars, control tower and radar stations. When an airport is only fifteen minutes' drive from enemy territory it necessarily combines civilian and military services, and Ben-Gurion had a ready supply of both.

"Mr. Green," the General began, speaking in unaccented English though he knew from Green's dossier that the man was admirably fluent in Hebrew and Arabic, "your commander has kindly given me this opportunity to ask you a few questions. Do you mind?"

"That depends on the questions," Green answered glibly, reluctant to admit his sudden nervousness, and determined to conceal it beneath an off-hand manner.

"Yes, of course." Charon showed no amusement. He sat behind the desk across from Green and opened a drawer, pulling a gun from it. Holding the weapon loosely, he said, "Do you recognize this, Mr. Green?"

What the hell? Green shifted uneasily on the foam cushion, his eyes never leaving the gun. Was someone trying to set him up?

"It's a Browning P-35, also called the HP—for *Hochleistungs-pistole*, or the GP—for *pistolet de grande puissance*, depending on the country you're in. Calling it the High Power refers not to its relative stopping power but to its large magazine: 13 rounds plus one in the chamber. The pistol gained immediate popularity following its introduction and has seen wide service. Using a 9mm Parabellum and with 14 rounds it is a . . . capable weapon."

"You have used this weapon?"

"Not that particular gun, no. But one like it. The Squad trains with every type of handgun in the Israeli arsenal."

"Where were you last Friday and Saturday?"

Blood rushed to Green's face and he clenched his jaws, striving ever harder to control his rising anger. There was no reason to humiliate him like this; Voight could have called him in for five minutes and given him a paternal lecture, he didn't have to let a man from Shabak do his dirty work.

"Relaxing."

"Where?"

"I was off-duty so I drove to Haifa, took a room in the Solomon Hotel, and enjoyed myself immensely with the local females."

"You went to Haifa and stayed at Solomon's, but I can't say you enjoyed yourself," Charon said, fastening his eyes on Green's tight features. "You visited your wife there on Friday morning then disappeared. Why? Where did you go?"

"Is this Shabak's business?"

"Mr. Green, be patient with us. We only want the truth. As a loyal employee of the government, is there any reason why you should withhold evidence from a ranking superior?"

"Evidence of what, General?"

Charon replaced the automatic pistol in its drawer. He was well-aware of Green's value to the Special Flying Squad and the high morale which he inspired among his associates; but in this instance, that only made him more visible as a suspect.

"How long ago did your wife die?" he asked tonelessly.

"Five years this month."

"How did she die?"

"In a plane accident."

Both men were determined to play the game out, regardless of the pain it caused. Charon knew the details of how Green's wife died; Green knew Charon knew, but disliked discussing the matter and mistrusted the General's motive in asking about it.

"A flight from Athens to Tel Aviv, wasn't it? A skyjacking. Your woman got in the way somehow. Shot down."

"You'd better read the report again," Green said coldly. The arms of his chair creaked ominously as his body tensed at the memories generated by this conversation. Where was it leading? The day had begun so auspiciously. And now . . .

"According to other passengers she intervened when one of the skyjackers physically abused an old man who refused to obey his commands. So the skyjacker shot her in the head. In a way it was fortunate, since if the bullet had not been stopped by her skull it might have penetrated the fuselage. The plane was cruising at peak altitude and decompression would have sent it into a fatal spin."

"Not necessarily. The pilot could put it into a steep dive, level off at 5000 feet, and structural damage would be minimal. The passengers could begin respiring normally in a matter of minutes. Too many people believe that decompression means the plane explodes or passengers are sucked through windows. Not always true."

Charon frowned. His gambit had failed: Green was visibly upset but otherwise controlling himself.

"Why'd you two never have kids?"

"That's not the government's business."

"Personal curiosity then."

"By your leave, sir, none of *your* business."

"Okay, Green, let's go back. Where were you after Friday morning last?"

"Going back, I was off-duty—that is, my instructions were to remain in Israel and keep my ears posted for the code-phrase which means I have to call in. I did both."

Charon smiled, learning forward. "But you lost your shadow. Why?"

"Was someone following me?"

"Don't play innocent. One of our best men had you tagged. He took you into the cemetery, watched you as far as the mausoleum. An hour later you still hadn't come out, so he radioed for a widow. She went inside and found only the caretaker. There's only the one door. How'd you skate, Green?"

"I saw the man when I got up that morning. He sat in a car across from the apartment building and kept glancing up at my window. I phoned Records and gave his license number. The owner turns out to be the Negev Fruit Exporters Company. A front for Shabak—so transparent a blind man could see through it. I did what I planned to do—visit my wife's tomb—then had my friend the caretaker let me in a neighboring burial chamber. All I had to do was wait for the tail to discover my absence, report back to—you? . . . then leave in my own good time. Simple."

"We have no indication that you followed it up. Weren't you curious?"

Green laughed, a soft, gentle laughter that trickled from the corners of his mouth. "My superior warned us about the overly-diligent bureaucracy at Shabak, that its counter-espionage units try to ferret out victims in the most unlikely places, especially in the other security services. Though I suppose that isn't so unlikely, since high-grade intelligence is concentrated in Mossad and Modiin. But the Squad? Really, General, you give us too much credit."

"Perhaps," Charon said, running a hand through his bristly steel-gray hair. "But we do spot-checks on all personnel. A continual house-cleaning, you might say. Most targets never know. Those who do either recognize it for what it is and dismiss it, or report it to their departmental head. You had to be different. You flew the coop, as you Americans say."

"I'm an Israeli now."

Charon ignored the rebuttal, continuing, "And now all I need to know is where you were so I can verify—and forget you."

"I left Haifa by car, driving as far as Nevatim, stayed at the Judea Hotel that Friday night, then went on to Eilat on Saturday, and stayed at the Hegel Hotel."

"On the Sabbath?"

"I'm not Orthodox. Anyway, security services don't operate according to fixed schedules. Our enemies rarely observe our religious customs except for seeking an advantage—as in 1973."

"I know that," said Charon, wearying of an interrogation which Green had managed to dominate through his peculiar obstinance and disrespect for authority.

"Then don't spring any of your Pharoah's-plagues on me. I didn't come all this way just for a job interview. I went through SB interrogation five years ago and was cleared. Since my activities have apparently been monitored before by Shabak, why the sudden interest in me? Was my shadow upset about being shaken? He did all he could, General."

"You're quite an independent fellow, aren't you, Green? Your case file bespeaks a radical personality, a man who likes to run things his own way and fortunately is blessed with an analytical and inventive mind which sees him through his mistakes. That's a fair estimation, wouldn't you say? In all modesty? When you went to Budapest with the South African soccer team and were spotted by a KGB recruiting agent for a bit of subversion in Pretoria, you forgot about your principal job of tracing an Israeli who disappeared while vacationing there two months earlier. You sucked the Russian dry until his superiors caught on and arranged that accident in Cape Town. You were lucky to get out with your life."

"As someone once said, 'Bad luck is merely a defensive and self-consoling synonym for inefficiency.' The thing in Budapest had nothing to do with luck, good or bad. Brake-fluid was all over the place. Any idiot could have seen that the car was fixed."

"The point is, you dropped your assignment and picked a new one for yourself. That indicates unreliability."

"It indicates responsiveness to valuable opportunities. If Shabak has a beef about that, why doesn't someone contact General Voight? Why drag me in?"

"Did you see those two men outside?" Charon asked.

"Sure."

"They've gone through the same questioning. I've been requested to find someone suitable for a particularly sensitive job. Mossad would ordinarily handle it, but all services have proposed those of their men whom they consider most qualified for handling the assignment. At the moment, I can tell you that you score highest in each chosen category—with the exception of one: willingness to follow procedure. That alone is enough to knock you off the list."

Curious, Green once again settled back into his chair. "What's it all about?"

"What do you know of the Alitalia hijacking last week?"

"Only what I heard on the radio. You think an Israeli was involved?" That seemed obvious if Shabak had taken an interest in the odd affair.

"We don't know. Until we do, we can't deny it. For either moral, political, or economic reasons, many governments are vigorously condemning the rescue, saying the double-cross could have had the same dire results as the German deception at Fürstenfeldbruck. The Premier agrees and wants to know which maniac in Mossad proposed such a dangerous operation without consulting him. Many jabbing fingers, believe me. Modiin has confirmed that the Syrians have intensified their army maneuvers along the Golan Front in an attempt to draw us out. Fresh units of PLO terrorists are crossing below the Litani and are expected to use the rescue as an excuse to send rockets across the border—which will lead, of course, to reprisals and a new round of condemnation against Israel in the UN."

Green stared at the Intelligence chief without blinking. His eyes had already focused on a possible prospectus for the work ahead; he didn't see the grizzled face in front of him, the shrewd gray eyes delving into his own.

"When do I start on it?"

Charon laughed. "Who said you'd been picked for this job? Besides, there are complications that prohibit an all-out attack with this assignment."

"The trail will only get colder."

"And it may lead to Washington—despite what the Administration there tells us. I know the CIA Director. This kind of operation would appeal to him personally, to hell with regulations. He'd send one man in if success could raise his agency's sagging morale. Doesn't matter that no one but him and the operator ever knew about the scheme. If you trace the man—something no other intelligence service has done, perhaps fearing he is one of their own—you want to avoid getting mixed up with him. Don't show yourself or your prints. Get the hell out once he's confirmed and report directly to me."

Though Charon had not intended admitting he'd already chosen Green as tracker, he now realized his warning remarks had indicated that very fact. He stood up, sticking his hands deep into his trouser pockets. What the hell. The Security Services Council wanted a bright, enterprising young man not directly traceable to Mossad's Special Operations branch, a man with a bloodhound's nose for faint scents and the versatility to artfully separate criss-crossing leads, following the correct strand until no doubts remained as to who initiated the rescue of the Alitalia DC-9 at Luqa. Green was a responsive agent, tested, imaginative, dedicated to the survival of his adopted country, his spiritual homeland. He would do well—certainly as well as the dull thugs in Mossad who kept Israel's enemies in constant apprehensiveness. Of course, dedication to country was not Green's sole motivation for accepting a mission and Charon knew it. His sensitivity about his wife established that clearly.

"I'll need a briefing."

"You'll get it during lunch. Shall we go?" Charon, relieved of his initial duty, was glad for the man's enthusiasm. Green could have complicated matters by asking why he was questioned about his activities the previous weekend.

Charon purposely held back during their lunch, sketching only a vague outline for Green.

When the waiter finally brought a telephone to their table, Charon pressed the receiver tightly against his ear and watched Green for an indication that he could hear the voice at the other end. Evidently he couldn't.

"Yes, this is Charon. What . . . ?"

"Nathan Green passes. He booked under his real name at both hotels, Nevatim and Eilat, on those dates."

"A double?"

"Hotel security photos match his dossier. No way he could have been on Malta in time to be involved in the operation. We've run a follow-up on all his close friends in the services and they check negative too. None of them were in contact with him from the time the Alitalia flight was seized."

"Anything else?"

"That's it."

"Right." Charon hung up and turned back to his new agent, who continued to lay waste to a bowl of green figs and cream.

Dmitri Sebilitov angrily pressed the lock mechanism and slammed the door behind him. A station chief for the KGB at the Russian Embassy in Beirut, he did not like being insulted by a lowly Arab, and he felt the sting more deeply because he was instructed against retaliating. It all made sense, of course: Moscow plays up to the Palestinians and thus gains control over the channeling of their disruptive acts, using the Arabs as mercenaries bent on terrorizing—if not destroying—Western societies.

But that still did not give one of Arafat's filthy lieutenants the right to give orders to a Russian. Bastard. The incident would naturally have to be reported to Moscow, and Sebilitov could phrase the message however he wished. Some relief gathered from that. Then it would be up to his superiors in the Executive Action Department to filter down their instructions on the matter. No hurry about it. No real pressure either felt or given. The PLO man could sit on his haunches outside the embassy until Lenin rose from the dead, for all Sebilitov cared.

How dare this desert peasant command him to locate Federico Basilia, the strange daredevil of Malta! For all anyone knew, the operation might have been ordered by Moscow to discredit and confuse the West. The minds at 2 Dzerzhinsky Square plotted stratagems with multivocal facets, often brilliant in conception, disastrous in execution. They never told him anything. How was he to know what they were up to, whether or not he'd be dropped into Siberia for even mentioning the name Basilia?

He paused at the top of the stairs and tried to remember why he had left his office in the middle of the day. Yes. To get some aspirin. Splitting headache and the damn Soviet pharmacologists hadn't perfected an effective aspirin. You can't complain or they'll say the headache is due to insanity and ship you off to a mental hospital, home of the Russian conscience. Sebilitov decided to buy Bufferin, transfer them to the aspirin bottle furnished by the embassy doctor, and pray none of his comrades discovered his taste for capitalist luxuries.

Nathan Green and General Yigael Charon again faced each other across a desk, now in the latter's Tel Aviv office.

"A gun will of course be issued to you by the Ministry of Foreign Affairs' Investigative Service in every country which you visit and where we hold diplomatic relations," said Charon. "You will be expected to leave it before you cross a state border. I doubt whether you will need a weapon—not at first, surely—but later it may provide comfort. Events will determine necessity."

"A P-35?"

"No, I doubt it. According to one of the hostages who claimed to recognize it, the Browning P-35 was the type of gun used by Basilia. That's why I mentioned it earlier. To determine how informed you were about the case. Embassy armories will doubtlessly offer you a choice of weapons.

"Now, as to specifics. Unfortunately, no photographs were taken of Basilia, but the Maltese have issued an Identi-kit composite prepared from descriptions. Don't put much trust in it: Basilia obviously disguised his appearance as well as his name and occupation." Charon handed the agent a copy of the composite. "Low forehead, black hair graying at the temples, prominent nose, dark complexion, sagging jowls, approximately 45 years old. Affects clothing too large for him. Speaks English with a Spanish accent, claims to be a journalist, is a deadly shot. As reported, he made the Maltese Foreign Minister's acquaintance, they became quite friendly, and soon Dom Lucas found himself following Basilia's lead. Applying as collector for a wounded woman onboard, he was tested by the Italians to show his inefficiency in recalling details—compared to the ability of an Italian commando. But like any good reporter, he passed at the top of the class, exhibiting a photographic-memory. Mind, Green, that can't be faked. That may help you trace him by removing many of the possibles. Photomnemonists are rare, I suspect. . . . Then when he got inside the plane—fireworks."

"How does this affect Israel?"

"Good question. The Arabs claim this is another sideshow like the raid on Entebbe. They want the world to condemn us, put an embargo on all trade with Israel. Our few friends may decide it's the only way to keep the oil flowing. So we have an obligation to ourselves to identify the man calling himself Basilia, gather solid proof, discover his motives and reveal our results to the world press. Having endangered our foreign relations he cannot be allowed to fade quietly away."

"And if he's CIA?" Green asked.

"Makes no difference. The President says he is not and we do not care to embarrass him by proving otherwise. But we cannot afford to—how do you Americans say it?—swing slowly in the wind? Locate him, discover his origins, motives, who sent him, how he got on Malta so quickly . . . well, you know your business. Find him but don't damage him. We're in enough trouble around here."

Charon touched a small plastic toy on his desk after Green, given his instructions and espousing his own ideas, had departed. It swung back and forth on its nylon strings, hypnotic in its motion. Charon had built the model himself, having been a sapper with the Palmach and seen the unwieldy "secret bomb" designed to blow an entrance in Jerusalem's wall. The weapon proved to be a dud, but the interest and excitement it had generated in May, 1948 still amused him. He'd carved the miniature from memory, polished it, hung it, and kept it near him all these years as a constant reminder of how easily technology can bedazzle men into believing they are superior to their creations. No, machines failed or succeeded only as men failed or succeeded in constructing them. To Charon there was no deeper truth than that the world is an extension of man and therefore malleable. God surely understood what He had done in giving Man fingers and an inquisitive brain, a desire to reach perfection and an inability to achieve it.

He abruptly dismissed the gloomy thought and pulled his desk phone toward him, dialing with stabbing thrusts. The Directors of Mossad and Modiin must be notified that Operation Moses had formally begun.

CHAPTER FIVE

The veranda of the Hotel Ancora was deadly quiet. Anyone stepping onto it would have wondered how the establishment managed to stay in business, because the restaurant had but one guest and this was the traditional time for dining. Only a solitary man sat among the round metal tables, almost invisible, his white sweater and white jeans blending perfectly into the brilliant white of the outdoor furniture, iron railings, canvas table-umbrellas, trellises, even the flower-sills that lined the entire veranda and brought the only colors to the place: violets, vulnerable and melancholy; chrysanthemums, shower-headed crimson blooms; multi-stamened azaleas looking gnarled but happy in the strong April sunshine. A humming swarm of bees danced among the flowers, and when one of them was attracted to the tall glass of light Puerto Rican rum and 7-Up on the man's table, the man in white would make his sole movement: a sharp snap of the rolled newspaper in his right hand that sent the insect crashing to the plank flooring. He never missed, though the blow was rarely fatal and often the bee returned to the glass only to be swatted again.

Beyond the veranda were the mountains, a purplish-brown range of craggy peaks reflected in the waters of a lake far below. Tiny white sailboats skimmed across its surface, operated by invisible sailors. No sound came up from them, no sound intruded onto the white veranda except the bees' gentle buzzing, and the man thought wryly of a silent movie and the drone of a projector. A blissful calm had settled over his environment, a Monet-like euphoria that encouraged langorous eyes and soft, muted tones. No automobiles churning past, no smokers walking by spreading pungent pollution, no planes streaking the limitless azure sky. Everything tranquil, peaceful; sleep beckoned nearer by anesthetic zephyrs, tempering the warm sun with cool flushes, the smell of wet grass and running streams.

The man's head dropped forward, dozing, his thick hair covering his ears. The hairs were dry and crisp, yet highlights of blond and auburn shone through the dullness caused by overwashing.

His *riposo* was interrupted by an elderly couple who came onto the veranda from the frigid depths of the hotel lobby. A young girl accompanied them, obviously the grand-daughter. The trio seated themselves at a table next to the man's as he looked up and returned their friendly smiles. Then his gaze sought the distant horizon, ignoring the persistent stare of the nine-year old.

The little girl was absorbed by the angular contours of his face, the straight sharp nose, the hollow cheeks, the large aquamarine eyes burning steadily from sunken pits, the jaw firm and slightly jutting. It was neither an ugly, nor plain, nor handsome face, but one that engendered interest by its uniqueness; the type of face that mural painters always choose to represent character, deep emotion forever lurking just beneath the surface.

The old couple chuckled merrily, reminiscing in Italian about the honeymoon they had spent in this same hotel forty years ago. Of course, then there hadn't been a veranda at the back, only a manger and an endless series of rock steps that led twisting down to a rickety pier on the lake. And the hotel had been *pensione*, 1400 lira a week. Times indeed had changed: every room fully carpeted, with a telephone, television and private toilet, and crystal chandeliers in the lobby and dining-room. It was hard to believe.

The man in white did not listen. His mind swept up the shards of the past week and tried to puzzle them into a meaningful form, a shape which he could recognize as whole—and then forget. But forgetting was impossible. All the scintillae struck off by the passing days, however short, were absorbed by the brain like so many iron-filings attracted to a magnet. Nothing was ever lost except one's most private secrets—and then only when you died, taking them with you. Everything else became a part of the universal experience, capable of being passed through generations like an old coin, a book—or a cremation urn.

A waiter, the inevitable wine towel folded across a bent arm, appeared beside the white-haired gentleman and muttered that a telephone call awaited him in the lobby. The old man followed him out, shrugging his shoulders in perplexity.

His wife stared after him, lines deeply etched in her forehead. As with all women who have lived long enough to bury many of their closest friends and relatives, she feared the unexpected call, the telegram that arrives on other than a birthday or holiday, the magisterial stranger standing at the door without a salesman's wares in his hands, the various dreams and odd coincidences that give psychic phenomena credence in a modern society. But the little girl released the mounting tension by taking her grandmother's hand and asking for *gelato*.

The waiter did not return to his post at the entrance to the veranda. During the afternoon slack period when most guests were picnicking along the narrow beach or sight-seeing by bus, the hotel kept only one waiter on duty. That was usually enough to cope with the odd tourist who started drinking early or had tasted the hotel's packed lunch and wanted something more agreeable than dry sausage and moldy cheese between two bread crusts.

Now the waiter was at the bar inside, checking whether the supply of ice would outlast the American gentleman's appetite. For two hours the fellow had sat there, sipping at three rum and 7-Ups and—to the waiter's amazement—eating his ice-cubes, then demanding more. Why couldn't he eat food like any normal human? But since the American tipped lavishly, the waiter's stomach did more growling than his mouth. He just hoped he got his lunch-break after the American departed, otherwise he'd lose the tip to his replacement.

Impatient with the service and worried by her husband's lengthy absence, the old woman finally told the girl to behave herself and stood up, looked at the quiet gentleman at the adjacent table (wondering whether he would agree to babysit while she was gone), then decided that with the current rash of kidnappings in Italy it was best not to flaunt the fact that little Angelina was being left unattended for a moment.

"*Signore?*" the girl said.

The man in white continued to gaze into the distance, his face bleached by the stark whiteness reflected from the metal table. A bead of sweat worried its way down his forehead, crossing the dense forest of hairs joining his eyebrows, and passed to the right of his nose, staining his cheek like a tear. He had heard the girl but thought it wise to ignore her. Why get involved? Her grandparents would return, enter into a conversation, ask questions. That could be dangerous.

Angelina persisted. "*Signore?*"

He turned in his seat to watch a bee hovering at the lip of his glass. His newspaper sliced the air, smacking the fat insect into the drink, trapping it among layers of ice-cubes. There was no escape.

He returned the girl's stare. She was dressed in a red pinafore skirt, long-sleeved blue blouse, and white knee-socks. A pale scar marked her forehead just below the hairline and added poignance to her large brown eyes as they concentrated on the drowning bee.

The man winced. "*Si?*"

"*Posso avere un gelato?*" she asked, unable to take her eyes from the struggling insect.

"*Que sapore voi?*"

A haze suddenly filled the air. The man tried to blink it away but it invaded his head, hissing along his sinuses as though an air-hose had been pushed into his mouth.

"*Fragole,*" the girl answered immediately, aware that the man had given her his undivided attention, and sensing the quick accomplishment of her desire.

Strawberry. What else? Of all the flavors in the world his Princess loved strawberry more than any other. An eidetic memory exploded behind his eyes, painfully contorting his expression. . . .

After Sunday school he and his Princess always walked four blocks to the drugstore, a remnant of the past that had somehow managed to survive competition from fast-food, fast-buck chain-outlets with their fancy waxed cardboard cups and machine-produced food wrapped in illustrated toilet tissue. She would climb into a high-backed wooden chair and coyly request the same thing every Sunday morning. And he'd bring it from the counter, setting the large-mouthed glass in front of her, watch her with pride as she started on the strawberry sundae, her rose-petal mouth hardly large enough to take an entire strawberry in one bite—though she certainly tried, much to her father's amusement. They would sit there for an hour or more, ruining her appetite for dinner and Daddy asking what she had learned in Bible class. "Jesus loves me, this I know, for the Bible tells me so," she sang; and Mr. Washenski the storekeeper stood her atop one of his old wooden tables and requested an encore. She loved Mr. Washenski; he loved her. Everybody who met her loved his Princess. She wasn't a bratty child like so many children with only one parent—or, for that matter, with two. Spoiled, yes, but more with love than a wealth of gimcrack toys and unchecked indulgences. She respected her father's authority, sensed his moods and often tried to cheer him up, shrewdly understanding what her father could not accept whenever he took Mommy's picture from his desk and held it to his chest, eyes closed, his shoulders heaving gently, struck by waves of sorrow. Yes—she understood; and her tiny hand would slip into his while she pleaded "Don't cry, Daddy, it's okay, it's okay." And he would fold her in his arms and feel ashamed at his weakness, humbled by the strength in his daughter and her concern for his misery. Then he would work even harder, dedicating himself to giving her as much security as possible if something should suddenly happen to him as it had happened to her mother. But nothing happened. He'd survived. The worse luck, the curse of an invidious God who wanted another Job to test. Well, he'd failed and he didn't care. The age of miracles was past and the sons of Cain had populated the earth. . . .

"*Signore?*"

"*Si. Qualunque cose che tu voi, Piccolina. Cameriére!*" he called, twisting his body toward the entrance where the waiter was certain to be lurking. And sure enough, at the sound of the man's resonant voice the waiter appeared at the door, chin tilted up in the common European gesture of inquiry.

"*Allora, posso avere il gelato con il fuoco anche?*"

The man smiled—until an image of what the girl wanted filled his mind. *Gelato con il fuoco* was a Friulian specialty, a dessert to charm children, amuse adults: a liquer-soaked sugarcube placed atop a bowl of ice-cream and set on fire, melting the ice-cream and giving it a carbonic flavor.

Fire. Raging, warping fire consuming everything; red billowing streamers blowing out the windows in a fiery holocaust that blackened the sky, the concrete, his life, the world . . . burnt alive; and like a witch turned to smoke she floated back to haunt him.

"*Signore!*"

The waiter stood beside him now but wasn't concerned with taking an order. Angelina was screaming, her face mutilated by fear. Both grandparents materialized from the lobby, running toward their young charge.

The man in white looked disinterestedly at the table, the shattered glass and clear liquid that drained across the surface. The ice-cubes moved crazily, jerkily, motivated by confused physics; and the liberated bee proved his tenacity by stumbling off the table and buzzing over the projecting edge of the veranda, apparently none the worse for his intoxicating swim. Blood streamed down the man's fingers, hitting and spreading in the spilled drink like a corrosive acid, dripping onto his Arran sweater and forming crimson polka-dots as he raised his left hand, inspecting the wound curiously. It looked worse than it really was, he concluded. A scratch leaving no scar, that tattoo of man's mortality.

"It's nothing. *Non importante*," he told the waiter bending over him with an expression that precedes vomiting. "*Niente*."

Before anyone could offer medical advice the man in white had disappeared into the bowels of the hotel, ostensibly to clean his wound and get a plaster bandage.

Crazy Americans, the waiter thought, always doing something foolish, always causing trouble. Being a good Socialist, he had what he considered an objective view of the American psyche; being interested in a better life for himself and his family, and knowing how deeply his country depended on capitalist tourists for its survival, he kept his views to himself.

He quickly mopped away the accident and vanished before the elderly couple could give him their order.

He was rinsing the gash across his left palm when there was a knock at the door.

It was the manager, a balding man, fifty years old

(forty-six to everyone but his wife), dressed in a morning coat and with the egregious air of one not born to serve but somehow stamped in that role by circumstances and fully accepting the fact.

"Afternoon, Mr. Erinys," he said, priding himself in his English and using the language with the flaying syntax bred of two years serving an American lieutenant-general during Italy's occupation after the last war. "Heard of your accident. Anything we can do? Brought iodine and Band-Aids."

The man in white stepped aside as the manager slithered through the doorway, his dark eyes searching the room for empty whisky bottles and soiled sheets.

"No thanks, I can handle it."

"Why don't I call a doc? You should get a tennis shot of that," and he jabbed at Erinys' hand bleeding through a towel.

"A what?"

"Tennis shot. Stops jaw-lock."

"Tetanus?"

"Yeah."

"Only need it if your glasses aren't clean."

The manager flapped his hand, laughing artificially. "They're clean, take it from me. Cleaner than a hound's teeth."

"Good. Then I have nothing to worry about."

"I'll leave these here anyway," the manager said, his eyes still cruising over the curtained room as he set a bottle of iodine and tin of adhesive bandages on the dresser. "We try to care for our guests as though they were our children. And since you plan to stay with us for several weeks, we especially don't want to give you cause to leave early."

"It was an accident. My fault entirely."

Seeing that Mr. Erinys wanted to be alone, the manager bowed, apologized for nothing in particular, and was departing when Erinys suddenly asked whether there were buses going south from Bellano.

"Sure. Several every day—to Milano, Firenze, Roma. Were you planning...? But your car..."

"Yes, I could drive my car. Maybe I'll take a trip to Venice."

"Early September is the best time for Venice," the manager said, anxious not to lose such an undemanding guest.

"If I went, I'd keep this room. I like it here. The climate suits me. And I'm not due back at the office for a good month."

"Are you married, Mr. Erinys?"

"No, why?" Erinys followed the manager's glance to his left hand, but it was covered by the blood-stained towel.

"Many beautiful *signorine* in Bellano, Mr. Erinys. No need to go looking elsewhere."

"So I've noticed. Thanks." He abruptly closed the door on the manager's smirking face.

CHAPTER SIX

Nathan Green disliked working with women. Though he knew from experience that they could do anything a man could, he doubted their capacity for reacting logically under stress. It was an old male argument; he accepted that. Yet being old and being espoused by men made it no less true in the Age of Women than a hundred years before Susan B. Anthony first raised a placard. Women might be wily enough to charm acorns out of a fig tree, but they disintegrated when put under pressure or—horrors!—jilted by a lover. Or so he believed.

Well, here he was, just off the plane at Luqa and met by Susan Meyer, his "front man." Why hadn't Charon prepared him for this? It made him wonder just how serious the Israelis were in their effort to locate the mysterious Federico Basilia.

"Have a nice trip?" she asked, and he could see his disappointment reflected in her oval blue eyes as he passed out of Passport Control.

"Nice enough," he retorted, heading for his baggage and forcing her to run to keep up.

"We'll be working together," she said needlessly.

"I thought you were stuck with our Italian embassy. Why'd Foreign Affairs put you on this job?" He spotted his single piece of luggage and heaved it off the metal container-tray. "You must have been a very good girl since that Yugoslav fiasco last February."

"Yes, that must be the reason."

"Do you have a car?"

"Outside. You'll be staying at the Fortina Hotel in Sliema, Tigne Seafront. You'll love the view. There's even a heated pool."

"Great." Stupid woman has lost her priorities already. "I suppose you've finished the casework on Basilia?"

"I'll tell you what I have while we drive."

Green was surprised to find she had done a thorough job of filling in the obvious blanks about Basilia's stay on Malta. He could think of very few follow-up questions.

"The subtle touch came when Basilia spoke Hebrew. As reported by Captain Montani, the remaining skyjacker stood at the rear of the cockpit holding explosives while Basilia sat in the second row of First Class seats. Basilia warned the Arabs—plural—of danger. Then he shot the skyjacker, politely told Montani and his co-pilot to break contact with Luqa Control for five minutes, and took off with his passenger—the injured Mrs. Weinbaum—in an army jeep."

"What language did he use with the pilot?"

"Italian. He spoke English at all other times, but with a Spanish accent. A Marseilles journalist reported that he asked Basilia where the men's room was and was answered in French. Quite a linguist, this Spaniard."

"Any fuller descriptions than what the Maltese and Italians gave out?"

"No. Not many people remember what he looked like, he fitted so well into the role of a rather dated reporter who wasn't on an expense account and probably needed a scoop on this story more than anyone else. Bad posture, bad teeth, and bad eyesight typify the descriptions. No photos have turned up on him, though there's hope until the wire services release their final load to the newspapers. It's hard to describe a man when he inspires no curiosity and people are more likely to look away after first sighting him."

"Yes—almost as though he planned it that way."

"I've checked with every hotel on the island. No one of Basilia's description registered at any of them. No one of his *general* description registered during the week preceding the skyjacking—at least that they remember. A lot of people move through Malta in one week and our man could be a suicidal member of a charter tour from Iceland."

Green dismissed the idea curtly. "How would he smuggle his gun through Customs? How did he have time to rig a false identity—with documentation—between Friday evening and Saturday noon? If he was suicidal, why did he disappear after killing the skyjackers? No, too much was at stake. Basilia coughed up a lot of money to get himself onto Malta with a gun and fake ID before his chance to act had passed. He has strong connections, friends willing to risk prison to help him. That suggests an organization, possibly a right-wing element with corporate backing that has decided to ride shotgun for society's stagecoach."

Susan Meyer looked at him in wonderment, uncomprehendingly. The American idioms baffled her. "What kind of group?"

"One that doesn't have a hell of a lot to lose if discovered. That's why I doubt if the big services—CIA, KGB, SIS—would dare involve themselves. Given the world situation, their motives would be self-contradictory. Unless," he added cautiously, "they wanted us down. Israeli discomfort means assured oil supplies."

He relaxed against the cushioned head-rest and tried to forget for a moment the conflicting directions his theories were pulling him. Without more evidence they meant nothing. He had to simplify the search. But how? Look for a mad killer or a professional assassin? Trace every Browning P-35 ever manufactured? Request data on every known criminal who could not establish his whereabouts last Saturday?

Susan drove expertly, an expression of tranquility suffusing her features. She had no intention of saying anything to hurt the man's ego. Too many hours at a desk in Rome had made her eager for field-work. Nathan Green wasn't going to make her botch this chance.

The coded message was deciphered and brought down from Communications. Unfortunately, Dmitri Sebilitov could not be found to accept it. All his assistant said was that the surly Intelligence Attaché had gotten a call from the local PLO officer and took none too kindly to it. His shouts had interrupted activity on the entire floor. Did anyone want to hear a tape of the conversation?

The embassy's security chief did; though after listening to it he reluctantly admitted it gave no clues as to where Sebilitov might have wandered. What was so important about the communiqué? Could he see it?

No. For Sebilitov's eyes only. Top-grade material from

Moscow. The decoding officer—by necessity—and Sebilitov were the only ones cleared for it. This rankled Basilki, the security chief, and he regretted not having put a 24-hour watch on Sebilitov instead of the usual tag from office to home, home to office. Worse yet, if something happened to the top KGB officer in Beirut—something like being crushed by a collapsing wall that CIA men had rigged—Basilki's head would roll. Damn the man! How had he gotten past the operative on the elevator? He had a key for the back entrance—but why would he use it? . . . unless he was meeting secretly with enemy agents and took pains to conceal his tracks.

Basilki shuddered and ordered his entire security contingent into the field.

Commander Albin of the U.S.S. *Oread* frowned, looked again at the fifteen rows of connected numbers, and told his radio operator to call in a helicopter from the carrier *Louisiana*, eighty miles west and heading toward Taranto. He doubted whether it was serious, but he wasn't willing to take a chance. The series of numbers at the end—100743744—were well-known to him and meant that either Andropov or his chief deputy had sanctioned the message. The CIA had been kind enough to circulate that information to Naval Intelligence, apparently realizing that unless America's military ears knew the importance of the coded signature they could not be expected to relay any subsequent—and relevant—information to their civilian counterparts.

When the helicopter arrived at the electronic surveillance vessel sitting 22 miles northwest of Beirut, Commander Albin climbed into a sling suspended beneath it and was drawn up into the hovering craft. He handed the *Louisiana*'s intelligence officer a sealed plastic envelope, was given a receipt, and then lowered back to his ship, the helicopter returning to its floating base.

Onboard the *Louisiana* a second code was used to scramble the message recovered by the *Oread*'s omnifrequency receivers, and with a brief introduction the double-encoded fifteen rows of numbers were beamed to an American radar station near Adana, Turkey.

The intelligence personnel situated there already knew of the message, but gladly accepted confirmation that it had reached Beirut. Considering it was a high-speed transmission squeezed between massive jamming signals sent out from the southern Ukraine to obliterate the broadcasts from Radio Free Europe and Voice of America, no one at Adana could be sure it actually reached its goal.

Computers had already begun tackling the code. Success came sooner than expected.

When they finally got the translated message, the resident CIA staffers ordered up the fastest civilian jet on hand and sent a senior officer to London where the DCI's personal representative would be waiting for him.

Dmitri Sebilitov sheepishly spread his hands, one of which held a bottle of Bufferin aspirin.

Though he ranked above Basilki, he feared the copperheaded security chief—who, it was rumored by those in a position to know, had been a principal in the 1940 massacre of 28 Poles near Konigsberg, and reinforced his vile reputation by kidnapping Soviet draft-dodgers during the Cold War and having them castrated.

"Well?" Basilki asked. "Where were you?"

"I had a headache."

"So you decided to give us *all* a headache by disappearing. Why don't you use Soviet aspirin?"

"I forgot to cap my bottle and they were moist. Useless. It was stupid of me and . . . I've got a right to come and go as I please. Intelligence does not have to answer to Security."

Basilki's eyes began to glow in the semi-darkness of the corridor leading into the embassy building from the rear. "Don't think you can pull rank on me," he said coldly, his lips barely moving. "I have been in my profession longer than you have been in yours. The Americans have posted permanent watchers to track our comings and goings. Everywhere you go, everything you do—and buy—is carefully noted, reported, and filed. You could become an embarrassment to us, comrade. A liability." He paused to let the veiled warning sink in, then said, "Now get up to your office. Moscow has sent an urgent message—your eyes only. I expect they want a reply. Hurry, you are keeping them waiting!"

Sebilitov's only retaliation was a derisive sneer. He made his way to his second-floor office, called for the decoding officer, and was handed the message.

Both the *Oread* and the post at Adana monitored the reply from Beirut, sent on a wildly oscillating high-frequency wave pattern which made immediate transcription impossible. The banks of computers in the Adana installation were fed a tape of the transmission, taking six minutes to connect the dots and, given the code-breaker, translate the message into something recognizably human in logic.

"Looks like shit," the computer-systems analyst said,

offering the results to a linguist.

"Looks like Polish," the linguist said. "But I don't know Polish," he added, slipping the piece of paper to the Station Chief.

"It's Czech," the Station Chief said. "Give it hand-to-hand to Bronocek. See what he makes of it."

"Looks like shit," the analyst repeated for his own benefit.

The ten F-15 fighter-bombers screamed low over the sea-green Mediterranean, so swift that anyone directly in line with their flight-path would have been unable to identify them before they disappeared, leaving no other trace than a wave of brighter heat shimmering across the placid waters.

When they flew over Beirut—the marrow-piercing screech of their engines far behind them—and the Eagles with blue Stars of David on their fuselage were recognized, telephone lines jammed as the Lebanese government invoked its status as a member of the UN to complain about this new Israeli intrusion into Lebanese air space and to alert its fellow Arab nations that war was again imminent.

Sebilitov cursed his luck, the Lebanese communications system, the Palestinians for provoking this awesome display of Israeli air superiority, and his superiors at KGB Headquarters for placing yet another responsibility on his already tired shoulders. Then he again tried to telephone an inconspicuous warehouse in the port city of Tyre—still without results.

Deciding at last that he would have to make a journey there by car, he contacted Basilki and asked for an escort.

Nathan Green was sifting through the clippings and reports which Susan had collected on the skyjacking and rescue. It was his second day on Malta, the tenth day since the four skyjackers were shot dead at Luqa.

No dramatic breaks had appeared in the search for Basilia. The Maltese and Italians were anxious to drop the matter, convinced they had done as much as they could. To the press they said that Basilia obviously belonged to a secret organization well-versed in covering itself, and their job was complicated by the sophistication and physical resources of said group. What more could they do? Every country with economic or military interest in Malta—now or in the past—was asked to help in the search. Few had refused. A reward had been posted by the Libyans for any information leading to the capture of Basilia, and no one had succeeded in claiming it—though many tried. How could Valletta and Rome be faulted when they were clearly up against a very determined, very sinister band of killers willingly paying anything to keep its men safe?

Green paged through the ballistics and autopsy reports with growing weariness. All they told him was that Basilia knew how to use a gun. Five shots, only one miss. Three fatal heart wounds, one fatal neck wound. Green couldn't have done better firing point-blank at a barn door. Using a large-capacity automatic had clearly been a protection against an unknown quantity of skyjackers rather than an amateur's need for sheer fire-power. In place of fire-power Basilia employed flat, soft-nosed bullets—dumdums—that expanded on impact, amplifying the lethality of the slug by increasing radial damage. All very professional. No idea where the ammunition had been purchased: 9mm Parabellum is a common calibre and can be used in a wide variety of handguns. No idea where the gun originated; hundreds of thousands were produced for such disparate parties as El Salvadore policemen and Nazi SS officers (when they couldn't get hold of a Mauser *Kuhfusspistole*). Basilia's weapon may have come from a forgotten WWII cache or a modern gun-dealer.

Untraceable through his gun, Basilia also had successfully prevented any physical evidence being left behind. Not a fingerprint on the plane that couldn't be accounted for or a piece of discarded clothing with a tell-tale laundry-mark. Basilia had not smoked, drunk, or eaten from the time he first appeared. He always kept a considerable distance between himself and a microphone so that his words would not turn up on the taped conversations between Dom Lucas and the skyjackers, leaving a voice-print which could be used to identify him. He spoke rarely, he shied away from other reporters, and he never used a phone to anyone's knowledge.

So where to start? Was this the fabled "perfect crime?" (Was it even a *crime*? What would the Maltese charge Basilia with if they caught him? Leaving the scene of a rescue? Using a firearm within city limits? Impersonation of an anti-terrorist commando? Use of excessive force? Fibbing?)

He stood up, scratching his scalp and trying to decide whether now was a good time to take a shower. He felt grubby, his hair matted with natural oils, a stickiness at his armpits in spite of the air-conditioning combating today's unseasonably hot weather. Susan Meyer would be back soon from her interview with Dom Lucas, no doubt full of old information about how humped Basilia's shoulders were, where Basilia's notes had gone, whether he used short-hand, what his nose could be compared to.

What Green wanted most was an explanation of how Basilia managed to get off the island.

Actually, there was no reason to assume he *had* departed. Because it seemed the obvious thing to do hardly warranted ignoring the less-likely possibility that Basilia was holing up in one of the many limestone caves on Malta or had a hide-out on Comino.

And yet the Maltese swore they beat every square yard of the islands and found nothing. Considering the abuse they would have received had they *not* searched intensively on their home-turf, Green was convinced Basilia had escaped from Malta and might now be laughing about his adventure while riding a Hong Kong jinricksha with his mistress or buying a late Easter gift for his wife in a Chicago department store.

The warehouse had seen better days. Viewing it for the third time in as many months, Sebilitov wondered how much it had cost the embassy's financial comptroller, how much some Arab estate agent had wheedled out of the Soviet Treasury; for nothing came free to the Russians even though they kept the government in power by supplying food and arms and training.

A three-story building of steel and concrete with large glass windows on the upper floors, the warehouse suffered greatly under retaliation strikes. With the coincident disappearance of the insuring company, it had been shuttered with galvanized tin sheets and forgotten—despite its strategically-attractive location. Then in 1975 the Soviets purchased it through the PLO, restored it, built a tall fence around the building, and went into business, only vacating the warehouse once—during the

Israeli occupation of southern Lebanon.

Basilki's agent rolled the aging Skoda to a stop before the guardhouse. Keeping one hand on a pistol hidden under his jacket, he presented the necessary clearance papers and was waved on. Then he parked the car directly in front of the warehouse and escorted Sebilitov to the entrance. Beyond here the Intelligence Attaché would be entirely on his own. Access was severely restricted and those without official business were strongly discouraged from trying to enter.

When Sebilitov stepped through the foyer and into the gymnasium, he realized how clever the Russian designer had been; the huge cavern-like space was fully insulated to control extraneous variables: temperature, noise, light changes. Without a watch, no one inside the building would have been able to tell the time. The ugly facade was a deception. The interior had modern facilities for most sports—and certainly those sports which could be used in the exercise of force; included were a firing range, a deep swimming pool for training scuba divers, mats for karate and jujitsu, and gymnastics equipment.

"Why did you not call?" a soft voice asked in Russian.

Sebilitov whirled. Two seconds before, no one had been near him. Where had the man sprung from?

"Ack, Yevgeny, you frightened me! Still creeping around on thick rubber soles, I see."

"What are you doing here, comrade? I thought it was agreed that the . . ."

"Yes, yes, I know. But I couldn't get through to you. The Jews put Beirut into a spin," Sebilitov complained.

"Bombing?"

"The capital? They wouldn't dare. No, they just passed over so everyone could see their obscene gestures."

The other man laughed heartily. "You people in Beirut should be glad you're not getting what we do. Napalm and concussion bombs, strafings, an invasion now and then, and the odd artillery round from a Falangist unit. But is that why you came all this way, comrade?"

Sebilitov winced. He'd never liked that word: comrade. It was so easily adaptable to sarcasm, so politically dogmatic, so reminiscent of the slogans in Orwell's *1984*—a novel he picked up one day five or six years before in a bazaar—which implied a uniformity among all humans, a concept Sebilitov abhorred as much as the beastly quality of Soviet pharmaceuticals.

"I came," he said, "because I have received a message from Moscow that involves you."

"Me?"

"I mean to say it refers to a man like you. I supplied the face and name."

"So Moscow has not recalled me?"

Sebilitov stared long and hard at Yevgeny Sholokov, his top counterespionage agent in the Middle East. He knew Sholokov had a family awaiting him in Moscow, and thought it ironically apt that the bureaucratic idiots in and around the Kremlin should be so detached from the conditions under which they forced their agents to work. Sholokov was a good worker because he was young and still believed that diligence had a reward—in this case, a shorter tour of duty. But no. The KGB spurred its agents on until they collapsed. Then they were discarded, mere shell-casings, useless and irritating, worthy of Siberia but graciously consigned to a numbing retirement in a secluded dacha.

"No. We have a job for you. Can we speak privately?"

Sholokov led the way across the ground-floor gymnasium, passing groups of Arabs engaged in various exercises, their sinewy brown bodies lacquered with sweat. The warehouse served as a preliminary training-ground for the teenage Palestinians. After completing instruction here they would be spread through the many refugee camps in Lebanon and Syria to recruit and train others in the art of guerilla warfare.

The two men crossed an office, then descended a row of straight narrow steps at the rear of the building, steps which led to a bomb-shelter.

Sebilitov marveled at the shelved stacks of tinned provisions, the huge water reservoirs and emergency power generators, the awesome vastness of the underground refuge. The concrete bunker seemed capable of withstanding anything less than an atomic bomb.

"Is this necessary?" he asked.

"What?"

"This shelter designed for our scientists at Novosibirsk."

Again Sholokov laughed. "Often we are asked to house important people here. It is their safest refuge. Arafat, Haddad, Dadoud—they have all taken sanctuary with us from the double threat of Christians and Jews. If the bugs don't bother you, you can pass a restful night down here." He pulled a cot from a shelf holding dozens of them, set it up, then did the same for Sebilitov. "There. Now—my orders . . ."

"The Alitalia rescue Saturday before last. Do you know about it?"

"What I have read. What my boys tell me. Not very objective, I'm afraid."

"Arafat is in Moscow right now. Did you know that?"

"No."

"The visit had been planned for some time. Arafat wants more sophisticated weaponry—what else? He also demands that Moscow locate the murderer of the four Palestinian Liberationists. Ordinarily one would not expect the PLO to ask favors for a splinter group of Habash's PFLP, itself an offshoot of Arafat's organization. Still, in these times the different groups must form a common front. Birds of a feather—isn't that the expression?"

"And?" Sholokov urged impatiently.

"Moscow agreed to take up the search. They posted inquiries to cells on Malta and were rewarded."

"With what?"

"I don't know. I assume it's a lead on this Basilia. Why else would they ask me to send my top man to investigate?"

"But why me?"

"You have survived exceptionally long for one so daring. You know Europe well. You need a chance to serve your country in a dramatic way. You are to take a Palestinian marksman with you; since you speak Arabic, that will be less of a chore. Take your pick."

"*Mokrie dela?*"

"Moscow says end-stop. No questions, no reversals. End-stop."

"When am I to be briefed?" Sholokov asked.

"Fly to Rome. You will be met there by a compatriot who will provide you with the developments. Apparently the Arab is not to be included until you spot the target. Moscow wants the matter closed quickly and to the Arabs' satisfaction, so you leave today."

"What about my school here?"

"Delegate responsibility. You must have someone

ready to fill your shoes. You probably won't be gone long anyway, Yevgeny. After all, finding a man should be easier than locating a zinke," Sebilitov joked, remembering from the young man's dossier that he collected wind instruments. "The Arab will be responsible for the rest."

Sholokov merely nodded, his dark eyes unfocused.

CHAPTER SEVEN

Enrico Festina owned a second-hand Seaworker 22, a round-bilge hull form fishing cruiser fitted with a 75 h.p. Ford/Merak 4-cylinder diesel that gave the craft a top speed of 16 knots. The boat was Festina's pride and joy, acquired after many years of scrimping and saving and hard, slavish work for other masters. But now he ran his own boat and made his own hours, hiring out his services as captain to the wealthy businessmen who came down from Monaco and Milano and Munich and Madrid to do a bit of sword-fishing in the unpolluted waters off Paradise Bay.

Though his enterprising spirit paid his bills and financially secured his approaching retirement, the 60-year old Festina was not a captalist. Over half a lifetime on someone else's payroll had burned out his love of the independent entrepreneur—despite his present endeavors—and replaced it with a radical trust in the power of the masses. Every wrinkle on his wizened face represented a day at sea, cooking, swabbing, pulling in the nets, firing harpoons, standing knee-deep in slimy fish, coaxing an obstinate diesel to start again after the ship's screw was immobilized by seaweed. He'd done everything a man can do aboard a water craft and it didn't make him rich or famous or even respected. So he became a Communist.

On Saturday, 5 April, at approximately 4:30 p.m. Festina was installing a new radar reflector on his boat, the *Mesquita*, when a tall, broad-shouldered stranger approached along the pier at Marfa. He asked Festina if his boat was for hire.

Yes, said Festina, but not to him.

"What do you mean?" Sholokov asked through the interpreter.

Well, Festina had had an offer the day before from an American who wanted to take his wife and son out for some shark hunting. Thought it would be great sport. Festina told him he must be crazy. If they brought back a shark the island's beaches would empty of bathers and tourists would flee in droves, precipitating a loss of jobs—not the least of which might be Festina's. The American grumbled, handed Festina a 20-dollar bill, and told the old captain to keep his boat free on Saturday in case he should decide on some other aquatic enterprise.

"Did he come back?"

No, not by 4:30 on Saturday afternoon. The stranger came instead. He was big, blond, spoke Italian with a German accent. He wore blue jeans and a yellow turtleneck sweater, and carried an Adidas athletic bag—orange or red, Festina didn't recall which. He said he wanted to go to Sicily.

Festina laughed. Cross the Malta Channel in *his* boat? What was he? Crazy?

Five hundred Maltese pounds crazy was what he was.

That's how much he offered for a one-way journey. Said he was doubling his first offer because he knew Festina would of course have to pilot the *Mesquita* back to Marfa, passenger or no passenger. This warmed the old seaman's heart—as did the money—and he told the stranger to return early on Sunday and he would take him as far as Siracusa.

"Did you know yet what had happened at Luqa?"

"The hijacking? Sure."

"No, the killing of the hijackers."

No. Festina always kept the wheelhouse radio tuned to a weather channel. He hadn't heard about the rescue until he was on his way back from Siracusa on Sunday; a bulletin requested that all shipowners report any passengers they had taken off the Maltese islands who answered the following description . . .

"Yes, Enrico, we know the description. It does not match your passenger's description at all. So why did you contact *us* if you had suspicions? Why not inform the Maltese police?"

Well, Festina said, it seemed more like a capitalist plot, something hatched by those bastards in Valletta. They might call themselves Socialists, but they were just stooges for big European banks. So he called the Maltese Communist Party headquarters in Paola and voiced his suspicions. The information might prove useful, and nothing would please Festina more than to see those assholes in Valletta hounded out of office.

"What about the man? Did he give a name? What did he say and do? Did he have any distinguishing characteristics?"

The stranger introduced himself as Mr. Derna. He said he had to get to Palermo by Sunday night to meet a business acquaintance. He insisted on leaving immediately or he would look for another boat. Festina therefore agreed to take him then and there. The weather reports were predicting unseasonably calm seas, and the thought of 500 pounds stuffing his wallet proved irresistible.

During the six-hour voyage Derna remained silent, spending most of his time in the small cabin. Several times Festina went down to see if he was asleep so his mysterious bag could be examined, but the fellow had no interest in sleep. He sat stiffly on a bunk, reading one of Festina's fishing magazines and with the athletic bag balanced on his lap. Festina thought at first he might be a drug smuggler, but no one smuggled drugs *out* of Malta. So he returned to the wheelhouse and imagined ways of spending his huge fee.

No, Derna had no distinguishing physical attributes. He was big but not *that* big; tall, yes, but no skyscraper; blond, but perhaps bleached by the sun. No visible tattoos or scars.

"Did he stoop?"

Stoop? He was as straight-backed as a flag-pole!

"Do you still have the money he gave you?"

Some of it. Festina handed the bills to Sholokov and the serial numbers were copied.

"Did he give you any idea as to his intentions once he reached Palermo?"

Only that he'd be seeing his business acquaintance. He never said anything about a family or friends, if that's what you mean. But he was in a damned hurry to get away from Malta. Festina asked him why he didn't fly to Palermo. The airport was closed, he answered, because of the hijacking.

Sholokov sat quietly for several minutes—thinking

that Derna should have killed Festina and thrown him overboard—then thanked the old seaman for coming so far. The Party would, of course, handle all expenses. "You've been very helpful, comrade, and we would only ask that you not repeat your story to anyone else."

"What do you think?" Alexander Yupn asked. He was the Soviet Embassy's resident intelligence officer in Rome and had personally brought Enrico Festina from Malta. Unwisely, as it would turn out.

"He appears to be telling the truth," Sholokov responded.

"Of course he's telling the truth. We contacted the port authority at Siracusa and confirmed that the *Mesquita* docked there during the night of April fifth. The immigration officer has two men getting off: Enrico Festina and Hans Derna. Derna carried a German passport. What I meant is whether you believe Derna to be Basilia. Is it possible?"

Sholokov shrugged listlessly. "Who can say? But it is our only lead thus far, comrade, and so we must investigate it. Otherwise, if Derna *is* Basilia . . ."

"What have you got?" Green asked as Susan Meyer entered the apartment.

She looked at the phone in his hand, the mouthpiece covered. "Plane manifests for the past two weeks. Interesting. Charon?"

Green nodded.

"Tell him you'll call back."

Green sighed, relayed the message, and hung up. "This had better be good. It just took me three hours to get through. God knows how many people had tapped in by then."

Five minutes later she completed her debriefing. The special government committee organized to oversee the search operations for Basilia knew Susan quite well by now, having confirmed her role as an Israeli representative when she first appeared before it; and she was denied nothing, the Maltese intent on wiping their own hands of the affair as swiftly—and painlessly—as possible.

"So," she said excitedly, looking for praise from her terse companion.

"So what? Yesterday this Festina flies to Rome, returning the same day. He happens to be the owner of a small fishing cruiser operating out of Marfa. I don't get it. Where's the connection with Basilia?"

"On the same day, Alexander Gregorovich Yupn flies to Luqa and leaves almost immediately on the outbound flight back to Rome. He doesn't even have time to leave the airport. And it just so happens that he is a known KGB agent working out of Rome's Soviet Embassy."

"And Festina is a Communist. I get it now."

"Do you?"

"Sure. This Festina is really Basilia. He did a job for the Reds and now they come to retire him, sending their top Italian fixer to hold his hand. In broad daylight already!"

"I'm tired of your sarcasm!" she suddenly spat, her eyes blazing. "You sit on your ass in here and expect me to do your job for you, then you use that so-called wit of yours to shoot at the evidence. You stupid bastard! What the hell are you here for? To boss me around? Well, I'm not some crummy slut who licks boot leather for five bucks an hour! You can go suck an egg, Mr. Nothing Green!"

She slammed the door behind her.

Green slowly rose and pulled the drapes, letting the afternoon sun burst in like burning phosphorus.

She was right, of course. He'd been acting like a clod ever since he stepped off the plane. Not expecting a female partner, he had let his antagonism and disappointment show—to his detriment. Susan was doing a spendid job; and perhaps because he didn't expect that—or resented it—he made every effort to prove himself right by proving her wrong. A stupid bastard. Yes. He'd been sent to track down Basilia, not pout like some misogynous schoolboy. Susan was intelligent, imaginative, and industrious. And she was putting him to shame.

He thumbed again through the material she had brought, pondering over her thesis.

Festina and his boat might have been instrumental in getting Basilia off Malta, but why would he have to go to Rome to tell the KGB station chief? Why didn't he just collect the reward money? (Obvious: The reward could only be given once Basilia was apprehended, and Enrico Festina was not a gambler.) Why didn't Yupn send a minion to collect the information instead of venturing out himself—and then only to escort Festina to Rome? Unless . . .

Unless someone in Rome wanted to question the boatman but couldn't afford being seen on Malta. That fitted in nicely with the information General Charon had just relayed: the Americans intercepted a radio message to the Soviet embassy in Beirut which ordered the resident intelligence officer to send an agent to Rome where he would receive further instructions. The key word was "Basilia."

Washington didn't know what to do with the information. If the CIA was caught trying to foil the KGB's man, Uncle Sam would be up to his goatee in trouble; American involvement in the Alitalia rescue would appear undeniable. Fortunately, however, the message from Moscow also ordered Beirut to send along a Palestinian. Yasser Arafat being in Moscow at the time, the CIA concluded that he personally forced the issue of finding Basilia and using a PLO guerilla to finish him. All for the sake of retribution—*el tar*—and tying loose ends. Anyway, mention of the Palestinian gave Washington the excuse it needed to inform the Israelis of the transmission's contents.

Now it was up to Green to discover what Festina had said in or on his way to Rome. Under normal circumstances that would not present much of a problem. But these were not normal circumstances. The KGB must not be aware that its Israeli counterpart was standing in its shadow. It must first lead Green to Basilia.

And then?

The first line of inquiry led to the car ferry that crossed between Messina and Villa San Giovanni on the Italian mainland. Hans Derna could have rented a car in Siracusa, taken a ferry across the Strait of Messina, and then lost himself in one of the larger cities. He would have avoided planes because they indicated his direction—if not his final destination.

Shown a composite portrait made from Enrico Festina's description, a freight-handler on the ferry remembered seeing Derna, but he hadn't come on with a car. The blond-haired man asked him how long the crossing took, and the laborer replied "Sunup till sundown"—and thought himself very clever.

That was on a Monday. The ferry didn't operate on Sundays, the day Derna would have arrived in Messina after hitch-hiking up the east coast of Sicily, anxiously looking for a means to cross. He probably could have paid a boatman to take him across the strait; though again that might have seemed too great a risk.

Sholokov put himself in Derna's place. Once in Villa San Giovanni he must find a means of locomotion. It was still less than 48 hours after the rescue and police in the Mediterranean states would be tightening their net. Would he rent a car, take a bus, or hitch a ride?

The report from the embassy's investigative staff was definitive. Presenting themselves as policemen, they said they were looking for Hans Derna, a German criminal wanted for extradition. Since he may have been using an alias, the KGB men offered copies of the composite.

On Monday afternoon Hans Derna rented a silver Ford Granada from a car rental agency on Via Stradio a Monte in Reggio di Calabria using an American Express credit card, said he would need it for three weeks and would drop it off at the rental agency's garage in Turin. His card had been issued through a bank in Frankfurt, and the agency spoke with the bank's manager to ascertain whether Derna was in good financial standing. The manager stated unequivocally that Herr Derna was quite solvent.

"So how is he a criminal?" the wide-eyed rental agent asked.

"He deals in stolen cars," the KGB investigator replied, smiling lugubriously.

Half an hour later the information came into Sholokov's hands. He passed the license number and make of the car to Alexander Yupn, telling him to uncover the car's present location—assuming it was still in Italy. This could be done simply and inexpensively by contacting branches of the pervasive Italian Communist Party (PCI) and requesting information on such a car, probably sitting in front of a hotel. There was no reason to assume the car was being hidden.

At 9:32 that evening the Soviet diplomatic mission in Milan received a phone call from an 18-year old bellhop at a hotel in Bellano, a peaceful and extraordinarily beautiful town on the eastern shore of Lake Como.

Wend Ergatz shook his hand warmly and motioned him into the waiting black limousine. As they were driven to the embassy, Ergatz offered what information he had been able to gather in the brief time allowed him.

"They arrived from Athens via Olympia Airways. You'd expect them to travel separately, but evidently they feel as pressed for time as we do. They're making big mistakes."

"Perhaps they've convinced themselves the Americans could never break their code, and so they have no need to worry about someone taking interest in them. After all, they've now using the trap-door cypher the Americans invented."

"Perhaps." It was a small point and Ergatz was none too familiar with codes. "Anyway, they were listed on the manifest as Mikhail Arpotin and Hani Rabat. Even sat next to each other on the plane. You wouldn't believe, Nathan, all the trouble this—"

"I believe it, Wend. What else? Have you kept track of them?"

"The Arab has disappeared. The address he gave on his immigration card is false, and we haven't been able to make him. Arpotin turns out to be our old friend Yevgeny Sholokov, coach to young killers in Lebanon. I

114

thought Mossad took him out two years ago—until I saw our photo department's slides of him eating a plate of spaghetti yesterday at *Il Terremoto*. Brazen as hell. He's a damn exhibitionist, if you ask me."

"Where's he staying?"

"He took an apartment off the Spanish Steps but spends most of his time at the embassy."

"Doing what?"

"How would I know? The place is as bugged as an old mattress and we still get no signals. I understand the Italians are losing their tempers about the microwave interference beeping out of the embassy during working hours. Maybe we'll hear something after they lodge a formal protest."

"What about surveillance?"

"Top-grade. We won't lose him."

"But no sign of Basilia."

Ergatz unhooked the waist-clasp on his trousers and allowed his protuberant belly to sink to his thighs. He shook his head. "This is guesswork, Nathan. We're just trying different approaches. Sholokov may lead us to nothing."

"That's not what Charon thinks."

"Charon is fifteen hundred miles away. Light-years. If it had been known the KGB was accepting the demolition job, Shabak would never have been given the brief. This is Mossad's type of work."

"We're not looking for old Nazis, Wend."

"Huh. By the way, where is your partner?"

"Miss Meyer? Back on Malta."

"Everything okay?"

Green frowned. "Yes, of course, everything's fine."

"That's not what I hear. I hear she's been cut from

the operation."

"One hears lots of things."

"You haven't denied it, Nathan."

"She got her period. It doesn't rain enough on Malta. She's returning to Tel Aviv to wash away the waste."

It was a crude remark. According to Orthodox tradition, during menstruation Jewish women are required to bathe in rainwater. The subject is not open to discussion between men. Yet Green showed no compunctions about insulting Susan Meyer.

"I didn't know ... I'm sorry."

"Forget it," Green said testily. "Just forget it."

He hated himself.

CHAPTER EIGHT

The bellhop told them Mr. Erinys was staying in Room 15. He had gone on a sight-seeing tour by bus to the Tyrolean Alps; but, according to the hotel manager, he was expected back in a few days. With what the bellhop considered typical American extravagance, Erinys had paid to keep his room even though he was not using it and could just as well have made a reservation for his return.

This fact drew Sholokov's attention. If Erinys wanted to hold his room he obviously had a reason. Was he hiding something inside it, something he couldn't carry with him?

The Palestinian took Room 16, an end room facing the corridor leading to the self-service elevator. Through the connivance of the bellhop there was no difficulty in obtaining this particular room, for it did not face the lake and was therefore hard to let.

Within an hour of bringing up the Arab's bags, the bellhop had unlocked Mr. Erinys' door and stood guard by the elevator as Sholokov and his partner, Hani Rabat, searched the American's room. The youth happily accepted the danger he put himself in, convinced that Erinys was a CIA spy trying to undermine the Workers' Movement. His friends would be astounded and envious when he told them how he helped the Cause, foiling another Yankee plot.

Sholokov expected to find a Browning P-35. He was disappointed. Except for a suitcase against one wall the room appeared empty. Even the bathroom failed to yield so much as a toothbrush. If Erinys was concealing anything it had to be in the suitcase.

The KGB assassin drew a thin plastic card from his back-pocket, examined the suitcase locks, and inserted an edge of the card into one of them, twisting.

When the suitcase-handle exploded, Hani Rabat was in the bathroom examining the toilet cistern. The dull thump and Sholokov's scream of pain sent him rolling across the tile floor, his Russian Tokarev pistol already in his grip.

Sholokov was sitting on the floor, his back against the foot of the bed. Spots of crimson blood freckled his face. His eyes stared down at his left hand. Blisters had begun to form beneath the seared skin, puffing up the fingers. Except the little finger—which was missing.

Rabat spotted the bloody digit atop a curtain-rod. He said nothing, rapidly returning to the toilet.

Sholokov sat dazed, watching the slow throb of blood from the darkened stump. If he needed any stronger evidence that Erinys was the man who mercilessly killed the four Palestinian hijackers, he had it now.

Only the bellhop seemed to have heard the detonation, and he was left to tidy the room while Rabat drove Sholokov to a doctor. Much to the Russian's disgust the booby-trapped suitcase—blown open by the explosion—

contained nothing but twelve identical copies of the *International Herald Tribune* dated three days before; that is, the day Erinys purportedly departed for the Tyrolean Alps.

Hani Rabat had seen it all, wanted it all, and—with the certainty of youth and three years of crossing international borders where they were least protected—thought he knew it all. He was a short, stocky young fellow, much like Sholokov, with large dark eyes and ears flat against his head. Though his thick muscularity indicated clumsiness, his movements were actually quick and almost dainty.

Joining Black September as an organizer in 1972, he soon brought attention to himself by his unusual intelligence. He had an amazing facility for linguistics and was spotted by Abu Daoud to help in the attack on the Olympic Village in Munich. The plan had been conceived by the Black Septembrists as an effort to gain recognition for their group and attention for their cause, and it was considered infallible. Preparations were exhaustive, largely due to young Rabat's imagination: he questioned every plotted movement, tested it against the probable reaction of the West German police, suggested the various requirements of the assault party, and generally made such a nuisance of himself that for the last week leading up to the invasion of the Olympic Village he was banned from contact with any members of the strike-force wherever they might be.

In 1974 he dropped out of the group, sensing that it had already seen its best days. He also decided upon a more active role for himself in the terrorist movement. Since only George Habash's PFLP offered him that opportunity, he joined it. No more empty days plotting logistics, no more excuses to his friends about what he was doing to further the cause of a Palestinian homeland. As with all men who have been tied to a desk he envisioned himself doing great, heroic deeds, his towering figure surrounded by heaps of corpses, his friends applauding his awesome courage and strength.

Now, several years later, he could claim two skyjackings and two assassinations to his credit. The skyjackings proved too easy and he dropped out of that section. If he had stayed, he told himself with modesty, the Alitalia hijacking would never have failed. The assassinations may have been routine—a rich Jewish merchant in Holland and an Arab diplomat in Paris who had unwisely supported Jordanian sovereignty over the West Bank—but at least they fired his jaded senses, making him feel more in control of his own destiny than that of a planeload of shaking, sheep-like hostages.

Soon the Action and Security Section would be retiring him for a younger man—not because Rabat lacked proficiency in his field (something no one dared say) but because other Palestinian warriors needed and deserved a chance to fight for their non-existent country. Hundreds of them must dream of filling his boots; and as a man of the world, one who saw, wanted, and knew it all, he understood their need. There were only so many Jewish targets to go around, targets within reach; they had to be shared among their murderers at a pace that frightened them, though not so fast as to raise a world-wide hue and cry of systematic genocide.

Rabat realized his active life in the PFLP was approaching an end when his immediate superior ordered him to join this stupid, clumsy Russian bear in Athens.

Before, he worked by himself, refusing—and proving he didn't need—a backup. Now it was different. Technically Sholokov simply came along to pin the target. In actuality Rabat was just another hired gun, condescended to and usually ignored by his partner; he had as much voice in this affair as a bomb in the hands of a madman.

So Hani Rabat felt no sorrow when the Russian agent lost a finger. In fact, it elated him. Now he was free of the man's leash, free to sit and plot and wait for the strange Mr. Erinys, the bastard who murdered four of his comrades, who walked away unmolested by the justice of Allah or man, and who must soon answer for his sins.

Three days passed uneventfully.

Yevgeny Sholokov returned to Rome, mending, experienced enough to remain unprovoked into revenge by his mutilation, and certain the Arab could handle the completion of the mission without his personal guidance. Unless Erinys failed to return no further problems were anticipated. The Turin garage, naturally, had been placed under separate surveillance in case Rabat failed to sight his target.

On the fourth night Hani Rabat went to bed early, as was his custom; he wanted as much rest as possible, and had instructed the bellhop to ask for the night shift so he could inform him immediately if Erinys chanced to return during Rabat's sleep. Another alarm was installed in his room: a sound-amplifier attached to the wall separating Rooms 15 and 16, with a lead-wire to a small speaker beneath his pillow. Various sundry noises were caught by the sensitive wall microphone but Rabat quickly grew accustomed to them and felt certain he would be awakened if anyone entered Room 15.

The bellhop, a pimple-faced boy named Alberto Zuccobachi, was smoking in the cloakroom of the darkened restaurant when the car rolled to a stop on the shore-line road below the Hotel Ancora. His thoughts were far-distant from keeping a watch for Mr. Erinys, from his duty to the Party that had forced his father's wages higher and helped pay for his mother's appendectomy. In fact, he was concentrating on the nude women in a magazine left behind by a guest, his hand feverishly rubbing the blood-flushed stem of his penis. He was quite oblivious to the man who stepped out of the car, walked up the stone steps leading to the veranda and rear entrance of the hotel, paused outside the hallway opening onto the reception desk, then carefully eased his way through the door, eyes and ears alert for the slightest movement or sound from the weary receptionist who rested her head on folded arms at the switchboard.

Hani Rabat awoke instantly. Springing from the bed fully dressed—wearing a casual outfit he had not removed since Sholokov left him four days earlier—he stepped to the door and peered through the peep-hole set in the center.

The corridor was empty. No one had knocked. The bellhop would have knocked if Erinys was back, or called up. But would Erinys return at 2:08 in the morning? Rabat shook his head to clear away the detritus of a bad dream, then considered Room 15. No sound came from the room—yet the Arab knew that *something* startled him out of his sleep. Could it have been the ashtray he wedged between the wall and front panel of the desk, so arranged that it would drop to the floor if anyone tried to pull out the locked drawers?

Not daring to turn on a light, he carefully felt along the string leading from a bed-post to a piece of gum stuck to the wall, indicating a spot directly above it where Rabat had bored a miniscule spy-hole.

Cautiously positioning himself, he located the hole with his sensitive fingers, bending low to peer through.

There was no light in Room 15; either that, or someone had blocked the pin-sized hole.

And then the beam of a hand-torch slashed across the hole, so surprising Rabat that he rolled backward on the thick carpet before pouncing to his feet and scrambling for the loaded Tokarev automatic concealed between the mattresses of his bed.

Alberto Zuccobachi meticulously wiped himself with a tissue. His mother always made crude remarks when she found the front of his underwear stained yellow, and Alberto did not care to explain the necessities of manhood or have her badger him with the Church's teachings on self-manipulation as a form of regenerative suicide. He therefore made certain his penis was emptied, zipped his trousers, stashed the girlie magazines in the trunk used for lost property, closed the small high window that he'd opened to free the acrid stench of cigarette smoke, then checked his shirt-tail. If one of the staff happened to be standing outside—very unlikely, but possible—Alberto wanted to look like just another conscientious employee dutifully keeping an eye on the hotel environs.

No one stood outside, so he headed directly for the toilets, intent on flushing the last drops of sperm from his organ by urination.

The toilets, reserved during the day for patrons of the hotel restaurant, were situated to the left of the reception desk. An aluminum drinking fountain stood between the twin entrances and was the landmark the staff used in giving directions to waterlogged diners; the hotel manager actually insisted on this point, rightfully proud of the quite un-European convenience which he had had installed against the better judgement of the Ancora's owner, and wanting everyone to know that the Hotel Ancora combined Old World charm with Holiday Inn hedonism.

Alberto passed the reception desk and noted its caretaker trying to earn wages in her sleep. Poor Monique! As horny as Alberto continually was, he seriously doubted whether she could ever seduce him. He had, of course, fantasized over that very possibility, but with such negative results that he was forced to return to his magazines or risk rubbing his flaccid penis to a cinder. Monique had the face of a pig—totally unsettling.

He also noted—in passing—the rows of numbered keys hanging from a wooden plaque above the switchboard. The keys told which rooms were empty or which guests were still out partying. The empty spaces indicated those guests who had retired to bed.

With a rising sense of panic Alberto realized that the key to Room 15—the key Mr. Erinys had left behind when departing on his trip—was missing from the rack.

Standing to the side so his shadow would not fall across the bottom edge of the door, Rabat slowly inserted his duplicate key into the lock and twisted. He'd oiled the mechanism three days before, even waxing the bolt so that it slid soundlessly in it housing.

The Arab had waited five minutes, hoping Erinys would either switch on a light or leave. He was convinced the man intended checking out surreptitiously; after seeing the condition of his suitcase he'd have no choice, not being in a position to afford a police investigation of his reasons for rigging the suitcase with a small bomb. Where had he obtained the plastic explosive? the *carabiniere* would ask. Where did he learn his booby-trapping skills? Why did he consider it necessary to employ them?

Rabat finally decided that his target might choose to exit via his small balcony. Hanging from the ledge, Erinys would have only a four-foot drop to the flagging below. From there he would be able to reach his car in thirty seconds and be on his way.

So Rabat turned the doorknob. As soon as the latch was retracted he would quickly slip his hand inside, touching the light-switch four inches from the outer edge of the jamb and momentarily blinding Erinys whose eyes were by now accustomed to the darkness of his room. Then the silenced Tokarev would deliver a just retribution—though not before Rabat had exacted full details of the assassin's mission, his superiors and organization, and the names of any accomplices.

Gripping the pistol in his right hand, he struck the door with his shoulder and fumbled for the switch with his other hand.

A heavy force slammed against the door from the opposite side, knocking him backward and trapping his left arm. Pain ballooned excruciatingly into his chest as he again hit the door, trying to free himself.

But the door was immovable.

When his quarry grabbed his hand and twisted crudely, snapping the wrist, Rabat fired into the door at chest-height, no longer caring whether anyone heard. He needed help and was—for the first time in his life—on the verge of calling for it.

The door abruptly swung open and the Arab fell inside the dark room, firing again as he struck the floor, not certain of his target as a deeper shadow moved from behind the door, merging into the blackness of a corner.

His third shot brought a scream from Room 14. The hard-nosed bullet had penetrated the adjoining wall and lodged in the left kidney of an elderly Austrian, here with his wife to enjoy a blessed retirement vacation. He had sat up in bed at the first heavy sound from the next room, switched on the bed-lamp, and shook his wife. She looked up to see him point at the wall, suddenly grimace and flail his arms behind him, then topple off the bed, a spreading dark stain on the back of his striped night-shirt.

Rabat pushed himself to his feet and retreated toward the partially open doorway. His hand shook, his knees quivered. Still no sound from Erinys. But that would change when Rabat flipped on the light.

Searching for the switch with the back of his limp left hand he sensed body-heat along his right arm.

Shrieking wildly, he swung the Tokarev around, but the knife-life edge of a hand collapsed his larynx before he could pull the trigger. Goggle-eyed, dropping his weapon and grasping his throat, he sank to his knees, never seeing the foot that fractured his skull and killed him.

CHAPTER NINE

Resting comfortably on the rim of a mountainous region known as Jebel el Akhdar, the Libyan city of Darnah emanates a smug satisfaction. Bloated by oil workers, tourists, and a farming community that expands in direct proportion to the increasing flow of water from a new desalination plant, Darnah has been assured a stable life. The winds of chance do not frighten it. A new store opens in the city of an average of every ten months. A mining consortium scratches through the rocky woodlands southwest of the city, buoyed by traces of uranium. The Trans-Libyan Railway, near completion, will at last connect Marrakesh and Cairo, bringing additional tourists and opening new markets to Darnah's enterprising businessmen.

The blessings from the pipeline terminal at Tobruk, less than ninety miles away, help of course. Darnah, smaller, less industrialized, more agricultural, receives the tourist benefits from its neighbor: foreigners who come to work in Libya's oil industry but want a place where they can relax, spend money in an atmosphere unpolluted by the viscous smell of crude. They, in turn, tell their friends of the city's pleasant hotels, excellent seafood, and unhurried way of life.

Darnah is the new Libyan Mecca.

Darnah is also the jumping-off point for Colonel Gaddafi's appointed sanctuary for Palestinian killers.

In the hills that roll behind Darnah there is a small camp completely surrounded by a high fence and members of the Libyan Army of Liberation. Few tourists ever glimpse the rough structures of clay bricks and corrugated iron, and certainly no journalists—should they venture beyond the government-approved areas around Benghazi and Tripoli and the resort spots—are able to question any of the transients who find a temporary home in the encampment.

Naturally, concerned governments wonder what happens to the hijackers who steal their civilian planes, the urban terrorist prisoners who are ransomed for innocent civilians, the mad bombers and snipers and cut-throats who infiltrate their society and extort a deadly revenge for undisclosed or curious political misdemeanors. Secret agents of these governments make discreet inquiries, spy-satellites photograph the changing face of the Sahara, and high-ranking emissaries demand satisfaction from the guardians of these radicals—yet nothing ever comes of all the fuss. The major governments pinpoint the terrorists' havens but are powerless to act against them as long as the host country is oil supplier to much of Western Europe.

On this early morning in April the camp was silent. The eastern half housed seventeen men, the western half thirteen women. Thanks to the ingenuity of one terrorist, an Arab chemistry graduate from the University of Utah, a large quantity of grape juice had been fermented in an oil barrel; but their low tolerance for alcohol proved incapacitating, the reason for the terrorists' silence. Occasionally one of the women would wake up and vomit, then drop back to sleep on her thin hard pallet. Even the guards, invited to join and accepting because they so rarely had the opportunity to do anything strictly forbidden, were quiescent, sitting at their positions and smiling for no apparent reason, perhaps thinking of the female company they enjoyed earlier that night. What else was there to do but sin in such a boring, uneventful place, protecting a gang of crazy youngsters from an enemy that could not even get near to it?

Having twin encapsulated 130 h.p. Volvo petrol engines with air ducts leading to ventilators on the aft deck, the special Swedish Albin 25 rides quietly on the water. Made in Kristinehamn, it can be fitted with a mast and sails, making it even more quiet to run.

The 25-foot model that glided into Darnah's harbor in the dead of night was so fitted. The harbor-master would not have even noticed it entering an open berth if his mongoloid son had not tugged at his sleeve, jumping and howling excitedly. Not that such a craft never appeared at Darnah. In fact, much more impressive yachts owned by European film stars and Arab oil sheiks were constantly putting into Darnah, becoming so commonplace that no one paid any attention to them.

Ahmed el-Gezzer had his duty, nevertheless; if it ever became known that he allowed a vessel to moor without getting its name, the pilot's and those of his passengers, a berthing fee, and passport information, he would very soon be back to his old job of repairing fishing skeins.

A well-lit esplanade bordered the water, and anyone coming ashore from the wooden piers that jutted into the harbor like blunted fangs would necessarily be seen from the small shack which el-Gezzer called his office.

Waiting patiently, the harbor-master watched a white figure shifting rubber bumpers against the cruiser's starboard side, looping his mooring lines around the metal-capped posts. The light coming from the esplanade's lamps barely reached the boat, but the scrawny Arab could at least see that only one man was nestling the handsome craft. Perhaps the others—the passengers and/or rest of the crew—were asleep below deck, for the boat showed no lights of its own.

The man in white finally finished, disappeared into the cabin, then re-emerged almost instantly and walked along the esplanade from Pier 2 toward the brilliantly-lit office of the harbor-master, a bulky canvas carry-all slung over his back.

According to the documents he presented to el-Gezzer, the man was Jean-Marguite Plessy, 39, a French entrepreneur who owned and operated the 25-footer now in the harbor basin, the *Écrasez L'infâme*. He told el-Gezzer that he was traveling from Benghazi to Tobruk to pick up a client's party and decided to take a breather in Darnah before completing his journey because his deckhand had suddenly decided to accept a job on a passing tanker, abandoning him.

Only half-understanding Plessy's French, the harbor-master paid his words grave attention, and therefore did not realize Plessy was positioned between him and the *Écrasez L'infâme*; for that reason he did not see the black figure that scurried off Pier 2, sprang over the low sea-wall, and vanished into the darkness of Darnah's narrow streets. His son saw; but being unable to speak he was frustrated in his efforts to make himself understood.

Plessy filled out the required forms and asked el-Gezzer where he might find a room for the night.

"Will you not sleep on the boat?" el-Gezzer replied in lieu of an answer.

The man paused, finally nodding. "Yes, I suppose. The bunks are like rock though," he joked.

"There are many hotels," said el-Gezzer, suddenly thinking that Darnah's tourist board might find his first remark disloyal. "You can surely find a room, regardless of the hour."

"No, no, I will sleep on the boat. But can you tell me where I can eat a good meal?"

El-Gezzer referred him to an all-night restaurant and wished him a *bonne fête*. He did not check Plessy's bag, assuming it was filled with a change of clothing. Europeans were all the same. Changing clothes every day, constantly taking baths, trimming their little pink fingernails. El-Gezzer began feeling very superior.

The police were baffled.

Three bullets were recovered from the environs of Room 15 at the Hotel Ancora. One had passed through the door, lodging in the opposite wall. Another was found in the wall-insulation at the corner junction of Rooms 15 and 16. The third was dug from the body of one Ugo Vescatzi, dead from peritonitic poisoning. At least that was the medical examiner's initial opinion as to cause of death.

The slugs were sent to the Crime Detection Laboratory in Milan along with the Tokarev, and the results of comparison tests would be available by mid-day.

Inspector Matan had little doubt, however, that the Tokarev fired the bullets: all one had to do was examine the magazine and chamber to see that only three more shells could be fitted into the pistol. He was certain as well that the dead man, identified as Hani Rabat, was the assailant. An examination of his room had undeniably shown that Rabat was spying on Room 15. Everything pointed toward attempted murder.

But if Signore Erinys, occupant of Room 15, was the intended victim, where was he now? Why didn't he present himself? He could justifiably claim self-defense. No one would dare doubt him after seeing the listening devices in Rabat's room, the spyhole in the wall, the notebook with Signore Erinys description in it.

And yet was Erinys involved? The receptionist said the room-key was taken while she dozed. The bellhop had brought it to her attention, then gone upstairs to find Rabat dead and Mrs. Vescatzi screaming her head off in the hallway. Would Erinys have been so secretive about taking his key?

No, said the hotel manager, rudely awakened by a report of two murders in his hotel and wondering whether they would hurt business or increase it through the morbid curiosity of tourists. After looking at the key to Room 15 which the police found in the door-lock, he stated unequivocally that the key was a copy, a crude duplicate probably obtained from Marchese's drugstore. Everyone knew Marchese had no scruples; even though he'd been warned by the manager to report any guests who tried to have copies made of the Ancora's well-marked keys, he continued to turn them out. For 750 lira apiece!

Marchese was pulled out of bed and finally admitted that he had indeed made the copy—though not very well. You see, his automatic key duplicator had a twitch in it. It didn't follow a groove. The original and copy came out looking similar, but the copy was harder to maneuver in the lock. That's why the man had taken the original and put the copy on the hotel's plastic key-chain.

"What man?"

Marchese described Erinys.

That effectively knocked Erinys off the list of suspects. If he had the original key to Room 15 there would be no reason for him to take the poor copy from the hotel rack. Even if he'd lost the original, wouldn't he logically have gotten the receptionist's attention and openly asked for the key to his room?

So what the hell was going on? Where was this Erinys?

Having taken Erinys' passport number from the hotel's file, the police contacted the American Consulate in Milan.

Twelve hours later the reply arrived: The passport number which the Bellano police had quoted belonged to a woman in Tacoma, Washington. She'd never heard of a man named Erinys. Neither had the State Department. If the Italians got their hands on Erinys and his passport, would they please contact Washington immediately?

While the police were still vacuuming the carpet in Room 15 for the tiniest shred of evidence leading to a motivation for the assassination attempt, Paul Justine, alias Jean-Marguite Plessy, alias Pierre Courbot, strolled along Darnah's Hassad Boulevard (formerly known as Sadat Boulevard). He turned left at the second alley-way he came to and deposited his heavy carry-all beside a rain barrel.

"Nine o'clock," said the man on the opposite side of the barrel.

"Be there," Plessy replied, reaching for an identical carry-all which the man in black handed to him. A shiver of worry suddenly tapped his spine. "Are you sure you can make it?"

"You had better hope I do."

"I wasn't thinking about the money."

"Neither was I. Just be certain the old geezer sees you off."

"The keys are in—"

"I know."

"Remember, you turn—"

"I know. Get out of here."

Plessy returned to the *Écrasez L'infâme* after chatting with the harbor-master for ten minutes and offering him some rolls which he had in his bag, saying he'd decided to eat onboard and so bought a take-away meal from the restaurant el-Gezzer recommended. All very pleasant. The old man and his son delighted in this diversion from the usual boredom of the night-shift.

Darnah used to be exciting, el-Gezzer told himself. Plenty of action as rival tribes battled for supremacy along the only fertile strip of coast-line in Libya. Not now. Things had changed. The old flintlocks and carbines he'd wielded as a youngster were replaced by long-range artillery, high-flying bombers, mammoth tanks. A man no longer saw the faces of those he killed or who killed him. War was impersonal, uncathartic. Blood was cheaper than water. The fire in a soldier's eyes once burned one enemy at a time, but now razed entire cities.

And why? What reason motivated men to war against their neighbors? Egotism, envy, lust for more power and land?

Yes, the same old motivations. They'd been the impetus toward brutal war when el-Gezzer was a child, and they were still operating. The same paradoxes continued in the struggle of the fittest and strongest killing each other, removing themselves from a race's genetic pool.

Before leaving the old man and his son, Plessy told them he would be lifting anchor at dawn. El-Gezzer tried to convince him to stay longer, fearing his earlier abrasiveness had upset the Frenchman. But Plessy had evidently made up his mind.

Plessy drew in his mooring lines only half an hour after boarding his boat. When the sun tipped the eastern Mediterranean the *Écrasez L'infâme* had disappeared.

Nathan Green only relaxed after crossing the border into Switzerland. Leaving Italy was not a move he had anticipated, but his instincts told him it was the only choice left open to him—for safety's sake.

The car, of course, would have to be ditched since someone might have noticed it parked below the Hotel Ancora—even though it was rented under an assumed name and could not be traced to him.

He had not wanted to kill the Palestinian, he told himself, though knowing all the time that that was the only reason he'd joined the Special Flying Squad. To think of his job objectively, free of darker motives, eased his conscience somewhat, made him feel less—what he considered himself during his despondent periods—the hired thug. Arabs were human beings just like Jews. They felt the same needs and ambitions he did. Why bother them?

A Palestinian also killed his wife in cold-blood.

Not being a Christian, Green suffered under no illusions that he must love his neighbor as himself, turn his cheek, forgive and forget. Doing unto others as they would do unto him if the bastards only had a chance made more sense, he admitted. Yet even an eye for an eye could not satisfy his craving for revenge, a need which he concealed from everyone but himself.

Wend Ergatz must be notified and get a message to Charon. The pages of information Green had torn from Rabat's pocket notebook would prove invaluable. They gave a concise version of the stake-out at the hotel, an unstated motive for seeking this man Erinys, and an itinerary of all tour buses operating out of Bellano. Erinys' description had been left behind to give the police another fact to chew on; it might also serve to lessen the heat on Erinys, who would automatically be eligible for a verdict of justifiable homicide, Rabat clearly having been the aggressor, the stalking hunter.

Though Green now recognized that he was tracking the right man, the Federico Basilia who rescued the Alitalia passengers at Luqa Airport, he felt no exaltation. Understanding why it was necessary to apprehend Basilia/Erinys, he still found his mission unsavory. For centuries the Jews had been accused of, hated and persecuted for the death of Christ; wrongly, as it happened, but a fact. Now a Jew was being asked to track down and render unto Pilate the saviour of a planeload of defenseless people. How would Israel excuse itself before the majority of the world's billions who silently approved of Basilia's action and applauded his daring?

What devious excuses would the Knesset give when the world learned the Jews were responsible for dire judgement falling on a brave, talented, obviously intelligent saviour of innocents? Would the exhibitionistic joy of young radicals affect the masses' opinion?

Fuck it, Green thought. Fuck the whole thing.

The Russian agent had been followed from the moment he left his embassy. He boarded a flight to Milan, was met there by a man from the Russian consulate, and joined shortly thereafter by Hani Rabat. Rabat drove Sholokov to Bellano and checked into the Hotel Ancora.

Within an hour of having gone up Sholokov emerged from a fire-door with his hand stuffed inside his shirt, Rabat accompanying him. The Foreign Ministry intelligence officer tailing him discovered specks of blood leading along the sidewalk where Sholokov had passed, and also learned from a discreet inquiry by phone that Rabat (going under the name of Alazar) had wanted an end room, preferably on the first floor. Since these rooms tended to be unusually claustraphobic, the obvious interpretation to be made was that Rabat wanted to be near someone. Room 17 being untaken, Room 15 must be the target.

The agent contacted his superior, and soon Green had replaced him. He waited three days for Mr. Erinys to return—as did Hani Rabat.

Finally growing suspicious that Erinys might have decided to forsake his return, Green attempted to search the man's room for evidence of where he might have gone and whether he was connected with the Luqa incident. Then Green could either prosecute his search in other directions or place the hotel under proper surveillance.

But Rabat messed things up by breaking into Room 15

while Green was examining it.

The two-lane ribbon of road wound deeper into the mountains. Lugano was an hour behind him, and still Green kept driving, rolling down a window, letting the cold, crisp mountain air slap at his cheek, honing his concentration to a fine edge.

Rabat hadn't even scratched him.

Bumping along the deserted road in an antiquated Land Rover, the man known as Mr. Erinys found reason to smile. True, the job had only begun, but he sensed that nothing could stop him now. The hardest part had been finding someone who knew the area around Jebel el Akhdar, someone who would willingly take a risk if there was enough money in it. That's why he had gone to Marseilles.

Marseilles is a smugglers' haven. The assorted riff-raff of the Mediterranean congregate here, always sure of finding the company of their own kind. With the attenuation of France's colonial empire, the French police hoped Marseilles' infestation would die out, sources of supply having theoretically dried up for the smugglers. But they failed to consider the new breed of criminal moving into the city's waterfront area: ex-Legionnaires who—lacking a job and its attendant discipline—expended energy in transferring tons of heroin and cocaine from Turkey and North Africa to the cities of Europe. They scoffed at the brutal laws which France's former colonies devised against them and laughed outright when confronted by border guards and narcotics agents armed with weapons inferior to their own.

These modern pirates had their uses, however: they

were in a position to gather information for French Intelligence about events in remote places, they could disseminate false information to France's potential and real adversaries, and they were not above snitching on crooks not in the trade if it meant an easing of police pressure on their own activities. This is not to say the French police like Marseilles' roughnecks, but they were willing to put up with them on short-term interest.

Finding the type of man Erinys needed had been ludicrously easy. Inserting 100-franc notes into grasping hands loosened mouths that were otherwise closed to strangers. A string of informants eager to please led him finally to *Le Diable Bleu* and M. Paul Justine.

Justine joined the French Army when he was eighteen, saw brief service in Algeria, refused a commission, enjoyed five years as a roustabout, then decided to use what money he'd saved to buy a boat and go into business as a hauler of dangerous cargo. This included gun-running to Cyprus and smuggling heroin between Fethiye and a secluded beach on the Cote d'Azur.

Though he earned a salary commensurate to the risks he was taking, he never considered buying a larger boat, one with more cargo space and greater sea-worthiness. His success depended on his seeming innocuous, vulnerable, lost and crazy; and the sight of his small craft plying the often testy waters of the Mediterranean gave this impression. Government agents interested in such things scoffed at the idea of Justine as a smuggler, wondering instead how he managed to keep his damn little rowboat afloat all by himself. He'd berth in Marseilles after a month on the watery road and immediately open his craft for inspection. Customs men would tramp aboard, sniff around, turn their dogs loose, come up with nothing, apologize as always for doubting a man with no police record, and leave, never realizing that a hundred kilos of heroin had been removed from *Le Diable Bleu* less than eighty miles away and were already entering the pipeline that led to street-dealers and junkies' arms.

What mattered to Erinys was that Justine was dependable. Erinys had no desire to be stranded in a hostile foreign country, blood on his hands, by someone who was incompetent or—worse—a coward. Having collected information on Justine and then meeting the man to propose a job, he'd been impressed by the smuggler's intelligence and quick interest; in fact, Justine treated the monetary offer with irrelevance, more concerned with the details of his employer's mission. He asked only pertinent questions and never sought to learn the man's true identity. Why his employer wanted to be dropped in Darnah and why Justine was being asked to carry arms and munitions were naturally important to him because he would be taking as much of the risk as Erinys, and so Erinys supplied him with the information unhesitatingly.

As for Erinys' motive, neither man spoke of it. Justine doubtlessly had thoughts on the matter, but he wisely kept them to himself, assuming his employer would tell him if the knowledge was essential to the ultimate success of the operation.

Erinys handed over 10,000 francs as partial payment for Justine's services. The smuggler absent-mindedly stuffed the roll of bills in his inner jacket-pocket and listened as Erinys gave him his instructions.

Changing its name and registration, he was to take *Le Diable Bleu* to Benghazi, apply for a permit to carry passengers in Libyan waters, wait for a call from a man called Haberstein, then buy a car or jeep under an assumed name and travel overland to a small city called Darnah. Somewhere near Darnah a number of Palestinian terrorists were being given sanctuary. He was to pinpoint their location by whatever means necessary, make a map of the area, leave the car parked in Darnah, return to Benghazi and be waiting with his boat in the port of Matrûh, Egypt no later than the 23rd of April. Erinys would meet him there before the 25th. Together they would proceed to Darnah, timing their arrival for midnight if all else went well.

It had. No hitches. After quick trips to Paris, Frankfurt, and several days' rest in Bellano, Erinys took a bus to Andermatt, Switzerland, rode a train to Geneva, then boarded a DC-10 flying to Rome. After that he hopscotched his way to Cairo, arriving just in time to receive his small trunk of china. Beneath the china lay a cache of weapons, compliments of M. Le Beau who, apparently enjoying his role as arms-supplier for a freelancer as much as the easy money it earned him, was not remiss in filling the man's orders. All transactions were designed to cover him, so he had no fear for himself—except if he failed to deliver. The stranger's threat to kill him should he inform the police had proved inspirational.

With his new weapons neatly stowed in a carry-all he took a train to Matrûh, sharing it with fresh Egyptian troops bound for the free-fire border zone around Salûm. The trip had been unexciting; the crowded, hot, smelly passengers were in no mood to bother him.

Justine had the good sense to book a room in one of Matrûh's three antediluvian hotels, using Sam Erinys' name. Erinys made ample use of the room, bathing and resting and bathing again to cleanse away the accumulated filth of his recent journey.

They departed that night, both men anxious to act, to know what fate awaited them. Justine kept his anxieties to himself, confident that if Erinys should fail in his mission—and what, really, could one man do?—the Frenchman had several excuses to offer the enraged Libyans who would be searching for an accomplice. Deep sea fishing equipment had been put aboard his boat for that explicit reason.

They arrived at Darnah Harbor several hours later than planned. Erinys was too intent on essaying his goal, however, to be stopped by the rigors of time, even though Justine insisted he would be caught in daylight. Erinys derided his partner for trying to hold him back, so Justine shrugged as only Frenchmen know how, turned to the wheel and guided his craft between the channel lights.

After that, everything began to fall in place. Justine engaged the crusty harbor-master while Erinys disembarked, then delivered the heavy carry-all to him, picked up some food, and returned to the boat. Erinys found the Land Rover waiting for him exactly where his assistant said it would be, and now . . .

He came to the diverging road which Justine had warned him to expect. It led east, away from the mountains and toward the mammoth pipeline that began in the Serir of Kalanshu fields and terminated at the port of Tobruk, and crossed a low range of hills—beyond which Erinys would find a garrisoned checkpoint.

Driving the Land Rover into a narrow wadi, Erinys spent the next hour burying the vehicle under sand, using a collapsible shovel Justine had left on the backseat. It was hard work, and by the time he finished he was coated with sweat and fine dust, despite the moist coolness of the air. The job looked unnatural, but would escape notice at least until the sun arose, and he expected to be out of the area long before then.

If all went well.

CHAPTER TEN

Yigael Charon, true to his regimen, awoke at 4 a.m. after five hours of deep sleep. He dressed, shaved, prepared his breakfast of toast, fresh orange juice, and green salad, kissed his sleeping wife, and went to the garage. As usual, his two bodyguards were awaiting him inside his car.

At his office on Palenta Street Charon found a sealed note, forwarded by the Foreign Ministry. He sat behind his desk, wondering if the message dealt with Olric Seizer, the traitorous Defense Ministry secretary who had flown to Dubrovnik for a holiday and ended up in Tirana, Albania, spilling out what little he knew to his curious comrades. The matter had been referred to Shabak for an investigation of Seizer's contacts in Israel—if any—while the Defense Ministry tightened its security. Charon didn't think much of the case, but Modiin insisted on a thorough back-tracking of Seizer's movements until the traitor could be eliminated or kidnapped back to Israel for interrogation and trial.

But the note came instead from Wend Ergatz, station

chief for Mossad's West Mediterranean Bureau. Much to Charon's dismay it had been forwarded effortlessly to his department, a sign that too many people knew its recipient. That worried him; in a country living under siege conditions one could never be too careful in retaining one's anonymity. A crowd of luckless Israeli politicians discovered that lesson the hard way, not realizing until too late that Palestinian terrorists like important targets just as much as ordinary ones and are quite willing to die to get at them.

Charon scanned the terse communiqué, grunting with displeasure when he read that the Russian agent had been lost.

Then he sat back in his cushioned swivel-chair, staring at the ceiling until the idea finally germinated and took root—just as he knew it would once he fertilized and watered the seed with logic, simplicity, and commonsense.

Why hadn't he thought of it before?

The two jeeps reached the first check-point just as sunlight came bursting over the eastern hills, gradually emptying the black hollows of night.

Lieutenant Sadamin, sitting beside his driver in the forward jeep, relished anew the miracle of dawn in the desert. Technically the desert did not begin until a hundred miles south, and these hills, partially covered by drought-resisting vegetation, short-stemmed grass and scrub-trees, were quite distinct from the roiled sands and bare rock of the Algerian Ahaggar where Sadamin had been born thirty-five years before. But they were—in his mind at least—near enough that he felt a pang of nostalgia when a blood-red morning sun first settled on his tough, creased face, driving needles into the flesh.

The two guards behind the white pole-barricade greeted him respectfully as his jeep pulled up in front of them. Since his promotion six months before, he had been assigned the inspection of Alabet, so he was well-known to both sentries.

"How are the vultures?" he yelled above the roar of the vehicles.

"As usual," the taller guard said, pushing his slinged Kalashnikov rifle to his back and raising the barrier. "They went on another binge last night, sir."

"Again? The commandant must be gone. I hope he hid their weapons before he left."

"He drove to Benghazi yesterday afternoon. And he didn't take their guns. They were shooting them off only a few hours ago. Must have been quite a party, women screaming, guns—"

Lieutenant Sadamin grimaced. He hated the *fedayeen*, considering them sexually immoral, disrespectful of authority and religion, and inclined to alcoholism. Yet because they were talented killers, Gaddafi shielded them from an antagonistic world; and Gaddafi ruled Libya. This in no way diminished Sadamin's hatred, though it nurtured his sense of political reality: Do your duty, keep your feelings to yourself. If the buggers want liquor, let them make it themselves. If they want to shoot up their quarters for a lark, let them. After all, they have to live there.

"Yes, I suspect it was. Someday one of them is going to get killed during their so-called parties. Anything on the perimeter?"

"Can't say. The telephone line to the posts must be down. I can't raise them."

"Did you call a repair crew from Darnah?"

The tall guard smiled stupidly. "Yes, sir. I tried, sir. But that line seems to be down as well. In fact, our electricity went out at about the same time the party really got started."

Telephone, electricity—out. Wild shooting. Screams. Sadamin motioned his driver to continue down the narrow winding road that led through the hills to Alabet, the terrorist camp. He was beginning to worry and unconsciously patted the Luger at his side, a prized gun his father had won from a German at Tobruk.

Of course, the *fedayeen* weren't above playing pranks on their guardians—all in jest, naturally—and Sadamin told himself they were trying to upset their hosts by cutting off the refuge from the outside world. That would be easy since Military Command, installing a telephone line to the camp, stupidly decided a radio was unnecessary.

After twisting around the base of several hills, the men in the two jeeps came within sight of Alabet. It crouched in a natural hollow, completely sheltered by the rocky mounds around it, and fed by only the one road which Sadamin, his military police and the replacement troops, now traveled. Crowning these hills and invisible except to the trained eye were guard installations scooped from the rock and covered by rubble, sand and brush over wooden planks. Alabet itself consisted of two long, low barracks on one side, a dining area and administration building on the other, all enclosed by a tall fence topped with barbed wire. Just outside Alabet and on a diagonal with it were two guard towers, one serving dual purpose as a water reservoir, pipes running from it to an open-air shower inside the fence and to the dining hall.

Already the sun had cleared the depression of darkness, revealing its drabness, the uniformity of its surroundings, the tangible prison-like atmosphere of Alabet.

"They must be sleeping it off," Sadamin said to no one in particular.

He had stood up and the jeeps pulled to a halt while he scanned the camp with his binoculars. Again he felt a shudder of uneasiness rake his spine. There was no movement at all among the buildings—nothing. If they'd been drinking heavily, he at least expected some of the terrorists to be stumbling toward the outdoor cesspool. Even the two guard towers appeared empty.

"Shall we go on, sir?" his driver asked, shifting nervously in his seat.

"We have to, Ibram. Something strange is happening here." He paused. "The phone is out, and if we returned to Darnah for reinforcements then found the *fedayeen* were only playing another of their nasty tricks, we'd be demoted three ranks or knocked out of the service as cowards. So drive on."

The khaki-colored vehicles stopped beneath the northwest tower which guarded a wide double gate into the compound. Sadamin yelled up to the twenty-foot high post, but received no response.

The camp was as quiet as a desert cemetery.

"Blow the horn," he told the driver.

Still no movement. The guard replacements were growing nervous in the second jeep, and Sadamin heard the snap of holster clasps.

He also heard something else, something besides the putter of the engines idling and the low scuffling of wind across the sand-floored basin.

"Cut the motors!"

Listening more attentively he again noticed a distinct and low-pitched hum coming from the camp.

"How are we going to get inside, sir?" There was but one entrance into the camp. It had to be opened from the inside. Yet the tower guards who usually unlocked the gate were not answering, their position could only be reached by a ladder within the camp, and no one else inside was answering the repeated blasts of the horn.

"Can you ram this thing through the gate?"

The driver squinted, examining the heavy metal brace securing the two sides of the gate together, the barbed-wire topping, the wooden stanchions just inside the gate which could rip out his engine if he lost control after breaking through.

"I can try."

Sadamin turned to the men in the second jeep and told them to investigate the three outposts on the surrounding hills and bring back the guards immediately. Then he and the two MPs in the rear seat got out.

Ibram backed up three hundred feet. He wanted plenty of momentum when he hit the stout fence; otherwise the gate might collapse inward and onto the jeep, and the barbed-wire at the top would surely saw his head off. He had done stunts like this before, but then he'd been drunk—an experience he did not care to mention to his Orthodox Moslem CO, Lieutenant Sadamin.

The jeep breached the fence at 40 m.p.h., expertly twisting the bracing rod and leaving both sides of the gate on their hinges.

Sadamin ordered his MPs to search both towers, then he walked to the smiling Ibram who saluted proudly.

"Good work, Ibram. Now let us see what our

Palestinian friends are up to."

As they approached the squat yellow-brick structure reserved for the males, Ibram grunted disgustedly. "Do you know who built these barracks, sir? A bad job. Brick captures and stores heat, and a metal roof turns a building into an oven. I could have built them a much better place."

"I'm sure. But the brick walls and metal roof are good protection against bullets, and electric air-coolers have been fitted on the opposite side."

"Then why did they break out the windows?" the driver asked, pointing to the three four-foot square openings on the wall facing them.

"Well, if the electricity went out, the air-coolers . . ."

But the electricity had gone out early this morning when the air was naturally cool. And besides, if they wanted they could have opened the door. No reason to break out . . .

"What is it, sir?"

"Shut up."

The humming had become louder as they neared the barrack. The insistent buzzing rattled in their ears, alarming both men.

Zzzzzzzzzzz . . .

Sadamin hesitated, then ordered Ibram to follow him through the door with his gun ready. The windows were set high in the wall, too high to furnish them with a preview of what they were getting into.

Zzzzzzzzzzz . . .

The building consisted of one communal room, low bunks shoved against the walls and the center occupied by a large table. There were no wash basins, all washing facilities being contained in the building housing the cafeteria. Every square foot of wall was taken up by chalked graffiti ranging from Marxist slogans to childish rhymes, swastikas, and crude drawings of impossible coital positions. A wool blanket lay on the floor near the table. On one of the ten chairs around the table was a neat stack of games: Monopoly, Paycheck, backgammon, an Arabic version of Scrabble, War Strategy, Othello, and Sea Battle, all housed in their cardboard containers. Empty soda bottles smelling suspiciously of wine and a rain barrel sat at one end of the table. Czech-made rifles leaned against the back of each chair.

Zzzzzzzzzzz . . .

Sadamin took in the scene quickly, having often visited the room before during inspection tours.

Zzzzzzzzzzz . . .

"*Allah!*" Ibram choked, staring over his CO's shoulder, then rushing out into the warm, sane world.

Bright rectangles of sunlight lit the dingy room, speckled by the shadow of myriads of flies disturbed by Sadamin's entrance but now resettling on the gaping faces of the dead men.

Lieutenant Sadamin holstered his Luger and walked slowly around the room, batting at the flies and noting emotionlessly that the bed mats and sleeping bags had soaked up most of the blood.

Though he looked closely for a sign of life, he soon realized all seventeen men were dead. Each had a fatal bullet wound in the head, usually just in front of the ear, in several cases through an eye or the mouth. No signs of struggle from any of them.

He picked up the wool blanket lying near the table and examined it, finding what he'd expected: powder and scorch marks, the reek of cordite. The assassin (if indeed there was only one) had apparently wrapped his gun with the blanket to smother its report. He probably used a silencer as well. Though considering the drunken stupor his victims must have been in, a silencer was probably unnecessary.

Wearily, feeling the weight of new responsibility on his shoulders, Sadamin left the room and found his driver retching beside his jeep. The two MPs sent to search the guard towers began yelling simultaneously as they caught sight of their CO from the pyramidal posts. He sighed heavily, forcing out the stench of blood and vinegary wine, called to the men to join him, and headed directly for the women's barrack, ignoring Ibram.

The women's building was identical to the men's, at least from the outside. The thirteen female terrorists at Alabet tended to care more for the environment they had to live in, however, and kept their quarters respectably clean.

Or had.

Sadamin nosed through the open doorway, his Luger again preceding him.

Whatever he expected, it could not have been what he found. As he was to say later, "A trip to hell should not come during a man's life-time. If it does, he should not have to feel responsible for purchasing the ticket."

Everything had been thrown into the center of the room. Including the occupants.

And set on fire.

For some reason the fire had burned poorly, consuming nothing whole, leaving corners of mattresses, bookcovers, a face, an arm, a nylon stocking untouched. The pyre had been a fizzle.

Nevertheless, the girls were dead. Sadamin was unable

to count them, thrown as they were upon each other then covered with anything and everything the killer considered combustible; but he knew intuitively that they were all there. They had died from gunshot wounds, not fire. The multiple and indiscriminate holes in their bodies and in the walls were clear evidence that a machine-gun slaughtered them; while the presence of a pistol still gripped by a blistered black hand told the officer that the women had time to react against their assailant, perhaps wounding him.

He picked up eighteen expended shells from the floor, pocketing them. Perhaps they would bring joy to a crime analyst in Tripoli. They certainly hadn't brought joy to these girls.

Turning to leave, he met Ibram just entering. "You don't want to see this," he said, pushing the young man outside.

"What happened?"

"They are dead. All of them."

The MPs joined their CO, relating what they had found: the guard in each tower had been shot dead at close range: the fence near the southwest corner of the camp had been cut.

Five minutes later the second jeep came rocketing down a hillside, pulling up in front of Sadamin. The four men aboard it were ashen-faced.

"Well?"

"They've all been murdered," the leader said hoarsely.

"Shot?"

"No, sir. They had their throats cut. Ear to ear. I don't think they ever knew what happened. Blood—blood all over."

"Had their guns been fired?"

"No, sir. I checked. What about here? Where is everyone?"

Sadamin explained the situation quickly and concisely, then ordered the four replacements to stand guard at Alabet until he could get word from Darnah to the Central Military Command at Benghazi. At the checkpoint two miles away he exchanged the two MPs for the guards and told Ibram to make the trip to Darnah as short as he could.

He spent the journey mulling over how the attack on Alabet had been mounted. It was obviously preceded by a detailed reconnaissance. Circumstances supported that view. The three spotters on the outermost perimeter were silenced first, the telephone and electricity lines were severed, and the attack force cut its way through the fence. After that the tower guards, probably having joined their guests in earlier celebration, were easily murdered.

The male terrorists, being considered more dangerous (wrongly, as the women had proved time and time again), would have received the first visit. But because of the muffled gun Sadamin wondered whether the attack had not been launched by one man. If there were several killers, why bother being silent? They could have simultaneously sprayed both quarters with machine-gun fire. But they didn't. So one could assume there was only one assassin.

Of course. He quietly killed the men then proceeded to the women's building. Electricity was out, so he would have been invisible in the darkness. Probably used a hand-torch or electric lantern in the rooms to sight his targets. Unfortunately, at least one of the women was awake—or awoke—when the killer arrived, and he was forced to resort to a weapon with greater fire-power.

Then, for some as yet undeterminable reason, the killer hauled everything to the center of the room and tried to set it ablaze, breaking out the windows to give the fire oxygen, returning to the men's barrack and breaking those windows but—again for some inexplicable reason—foregoing an attempt to burn the evidence of the massacre as in the women's quarters.

Thirty-five people dead. Thirty of them the rowdy elite of the terrorist army's youth division—troops tested by adversity, proven adepts experienced in dynamiting Jewish nursery schools, hijacking planes, assassinating diplomats, and making fools of civilized nations. And now their barbarism caught up with them. They probably never believed cold blood ran in veins other than their own.

Bearing north-northeast he spent just over two hours making the eight-mile journey, most of the time in an easy jog over sandflats and rock outcroppings. The windsprints and long-distance runs in Paris served him well; the searing heat and the satchel of weapons tied to his back would otherwise have held him to a walk and he never could have made his rendezvous with the *Écrasez L'infâme* in the little cove six miles southeast of Darnah and on the Gulf of Bunbah.

Paul Justine, unwilling to arrive or stay later than the agreed time of 9 a.m., was early. He allowed his craft to drift in the minimal shelter of the cove as near as possible to the gravelly shore, and anxiously awaited Erinys' appearance. Not sure whether Erinys or the Libyan Army would arrive first, he threw out several fishing lines, undressed to a pair of swimming trunks, and sat in an aluminum deck-chair atop the foredeck, holding a book but keeping his shaded eyes on the jagged horizon half-encircling the shallow cove.

At first he failed to recognize the tall burnoosed figure that materialized among the rocks, running for the water; but then he saw the familiar carry-all which he'd handed to Erinys in Darnah less than eight hours before. He threw the deck-chair aft, dropping through the sun roof and starting the engines as Erinys waded toward the craft. With a draft of 2 feet 4 inches, the cruiser was boarded without Erinys dampening his cord belt.

As soon as his passenger was on, Justine gunned the engines, pointing the boat toward the open sea. After they were a mile out, he gave full throttle to the powerful outdrives, urging them to a maximum speed of 35 knots. He knew his most important task was to put distance between the boat and Libya, first by losing the boat to shore observers, then by moving into Egyptian territorial waters where the Libyan Air Force and Navy would be loath to venture.

During this time Erinys had stripped off his Arab garb in the forecabin, stuffing it in his carry-all and dressing in jeans and a blue T-shirt. He washed his hands and arms with an industrial cleanser, scraping away a layer of skin and callous, massaged them with a skin moisturizer, and finished by liberally sprinkling cheap cologne over his body.

He then proceeded to the aft-deck, crushed the air from his carry-all and flung it overboard. Weighted by fifteen pounds of weapons, it sank immediately.

"Why did you do that?" Justine asked when the man sat beside him at the wheel. "Why didn't you bury it instead of carrying it all the way to the beach?"

"If an alarm was raised before I reached you and they sighted me, I had no desire to be defenseless," he said, pointedly surveying the *Écrasez L'infâme* which, according to instructions, Justine had spray-painted marine-blue down to the water-line during the early morning hours, making especially certain all chrome and aluminum furnishings were covered.

"Everything go to your satisfaction?"

Erinys merely smiled and asked for a cigarette.

"Better not light it in here. Go aft. This galleon is nine-tenths gasoline right now."

"Will we make it to Candia without refueling?"

"Not if we go for Egyptian waters first. And unless we do, we may be shot right out of the water. I have a fair idea what went on at Alabet, and I know the Libyans won't mind strafing us if we fail to turn back on their orders."

"That's assuming they find us. Without its mast and sails and painted blue this boat is practically invisible. Once we enter the major shipping lanes and join the traffic, radar will have a hard time ferreting us out. I estimate we can reach Crete in six to seven hours," Erinys said.

"Nine if we don't blow a water-pump, we don't catch fire with all that polyurethane foam and glass fiber crammed in the engine box, the weather holds, and we're not torpedoed. Ten and a half if you expect to be dropped near Candia. Remember, I have to worry about fuel consumption. Straight out, she'll burn 23 gallons an hour. I've got petrol in two tanks, the bilges, stored in barrels in the cabin. She'd probably make it but with no safety margin. *Merde*, I have 180 gallons stowed in her. Do you know how much that weighs? Roughly 1320 pounds. That's why we will have to plane down, burn off some weight, why the trip will take longer and we can't get away as fast as we would like. Sure, there are plenty of other things that can go wrong, so why worry about them until they happen? By the way, I taped your documents under the sediment bowl."

"Thanks" was Erinys only reply. The documents referred to were Hans Derna's passport and visa, both of which Erinys intended burning as soon as he left the Frenchman, using instead fresh documents provided by Pierre Le Beau's master forger.

"Crete then?"

"To Krētē, Ulysses."

Word of the massacre sped rapidly to the highest levels of government in Tripoli, horrifying the military committee that ruled the country.

An investigative team was sent to Alabet with the task of uncovering solid evidence as to who committed such a blasphemous crime against the Arab people. The seventeen detectives were given the impression that their return would not be appreciated unless they met with success.

The air base at Bardia—on the border with Egypt— became increasingly active, search-and-destroy sorties constantly being ordered against any unidentifiable plane, ship, or land vehicle attempting to cross east along the longitudinal border 25° E. and between latitudes 28° and 32° N. Always suspicious of the Egyptians, the Libyan commanders assumed the assassins' escape route would lead through Egypt, probably by land. A plane would appear on radar and a boat was too slow; but a truck or jeep was very difficult to spot, especially if it had been camouflaged. Reinforcement units were sent to strengthen the army post in Bardia on the supposition that the treacherous leaders in Cairo might use the heavy air traffic along their western border as an excuse to wage another mini-war against their neighbor, and this added to the resulting confusion as the search got fully underway.

Since both domestic and foreign journalists' reports were censored and international telephone calls were either forbidden or carefully monitored, the reason for the sudden surge of military activity in Libya was kept secret from the rest of the world. The ruling junta, embarrassed by their inability to protect Alabet or locate the calloused assassins who massacred its inhabitants and all but two of the guards, did not want their impotence to enter the public forum; not, at least, until they had no other choice but to ask for outside help.

Yet, as night fell and Libyan troops moved into the urban areas between the Bay of Bueb and Gulf of Bunbah for a house-to-house search for illegal aliens and weapons, as the *Écrasez L'infâme* rounded Crete's Cape Spatha and headed southwest, as the crowd of investigators at Alabet concluded their quest and started back toward Benghazi, as half the world slept and the active half remained ignorant, a Darnah seller of ropes, baskets, and spices went down to his basement storeroom, moved a pair of bulky crates hiding one wall, pushed against a knot in the wooden paneling, and slowly lowered a hinged radio transmitter from its snug niche.

An emergency meeting of Israel's Intelligence Directors was called that night for 11 p.m. Since the Premier requested the session, those invited made certain they were on time.

Yitzhak Beitel, head of Mossad Aliyah Beth (Organization for the Second Immigration) convened the special gathering at his headquarters off the Herzlia Road. Fifty-two years old and bald as a bowling ball, a man with an agile yet disciplined mind, he hated appearing alarmist and would rather have spent the evening with his third wife than keeping his peers from their homes. Still, events of the past twelve hours precluded the idea of business as usual. The news was spreading and something had to be done.

"Mr. Premier, gentlemen," he began, coughing a cloud of smoke, "information has come to my attention—perhaps to yours as well—that Israel may be in extreme danger during the next few days. The Americans have been kind enough to forward a series of detailed satellite reconnaissance photos which they rightly felt would be of particular interest to us. These photographs cover the northeastern region of Libya known colloquially as The Hump. Our attention is drawn to the area called Alabet, located midway between the villages of Martubah and Al Makili."

At this point he removed twenty 12×15-inch gloss-finish photographs from a quarto file. They were clipped into groups of five, and he dispersed these among Yigael Charon of Shabak, the Premier, General Tomas Badon of Modiin, Shaul Vennori of the Ministry of Foreign Affairs' Investigative Service, and Zeev Tanai of the Persecuted Jews Bureau.

"Alabet has been a refuge and training camp for Arab terrorists since 1969 when the experimental farm on the site was suddenly closed down. Though the camp is poorly defended, lacks sophisticated security equipment, and has a totally undisciplined population, we—and I am speaking for all of us since it was a collective decision at the time—believed the sending of an elimination squad too dangerous to risk. The problem was getting inside and finishing the job before their air units could react. Israel does not want to provoke another Middle East war by shooting down the Libyan Air Force."

The assembled leaders joined in laughter, confident of Israel's military prowess. Though knowing the IAF could probably have bombed Alabet into ashes without suffering a casualty of its own, they also realized that world opinion would swing against their country, overpowering any pleasure gained from destroying a coven of enemies in its nest.

"As you will note from the circles on these satellite photos, sudden and intense activity has developed around the camp. Armored troop-carriers, tanks, and planes were scouring the area at noon today when these were taken. We have other indications of a military build-up along the Libyan-Egyptian border, begun by Gaddafi's storm-troopers and countered by our reluctant friends in Cairo. Also, one of our electronic surveillance ships picked up a radio message from a sleeper which Mossad planted in Darnah, Libya twenty years ago, and he confirms our earlier reports."

"Any reason given for this hubbub?" Shaul Vennori asked.

Beitel smiled. "Fortunately, yes. At least for us. Rather unfortunate for our man. His son was a guard at Alabet."

"So?" Charon said impatiently, following a long pause by Mossad's Director. "Are we supposed to solve the riddle by ourselves?"

"A moment, Yigael, please. I like to savor a success as much as you do." He paused again, but only long enough to light another cigarette.

"An army officer appeared at our man's home tonight to express his condolences that the son had been killed at Alabet—along with four other guards and the entire population of terrorists."

The men broke into expressions of surprise and alarm. Their immediate conclusion was that Mossad had run its own operation without consultations with the other services. But then why did Beitel need to refer to CIA photographs and a sleeper's report?

Reading their minds Beitel said, "Mossad had nothing to do with this, gentlemen. And after speaking with the Premier I know that none of you here are implicated in this affair. Israel can wash its hands. We have no *de facto* knowledge of what occurred, only reports."

"How many were killed?"

"According to the Darnah report, thirty-five."

"Whew! That will cause a stink. And who do you think will be the scapegoat?"

"Right now it seems to be the Egyptians. Relations between the two countries are touch-and-go. After a while, Tripoli will look for an outsider—a non-Arab group—but solid evidence will have to turn up to make it stick. All those innuendoes after the Luqa rescue may have worked once—but not twice. Incidentally, Yigael, any luck on tracing that character Basilia?"

Charon looked up sourly. "Not so far. I decided to recall my principal agent and leave the paperwork to Shaul Vennori's sleuths, then try to develop a motive from this end by going through every Intelligence file in Israel, Europe, and America."

"That may take a few day," Vennori dryly remarked.

"It's an inspired idea, all my own. And of course if anything comes of it I'll mention it at our regular meeting."

"Yes, let us know, will you, Yiggy?" Beitel joked, sinking into the Old Boy humor of those who had fought together through the streets of Haifa, the hills around Tiberias, and the sandy flats of the Negev; the Haganah and Palmach warriors who won the Holy Land from the Arabs in 1948.

"It wasn't a complete waste," Charon continued, as though he hadn't heard Beitel. "By a fortuitous circumstance we noted the arrival and departure at Luqa of a Russian agent from their Rome embassy. He came to escort a Maltese boatman to Rome. Suspecting that the boatman, a Communist sympathizer, was instrumental in getting Basilia off the island and that Basilia might actually be a KGB man—despite the evidence against it—my tracker flew to Rome where he was assisted by Shaul's venerable forces."

Shaul Vennori inclined his head in recognition of the compliment.

"We came upon another startling fact. A Russian from Beirut and a Palestinian killer were in the country, arriving—so we learned—to seek out Basilia. The Russian checked into his embassy at the same time this boatman was there.

"Mean something? It didn't seem to. Nothing definite, anyway. So my tracker contacted the old boatman when he returned to Malta, said he had some follow-up questions, and wormed out the fellow's story. As it happens, the boatman unwittingly took our probable target to Sicily the same day the Alitalia plane was rescued. Obviously—and much to my disappointment, actually—Basilia is not a Communist agent. Whatever he is, he changed his name to Hans Derna."

The room suddenly fell silent at the sound of the name. General Badon stopped scratching his beard in midstroke.

"Do you know what you're saying?" Beitel finally said, finding his voice.

Not having been informed of the events in Libya until a few minutes before, Charon had failed to make a connection. Of course it might be a coincidence. He'd heard of far stranger synchronous occurrences. Who was to say . . .

"Perhaps Yigael should finish his narrative," the Premier said quietly.

"Well, we couldn't locate this Hans Derna, so we stuck to the Russian agent—an assassin named Sholokov—hoping for a break. The Communists have a phenomenal grass-roots grapevine and it turned up with results, for soon Sholokov flew to Milan, was joined by his Arab partner, and then drove to Bellano on Lake Como. My man had no idea what was up there, but the sensible thing was to follow his instincts, so he kept tailing.

"The Arab was dropped at a reputable hotel and just sat in his room days on end while my agent from the Flying Squad tried to discover what his intentions were."

The other men in Beitel's underground office leaned forward with growing interest. As these events were so recent and they normally gathered only once a week for a Session, they had heard none of this before.

"Simple deduction led him to believe the Arab was waiting for a Mr. Erinys. Erinys had the room next to the one the Arab took, but had left on a tour the previous Saturday, intending to return soon. The only way to certify the connection was to search Erinys' room for evidence that might link him to Luqa or the man called Derna and—hence—Basilia, since my man felt they could be one and the same.

"All very confusing. Then *and* now. However, it cleared a bit when my tracker started searching Erinys' room last night. The Arab burst in and tried to kill him—assuming, I think we can agree, that *Erinys* had returned. Thus we have the motive for Russian interest in the Luqa affair: the Reds want to liquidate Basilia. Though we had already guessed that."

"What happened?"

"My man killed the Arab and raced across the Swiss border."

"And the Russian—Sholokov?"

"We lost him, Mr. Premier."

"So you're planning a different *modus operandi?*"

"Yes. I'll have it ready for discussion at our next Session."

Beitel stirred in his seat. "We have wandered a bit from the reason for calling this special meeting. I suppose I should ask for suggestions as to how we should handle our response to the raid at Alabet."

"The best response in these matters is no response," the Premier said. "Being a politician, I know if you deny an accusation no one believes you. If you confess your guilt you crucify yourself. But keep silent and time reduces your opponents' arguments to the absurd."

Screaming Israel's innocence, the Intelligence men agreed, would do no good—especially as no one yet had pointed a finger at the Jewish state.

"A minute, my friends."

The voice stopped the meeting just as the men were preparing to adjourn. Everyone looked to tiny Zeev Tanai, head of the Persecuted Jews Bureau, an Intelligence service devoted solely to the documentation and research of cases where Jews around the world have been immobilized or persecuted for their beliefs. He was an exceedingly erudite man, his diction and vocabulary marking him immediately as one who is accustomed to leadership.

"This matter of the man's name. It just occurred to me—"

"Rather slow today, aren't you, Zeev?" Beitel laughed. "We already touched on that."

"No, no. I don't mean Derna, the old Latin name for Darnah. That is too obvious. I am referring to the two other names before us." Being a lexicologist by inclination, Zeev now inspired the rapt attention of his fellows.

"Basilia. An interesting name which one could almost alter—subconsciously—to Basilica. Silica. Basil. Mmm." He paused, wetting his lips. "Assuming Basilia to be a diminutive of Basil, we still have the word "basil" deriving at farthest reach from the Greek *basiliskos*."

"And what does that mean?"

"It is a diminutive of *basileus*, meaning—a king."

"So we go looking for a man with delusions of grandeur. Simple, Zeev. Thank you."

"Ah, but it also refers to the basilisk, a tiny monster described by the Roman Pliny as having lethal eyes and breath. The name has accrued to a crested lizard of Central and South America."

"That may be grasping at straws, Zeev, but I'll take it

into consideration. Thank you," Charon said, numbed by the little man's encyclopaedic mind.

"I am not finished, Yigael. If you need more proof that the man is playing a crafty word game, look at the third name before us.

"An Erinys was a Fury, one of the Erinyes. There were three, known euphemistically as the Eumenides: Alecto, Megaera, and Tisiphone. The seventeenth-century English poet John Milton metamorphosed them into, simply, the Fates. But their origins are much darker. They were the goddesses of vengence, of retribution and murder."

PART TWO

What shame or stint should there be in mourning for one so dear?
—Horace, *Odes*, I, xxiv, 1

CHAPTER ELEVEN

The Renseignements Généraux, responsible for France's civil and criminal archives, found nothing on a Jean-Marguite Plessy. No one of that name had been born in France. Sorry.

The reply was returned to an assistant for the Minister of State. Its bluntness hinted that the RG's Director would have preferred the request to come through normal channels, and that he was singularly unimpressed by the condescending use of rank.

A second and even more formal query went to the offices of the Direction de la Surveillance du Territoire, asking if the department possessed any knowledge of a Jean-Marguite Plessy or a boat known as the *Écrasez L'infâme.* Description appended.

Notified of the top-level request for information, the head of the DST arranged a meeting with the Minister of State. His first words were a polite demand to know how Plessy had sparked such interest so high in the government.

"Then you have at least heard of him? *Bon!* As for our

reasons for wishing to locate him, you must take them on trust. The Sûreté is interested in him because a friendly power is interested in him. I can say no more. Now where is this man Plessy and who is he?"

"Plessy is an alias for Paul Justine, a former French soldier, served with distinction, presently operates a boat out of Marseilles called *Le Diable Bleu*. Didn't the RG have this?" the DST Director asked.

The Minister waved his hands deprecatingly. "You know how stubborn Marvaux is. He'll punch out the name on his Univac and if the screen remains blank he goes out for another meal."

"Do you want Justine picked up?"

"Where is he?"

"We haven't had time to check. He rents out his boat and services to the small-time winners on the Cote d'Azur, picks their pockets, sometimes hauls small cargo. Keeps his nose clean generally, but there are suspicions he smuggles drugs—narcotics. Never caught at it though, so no formal dossier on him."

"What about the alias?"

"We've known about that for several years, only we've always failed to turn up with his false passport. Without it we can't bring charges."

"Why does he use it?"

"One of our men asked him that. He admitted—lot of fire in that boy—that he often did business along the north coast of Africa and the Arabs thought his name sounded Jewish. So he changes it every time he crosses the Thirty-seventh Parallel."

"*Is* he Jewish?" the Minister asked quickly.

"No. Both parents were Catholic."

"Ah." Disappointed, the Minister asked the head of

170

the DST to hold Justine for interrogation once he was located. "I want to know where he has been and what he has been doing. My assistant will fill you in on the rest. And don't waste time."

Four days later, on 2 May, *Le Diable Bleu*, sporting a fresh coat of white paint and with its chrome finishings sparkling like new, pulled into its rented berth in Marseilles' Bassin de la Joliette. As soon as the pilot and passengers handed their disembarkation cards to the Immigration officer, three heavyweights approached and asked politely that they accompany them to the police station.

Since the two passengers were an American couple— both in their sixties—an English-speaking agent of the Sûreté Nationale, the bureaucratic overseer of France's principal law enforcers, was called in to supervise the interrogation so the Americans could be released before their patience expired.

Q: Where did you and your wife board M. Justine's boat?
A: (man) At Canea. That's on Crete.
A: (woman) Candia, Harold. He's always getting names confused, aren't you, Harold? Guess we're all growing older. We flew there from Athens. We've never been to Crete before, and Harold says—
Q: How did you happen to meet M. Justine?
A: (man) We were in Paris. We have an apartment there, you know, right near the Louvre, as a matter of fact. Like Maud says, we'd never been to Crete. I've been retired for four years now and we've been trying to make up for lost time.
Q: Yes, of course. But where did you hear of M. Justine?
A: (woman) We heard of him in a cafe in Montmartre,

actually. A nice lady at the next table overheard Harold and me trying to decide how to get to Crete. We wanted to do it differently.

Q: Differently? But you flew there, did you not?

A: (woman) Yes, but we had to. Paul—

Q: Maybe you had better tell me about the woman at the cafe, *eh!*

A: (woman) She told us she knew a man who did boat charters and that he would probably take us there for a reasonable price. The idea simply *intrigued* us—traveling the coast of Italy and Greece. And we had plenty of time. So we got Paul's name and phone-number from the lady and gave him a ring.

Q: What did he say?

A: (woman) Nothing. He wasn't there. A friend of his answered and said that he'd gone to Benghazi—that's in Libya—to pick up work. But the nice man said Paul might be interested in bringing us back from Crete since it was so near. He gave us a hotel number in Benghazi which we could call.

Q: Did you reach him?

A: (man) Sure did. Said his prospects weren't too good and he'd be glad to pick us up in Canea—

A: (woman) Candia, Harold.

A: (man) —on such and such a date and return us as far as Marseilles. Sounded marvelous, didn't it, Maud? So we flew to Crete via Athens, had a *great* time, and Paul met us just like he said he would. Great guy, Paul! What's this all about?

Q: Where did you put into port during the trip?

A: (man) Oh hell, I don't—

A: (woman) Harold!

A: (man) Well, we stopped in several ports—to refuel,

172

you understand, and take on provisions. Stopped in Anzio, I remember. I landed there during the last war and I wanted—
Q: Yes, I understand, M. Haberstein. I wished to know whether you disembarked during—
A: (woman) I wouldn't let him. I love a nice cruise, but the trip from Candia would have taken *forever* if we kept getting off in every port.
Q: Do you mean M. Justine piloted his boat without taking time to sleep, all those days?
A: (woman) Of course he slept! When we didn't have to cross large bodies of water—I mean when we were cruising along a coast—Paul would let Harold take the wheel, then go below for a nap.
Q: Have you ever piloted a small boat on the open sea before, M. Haberstein?
A: (man) I was in the U.S. Navy, sir!

When the SN agent questioned Paul Justine, the boatman repeated what the Habersteins had said. A check of phone-calls made between Paris and Benghazi on the day in question confirmed that Harold Haberstein had placed a person-to-person call to a M. Jean-Marguite Plèssy staying at the Hotel Al Hamra in Benghazi.

Q: What explanation did you give the Habersteins for your change of name?
A: None.
Q: How did they know whom to ask for when they phoned Benghazi?
A: My answering service obviously told them—and why it was necessary to ask for M. Plessy.

Q: Didn't they find that hard to believe?
A: Not to my knowledge. Why should they?
Q: Didn't they think it strange?
A: I do not read minds. I have no idea what they thought.
Q: What's your game, Justine?
A: Game?
Q: We aren't fools, you know. We have a good idea what you have been up to this week.
A: You should. The Habersteins told you, I told you . . .
Q: Did they ever mention to you that using an alias because you thought a perfectly good French name sounded Jewish—that that was ridiculous?
A: No.
Q: No?
A: Libya is fanatically anti-Zionist. I'm not Jewish, but the Habersteins are. They understood my reason for changing my name.
(A long pause as the SN agent digests this information and curses himself for falling into such a simple trap.)
Q: Very well, M. Justine. And do you know that using falsified travel documents is against the law?
A: So is suicide.

The head of the DST was not amused when he listened to the tapes that same evening. Paul Justine, alias Jean-Marguite Plessy, had been released since there was nothing to prove he was involved in the murder of five Libyan soldiers, and that meant a call to the Minister of State who then would have to inform his Libyan counterpart that the suspect had been cleared at this end. He simply was not the type to go around murdering Arabs, alias or no alias.

Naturally, the DST chief had no way of knowing what the Habersteins said as they rode a train back to Paris. It is doubtful whether he would have been much enlightened even if he had heard their gales of laughter. They only knew that on the first day of April a messenger arrived at their apartment with an envelope full of American dollars and a typed message telling them to be near their phone at 10 p.m.

As it was April Fools' Day, the Habersteins suspected one of their fellow expatriates might be playing a very hilarious joke on them.

But the voice on the phone that night was a stranger's. It told them they could keep the $1,000 if they joined in a little adventure, and an additional $3,000 would await them when they returned from their trip. Washington, the voice said, likes to show its appreciation for services rendered. Nothing you will do will be contrary to international law.

Harold Haberstein, a conservative Republican who had spent half his life dreaming of an opportunity to help the CIA, agreed "unconditionally"—as long as his Maud would be put in no danger.

The voice gave explicit instructions, telling Haberstein that two air tickets to Athens would be awaiting the couple at Charles de Gaulle Airport on the day chosen for their departure. They must make their own arrangements for getting to Crete. They should take a bus to Canea on the agreed date, and there await a boat called the *Écrasez L'infâme*. The boat would continue to Candia, refuel, and return to Marseilles from where it came. Further instructions would be given by the pilot, Paul Justine, whom they must call in Benghazi, asking for Jean-Marguite Plessy.

Curious and excited, the Habersteins busied themselves in preparation. The defense of democracy was not something to be taken lightly, they told each other.

The Libyan government managed to keep the massacre at Alabet a secret. Inevitably the whole story must surface, but perhaps by then the globe-trotting detectives whom the ruling junta finally—in desperation—hired to break the case would have found the assassins.

Aware that too much military activity could provoke the Egyptians into another pre-emptive strike against their eastern air-fields, the Libyans eased up. No indication of who attacked Alabet, why, or where the killers were, was found, though it was generally assumed they had escaped the country.

A routine check of foreigners in Libya at the time of the massacre produced Plessy's name and passport number. The French government kindly furnished results of its investigation of M. Plessy, real name Paul Justine, and concluded that the Libyans might wish to check the Crete connection.

They did.

Much to their surprise and delight, the Libyans were informed by their hired investigators that the *Écrasez L'infâme* put to port in Canea before proceeding to Candia. One man had gotten off while the boat was fueled, and two people had later gotten on.

Acknowledging its oil debt to Libya, the Greek government generously opened its immigration records, and a name appeared which sent the private investigators rushing for a phone and transportation.

The man was quickly located by Athens police; but since he was in a hospital with a mild concussion they refused to allow him to be questioned. They did, however, permit photographs to be taken and forwarded to Paris.

"Yes," the head of the DST wearily admitted, wincing at the harsh Gallic curses of the Minister of State. "Yes, we goofed. The man in Athens is definitely Paul Justine, we have that from several independent sources. Our men just assumed—since the pilot of *Le Diable Bleu* held a passport with his photo and the name of Paul Justine—that he *was* Paul Justine. We have no dossier photo because Justine has no dossier with us, but the picture matches that in his army file.

"No, I have no idea who was impersonating him. I'm sure the Habersteins knew him only as Paul Justine. And we can't question the real Justine until he's released.

"The method? Justine must have picked him up in Libya. In Canea they exchanged roles and Justine disembarked just before the Habersteins boarded. Yes, I know what they said. But remember that the husband thought it was Canea while his wife insisted on Candia. No doubt an innocent mistake of getting similar-sounding names confused."

When Justine recovered sufficiently to walk around his room unattended, two members of the SDECE were admitted and allowed to ask questions.

According to Justine he met a fellow Frenchman in Benghazi who expressed an interest in part-ownership of his boat—if he would change the name. Down on his luck and unable to find clients, Justine accepted the offer despite his misgivings about the stranger.

Still, the man knew how to handle a boat. And when the Habersteins phoned with their request, Justine decided to take his craft (renamed *Écrasez L'infâme*) as far as Canea, spend a week or so vacationing on Crete, and let the stranger steer the Habersteins to Marseilles. Everything would have gone fine if he hadn't fallen down those brothel stairs.

Justine was shocked to hear that his partner was impersonating him. This was the first he'd heard of it.

"What was his name?"

"Henri Jarret."

"Description?"

Justine looked at the two inquisitors for a moment and then artfully created a single man by combining their features, laughing uproariously when they said the description differed somewhat from that which the Immigration officer and SN agent had given in Marseilles.

"No, Monsieur le Minister, we do *not* have a Henri Jarret on record. And would you please convey my extreme displeasure with the continual implications of our Libyan friends that the man they are seeking must be a Frenchman! We have not been able to locate this Jarret with his Identikit photo because he is not a Frenchman and he is no longer in France. Yes, we are showing the photo at docks, airports, train stations, and border crossings. Without results, I might add. If you want my opinion, he looks like a low-born German!"

"A very clever customer. Damned if he didn't clean his fingerprints from the boat. No sign of him in France—or having left. I wouldn't trust the description this fellow Justine gave, either. He's staying in Greece, playing sick so the French can't extradite him and use their medieval interrogation tactics. For someone who claimed he was down to his last franc in Benghazi, he must have earned a neat sum from the Habersteins."

Green found Charon's playful ramblings a bit unnerving. Coming home with blood on his hands but no new leads on Basilia, he had expected to be dropped from the case.

"Where's this from, General?"

"French Intelligence. We had to tell them we are possibly looking for the same man before they'd give it. But they did, and I think it's because they feel lost. To them, the only crime Jarret committed was entering the country illegally. Anyway," he said, suddenly laughing and throwing himself against the back of his plushly cushioned chair, "I am happy to see you, Nathan. We have a lot of work ahead of us."

"Then why was I stuck in Haifa for the past week—*incommunicado?*"

"I wanted to make sure your trail was absolutely cold before you stuck out your head," Charon replied, his face growing tense. "When you travel abroad you represent Israel; and Israel must not be accused of killing Arabs in Europe, even in self-defense. You seem to have covered yourself well, though. Wend Ergatz has sent word that the Italian police have all but given up on the Rabat case. You are to be commended."

"I'm not sure I deserve it. If Sholokov had been around . . ."

"Indeed, indeed. He has a well-earned reputation. If his official credentials were not so impressive, I would wonder why Mossad doesn't check him off. But that's a paradox of the trade."

Charon reviewed his new plan of action and what work had been completed so far, the reasons for it and the present results, squeezed from several hundred man-hours of tedious research.

"You gave me the idea, Nathan. Indirectly, of course. After receiving word of the debacle in Bellano—and I'm not blaming you for anything, son, just noting that things might have gone better—I tried to visualize what you would do if you were this man Erinys and if Basilia, Derna, and Erinys were all the same man. I found it impossible to imagine without first deciding upon one thing."

"My motive."

"Exactly. Once that was determined I could write my scenario. In your case you have a built-in motive: to avenge your wife's death." Charon saw pain lance across Green's visage and quickly said, "You'll forgive me, Nathan. I know you don't like to be reminded. Nevertheless, it is a fact one must face, an obtrusive reality one cannot ignore. I understand your feelings and mean no disrespect.

"Suppose that Erinys has suffered a similar loss. His warped mind conceives ways of retaliating against those whom he thinks responsible. He is willing to take unusual risks to achieve his ends. He possesses no conscious death-wish and carefully plans his means of escape and survival; but at the same time he has no fear of dying except inasmuch as it thawarts his vengeful desires.

"Put yourself in his place, Nathan. What would you do under the same circumstances?"

"I'd look for my wife's killers," Green answered tonelessly.

"How?"

"That depends on the circumstances of her death."

Charon stood up, walking to the window looking out

on Tel Aviv and the shimmering blue Mediterranean beyond. He spread the Venetian blinds with two fingers and said slowly, "I know this is hard for you, Nathan. Just try to remember that other men have been made widowers by the *fedayeen*. Every Jew has suffered in some way. I ask only that you try to identify with the man we are after."

"Why?" Green shouted, his anger flaring against the four walls. "Why is it so important to find him? He's doing us a favor. Why waste our resources on locating an ally? Let him go, let him kill the scum who murdered my wife. He is not a danger to the state of Israel, but an asset."

"Other people think as you do," replied Charon calmly, unwilling to show his accordance with the young man. "That is why we must find him. Our friends at the CIA believe he could prove a de-stabilizing factor in the Middle East. If they begin thinking he is an agent of Israel and then he acts irresponsibly—perhaps killing innocent bystanders or Libyan troops performing their ordinary duties—we will be put to task. We neither need nor want him as a surrogate, a mercenary, or an independent ally. What, for example, would you be thinking now if he'd failed at Luqa, if the plane and passengers had gone up in smoke?"

"I would deem him inept and stupid. The point is, he succeeded."

"A matter of luck."

"And at Alabet? For a man depending on luck, he must be blessed with nine lives. Why don't we simply admit that so far he has proved too clever for every Intelligence service put up against him? He wields enough monetary power to purchase high-grade intelligence of his own, he's a master of disguises, and he has a growing amount of practical experience."

"Nobody's perfect, Nathan. He'll make a mistake as we all do. Already Erinys has had to rely on others for help. When the reward is high enough they cannot be expected to keep silent. Someone will talk, either for the money or because of vanity. Then our mystery man's house of cards will tumble. Our job is to find him before everyone else, with or without informants."

"Then what? Will he be let off with a lecture?" Green sneered contemptuously.

"Perhaps you are identifying with him *too* closely. No, we only want to bring him to the notice of the police in whatever country he is found. His means of disposal will be left up to them. Israel will be off the hook."

"Unless he is an Israeli."

That possibility occurred to Charon more times than he cared to admit. Shabak had made continual checks on Israeli nationals abroad, ascertaining their whereabouts, their business, their personal resources, as well as the obvious facts of age, sex, and appearance. There was no longer any reason to believe Basilia-Derna-Erinys held an Israeli passport. Realizing its importance, Charon had made sure of that fact.

"He isn't. Nor, I feel safe in saying, is he from one of the Communist countries. They keep a tight grip on their citizens; and even a rogue KGB agent has only very limited resources upon which he can draw without consent.

"It is quite strange," Charon continued, "that we can know so much about our man and yet so little."

"I think we know *very* little," Green countered.

"At least we have an idea of his psychological makeup.

But because he is a consummate actor and appears to own a crowd of different passports, a description which might lead to a name has been impossible to achieve. However, shall we return to my original hypothesis? If you were Erinys, what would you be doing right now?"

"Planning my next attack," Green said, a touch of humor in his voice.

"Yes, I'm afraid of that too. Until we compile more useful information time is definitely on the side of Mr. Erinys. We can guess at his next targets, but their defense will be wholly the responsibility of the Arabs."

Charon moved away from the window and took his seat. "For the past week I have been conducting a research project, drawing help from our public archives, the IS archives, major newspapers, and civil aviation agencies around the world. A short-list has been complied which contains the names of all known victims of Arab terrorism during the last two years who either survived their injuries or left relatives to mourn them. Names and addresses of relatives are still being collected, and then begins the job of working through them to locate our man."

"If he's there, if he's not simply a devoted friend of the victim rather than the victim himself or a blood relative, if his motive is vengeance."

"Oh, I think we can agree on that. And I doubt if he could hold grudge longer than the two years without having acted before now. Assuming he lost someone by an Arab bullet or bomb, we'll identify him eventually. Then it's only a matter of time until he is located."

"Is this above-board?"

"Certainly. We couldn't ask a country's internal security service for information on its nationals without giving a reason. So far we've had no complaints. The American FBI, to take but one example, has offered its help, requesting only that we stamp TOP SECRET on whatever is given us. Though the FBI can justify its investigation of U.S. citizens, for political reasons it prefers the matter to be handled with utmost delicacy. Understandable after the revelations five—six years ago. Big Brother and all that.

"Just a few more words before I let you go off to lunch, Nathan. I want you in on this as much as possible—from *now*. Obviously, I have other things to attend to, things which I had to delegate to others while I tried to bring results on Operation Moses. The Premier wanted something positive. Now that that seems less impossible I'm turning the matter over to you. Naturally I'll expect regular briefings on your progress."

"Naturally." Tugging on the other side of his devotion to duty was a cold realization that Charon kept him on the case because he knew he would need someone to verify Erinys' true identity by a face-to-face confrontation. Green's personal feelings had no stake in the matter. And if they did, the head of Shabak had certainly plotted them among the intricacies of the search with only one thing in mind: an accelerated time-schedule. Perhaps he hoped his recruit would be spurred by curiosity, intrigued by the phenomenon of someone so like himself.

Charon understood that the majority of investigations depended for their success on long hours of sifting through minutiae, reams of incidental facts that might possibly render up a single clue—if you were lucky. Knowing that, he still had sent Green to Malta, hoping the ace of the Flying Squad could break the case and be home by the next Sabbath.

It hadn't been that easy. Green's principal discovery was the parallel but rapidly converging interest of the Russians and their rabid clients, the Palestinian Arabs— an interest which might well prove fatal for the elusive Mr. Erinys long before Green could reach him and extend his hand in fellowship.

The second personal visit proved less frightening.

Though Pierre Le Beau increased the security around his chateau near Moret after his unscheduled meeting with M. Rapière—as he now called the stranger with the sword-cane—it had been wasted effort.

Returning from a three-day holiday in Nice—and still happily reflecting on the expertise of the mistress he kept there—he was startled to see a sword-cane propped against his desk as he entered his home office. He turned to signal his bodyguard who had checked the room only minutes before and was now returning to his post at the front entrance; but Le Beau decided against it when he saw M. Rapière's gun-arm slowly rise from a dark corner, a polished barrel stuck in the hand.

He closed the door behind him and, acting as casual as he could in such a situation, strolled to his chair at the huge oak desk, saying "Ah, m'sieu, what a surprise! *Comment ca va?*"

"Keep your voice lowered," M. Rapière replied, retaining a fix on his moving target. "If your guard returns you know I will have to kill him. And do not turn on a light," he added when Le Beau stretched a hand toward a floor-lamp beside the heavy, blue velveteen drapes. "You can see me well enough to speak in my direction."

"As you wish, m'sieu." Le Beau was amused by M.

Rapière's insistent use of a gruff Norman dialect. He was French, but he certainly did not come from Caen.

"I am here with some business."

Le Beau hurriedly said—clipping his vowels—"I followed your instructions to the letter, m'sieu. Were the items not delivered even as you requested—in perfect condition? Despite the dangers imposed by sending them by commercial transport? We made a compact and I have not abused it. The police have asked me nothing, I have told them nothing."

"No one is accusing you. Anyway, why should the police be interested in asking you questions about me?"

"No reason, m'sieu, no, none at all."

"Have you said anything to anyone?"

"Mon Dieu! Do you think I am so foolish?"

"What about the forger who made up the passports?"

"Other than you and me, he is the only one who knows what names are on them, and he is paid to hold his tongue. Because the fellow reads newspapers, his price has increased since he learned what you had done and the reward was offered for your capture."

"What do *you* know of all this?"

"What I have read, no more. The police have been seeking a Federico Basilia. You ordered a Spanish passport in that name, so . . . but it is no business of mine. As you instructed," Le Beau said, his voice dropping to a murmur, "I read the obituaries in the Paris papers the day after you first came here. Nothing. But there was an article on the strange death of a former mugger in a Paris alleyway. Henri Blanche was a friend, m'sieu. Was it necessary . . . ?"

"I have no idea what you are talking about."

A cunning fox! He admits to nothing. And wisely so. "I

see your point, m'sieu. He did indeed leave a message which I have since taken to heart. Reward money is of no use to a dead man, *n'est pas?* Now—how may I be of service?"

M. Rapière dropped a manila envelope on Le Beau's desk then retreated to the shadows from which he had materialized. The director of the Corporation had only a fleeting glimpse of his face, and was shocked to see it almost entirely hidden by hair. Like a werewolf's, thought Le Beau, shuddering.

"Enclosed are my directions and your normal fee for producing the required items. You will hold them until you receive my delivery instructions. That may mean a wait of several weeks. I will telephone."

Now, five days after that second bizarre interview with M. Rapière, Le Beau received his call.

At noon tomorrow a large canvas bag (with a small rip in a corner and the name Gino Abrelli printed on the bottom in red ink) holding M. Rapière's purchases should be checked in at the left luggage department of the Gare du Nord. The receipt-stub must be handed to a black porter named Ogambe who will be standing at the entrance gate to Platform 5. The porter should receive a tip of 100 francs, otherwise he will not hand over the envelope containing M. Le Beau's bonus for a job well-done.

Having taken the call in his bedroom, Le Beau dressed, told the two women lying nude on the bed that he would return soon, and crossed the hallway to his study, locking the door behind him.

He sat among his law books for nearly two hours before reaching a decision.

M. Rapière must take me for a fool, he repeatedly told

himself, hoping that anger would fire his dormant courage. The radical Palestinians offered a reward of $20,000 for information leading to the apprehension of the man called Federico Basilia; and with the Saudis bankrolling them they would probably go higher. Now the Libyans, stymied for two weeks, were publicly advertising a reward of $100,000 to anyone who could furnish positive information as to the identity and whereabouts of the man who murdered five Libyan troops. Why not tell them?

Le Beau greatly feared that someone might claim the reward before he did. His master forger, for example. The man had been warned that a slow death would be his greatest reward if he ever mentioned the special jobs he'd done for Le Beau; but the fellow had no scruples, and the threat was losing conviction as the amount of money involved grew steadily. He could, of course, be eliminated, a thought Le Beau mulled over several times, always hesitating because of the forger's professional value to the Corporation.

Too, there was an outside chance some mastermind of the Union Corse might trip over the idea that Basilia's false passport had been made up by a Paris-based forger, then send a couple of goons there to interview all known paper artists. Le Beau's man would certainly spill his guts when they started scraping out his teeth with a pen-knife.

Deeming his criminal cohorts more dangerous than the solitary M. Rapière, Le Beau made the only possible decision left to him. He hated violence, had hated it ever since his two youngest brothers were ambushed while searching for a unit of the ALN in the mountains around El Bayadh. The sight of blood made him physically sick. He preferred being a recreant rather than a hero. After all, his disloyalty affected only M. Rapière, and once the Arabs sank their claws into the killer he would never again be in any condition to harm Le Beau.

Le Beau did not know M. Rapière's true identity or where he was staying. The head of the Corporation would have to be especially cunning to get his message across and earn the reward without opening himself to felony charges: counterfeiting government documents, dealing in stolen weapons, concealing information from the police, and serving as an accomplice in multiple murders; though he doubted whether the Arabs would care to pursue the matter beyond M. Rapière's body.

He stepped up to his bookshelves and took down a hollowed-out copy of Hugo's *Les Misèrables*. Inside was a key.

Walking into his adjoining office, he used the key to unlock the top middle drawer of his desk. It was filled with paper-clips, pencils, an address book, a half-empty pack of Citanes, a six-inch Havana cigar in a glass humidor tube, a stapler, a packet of three lubricated condoms, a guidebook to St. Moritz, and a red foil Christmas bow. He moved these items to the desktop then pulled out the drawer's lining paper.

On the back were five phone numbers, each with its separate code. He divided the first number by two, paused for a moment as if unsure of his next move, then grabbed the phone from its cradle and dialed the dividend.

While waiting for his call to be answered, he multiplied the second number by two, dividing the result by three as a voice at the other end of the line asked suspiciously, *"Oui?"*

"Oú êtes-vous?"

"Je suis ici."
"Qui es-tu?"
"L'homme de Verdun. Pipi. Qui êtes-vous?"
"Le cheval mort."

Convinced of each other's identity, the two men spoke freely for two minutes.

"Yes, the merchandise is ready. But I thought it was not needed until June or later."

"A change of plans. Here are your instructions." Le Beau conveyed M. Rapière's orders for the exchange, adding, "I want you to wear a blue suit tomorrow morning. Do not ask why, just do it. After you hand the ticket stub to the black man, you will board a train for Calais. Stay at the Hotel Meurice until I call you. Contact no one, especially not me. You may have to wait a week or ten days. And make certain no one follows you, Pipi."

He rang off, took the result of the second equation and dialed the number.

"Hallo?"

This conversation lasted ten minutes. He petitioned the listener with his many reasons for retaining his anonymity, and thus the necessity for a rather unusual transfer of the reward money from the Libyans' coffers to his Swiss bank. Before divulging his precious secret, Le Beau wanted to make certain he was not cheated of his due reward, passing on his account number—all that identified him to the bank—and the name of his Zurich banker.

"But you cannot expect us to give you the money until we receive some assurance your information is trustworthy," the somber voice protested.

"Listen. When you hear what I have to say you will be very happy to give me the reward. I will tell you certain things which you may easily check and which could only be known to someone who has had dealings with the man whom you seek. After two hours—which should make the time approximately midnight—I will call again. You can then tell me if you care to make a deal. If you do, you will deliver as security $30,000 in cash to my banker's home before 2 a.m. tomorrow. When I have verified that this has been done, I will give you explicit details as to how you may capture Federico Basilia—who, you must know, also goes by the name Erinys and the name Hans Derna. A cargo crate arrived for Hans Derna in Cairo, a consignment of china delivered through the Longaville Shipping Company of Toulon. Packed with the china were five M79 grenades, a .32-calibre Skorpion submachine-gun, and a SIG M1950 pistol. Five magazines were sent for the Czech gun, five for the 9mm Swiss weapon. Assuming the weapons have been found or the slugs recovered, I doubt if confirming my information will prove very difficult for you."

Le Beau brusquely hung up. His hands were shaking and a thin line of sweat had formed along his brow-bone. This wasn't his usual way of doing business. The backhanded betrayal. Once, perhaps—when he'd first begun organizing the Corporation and the necessity for weeding the slackers from the workers proved a good enough reason to play Judas. Then it came easily. His appetite for wealth had fed his ruthlessness. But those days were gone; he had more money than he needed. And so now he felt off-balance, not sure of his true motives, not comprehending the rules of the game he was playing and therefore trying to change them.

He thought of going to the bedroom, telling the girls they might just as well leave; but they were probably asleep by now and he felt an uncharacteristic desire to let them be, let them slumber while the mad world of armed men, blood and hypocrisy, fear and betrayal danced around them. It would be a long night for him. Why ruin it for others?

The pretty Air France stewardess smiled warmly, handing him a steaming cup of black coffee. It was the first and only thing he had asked for during her graveyard-shift on this run, and she wished all of her passengers were as undemanding. Most of them knew the two-hour flight would not give enough time for a nap, so they decided to celebrate, have a flying party, bedevil the stewardesses with constant orders for drinks, sick bags, blankets and pillows.

The passenger in 27B, however, kept to himself. He took no interest in his fellow travelers: French novitiates whose Mother Superior had missed the plane, leaving the giggling girls feeling liberated; the two American couples trying to outdo each other with long-winded recitations on the scope of their European Grand Tour; the businessmen and students and miscellaneous holidaymakers. He concentrated instead on the eastern horizon and the thickening line of brightness glossing over it.

"Have you friends in Paris?" she asked in Italian, for he had used that language when asking for the coffee.

He shook his head, frowning. Stupid woman, why does she bother me now?

"There is a hotel booking agency at the airport if you wish to make a quick reservation."

"Thank you. You are most helpful."

"What happened to your hand?" she asked, indicating the gauze wrapping which bound the fingers of his left hand together, crossed over the palm, and was tied at the wrist. "Is it painful?"

"No," he answered, turning back to the window.

She got the message, blushed, and went to help an old woman trapped by her seatbelt at a time when she least needed obstacles on her way to the rear toilets.

Yevgeny Sholokov stared over the Savoy Alps and into Switzerland. The jagged horizon grew starker, bleeding the purple sky and raising snaggle-toothed mountains against a golden-hued background. Such a sight might move a man to thanksgiving for being alive; but Sholokov seemed only bored, his eyes as cold and devoid of feeling as ice-chips.

He felt tired. A throbbing pain beat in his left hand and up through his brain. He wanted to scream, to kill someone, anyone who dared look at him. It was an irrational impulse; and knowing that, his anger increased. He was acting like some cabbage-head just out of the Komsomol.

A call had come at three o'clock that morning from Sholokov's European control, Alexander Yupn. The Libyan embassy in Paris had received a tip regarding both the Luqa and Alabet incidents. Apparently the informant knew what he was talking about; he offered corroborative evidence which proved his knowledgeability. Federico Basilia would be accepting a new consignment of weapons—source unknown, but thought to be the informant—at noon in the Gare du Nord.

Without the proper men to handle this operation on short notice, the Libyan intelligence officer notified his Russian counterpart in Paris, requesting help. The KGB man contacted Moscow and was referred to Yupn, who was overseeing the search for Basilia from his base at the Rome embassy.

Yupn, in turn, ordered the caller to put a three-man shadow squad in place until he could get his own man there. Then he shook Sholokov out of bed to tell him he had a reservation on the earliest morning flight to Paris.

So here he was, nursing his wound and streaking toward the man who gave it to him. He felt no enmity because of the booby-trapped suitcase; in fact, he thought his quarry quite clever for having planted the device.

Mixed with his admiration was a humiliating embarrassment: he should have known Derna—or whatever his name was—would, after leaving a suitcase with an explosive charge buried in the handle, never return for it. Obviously someone had killed Rabat, someone had been in Room 15; but Sholokov doubted whether it was Derna. The man would be stupid to return. If an innocent person—say, the chambermaid—fell victim to the tiny bomb, the police would have the hotel staked out.

Then who murdered Rabat? So confusing. Did Derna work with a partner? Unless Basilia was a master at disguise, at least two different men were involved in the Luqa rescue. But no one believed that. One man had left Malta under mysterious cover. Who else could it be but Basilia? And Basilia became Derna when he hit Sicily, and Derna became Erinys when he registered at Bellano's Hotel Ancora. Damn!

Sholokov hurriedly closed the plastic shutter as the sun peeked over the mountains, filling the cabin with sulphurous radiance. He pushed back his seat and waited for the stars to wash from his bloodshot eyes.

The uniformed doorman bowed slightly as the man exited from the Hotel Shalimar. Usually the handsomely-dressed Englishman had a kind word for him, joining the doorman in a cheery repartee about the weather, humorous anecdotes on the present state of French politics, or the lousy breakfasts hotel chef André always fixed especially for his English patrons, little knowing that kippers in a rich cheese sauce topped by a poached and shredded egg is not the morning meal of most Britons.

But not today. Ordering a taxi, the man was polite but reserved.

As the doorman watched the taxi disappear, he glanced at his watch, searching for an explanation beneath the scratched crystal. Ah, of course. It was 11:05. The Englishman was usually out by nine each morning. Today he slept late. And since the doorman had heard him order the taxi to the Gare du Nord, it was as clear as day that he'd missed his early train and was upset.

That explained it. Of course.

CHAPTER TWELVE

Green entered the bureaucratic machine without relishing the task set for him. To be cooped up with twenty wet-eyed paper-pushers for a week had shoved him one more move nearer resignation. He simply could not understand why Charon insisted on his presence during the routine checking, the collations, the informal but carefully worded requests to various foreign agencies for information on certain of their subjects.

The first week in the basement of Israel's National Archives was spent collecting further information on known victims of Arab terrorism during the past two years.

If a victim was injured but recovered, the task of gathering information on that person became more difficult. A formal query had to be lodged with the affected foreign intelligence service, requesting the present whereabouts of said individual or, if it happened to be a woman, the whereabouts of her close male relatives between the ages of 20 and 50.

In such instances where the victim had not been

physically harmed, directly or indirectly—as in the case of a skyjacking in which the hostages were freed before the terrorists fulfilled their threats—he or she was struck from the Israeli research team's list.

By week's end 240 names remained on the master roster from an original 712. These were victims who suffered wounds or death at the hands of the terrorists, and who were believed to have male blood relatives between 20 and 50 years of age. Additional information was required on each victim, and particularly on whether or not those who survived had taken a trip outside their country or been inexplicably absent from home or work at any time during the month of April.

The results from this line of inquiry were still coming in from the FBI, Scotland Yard, the Sûreté National, as well as internal security agencies in South Africa, Italy, Belgium, Spain, and the Scandinavian countries. Yet they would not offer a comprehensive study of *all* possible suspects; family members and friends might have to be interviewed, and their governments would certainly balk if asked to spread the investigation that far. Lacking a more substantial excuse than that the Israelis' quarry was *possibly* motivated by revenge, these powers could not—due to political considerations—be expected to quiz the tragic victims or their survivors about whether or not they'd been to Malta and/or Libya to exact a just revenge, whether they had the resources and physical capacity to carry out such an operation, whether they felt guilty about anything in particular. These questions would have to be answered by data supplied by Immigration and Passport Control, the internal revenue service, bank statements, and nosy friends—which took time to collect, accepting that the government concerned was even willing to spy on its law-abiding citizens.

Green angrily struck the back of his neck with a stiffened hand, a gesture designed to drive out the tension headache which had been creeping up from his trapezius muscles all morning. Too much coffee, the fluorescent lighting, the pages of names, addresses, necropsy reports. The job was too exhausting, too claustraphobic for his outdoor spirit. Depressing was what it was. Goddamned depressing. The innocent dead, victimized first by Palestinian terrorists, now by their own prying intelligence services; the walking wounded, wanting to forget how they got that scar or lost this arm or grieved for a spouse and being reminded by emotionless inquisitors that it was not over, not over at all. So depressing.

Yet in spite of the tedious nature of the work, progress was being made. Name after name dropped from the list as the researchers were informed of victims who had been permanently incapacitated and victims who were at work all during April; of relatives of dead or surviving terrorist victims, sons, brothers, fathers, husbands, nephews and uncles between the designated ages but who could be accounted for during April; of victims whose deaths marked the end of their blood-line; of survivors and relatives who had taken vacations during April but who either lacked the resources to finance a campaign against the Arabs on their home ground, lacked the contacts to smuggle weapons around Europe for them, or had simply taken their vacation in a resort distant from Malta and were remembered by hotel clerks, waiters, and bellboys.

And then, of course, there were those people who

survived Arab bullets and bombs only to be knocked down later by cars, cancer, heart-failure, or some other normal hazard of modern life.

By Monday noon, 12 May, the catalogue of 240 names had been whittled down to 23. Of these, 7 dead had at least one relative who could not at present be contacted but who appeared to have been at home and work during most of April; 3 dead each had at least one relative whose whereabouts were unknown. Among the survivors of Arab terrorist acts from the past two years were a man and wife, presumably lost at sea off the coast of Venezuela the previous February, 6 people whose present addresses were known but who could not be reached at them, and 5 survivors whom their governments were unable to trace to either home address or place of work. Personal dossiers to follow where applicable.

Green crossed out the two presumed drownings and was typing his reason on the file report when the telephone rang.

It was Charon.

"Keeping busy, Nathan? I must have missed your call yesterday."

"I'm keeping busy and that's why I didn't have time to call. Listen—"

"I'll hear your report over lunch. Same place. Half an hour. See you there."

Two days earlier, Pipi, dressed immaculately in a new blue serge suit, salmon-colored shirt and black clip-on tie, checked his watch against the clock suspended above the magazine kiosk, then walked with determination across the Gare du Nord's main concourse toward the left luggage office. In his left hand he carried a brown canvas-sided travel bag, a tiny rip in one corner and the name Gino Abrelli painstakingly printed on the base in red acrylic paint, the Bic red-ink pen having proved useless when applied to stiff laminated cardboard.

Immediately he noticed the dark-faced lounger standing awkwardly in front of a shoe repair shop, not thirty feet from the gate of the baggage holding station. The man's eyes were shrouded by sunglasses and he held a newspaper folded once across the center.

Pipi read the headlines as he passed, smiling to himself. Unless his glasses were of a most unusual type that could invert printed images, the fellow was reading today's *Le Figaro* upside-down.

Setting the bag on the tagging shelf, Pipi momentarily thought of canceling the delivery. But he knew it was important, otherwise the boss would not be handling it; and if the bag failed to change hands, serious complications might arise—none of them pleasant for Pipi. Anyway, this Corsican amateur looking in his direction did not seem much of a threat. Nor did those two hairy apes eyeing him from in front of the toilet marked FEMMES.

A surly attendant grabbed the bag and put it on a trolley behind him. *"Trois francs."*

"Trois?"

"Trois, trois. Oui ou non?"

Pipi passed the coins to the waiting palm and received a receipt-stub in return.

"Merci."

The attendant ignored him, pushing the tiered trolley up a dimly-lit passage bordered by high racks of wooden cubicles.

Pipi turned and headed toward the men's toilet, walking swiftly. When he was certain the three gorillas had no intention of following him inside, he stripped off his jacket and tie, opened his collar, and slipped on a pair of thick-lensed spectacles. Then he waited until an old man had finished his duty at the urinals and escorted him out.

The three dark-faced men were nowhere in sight.

Pipi disengaged his arm from the old man's and made his way to Platform 5, putting on his jacket as he went and returning the distorting spectacles to their case in his inside breast-pocket.

The black man was leaning on his metal luggage cart near the gate. From his instructions, Pipi thought the man would recognize him. Why else should he wear a blue suit? But the porter gave no sign of either recognition or interest when Pipi stood in front of him and stared at the plastic ID plate on his chest. It read: PHILIPPE OGAMBE.

Pipi held out the receipt-stub, the fellow took it, stuck it in the sweat-band on his cap, pocketed the 100-franc note—and that was that. Mission accomplished.

As he steered for an exit, he saw one of the gorillas, the one who read newspapers upside-down. A less experienced man would have stopped in bewilderment, puzzling over what he should do next; but Pipi had done enough shadowing to realize that the greatest mistake a target can make is to reveal an awareness of the surveillance. If you were to be nailed, confrontation only hurried the process. No, walk on, merge into a crowd, get inside a large department store with several exits, take an elevator up, descend by the emergency stairs, leave the store by a different exit. If it was covered, at least you were splitting the surveillance team.

Pipi left the train terminus, stopping at a phone-booth and miming an animated conversation.

The dark-faced trio did not appear.

Curious, Pipi waited five minutes then re-entered the station by another entrance and came upon the three shadows from behind. The reader was positioned just as before, leaning against a mailing-box, one arm supporting the other which held the newspaper. His two buddies were standing beside the closed gate to Platform 8 and talking to each other.

What ridiculous amateurs! But they are no concern of mine, Pipi thought, noting that their attention was brazenly focused on the black porter who had just been accosted by a shrill-voiced German frau with few manners and less French.

They want the African, not me. And that can only mean they are following the receipt-stub. Are they after the cargo or this Abrelli who is looking for delivery?

Pipi did not know or particularly care. He was paid to keep his curiosity at a minimum unless instructed otherwise. The boss said nothing about handling the bag like a registered letter, verifying that it reached who it was supposed to reach. So why bother? Get a ticket for Calais, hop the train—making sure none of these bums join you—and relax on your expense account. Summer is not far off and Englishwomen will be filling the streets, all in search of one of France's renowned lovers. Like me.

Yes, I deserve a paid vacation, he assured himself.

Sholokov watched the three Libyans from his table inside a small glassed-in café that fronted on the main concourse, dully wondering who had chosen them for this task. From their manner, they must have been drafted from the secretarial pool. What fools! What incompetent asses!

Since their brief did not include the appearance of a Russian secret agent, Sholokov had no way of calling them off quickly. His quiet explanation would not faze them. They were too dumb to possess imagination, and might, out of fear that *he* was the man they sought, blast away with those elephant-guns so ill-concealed beneath their thin jackets. His only recourse was to phone his Paris contact, have him get in touch with the local Libyan intelligence officer (praying he wasn't one of the men out there) and tell the bastard to pull his dogs off before they blew the case. Basilia might be laughing at them even now; he certainly would not recover the receipt-stub while they were hanging about, as obvious as eyeballs floating in a shot of vodka. Why, the man in the blue suit had caught on to them immediately! What the hell kind of operation was this?

He decided to make the call. It was 12:15 p.m. and Basilia might not have arrived yet. Perhaps he had no intention of collecting the stub at the Gare du Nord. But if the Libyans' informant could be trusted, Basilia wanted the weapons ahead of schedule; he would not let them lie fallow for long.

Sure that the Libyans would at least be able to keep an eye on the porter Ogambe while he was gone, Sholokov made his way to a telephone.

Thirty minutes later a young hook-nosed Arab walked up to each member of the surveillance team and murmured in his ear. Wordlessly they departed, backs stiff with injured pride.

They are unable to do even that correctly, Sholokov

thought in exasperation. He made a resolution to inform his superiors of the horrible state of Libyan Intelligence. The Libyans may have been trained at the Kiev KGB station, but they hadn't learned anything. No wonder they could let one man slip into a guarded terrorist camp inside Libya and murder the entire population, then escape to France without a problem. They would have done better to follow their usual practice of putting up Palestinian terrorists in luxury resort hotels.

Ogambe spent the remainder of the afternoon going about his business: assisting disembarking travelers with their luggage, rolling it to the sheltered taxi-ranks outside, giving directions to flustered youths (the older generation reserved their queries for white porters), and keeping a steady flow of coffee going from a café to the lazy ticket-takers at the gates.

Sholokov reminded himself that Ogambe had probably been given no reason to suspect surveillance and would be unable to spot it even if he did suspect. Basilia was different: cautious, perceptive, experienced, and cunning. He would be watching for anything out of the ordinary. So the Russian carefully masked his different positions.

Hours passed. The receipt-stub remained on Ogambe's cap, clearly visible. No one remotely similar to the description of Basilia, Derna, or Erinys came near the porter.

At exactly five o'clock, having been unengaged for the past quarter-hour, Ogambe wheeled his cart to a loading depot. Other porters with their carts were already there, racking them together. Ogambe pushed his cart into line, said a few words to another black porter, then entered the main terminal again.

Sholokov followed him with his eyes into a public toilet, debating whether he should risk going after him to make certain the exchange did not take place when—

Ogambe came out within ten seconds after entering and headed back toward the loading depot. The receipt-stub was missing from the band on his cap.

Consciously feeling the weight of his 9mm Makarov suspended in the shoulder-holster, Sholokov sighed heavily and started for the toilet. He had checked all of the men's rooms when he first reached the station, as well as other public facilities where an exchange might be made. He knew the windows on these toilets were too small and high to provide egress for a man. Whoever had accepted the stub was still inside. Either that or Ogambe had hidden it for Basilia to pick up later. In any case, the porter had not visited the toilet just to pluck the stub from his cap and pocket it, nor had he taken enough time to urinate.

The toilet facilities consisted of five stalls and a line of step-up urinals furnished with a plastic splash-guard. Facing the stalls were six washbasins. Despite the reek of disinfectant, the place was filthy. There was no attendant in evidence.

Sholokov knocked open the door to each stall but found no one. Then what—?

The yellow receipt-stub was wedged in the lower right-hand corner of the long mirror running above the washbasins, plainly visible to anyone who entered.

The Russian freed it, turning the slip of paper over to see if a message had been written on the back. No. Nothing. Why did the porter leave it here, conspicuous and unattended? Surely he could have found a place to hide it.

If he wanted to.

Sholokov ran all the way to the left luggage desk, cursing his stupidity. Moscow would be most unhappy if he lost Basilia a second time—especially when his superiors learned that he had dismissed the Libyans working surveillance. Being withdrawn was not so bad in itself—it meant seeing Tonya and the boys much sooner than expected—but his perquisites, travel visa and additional living expenses, would be lost, his reputation sullied. The humdrum life of weapons instructor would begin, resurrecting his envy of all those younger agents being sent on field operations. His family would be forced to foreclose on its present life-style, every ruble would have to be stretched. And all because of his damned overweening pride in his ability to handle this matter by himself!

"Yes, monsieur?"

Sholokov handed over the receipt-stub and watched the attendant disappear down the passageway leading to the storage cubicles. He was a different one, not the same youngster who accepted the brown bag from the man in the blue suit.

Sholokov spun on his heels, staring anxiously at the passing crowds as though he were being examined by hidden eyes—laughing eyes above a humorless mouth. His nerves were taut and the rhythmic pulse in his left hand began again. What would Tonya think of a nine-fingered man? Could she love me? You're being silly like an old woman. Like your wife's anile mother. Control yourself. Everything is fine.

The attendant returned, a puzzled expression creasing his low forehead.

"Could you describe the piece of luggage, monsieur?"

Sholokov knew the little game was over. Basilia had won. My congratulations, sir. And yet we must know *how* you won, so that next time I come up against you the game will be fairer. If there is a next time for me . . . for you.

"It is brown canvas. Small. A tiny tear in a corner near the bottom. My name is on the base—Gino Abrelli. In red ink," Sholokov added, struggling with his French.

The attendant eyed him suspiciously. "Ah, yes. I remember now." He held up the stub. "Where did you find this?"

"What do you mean? I was given that as a receipt for my bag."

"Yes, monsieur. Wait a moment, if you please. A gendarme will be interested to hear your story."

"I want my bag. Explain yourself or *I* will summon a flic. I have a train to catch and I do not intend to miss it because of your insolence and stupidity."

The attendant replaced the phone in its cradle and turned back to his angry customer. "Forgive me, monsieur. If I have made a mistake I apologize. But—"

"Where is my bag?"

"Another man came to me, said he lost his receipt but that he could describe his bag in detail. He used the same words as you have—tear in a bottom corner, name in red ink on the base. So I gave it to him. Who else could know such things?"

"When did he pick it up?"

"Shortly after I came on duty. I was late to work, so it would have been a few minutes after twelve. Jean—the guy before me—had just gone off."

"Can you describe the man who took my bag?"

"Ah . . . tall, thin, had a large moustache, wore a dark-blue trenchcoat. I mean—he seemed honest, even showed me an identification card with—" The attendant's mouth flopped open, his eyes taking the same round shape. "Just a minute. Maybe *you* had better show me some identification. If he was Abrelli, then you must have found . . . but then how could you . . . ?"

Sholokov was already on his way outside, his face a slide-show of shiting emotions, a pasty-white lump revealing varied aspects of rage, disappointment, amusement, and fear. His self-confidence dissipated and he was left with the hopelessness of his situation, convinced that this was the end of the line for him; he would never have another chance to catch up with Basilia, Yupn would have him shipped home on the next Aeroflot flight from Paris.

Fifteen seconds after he emerged from the great train terminal, a mint-green Triumph TR-6 pulled out of a space on the opposite side of the access road and bore down on him.

Sholokov jumped back as the car swerved at the curb and stopped. The passenger door swung open and he got inside.

"Where is he?" the driver asked excitedly, glad for some action after over five hours of sitting alone in the Triumph, chain-smoking, listening to the radio, and pissing into an empty Beaujolais bottle.

"I missed him."

"What!"

"He picked up the goods while I was keeping an eye on the receipt. Assuming he would have to show it to get the bag, I discarded the idea that he might use false identification to claim it."

"Discarded" was the wrong word. Actually, the

Russian never imagined Basilia could extricate the bag without using the receipt, and thus he dismissed the inept Libyans and centered his attention on Ogambe. All for nothing.

"What are we going to do?" Rashad whined. "Our organization has been fully mobilized for this operation. What do we do?"

"Perhaps your informant can give us some additional help. He obviously knows more than he told your embassy. He will call again when he discovers we missed Basilia and his own life may now be endangered. You can be sure of that. There is an old saying that the third attempt is charmed. Trust in it, comrade. Trust in it."

CHAPTER THIRTEEN

Miraculously, the list had been pared down to five names by Friday, only four days after Green's last progress report to Yigael Charon. Foreign governments, though confused that the Israelis should be so intent on locating a devilish enemy of the Arabs, were eager to remain "neutral" in the matter, and so had offered considerable assistance in the investigation.

With the list of victims already in hand, the task had been comparatively simple: either the suspects were located, interviewed, could or could not account for their movements during April, or were not located. The first group inevitably included a few independents who refused to answer questions until they were apprised of the reason for them, as well as some people who despised all forms of authority and kept silent on principle. Just as inevitably, these dissidents' names were checked with Immigration Control, their tax records were examined; and—in the case of two Americans who had been abroad in April but would not speak to the FBI agents who turned up at their homes—a court order required their banks to produce a detailed account of their deposits and withdrawals during the previous year. (The result: both Americans were cleared of involvement in the Alitalia rescue, though one was subsequently charged with tax evasion.)

The second group—those who could not be reached—was naturally much smaller. Since a missing person cannot be questioned, a brief biography was compiled on each of the absentees, sent by courier to the nearest Israeli diplomatic mission, and forwarded from there to the basement headquarters of the research team at the National Archives in Tel Aviv where a decision was made on whether the person could be viewed as a possible suspect or—as with the two Venezuelans lost at sea—was probably missing forever.

Green pulled the phone and its scrambler-box across his desk, started to dial the Shabak Director's number—then hung up. Charon would be impressed by the results, but five names still would not satisfy him. He wanted only one.

"Well, that's tough," Green muttered. If Israeli Intelligence wanted this guy badly enough—and it obviously did, having spent thousands of pounds to locate him, money better employed in other endeavors—it would simply have to send out field agents. That was the only way. Sure, it could badger various governments into running down the missing suspects, but without any guarantee that the job would be handled properly. Why the hell bother with one of your nationals who is making monkeys out of every intelligence service on half the planet? Why try to foil this human chameleon who is freelancing against international terrorists in a sanguinary and totally effective manner closed to you by the restrictions of morality and politics? Because he plays with the same total lack of ethical precepts as does his prey? Because he is setting a bad example and will have every nut-case not in an institution waving a pistol, attacking hijacked planes wherever found? Bullshit. *Bullshit*. Not even Charon believed that. The head of Shabak said the Americans were getting worried. The CIA thought Basilia was—using a technocratic term beloved by Yankees—"de-stabilizing" the Middle East. So? Green had not heard the Americans demanding this, that, and everything else, turning the world inside-out to put a tag on Basilia. Were they protecting one of their own—a CIA man, perhaps, who'd gone bananas? If so, Green might as well throw in his hand; the real Basilia would never be identified, never be found. He'd remain as anonymous as an ant in an ant-hill, a grain of sand in a sandstorm—visible only when it strikes your eye, invisible among the multitudes until it does its damage.

He stared again at the five sheets of paper spread out across his desk, each containing a summary of what Green considered the most pertinent details that would, eventually, mark the suspect as innoxious or iniquitous.

Looking a the names, he thought about the psychiatrist Charon had brought into the case a week before. From Hebrew University in Jerusalem, Dr. Wona Splenion possessed enough credentials to make her studied opinion important to Charon, and the Shabak chief impressed upon the research team that her description of Basilia's psychological makeup must be taken into account as they hashed through their lists of names.

Splenion had said: "Basilia—the man who at one point called himself Basilia, or I should say the man who presented himself as one Federico Basilia immediately before and during his rescue of the crew and passengers of an Alitalia plane at Luqa Airport on the fifth day of April last"—Dr. Splenion disliked ambiguities and, when speaking in front of a group of laymen like these, made tiresomely certain that, once she had finished her lecture, no one would be able to confront her with a question—"is not a homicidal maniac. From a close examination of information furnished to me by Mr. Charon and dealing with Basilia's known behavioral mode—as well as present conjectures on Basilia's possible motivation adduced through a scrutiny of his past actions—I have concluded that Federico Basilia is a well-oriented, intelligent, and fun-loving man."

Her audience roared with laughter, Charon turned a robust maroon, Green wanted to say he didn't need an academic to tell him the obvious, and Dr. Splenion winced, doubling the patchwork furrows of her face.

"I mean . . . I meant to . . . I meant, in calling Señor Basilia a fun-loving man, that he considers his lethal actions a game. I seriously doubt whether he is *amused* by his murders; but assuming his motivation is revenge—an assumption which I believe we are entitled to make in the absence of any contradictive evidence—then we can qualitatively affirm that he finds pleasure in such actions, a pleasure unconnected to the vulgarism "bloodlust." He is highly selective in his choice of victims; he cannot slake his thirst for revenge on society as a whole—even though he may feel absolved from guilt for his actions by that society's disinterest in his anguish—but only that part of a society which has engendered his compulsion toward violent reprisal.

"As for specifics," she continued, consulting her

notes, "you would be justified in looking for a man who has suffered a grievous wrong, whose basic instincts of fair play have been violated, whose belief in God and man has been cauterized by a severe loss and its attendant loneliness. He is now an inveterate ascetic, denying himself peace as long as his craving for proper vengeance has been unsatisfied.

"In other words," she said, evidently suspecting she might have opened herself to question, "Basilia has not, shall we say, foreclosed on his sanity. He is logical—totally. He sees his cause as impugnable. And yet he lacks the monomaniacal fixation of grandiose invincibility; he realizes his mortality and guards against his own death in a deliberate and incisive manner which will allow him to retain full freedom of movement at all times.

"How can he be identified? The task will not be easy. I would say he has suffered a direct loss: a brother or sister, a wife or child. The loss of a parent is painful enough when it is *not* the result of unnatural causes. But since we unconsciously admit that those who are older will die before we do, the motivational stimulus leading to retributive violence is less developed and harder to invoke. The chance that Basilia is a revenging uncle, cousin, grandson or in-law diminishes in direct proportion to the propinquity of the relationship, and for that reason can be discounted in your investigations—unless Señor Basilia was psychopathic to begin with, a proposition which seems untenable in the light of his present deterministic behavior. Unlike the true theriomorphous psychopath unremittingly aggravated by a stimulus or set of stimuli into revealing his disorder, the man you are seeking acts according to a preordinance which we can only guess at, tightly controlling himself to the point where he can disregard expediency. Hence, he is a confident man."

"Then how can psychoanalysis help us locate him if, for all intents and purposes, he acts quite normally?" Green asked, bored by the woman's repetitious pretentiousness.

Disapproval sparkled in Dr. Splenion's eyes. "Is this an interpellation, young man?"

"A what?"

"Do you consider my disquisition a debate?"

"I just asked a question. All I need is an answer."

"Because if you do, you are mistaken. I was asked to bring forward my professional opinions on methods of psychological identification as relate specifically to a man called Federico Basilia. I believe I have done so to the extent that such an enterprise is possible during the opening stages of investigation."

"I realize that. I—"

"Considering the man's deliberate secretiveness, his cryptic psychological profile, his theatricality, no one in the world could—without actually living with Basilia (something I hope you are not implying I should do, young man)—adduce more details than I have. If he appears normal to you, it is a fault of your perceptive powers."

"Dr. Splenion," Green began, taking up her point, "I do not wish to debate such a simple question. *You* have repeatedly implied that Basilia will not openly manifest his antagonisms except when he is willing, and for that reason he will appear ordinary to us until he pulls another stunt. I infer from those remarks that you have no specifics to offer us other than what we can gather from the physical evidence he leaves behind."

"If you insist. Behavioral psychologists produce their best work only when they can come into contact with a subject. If that was your point you have made it—though it has no bearing on the present matter."

Green gave up and settled back in his seat for the duration of Dr. Splenion's monologue. Charon had invited this windy old bag and he would have to answer for her—for the time everyone was wasting by staying to listen.

Now, a week later, Green knew his boss would start foaming at the mouth if he reminded him of that episode. The thought gave Green perverse pleasure. Should he mention Dr. Splenion? Infuriated, Charon might send him home to the Squad—which was what he wanted.

His tired eyes wandered back to the first page.

ANDERSSON, HALVEK: Born 1933; Stockholm, Sweden. Blond hair, blue eyes, 5'11", 180 lbs. M.S. in Mechanical Engineering from University of Uppsala, 1956. Served in Swedish Army, 1956-58. Married Ursula Dvanmuss, 1959. Children: Anna, born 1962; Thor, born 1965. Employed by Aardholm Construction Co. of Goteborg, 1959-65; Karsund Manufacturing of Stockholm, from 1965 on. Wife and daughter killed by a terrorist bomb planted in the Korko Restaurant, Stockholm, June of last year. Bomb intended for Israeli Ambassador to Sweden, known to frequent restaurant; his wife was ill that day and he stayed home. ANDERSSON was late for his luncheon date with wife and daughter, thus was uninjured. Two other people died in blast. The PFLP and PLO denied responsibility, though two Palestinian students at the

University of Stockholm were later detained by police before being released for lack of evidence. Detectives who handled the case are still convinced the two (Aled Kharif and Mohammed Demullid) were guilty. Following the funeral of wife and daughter, ANDERSSON resigned from his executive position with Karsund Manufacturing and, according to friends, sank into debauchery. In August of last year son Thor reported him missing from their home. A subsequent check of airlines revealed that ANDERSSON purchased a one-way ticket to Frankfurt via Brussels, but Sabena Airlines had no record of him flying the second leg. Subsequent inquiries showed that he rented a small motorboat in Antwerp, provisioned it with food, and stated to the rental manager that he intended a day-trip up the River Schelde. Wreckage recovered near Knokke, Belgium three days later, but no body. He has not been heard from since. Thor is under the guardianship of maternal uncle. Languages: ANDERSSON's school records reveal a proficiency in Norwegian, German, Spanish, and English. Weapons proficiency: Marksman. Assets: home in Stockholm; checking and savings accounts untouched.

Green turned the page face-down and wearily set the second sheet on top of it.

DALTON, PERCY HAROLD KEITH: Born 1948; Haddiscoe, Norfolk, England. Brown hair, grey eyes, 6'2", 168 lbs. Quit school at the age of 16. Joined Royal Marines in 1966; voluntary discharge in 1968 after suspicion of homosexual procuration. Until this March DALTON worked as a bank clerk at Lloyd's, Hammersmith. In previous September his brother (Edwin James George, born 1952) was accidentally (?) killed by a stray bullet during an attempt on the life of the Egyptian diplomatic attaché in Lisbon's Mansanto Park. The Egyptian escaped uninjured. DALTON left London on 28 February for a week's holiday in Gibraltar, returning on 7 March. On 10 March, during a routine accounting, bank examiners discovered a discrepancy of £28,000 on the bank's sheets. DALTON, having progressed in rank at Lloyd's, had been assigned the tasks of day-to-day accountant—checking tills, balancing books, and generally overseeing the management of the bank's resources during the manager's frequent absences. He was therefore held responsible, especially since he had disappeared. On 14 March the British Home Office reported that a dead man—one Edwin James George Dalton—boarded an Air France flight from Heathrow to Venice on 10 March. Also noted was the fact that Edwin Dalton applied for and was issued a new passport in July of the previous year, reporting his previous one had been stolen or lost. The logical assumption was that PERCY DALTON carefully planned embezzlement and escape from England and stole brother's passport on that eventuality, knowing he would be discovered but hoping to give himself a safety margin. Present whereabouts unknown, though Italian immigration officials have no record of his having left their country. Languages: studied French and Italian in state-schools; proficiency questionable. Weapons proficiency: routine, unremarkable. Principal assets: 40-acre farm near Haddiscoe; checking and savings accounts closed on 8 March and added to the embezzlement, amount to £44,632.

It might mean something, Green thought. That was enough money to buy weapons and false documents, plane trips and the silence of a confederate like Paul Justine.

But a lot of facts were missing. Others didn't jibe.

Green dialed a three-digit number on his inter-office phone and listened to it ring on the other side of the huge subterranean labyrinth.

"Lenny? Green here. You typed up the final five summary bios, didn't you?"

"Yeah. Locked them in your desk at seven this morning," Leonard Talmai yawned. "Kept me up all night, Nat. No rest for the wicked. How much coffee have *you* drunk in the last 24 hours?"

Green liked Talmai's subtle sense of humor, his industriousness and dedication to duty. He was information coordinator for what had now come to be called the Luqa Project, and he proved a major linch-pin in Yigael Charon's ongoing strategy. Other staffers said—with justification—that what Talmai did not know was probably not worth knowing; no one who knew him was willing to dispute that generalization.

"I want to know everything you dropped from the summaries, Lenny. Can you come over for a minute?"

"Why? Been talking to the Old Man?"

Green blinked slowly. "No. What makes you say that?"

"Called me at six this morning. Somehow he knew I'd be in. He must have video cables from here to his palace. I heard he gets up at four every day, probably to the thunder of my bare-boned fingers hitting the keys. Anyway, he wanted to know about our short-list: who was on it, their last permanent address, their ID tags, *et cetera*."

"What did you tell him?" Green asked, consciously tensing against his desk, wondering why Charon felt he had to go under Green's head and pick a subordinate's brain.

"Nothing, Nat. You know me."

"Maybe you'd better get over here and explain."

The surprising thing about Leonard Talmai was not his sponge-like brain but his child-like body. Standing rigid, he measured only 40 inches tall from his miniscule toes to the heavily mattressed crown of his cantaloupe-sized head. He smiled warmly as he eased himself backward into a chair across from Green, always careful not to embarrass others by treating adult furniture like an obstacle course.

"As I was saying, Nat, I told Charon we weren't finished with the comprehensives, photos hadn't arrived, and verification checks still had to be made. Operative summaries would be unavailable until later in the day, perhaps not until tomorrow."

"Why?"

"I don't know what possessed Charon to put you on this case," the midget said, his squeaky voice surprisingly strong, "but Shabak has information on all operatives in its brother services. I peeked at yours. You don't belong here."

"Why?" Green asked again, amusement tugging at the

220

corners of his mouth.

"Why? Because you're an active agent, not a desk clerk like the rest of us." And he swept a stubby arm in a swath that covered half of Tel Aviv. "Here, we're all perfectionists because we operate with paper, mathematical certainties, coincidental probabilities. It's easy for us. In the field, perfectionists are harder to find. Answers worked out beforehand can be altered by a sudden change of weather. That requires adaptability, resourcefulness under pressure, physical as well as mental acuity. You seem to have those qualities plus a motivational stimulus: an untarnished record of success. Pride, that's what you have. Why report to Charon if he already knows what you're going to say?"

Green threw his head back and laughed. "You should write a primer for would-be commandos and spies, Lenny. It would sell like hot cakes."

"Hot cakes?"

"An American expression."

"Oh. Well, I don't know about that. I'm afraid our enemies might buy a copy." The diminutive man, dressed primly in a three-piece brown suit that had worn thin at the elbows and knees, frowned, giving his face the contours of a raisin. "You wanted to know what I excised in developing the summaries."

"Yes. You present a concise analysis of a suspect's reason for disappearing—good enough—but there is no follow-up. We cannot presecute an investigation unless we know the latest details on that suspect—bits and pieces his government may have picked up, for example, or Interpol bulletins. . . . Something more timely than an old rap-sheet."

"I understand that. But, like it or not, only two of these men are wanted by police in their country of origin. A third simply disappeared, and it's being treated like any other missing person case. No one except Andersson's son is going to be dogging tracks across Europe. The fellow committed no crime. He even left his money behind for his son's upbringing."

"I read the summary," Green said laconically.

"The remaining two gentlemen are not at home and so we have been unable to contact them. That's why they are on the list—well, one of the reasons. Still, we possess no compelling basis for warranting a world-wide search for them. Since they have not broken any laws—to our knowledge—obtaining cooperation from foreign intelligence bureaus has been difficult. The Freedom of Information Act in the United States, for example, allows any interested American citizen to read all information the various departments of government have collected on him. Should either of our two American suspects discover that the FBI interrogated their acquaintances and examined their financial records, they might sue, claiming violation of privacy."

"So you think we have pressed them as far as they will go?"

"I'm afraid that's it. Further inquiries should be handled discreetly and floated on bribes. We won't have any luck otherwise."

Green glanced shrewdly at the five sheets in front of him. "Who do you think it is, Lenny? Of these five. Off the record."

"Easy. Andersson or Murphy."

"Andersson? You just said—"

"—that not many people are going to be looking for

him. Sure, we suppose he's wandering barefoot and penniless through the streets of Frankfurt. Where would he get the money to finance an operation—even a one-man operation? Steal it. He's a mechanical engineer noted for his practical solutions to difficult problems. When his wife and daughter go up, he decides to do something about it. First, being a clever man, Andersson has to protect his good name. He has no particular regard for his own life; but if the Palestinians were to uncover his identity, they might seek out his teenage son. So he goes to the old drafting board and plots a course. He must disappear in such a way that a detailed search will not follow—or, if it does, will prove misleading. So he fakes a drowning at sea."

"Then turns bank-robber," Green commented wryly.

"Maybe jewel-thief. There are many ways of getting quick money if you have the nerve, Nat."

"What about underworld contacts to furnish the hardware?"

"If he finds a fence, he finds a dope peddler. If he finds a dope peddler, he finds a smuggler. A smuggler can deal in many things. Once he has a reputation and enough cash, Andersson can find someone to sell him a bag of Martian ice if he wants it."

Talmai's argument had substance, Green thought. Andersson spent August to April gathering money for weapons, documents, and a safety-net, then was suddenly blessed with a golden opportunity at Luqa. He knew Spanish well enough to pass as a Spaniard, and would be rusty with guns but also quickly adaptable, having had experience with them in service.

As for Murphy . . .

MURPHY, JAMES MERTON: Born 1944; Los Angeles, California, U.S.A. Ph.D. from Univ. of California, Berkeley. Expert in Romance languages. Enlisted in U.S. Army, 1964; served one tour of duty in W. Germany as interpreter. Married German native, Elke Hausmann, 1967. One child: Rebecca Lynn, born 1970. Returned to U.S. and joined faculty of San Francisco State College in 1972. Wife died in April of last year when an altitude bomb exploded in luggage compartment of Lufthansa 747. Elke Murphy was returning to San Francisco via London after visiting relatives in Bad Homburg. Though he was untenured, MURPHY was allowed a year's leave (unpaid) during which time he could recover from his loss and arrange his affairs. Until this past November he was living in San Francisco, ostensibly working on a collection of scholarly essays. At that time he left daughter with a friend's family and flew to London, purchasing a cottage in Lower Swell in the Cotswolds of England. He returned to S.F. last January, then flew to London with his daughter in February, having sold his home and closed his bank accounts. A governess was hired to look after Rebecca Murphy, and has been doing so since mid-March when MURPHY went to Continent to gather research material. He regularly sends postcards to his daughter from various countries (France, Italy, Spain, Switzerland, and Austria) but without giving information as to how he may be located in an emergency. Last card postmarked Limburg, Germany. No other evidence of his having stayed in that town. Present whereabouts unknown. Languages: fluent in Portuguese, Spanish, French, Italian, Romansch and German; known as a "quick study;" doubtlessly versed in various dialects as well. Weapons proficiency: mediocre; trained with LMGs, other ARs; due to language proficiency, transferred to staff section as interpreter. Assets: Br. govt. unwilling to furnish information; Americans estimate his worth at time of departure to England at $107,000; cottage in Lower Swell; royalties from two books. Additional: Brown hair, blue eyes, 5'10", 190 lbs.

"You also mentioned Murphy. What about him, Lenny?"

"Record speaks for itself. He's still in his prime, apparently has a photographic-memory, love of languages, possesses plenty of money and motivation. All the critical factors."

"He seems a bit short. I notice you almost forgot that."

"Short for him? Basilia?"

"No, Hans Derna. The boatman who took Derna to Sicily said he was at least six feet tall. The immigration officer at Siracusa echoes him. Tall and blond, German passport."

"Maybe he wore elevators like I do," Talmai suggested, grinning broadly. "Though I need *stilts*."

Not knowing if his rejoinder would be appreciated, Green kept silent, sliding the fourth suspect's summary biography across the green blotter.

SHELLEEN, THOMAS GEORGE: Born 1946; Duncan, Oklahoma, U.S.A. Brown hair,

"Hell, Lenny, there are all *kinds* of brown hair! Can't we get something more specific? I have four browns, one blond!"

"Blame their parents, not me. I just pass on information. I can't pass judgement on passport details."

green eyes, 6'3", 190 lbs. B.A. in Liberal Arts from Univ. of Oklahoma, Norman, 1967. Married Annabelle Criar, 1966. One child: Molly Jane, born 1970. Drafted in 1967, enlisted in U.S. Marine Corps, served in Vietnam, two Purple Hearts, cited for bravery. After discharge, SHELLEEN moved family to Berkeley, then to Tarzana, California; got a job as stuntman for Universal Studios. Career began moving in 1972 when he starred in quasi-documentary called *Stunting*. SHELLEEN repeatedly refused offers of larger roles, preferring stunt work more. Co-produced several highly-successful films between 1973-77, usually two each year; retreated after each with wife and daughter to frontier home near Reindeer Lake, Saskatchewan, Canada. SHELLEEN and wife divorced in 1976 on grounds of adultery. Annabelle Shelleen was granted alimony, half of communal property, house in Saskatchewan. SHELLEEN given custody of child on assurance he provide her with a normal home-life; alcoholic mother (i.e., A.) allowed visiting rights and did not challenge court's decision. After enforcement of court's ruling six months later, SHELLEEN left daughter Molly Jane with parents who had retired to Melbourne, Australia. In London last December for promotional work on new film, SHELLEEN asked her grandparents to bring Molly to London for Christmas. Due to a recent heart-attack, SHELLEEN's father could not go and his wife was unwilling to leave him alone; so sent Molly with friends who were flying to Britain to celebrate holidays with relatives. Stops made at Singapore and Bahrain to refuel. British Airways flight hijacked over Syria and landed in Beirut, then flown to Algiers. PLO responsible for initiating skyjacking, and demanded release of all Palestinians held in Egypt, France, Germany, Italy, and Britain. The various governments hesitated—though were in agreement that their prisoners would have to be released. 342 innocent lives were at stake. Plane flown to Benghazi, skyjackers fearful that Algerians bending to international pressure and would allow foreign commandos to attempt rescue. A better reception expected in Libya. Day after 747 touched down, Palestinian terrorists released in Britain and Italy. Skyjackers not convinced; apparently against PLO leadership's instructions they left plane, ordered it refueled, then shot two bazooka rounds into fuselage. Belly tanks ruptured and ignited within seconds; 747 exploded and rapidly burned. 342 deaths. No survivors.

"God, what a sad story."
"Whose is that?"
"This man Shelleen."
"They are all sad, Nat—each in its own way. All possess a common characteristic: motivation for murder."

Common to me as well, thought Green. But if I had

ever intended revenge, I wouldn't have waited five years. Plenty of chances to kill Arab terrorists while on duty. Yes. A good excuse. Hired assassin. Saviour of the realm. Shashana could never blame me for shirking my duty to country, could never know that every time I killed one of those bastards I thought of her.

"Feeling all right, Nat?"

"Huh? Yes. I was . . . just wondering why you went into such detail on how the victims died."

"Had to fill the page *somehow*, didn't I? Actually, I figured the descriptions might give some clues as regards Basilia's predilection for certain targets."

SHELLEEN unwilling to take week's leave because of film's shooting schedule, and has been at work ever since. His co-producer is presently seeking financing for new film and reports that SHELLEEN has been scouting locations in Africa since mid-February of this year. Exact whereabouts unknown. Languages: not known; believed fluent in Italian. Weapons proficiency: excellent combat record; has come into contact with most U.S. military firearms; known to favor the 7.62mm M21. Assets: $562,000 in U.S. bank accounts ($1,200,000 withdrawn in February, but not unusual as he assumedly would be investing larger part of it in his new motion picture project); stocks of undetermined value; homes in Tarzana, London, on Fiji and Isle of Barra. Br. govt. will not release info on SHELLEEN's financial position in Britain without consent.

"A cool fellow, this Shelleen," Green commented.

"His father has a heart-attack and T.G. orders him to London rather than going to see the poor old fellow. Then his daughter is murdered and he goes about his business as though nothing happened."

"We don't know what he felt, Nat. That's why he is on the list. But what do you think of Usil?"

USIL, JEAN-CLAUDE: Born 1935; Capbreton, France. Brown hair, grey-blue eyes, 6'1", 175 lbs. Athletic scholarship to Univ. of Bordeaux; never graduated. Took over father's ailing vineyards in 1957, built local winery into thriving concern. By 1960 USIL was a franc millionaire. Married Matilde Mondeville, 1963. Children: Alexis, born 1965; Colette, born 1968; Jasmine, born 1970. Avid hunter and connossieur of Impressionist art, USIL lived a care-free life and amassed a sizeable fortune. Then in 1969 Alexis died of rheumatic fever and Colette blinded in an accident. Rapid expansion overtaxed USIL's resources and his small empire began to contract. In 1971 he attempted suicide. After recovering in a sanatorium outside Toulouse, he returned home to discover Colette dead. By 1975 his fortunes were much improved, USIL having apparently learned lesson about capital investments. Last year, in January, Mme. Usil drove to airport two miles southeast of Biarritz to pick up friends arriving from Paris. Two wealthy Palestinians, who had been gambling at one of the casinos on Boulevard Mal. Leclerc and losing heavily, tried to board a plane while carrying handguns. When security police sought to capture them they ran from the terminal building and spotted Mme. Usil parking her car. They ordered her to help them escape. Instead, she locked them out and attempted to drive away. Both men fired through windshield, hitting her eight times in head and chest. Ensuing gun battle with airport police resulted in deaths of both Palestinians. Mme. Usil's car caught a bullet in fuel-line and burned. The following March a letter-bomb addressed to Syrian ambassador in Paris was traced back to USIL. He refused to admit guilt, his attorney brought forward the record of his stay at Toulouse sanatorium, judge ordered a psychiatric evaluation. USIL committed to hospital care in Toulouse as a result until such time doctors felt he had been satisfactorily treated. His recovery appeared rapid. He was allowed two-day trial visits to friends and surviving daughter Jasmine. After one visit in October USIL failed to return to hospital. Police were alerted. Discovered he had visited his deserted home near Labenne; missing were hunting guns—imprudently left there after his arrest—and whatever had been contained in a metal box pried from beneath floorboards in the chicken-coop. Police suspect he crossed Pyrenees on foot. Last March they learned during a routine reappraisal of the case, that a JEAN-CLAUDE USIL was aboard an Iberia flight from Madrid to Munich in late February. German authorities informed—without results. Present whereabouts unknown. Languages: Provencal, Spanish. Weapons proficiency: hunting partners concur that USIL is an excellent shot, but his only known experience is with small-caliber hunting rifles and shotguns. Assets: home and farm near Labenne; vineyards near Capbreton; 413,600 francs in bank accounts; resort home at Evian; art works appraised at 160,000 francs; municipal stocks.

"What about the girl—Jasmine?"

"Remember those people Usil's wife was supposed to meet at Biarritz? They felt responsible. Since there was no one else . . ."

"And you still think Basilia is either Andersson or Murphy?"

"You've already thought this one out, Nat. Why ask me?"

"Maybe I need confirmation."

"Right." Talmai pulled the creases out of his tiny vest and stared at the fluorescent-lights. "Dalton steals his brother's passport *before* the guy is killed, which means that he wanted the bank's money for some other purpose than revenging. He didn't give a damn about his brother.

"Shelleen obviously loved his little girl, but I doubt if he has the intelligence to handle an operation of this magnitude. He seems to have a one-track mind, ambition before all else. He'd try to bury his suffering under a ton of work—which appears to be exactly what he has done, going off to do his crying in the jungle now. Basilia, in contrast, may be a smooth operator, but every action he has taken shows the scorch-marks of hot passion.

"As for Usil, the paramount reason for his being on the list is, simply, his unknown address."

"He lost his wife," Green said coldly.

"Yes, true, she was killed by Arabs and Usil built up a hatred against all Arabs on that foundation. Yet he is unstable, too apt to trip himself. Remember that the police traced the letter-bomb directly to him. Basilia would never be so clumsy."

"What did he do—print his address on the back?"

"Almost as bad. He registered the letter to make certain it reached the ambassador's hands before being opened. It did, but the detonator cap failed."

"You're right. Either Usil is a true imbecile or a peerless actor who has managed to deceive not only the staff at the Toulouse sanatorium, but us as well."

"And I don't think our hero would point a finger at himself quite so obviously. You heard what old Splenion said when—"

"Crap." The two men smiled at each other.

"Okay, Lenny, summary time. Let's look at this chronologically. Last year: January, Usil's wife is killed. April, Murphy's wife dies when an altitude-bomb goes off. Being exactly a year before the Luqa rescue, that may be significant or beginner's luck. In June, Andersson's wife and daughter pick the wrong restaurant. Two months later Andersson vanishes. Dalton's brother gets in the way of a bullet in September. Then in October, Usil disappears. That December, Shelleen's daughter is killed."

"In time for Christmas," Talmai said solemnly. "The plane was hijacked on the Twenty-first of December, in Algeria the next day, flown to Libya on the day following, and set afire on Christmas Eve. What a year!"

"Yeah, what a year. This one seems to have been made from the same mold. And you know, of course, who everyone is going to blame: Israel. Because Basilia suddenly showed the terrorists that two can play at their little game, the shitheads are crying foul and everybody's agreeing. And we—*we*, goddammit!—are supposed to finger Basilia. It's crazy!"

He hadn't meant to blow up. Maybe it was the pressure of the last two weeks, the boredom, inactivity, the restless longing for fresh air.

"That's politics, Nat. The rules are crooked because no nation is selfless. Each has a different perspective on morality, changing according to personal expediency. Israel has to save what it can from the wreckage. Our friends are few, so we condescend to their wishes or stand alone."

"What's so wrong with that?"

"Israel would rather lose a finger than its life. The choice is clear. Basilia is an enemy of our enemies, but he is not a friend. We have to live with that paradox," Talmai sighed.

"The choice?"

"Put up an appearance of seeking our enemies' enemy and keep our friends—or forget Basilia and lose our friends by letting them think we use executioners."

"Executioners. That must have the Russians rolling in the aisles."

Talmai, seeing Green's expression, steered the conversation back to their five suspects. "You were giving a chronological summary, Nat. What about this year?"

"In February, Shelleen disappears. The next month Dalton cuts out with Lloyd's money and Murphy vaporizes. Late winter seems to have been a favorite time for putting all your troubles in your old kit-bag. Destinations?"

"Shelleen flew to Kinshasa, hired some guides, and went out among the cannibals. No word on whether he made the menu. Dalton apparently flew to Venice. The top-heavy Italian bureaucracy makes it impossible to know whether he flew out again or is living next door to the police commissioner."

"Wait until the Communists come to power, Lenny. Then we'll really see bureaucracy at work."

"Don't laugh. They put a tag on Basilia soon enough." He paused. "As for Murphy, his last stop seems to have been Limburg, Germany."

"The others?"

"Andersson apparently lost at sea off the Belgian coast."

"But he had intentions of flying to Frankfurt."

"Possibly a ploy. Possibly not. Usil reportedly flew from Madrid to Munich in late . . . February . . . *My God!*"

The idea penetrated Green's insouciance too. He grabbed the inter-office phone, dialed, and ordered large-scale maps of West Germany and northern Italy. He could hardly suppress his excitement.

When the maps arrived, he spread them across the desk so they faced Talmai, then he pulled up a chair beside the intelligence coordinator.

"Let's take them one at a time, Lenny."

"Andersson. Bought air-ticket for Frankfurt via Brussels last August. Arrived in Brussels. No-show for Frankfurt."

"Maybe he came early to organize. Didn't want a trail."

"Shelleen. Left for Africa in mid-February. No report since. But we can't track him everyplace, so he might have made it back. And Usil. Flew to Munich in late February."

"An easy 239 miles between Munich and Frankfurt on the autobahns."

"Dalton. Flew to Venice in early March."

"Could have caught the E6 straight into Munich . . . 295 miles. Possibly continued to Frankfurt with Usil."

"Murphy. On the Continent for research purposes. Last reported location—Limburg, Germany."

"Which is approximately 35 miles northwest of Frankfurt on the E5. So we have two suspects positively in Germany, one earlier intention, another easy possibility, and a question mark. At least four—possibly five men converging on Frankfurt for a March summit."

"Less than a month before the Luqa incident."

"Yeah." Green dry-washed his face with a shaking hand. "And all of them with one thing in common: they lost close relatives to Palestinian killers."

"Do you think it will stand up?"

"Stand up? Charon will shit his pants when he hears this!"

"There are still—"

"We thought we were after one man," Green laughed, dialing Charon's number. "But there are *five! Five*, Lenny! Maybe more!"

"He won't believe you, Nat." Talmai's little tinny voice was a mere whisper among the hissings of the fluorescent-lights, the distant rumble of the air-conditioning unit on the floor above. "You know that, don't you?"

CHAPTER FOURTEEN

Cynthia Pryor, twenty years old and a student at Exeter University, looked across the empty seat to the man crumpled against the window. He had a handsome profile; Cynthia was observant in such matters for she had just spent three lousy weeks in Paris without getting laid, so that now every male she saw was a masked Adonis.

A pretty girl, Cynthia would have had no trouble in finding a "nice boy" (her mother's phrase—distasteful and quite meaningless these days) if it were not for her rabid female chauvinism. She enjoyed putting men down intellectually even as they bedded her; though her amours rarely progressed that far before the male, his ego flattened and bleeding curses, made a hasty exit.

Believing this fault a virtue, Cynthia explained her attitude as "modern woman's idiosyncratic need for primeval beast-man," and laughed condescendingly when her friends asked whether that meant she condoned bestiality. They were fools. Most of them couldn't *read* properly, and their articulation was absolutely *appalling!*

The traveler across from her was immersed in a yellow paperback entitled *Teach Yourself Hebrew*. She could see several Teach Yourself books sticking out from his travel bag under the seat in front, and casually wondered whether he was some kind of language freak. She'd never been out with a language freak.

I wonder how a language freak makes love, she thought. With twelve different tongues? She contained her giggles and reached into her purse for a cigarette.

Should she ask him for a light? That was the usual way of initiating a conversation. Have a match? Nice flight, huh? You live in London? Alone? You *too?* Want to come up and listen to my records?

On second thought, it might be better to try the second approach—see what the guy's made of. Ask him a few dumb questions to see if he's on the ball. If he passes, go on to the hard stuff. Not much chance he can stand up to a 168 I.Q. Of *course* that'll turn him off. So what? There's that cute prick across the aisle and two rows up— probably an American. A sure dumbo, but good for a quickie if you can ever get him to your flat in Kensington.

Cynthia felt her crotch dampen unexpectedly.

"Excuse me."

The face that turned toward her was not handsome at all, she discovered. The realization startled—for she prided herself with having a discerning eye—and disappointed her; a man who paged through a language text as though it were a comic magazine might have proved a challenge to her genius. But that *face!*

Beneath a shaggy mop of brown hair, the face was divided into two distinct halves. The right side held a faint smile, the corner of the mouth lifting into a series of tiny dimples like water ripples; the left side frowning, mouth tilted downward, the dark grey eye dominating, flecks of blue in the iris like bits of sky seen through a thundercloud.

"Yes?" The voice was deceptively soft, as though the man were consciously controlling a deep baritone.

"Have a light?"

"I don't smoke." He turned back to his book.

Peeved, Cynthia asked, "Why didn't you get a seat in the No Smoking section?"

The Hyde-and-Jekyll face again pivoted in her direction, cold eyes focusing on her mouth with the intensity of a lip-reader. "I enjoy sitting at the rear."

Not "I like" or "I'd rather be," but "I *enjoy*." What a strange man, she thought. And that accent. Hard to place. A mixture—as if he had lived nowhere very long and everywhere at least long enough.

"Have you been to London before?"

"Why?"

She shrugged. "Just curious. June's a bad month for London. Tourists start taking over. Have a reservation?"

For once, both sides of his face smiled simultaneously. "I have a place, thank you, miss."

"Cyn. Friends call me Cyn. Because I'm such a bad girl," she giggled, taking a box of matches from her purse before she realized her *faux pas*.

"Found a light, I see," he noted blandly, resuming his reading.

Cynthia was mystified. The man's disinterest in her proved intriguing and a stimulus for continued battle. She was determined to get a rise out of him by the time they crossed the Channel—even if it meant whispering dirty words in his ear.

She lit her cigarette and said, "I hate being forward, but my name's Cynthia Hunter. What's yours?"

He didn't even look at her this time, but kept his long nose buried in the primer. "I take it the P is silent then."

"What?"

"The embossed initials on your cosmetic case: C.P."

"The man made a mistake when he put them on," she said lamely.

"Yes, of course."

"He did! Don't patronize *me!*" Cynthia felt blood suffusing her cheeks. She had never been much good at lying; yet she despised this man for making her lies seem so horribly transparent, for graciously bowing to her conceit while he laughed behind his hand.

"You *hear* me?"

"I profoundly apologize for not making myself perfectly clear, Miss Hunter."

"*Miz* Hunter."

The man made no further statements, so Cynthia decided to turn her charm on the kid sitting two rows ahead.

Her failure to arouse his interest as much as he inspired hers continued to nag Cynthia. Admittedly, her approach had been rather tough, designed more to bludgeon the man into conversation by aiming for that god-almighty male ego than to lure by subtle enticements; yet he showed no damage from her efforts. And that apology of his. All he said was "Yes, of course." Why apologize? Why say he hadn't made himself perfectly clear? Unless he was putting her on.

That resolved the matter. She would make certain where the fellow was staying then accidentally bump into him sometime. He couldn't get away this easily!

Being a British citizen, Cynthia Pryor passed through Heathrow's Customs and Immigration quickly and waited in the Arrivals lounge for the tall man to appear. Now she at least knew he wasn't a member of the Commonwealth or an EEC country, for she had seen him join the queue marked ALL OTHERS.

When he came through the sliding doors, tall but curiously stooped, she was surprised to note that his only luggage was the blue handgrip he had carried on the plane, stuffed with paperbacks. Apparently he was either already situated in Britain or had come over for a short visit.

He went directly to a newstand and bought a copy of the *Times*, scanned the front page, then headed for the Underground entrance, using the moving ramps and not once looking behind him. If he had, he would have seen Cynthia, cosmetic case and bulging travel bag, vainly trying to look inconspicuous.

And between them a stocky figure, copiously endowed with body odor, who made every effort to seem at home in this modernistic environment but appeared falsely nonchalant instead.

Cynthia, naturally intent of keeping her fellow passenger in sight, was quick to notice the stocky man paying altogether too much attention to *her* quarry. He rudely pushed through streams of travelers in order to reach the man before he gave his destination at the ticket office, then disregarded the queue by breaking in and ordering his own ticket.

She purchased her tube ticket and hurried after the two men.

At the platform entrance the stocky man was greeted

by a couple of bored young Arabs, clearly identified by their dark features, bushy black hair, and carefully clipped mustaches so perfect and identical that they looked store-bought. Both men wore expensive grey suits, and one had a red carnation pinned to the lapel.

The short, stocky man handed over the briefcase he had been carrying, then motioned that the Arabs should follow him. His head remained fixed in the direction of the tall man who was still moving along the platform, oblivious to the multiple pursuit and evidently uninterested in the six-carriage train sitting on the tracks, its doors ready to close at any moment.

Cynthia decided not to take the gamble, and she boarded the nearest car, standing at the door and staring down the platform.

The thick-set man and his two companions were in a quandary. The Arabs wanted to get on the train—but their leader refused, waiting for the tall man to make the first move.

Speaking to members of the Metropolitan Police two hours later, Cynthia vividly recalled the next moment.

Four things happened almost simultaneously: a green signal light blinked at the head of the train; the tall man leaped into the second car; his three male pursuers, walking Indian-file, sprang for the nearest doorway; and the train-doors slammed shut with a pneumatic hiss.

One of the Arabs did not make fit. His hand caught between the doors, he jerked it free and stumbled backward. The doors retracted for a split-second then closed again before he could assay a second jump.

Perhaps afraid that they too would be left behind or their prey would spot them, the remaining trackers made no attempt to move nearer the tall man's car—though

Cynthia did notice that at each stop they took pains to watch for his possible debarkation, the frizzy black top of the Arab weaving sinuously as passengers tried to get by him, the squat man's head rooted at the door as though it were a permanent fixture of the train: a round warning paddle that extruded every time the doors slid open.

The tall man did not show himself until the train reached Green Park Station, at which time he calmly stepped off. A large number of travelers were getting off with him and so he was momentarily lost among them.

The stocky man and the young Arab had seen him and also stepped off, as did Cynthia—who was already phrasing the story in her mind, wondering how best to astound her friends with tales of her daring exploit.

Suddenly the doors were closing and the tall man was out of the crowd, hurling himself on the train.

The Arab shouted wildly and beat on the door of the car he'd just left. His companion stood motionless, his thick arms frozen at his sides, watching the underground train pull out.

Cynthia wanted to cry. It couldn't end this way. Not before she knew what it was all about. Not before she had a chance to tell the tall man he was being followed.

But he knew that. Somehow he must have sensed it.

The platform was almost deserted when she walked up to the squat man and boldly asked—surprising even herself—"Why were you after him?"

He has a good-looking face under that mean expression, she thought. Just like old Dad. And he'll probably tell me to mind my own business, miss, and I'll say "Miz" and walk away and leave him with egg all over his stupid copper's face.

But he merely stared at her vacuously.

The Arab came up, his glance flicking back and forth between his partner and Cynthia, sizing up the situation. He said something in Arabic to his companion, who shrugged.

Turning to Cynthia, he asked—in thick-accented English—"What do you want, lady?"

"I want to know why you were following that man."

His eyes narrowed, giving him—with the addition of a sprouting goatee beneath his mustache—a saturnine appearance. "What man?"

"The man whom you were after."

"You must be mistaken, lady."

Cynthia was growing impatient. Her luggage felt like a ball of lead stretching her arms out of shape, she was hungry, she could smell the acrid musk of her period, and this camel-jockey was being deliberately obstructive.

"The man who sat near me on the plane, who you followed from Heathrow, who just made an ass of you and Harpo Marx over there."

The key word must have been " Marx," for at the sound of it the Arab's companion began jabbering violently, spitting out the syllables in an oral frenzy.

The Arab tried to console him, then again faced the girl. "Do you know the man we . . . followed?"

That's better. "Why?"

He looked down the platform. Ten people were awaiting the next train, more arriving. No one else had reached this end, however.

"Tell me now, lady."

"Miz."

His right arm casually dropped over her shoulder and he moved her toward the wall.

"Don't touch me, you dirty shit, or I'll scream!"

243

The stout man had moved to her other side, screening her from the transients on the platform, as the Arab's left hand seized her throat, cutting off her air.

She dropped her luggage and tried to wrestle free, but he was strong and his grip continued to tighten until her body relaxed, her face a bright red matching her hair.

"Where does he live?" he asked, loosening his hold.

"I—don't know. . . . I swear it," she gasped, all resistance frightened out of her, leaving only stark terror.

"Why did you follow him?"

"Saw . . . on the plane. . . . I was curious."

"Do you know his name?"

"He . . . never told me."

The stocky man asked the Arab something, was answered curtly. He suddenly seemed to lose interest in the girl.

"If you talk to the police, we will kill you," the Arab said. "Do you understand?"

Cynthia nodded vigorously. Then the Arab cocked his elbow across his body and slammed it into her breast, still holding onto her throat and stifling the agonized scream.

His companion shook his head and, lifting the girl's slumping figure in his arms, brought her to an unoccupied bench nearby, propping her back against the curving wall and leaving.

After recovering, Cynthia took an escalator to the surface. She felt groggy—and angry. A distasteful sense of violation filled her, made her feel impure. She wanted revenge against the men who had treated her like they would another man. Being threatened and beaten like "one of the boys" was not her idea of sexual equality.

Cynthia found a police constable making his rounds on

Albemarle Street and told him her story. Knowing there was now little chance of apprehending the two men readily, but considering her story of sufficient importance to warrant a fuller investigation, he led her to the police station on Boyle Street where she was questioned by detectives.

Convinced she had no ulterior motive in seeking out the man who had been followed, they contacted New Scotland Yard. Within half an hour another detective was coaxing her through her narrative. Then she was released and told she would be needed later to help identify her attackers.

Getting the tall man's name was relatively easy. The police merely contacted the Heathrow headquarters of British Airways, gave the girl's seat number, and asked who had sat in the window seat two spaces over. With the name, they were able to locate the immigration card which the man surrendered when going through Passport Control.

Cynthia Pryor's story indicated the short man may well have come off the same flight. If he had been waiting at Heathrow for the tall man to appear he would not need a bulky briefcase, nor would his organization be so deplorable: it would be unnecessary for him to point out the quarry to his cohorts or buy a tube ticket for himself, and he'd probably be acquainted with the boarding and departure procedures of underground trains.

And he was a European-looking foreigner who apparently spoke little or no English but who was fluent in what the girl thought to be Arabic. All of which made him a very interesting character indeed.

The complete passenger list and seating arrangement for Cynthia's flight was ordered from British Airways and brought to New Scotland Yard. Three stewardesses who had operated on the flight were contacted and requested to visit the Yard, where they were given a description of the short man. None of them knew his name, but two remembered having served him. He seemed nervous about flying (so they thought at the time) and gestured that he wanted water. He evidently carried his own supply of dramamine, for he popped pills all the way from Paris to London. Both stewardesses recalled his seating position in the aircraft and he was soon identified.

Further inquiries were directed to the Home Office's Immigration Department in Croydon and the Aliens Registration Office on Lamb's Conduit Street, as well as to the CID's Identification Bureau with its massive computer banks on all known and suspected criminals in the U.K. and Eire.

By six o'clock that night Scotland Yard was ready to act. The tall man had given an address which turned out to be a science-fiction bookshop in Soho. No one there had ever heard of him. The stout man gave an address on Sussex Place in Paddington, a bed-and-breakfast establishment with dormitory-style quarters: rows of bunk beds set in strict formation and carefully administered by a gentle old Irish woman, Fanny MacDougall.

Miss MacDougall invited the two plain-clothes policemen to her basement flat, brewed some tea for them, then finally said, yes, she did have a Hungarian staying in the hostel's only single room. He had signed in that afternoon, giving his passport number willingly when she explained she had to take precautions in case something was stolen.

"Is he in now, Miss MacDougall?"

"No, no, he's a strange one. Paid up a week in advance

then said he might be gone for a few days. Seems a nice enough man. Doesn't understand much English, though. Had to have one of his friends translate it into Hungarian."

"Friends?"

"Yes, four very tidy Arabs. Very clean. One of them reserved the room for the gentleman this morning. Said he was his professor or something of the sort. The Arabs have been here for a couple of weeks, I think. Always so polite, never cause any trouble."

"These four—are they in?"

"Well, I don't know. They may be. They rarely go out except on Sundays. They said they start school next week—studying English, if I remember."

"Where do they go on Sundays?"

"Speakers' Corner, I think. They like to listen to those silly speeches. Some of their friends or kin blabber about this and that on their boxes, I suppose. These young people have such strange ideas," Miss MacDougall sighed.

"Do you mind if we take a look at their rooms, Miss MacDougall?"

"Well, I guess it would be all right—if I'm there. Have they done something wrong?" She rose to her feet wearily and searched for her keys in a cigar box atop her vanity dresser. "The other policeman wouldn't say."

The two detectives looked at each other, puzzled.

"What policeman was that? A PC?"

"No, he didn't wear a uniform. Why, bless me, I don't think he ever gave his name! Tall gentleman, he was."

The Special Branch—given the case because of its expertise in dealing with foreign malefactors operating in

Britain (and because the Commissioner of Police wrongly believed it to be less overworked than its brother services)—reached some conclusions by ten that night.

The four Palestinians had obviously been assigned back-up roles for the Hungarian: two at the underground platform, perhaps one with a car parked near the terminal entrance, another assigned to the little-used bus ramp.

The wily American wisely chose the underground route, knowing he would have the advantage and protection of surrounding crowds. And then he proceeded to lose himself. He'd probably gotten off at Piccadilly Circus, rushing back to Green Park Station in time to catch the Hungarian and his friend as they came out, and following them to their Sussex Place address.

Which said several rather interesting things about the American: He could spot a tail and shrug it off effortlessly; he knew human nature well enough to realize his trackers would momentarily be immobilized by surprise and the shock of failure; and he was familiar enough with London to know that only a third of a mile separated the two underground stations and which street he must take to get from one to the other. This coincided with information from the Aliens Registration Office which revealed that he was granted a twelve-month visa the previous November to do research work in Britain, and had been in and out of the country several times since then, leaving once for the States and twice for the Continent.

Checking his original application for an extended visa permit, the police found his second British address. It was in Gloucestershire. Two CID men drove out to the tiny village near Stow-on-the-Wold, located the cottage with some difficulty, and spoke with the lady of the

248

ouse—a governess looking after the American's young daughter. She had not seen the father since the middle of March when, having given her a generous allotment from which to draw her salary and pay bills, he left for Paris. The little girl had received several postcards from him since then, postmarked from different European counries. Was it necessary to go through all this a second time?

As before, the detectives discovered they were not the first to approach this particular angle of the case. Investigators from the Foreign Office had already been here. Why?

By midnight the Foreign Secretary had stuck his nose in the matter. Blunt inquiries from Scotland Yard were raising hell at the Ministry, no one wanted the responsibility of furnishing answers, and so the Foreign Secretary found himself rudely jerked from a meeting of the Explorers' Club by no less a personage than the Prime Minister who—for reasons he was unwilling to divulge—had been drawn into the affair.

The Foreign Secretary, apprised of the ongoing police investigations, pointedly demanded to know if the American in question had committed any crime under British law.

Yes—giving a false address on his immigration card.

"Look, geordie lad," he said, for he and the Commissioner of Police were old RAF buddies who had flown Spitfires in the same squadron, "I have it that that bookstore has been shaped out of an old tenement flat, and not so long ago. Besides, it may have been an unconscious mistake on the part of our American visitor. He *did* give his correct address to the Home Office. You can't charge him with *that*. So what else do you hold against him?"

"Well . . . nothing. But what are we supposed to do then?"

"You apprehended the Arab who assaulted the girl, what else do you want? Your major effort was directed at that, am I right? Forget the American."

"You're holding out on me."

"Of course I am. He's ours."

"He works—?"

"Don't be silly, old boy. We simply want to locate him. All hush-hush."

"For extradition? Then it's our—"

"Listen, lad, when we need your help we ask. And vice versa. If you find him, fine, stay away from him, contact the Ministry."

"Why the mystery?"

"The Israelis have sent out flyers on him, the Americans are looking for him, and I have a horrible suspicion the Arabs want him more than anyone. Losing our aspect of neutrality at this point—regardless of North Sea oil—could well prove economically disastrous for Britain. But . . ."

"You intend wiring Arab capitals and asking if he is wanted in those countries."

The Foreign Minister paused before admitting, "You are a very clever fellow tonight, old friend. But don't take this too far."

Green was in no mood to carry on a lengthy conversation. Several times he had been on the point of leaving Charon's office and forgetting his troubles with another bottle of bourbon; but Charon's voice droned on, always manipulating his curiosity.

"What do I care what Mossad's contacts have discovered? I quit this job a week ago. I'm through. *Through!*" Yet Green cared very much to know what Charon was dangling in front of him; he was too dedicated to ever quit the Squad. And he still waited for an apology.

"Nathan, I understand how you feel. I was impressed by your efforts but your conclusions were . . . far-fetched as regards the Luqa Project. I simply could not ask the combined services to mount an investigation that was bound to blow up in our faces. Besides, the German government was extremely forthcoming, checking our details and offering denial or confirmation. With a photograph of Jean-Claude Usil furnished by French Intelligence, the Germans located him."

"What? Where? What did he say? When did you find out?"

"Two nights ago."

"Why didn't you tell me?"

"You quit, remember?"

"But you're telling me now."

"We've entered the end-game." Charon paused, heightening the suspense. "Usil was registered as an anonymous in a Düsseldorf hospital. He had been picked up as a vagrant. When the police put him in a cell for the night he went berserk and was removed to the mental ward of a hospital on Ulmen Strasse. He had no identification and refused to speak, so there was no one to notify. Not until the government circulated his picture and a Düsseldorf policeman recognized Usil as the man he sent to the hospital did anyone discover his identity. By that time Usil's manic-depressive condition had degenerated into clear-cut paranoia. He cannot or will not speak. I'm afraid he's quite insane, Nathan, and could not offer us any answers even if he had them—which I doubt. He has been confined at the hospital since early March."

"I see."

"Even if we are on the right track, that discounts one suspect."

"Fine. What does all this have to do with me? I've retired. Maybe I'm a security risk."

"I wouldn't have any reason for telling you this unless I had a job for you." Charon leaned back, folding his hands behind his head. "Early this morning one of Modiin's mobile electronic surveillance units in the Golan intercepted a radio transmission originating in northern Lebanon. It seems the British have located our Professor Murphy and want to know if the Arabs are looking for him for any particular reason."

Green slammed his fist against the arm of his chair. "How in hell did they get that idea? *We* are the ones who requested further information on him!"

"They can put two and two together as well as anyone, Nathan. I don't know the whole story, but it seems Murphy was traveling under his real name and someone was already on his tail, someone who made a few bad mistakes and drew the attention of the London police—which, in turn, brought Murphy into the picture. The Foreign Office got wind of it, knew we wanted Murphy, and decided Britain's interests lie more with the Arabs than with us. That's nothing new."

"Who was following him?"

"Our Jewish friends in the CID were very helpful when they discovered the extent of their government's duplicity. Murphy was being tracked by two Palestinians who picked him up at Heathrow Airport."

"How did they recognize him?"

"He was fingered by the man who followed him over from Paris—our abiding nemesis traveling on a Hungarian passport, Yevgeny Sholokov. Sholokov and his buddies managed to lose Murphy, beat up a girl, and get themselves followed by Murphy all in the space of one day. The Palestinians were picked up in London last night. They were questioned, but I don't have the results yet. Sholokov is loose. So is Murphy."

"You know what this means, don't you, Chief?" Green's eyes were both worried and cautiously excited.

"It means you have to get to London today. It also means . . ." Charon did not want to speak the words. "It also means we undoubtedly have a leak in our research team, someone who passed on the names of our suspects to the Russians. Otherwise, how would they know to look for a James Merton Murphy? If Murphy *is* Basilia he's much too damn clever to ever allow even the rumor of a connection between the two names. Plugging that leak is my worry, though. Yours is flying to London and finding Murphy."

"Why? What's the purpose now? The Arabs get him, we can stop worrying about his effect on Middle East tensions."

"Your sarcasm is well placed, Nathan. We should wash our hands of the affair. But Murphy may be innocent."

"Let British law protect him."

"You must be joking. With Sholokov after him? Sholokov doesn't give a damn about British law, innocence or guilt. His brief is probably a check-list of five names. Only when he has crossed them all out will his superiors be satisfied he got the right man. Obvious[ly] we cannot be expected to act as international bodyguard[s] for these men. But the thinking among the General Sta[ff] of our Intelligence is that we may be able to both clea[r] ourselves and embarrass the Russian-Arab coalition if w[e] can gather evidence that they are operating assassinatio[n] teams in Western Europe. Some of us are especiall[y] anxious to implicate Britain by showing that she aided— if not abetted—these killers by providing them wit[h] crucial information regarding their target. We older fol[k] remember only too well Mr. Ernest Bevin and how h[e] tried to foil the creation of a Jewish state."

"What is expected of me?" Green had accepted the ca[ll] of duty, forgetting the angry speeches he made to himsel[f] in the mirror that morning.

"You will board an El Al flight waiting for you now a[t] Ben-Gurion. At Heathrow you will be met by a contac[t] and given all information from our lines into the Britis[h] police services and diplomatic agencies. The rest mus[t] come from your own evaluation of the material. And fo[r] godsake, Nathan, if you go in the field I want you to sta[y] low. We can do without heroics. Should you come acros[s] Sholokov, only get rid of him if you can see your wa[y] out."

"And Murphy?"

Charon paused, then touched the model bomb on hi[s] desk so that it swung gently upon its suspending wires[.] "Do you know what satyagrapha means?"

"No."

"Reliance on truth. It was used to describe Gandhi'[s] policy of non-violent revolution, passive resistance t[o] the oppressor. I want you to use a little satyagrapha o[n] James Murphy if events should prove that he is Basilia[

Talk to him, warn him of the dangers closing in on him, tell him everything you know and everything his enemies probably know about him. Worry him. Make him feel alone and deserted and unloved and hopelessly outnumbered by sadistic bastards."

"Pardon my saying so, sir, but I'm sure he is aware of that. He hasn't come this far by relying on the Chinese Army. I doubt if I *could* worry him, especially if he feels confident enough to use his real name."

"Which wouldn't mean a thing if he *wasn't* Basilia. Anyway, I'll expect to hear from you from time to time. Send it by diplomatic courier if it's not of immediate importance." He frowned, wagging his finger. "And try not to leave a trail of bodies, Nathan."

CHAPTER FIFTEEN

Heinrich Almbach slowly dipped his spoon into the steaming bowl of *lungenstrudelsuppe,* sipped, and looked again at the dark River Inn swiftly flowing opposite the small restaurant on Hertzog Otto Strasse. When he finished with the thick soup, a plate of *palatschinken* was set before him, each golden pancake filled with strawberry jam and bathed in butter.

It was his favorite dish, but he ate it without interest, his eggshell blue eyes focused on the rippling surface of the river with an intensity that worried his waitress. She liked him—not only because he was a regular customer who tipped generously and minded his manners, but because of an ineffable sadness that permeated his quiet nature, awakening her maternal instincts. He seemed to need friendship—love—which, for a man with his good features and refinement, should have been easy to come by. She would gladly have provided it had he shown any willingness to accept her.

But he never did. The wedding band of white gold on his left hand evidently meant too much to him, held too many memories. Poor man. A widower, surely. Poor Herr Almbach. So kind-hearted, so dedicated to his work on the new ski resort area between Innsbruck and Axams.

Almbach was thinking about the girl who broke her leg on the ski-jump today, about her stupid mother who was convinced she had spawned a skiing champion and wanted everyone to know it. And of course there was only one way to affect that: push the girl into a stunt she was not capable of performing even in her best moments.

The result had been disastrous. She barely reached the bottom lip of the incline before her nerves and body collapsed, sending her rolling over the edge in a flurry of poles and skis and screams. There was not enough loose snow at the bottom to fully cushion her fall, and she had no experience in landing—so she broke a femur and perhaps lost confidence in herself for the rest of her life. All because Mama wanted to brag at her martini parties, wanted some trophies to put beneath her Matisse in the drawing room, wanted her children to prove something about their genetic inheritance.

How to train a coward in one easy lesson! Herr Almbach thought bitterly, realizing that the basis for his anger came from resurrected memories of Ursula and Anna—how his wife would never have endangered their daughter in any way . . . let alone deliberately and for the sake of self-aggrandizing pride!

But Ursula and Anna were characters from another world, another dimension where he had been known as Halvek Andersson. Years ago. How many? Even two? Even so many as two?

Thor must be wondering what happened to his father, why he suddenly deserted him only to drown in the

English Channel. It must have been hard for the boy, his entire family leaving him. He could never be expected to understand.

Understand what? Almbach liked to ask himself, finding relief in these rhetorical arguments spinning out of his guilt. Understand that Halvek Andersson died every time he looked at the youth, seeing his mother's eyes, the same chubby pink cheeks of his sister that had been studded with glass fragments and nails when the shrapnel bomb exploded? And always the same answer: Understand I cannot live with the constant reminder of that tragedy; that I must go, forget myself, my past, where I came from and where I am going.

Andersson had thought of suicide, but never found the nerve for it; nor did he wish to leave a stigma on the family name—though Thor may have understood his father's suicide more easily than his desertion and death at sea.

Of course, Andersson really hadn't planned it that way. The lure of a high-salaried job in Frankfurt was the initial impetus because he knew he must leave an inheritance for Thor and therefore needed a good job awaiting him. But en route he changed his mind, saw the dangers of remaining alive to his son. So he arranged his "death," then made a slow progression toward Austria. He knew and loved the country, spoke the language, and decided it was as good a place as any to bury himself.

And now it was Heinrich Almbach who remembered his past—and hated himself for it.

Something else was happening, something he could find no explanation for: the search had been renewed. Ursula's brother, the one person Andersson had confided in and who had assumed guardianship of Thor, phoned him last night and said the police were again asking questions not only about his disappearance but about his schooling, his fluency in foreign languages, and the value of his estate.

Why would they be interested in those things? What the hell were they thinking?

The man knew he had been tricked.

He thought about who might have double-crossed him. The possibilities were limited. Only one person knew his real identity, and he considered his trust well placed in him; but the others, however ignorant, still could damage his plans by revealing what little they did know.

Paul Justine, for example, knew him as Samuel Erinys, alias Hans Derna; knew he was responsible for the killings at Alabet. But that was all. Enjoying himself in Greece with his bonus for a job well done, Justine had no reason to admit he was an accomplice to murder. He had no chance of collecting the Libyan reward money by opening his mouth; though he might collect an Arab bullet.

The same rules applied to the Habersteins. Since they were safe as long as they remained silent, they would simply settle back into their Paris apartment and forget the matter. If they were smart enough to somehow connect him to Alabet, that fact would frighten them enough to insure their reticence.

Pierre Le Beau and his counterfeiter were different. He hadn't trusted either one, and so had established contact with a German forger in Hamburg at the very beginning. Le Beau could lead police only as long as the man used passports the Corporation's forger had prepared; hence, his effect was now nil: the man had destroyed all the passports he purchased through Le Beau, flushing the ashes for good measure.

He thus remained perplexed as to how the Hungarian Mikhail Arpotin managed to follow him to Britain. He remembered seeing him at the Gare du Nord, but was certain he hadn't been spotted himself. The only way Arpotin could have tracked him was if the French and German forgers collaborated in a double-cross. Fortunately, the chance of that happening was infinitesimal. The German thought of Frenchmen as a peculiar, reptilian sub-species.

And yet Arpotin still lurked in every shadow. The tall man should have known better than to follow him to his London quarters, wait for him to leave, then pretend he was a policeman and ask the landlady about her squat boarder. For when the man departed, it was Arpotin who followed *him*.

The tall man really didn't care who Arpotin was or what organization he belonged to. The Hungarian had allied himself with the Palestinians. That was enough to make him a deadly enemy.

When the taxi pulled up in front of Euston Station, the man jumped out with his small American Tourister suitcase in hand and dropped a £5-note into the cabbie's lap. He walked quickly inside, purchased a First Class ticket, then went out again and hailed another taxi.

No use in making it easy for Arpotin if he's still around, he thought. He felt no particular worry that the Hungarian still dogged his tracks, only a dull resignation that sooner or later he would have to kill the marplot.

Sholokov waited patiently in the terminal for Murphy to return, feeling a bit uncomfortable in the modish double-breasted suit the London KGB station had tailored for him. The pants were too tight at the crotch, the shoulders were too tight, and the necktie his control insisted he wear was like a garrotte. True, the right breast was padded to balance the bulge of his holstered Makarov automatic, the hem in the sleeves had cyanide and chloral hydrate capsules sewn into it, and a 6-inch hatpin was cleverly hidden in the side lining of the jacket; but these were incidentals. If you felt uncomfortable wearing the suit, you looked uncomfortable. And if you looked uncomfortable, you brought attention to yourself.

So far, Murphy had not noticed him. He might be clever but he was still an amateur playing at a professional's game. When Sholokov did not want to be seen, he was *not* seen.

The Paris contact never came through again. Probably frightened when Murphy—then known as Abrelli—made off with his hardware at the Gare du Nord.

Sholokov didn't like thinking about that incident. He'd been at fault and admitted it, and his superiors decided to give him a second chance (which was really his third, but he didn't like thinking about the Hotel Ancora either) when the new information came in from Moscow's Tel Aviv man: a sleeper—so the joke went among the staff in Beirut—who was green, 3-feet tall, and granted a wish to anyone who caught hold of him.

The KGB's agents based in Western Europe were instantly put on alert. Penetrators lodged in social and police services, and Party members working in transportation were told to look for five men. The search in West Germany was especially vigorous.

In Paris an airline reservation clerk spotted Murphy's

name on a passenger manifest and, being loyal to the Workers' Struggle, notified her Communist Party local, which then forwarded the message to the Russian embassy.

Being in Paris and available, Sholokov was assigned the task of following Murphy until he could properly be dealt with. Since Murphy had given no Paris address, he would have to be finished in his country of destination.

From then on, Sholokov had enjoyed himself. Even when his two Palestinian helpers bungled their job he remained confident. He had no choice. If Murphy once got loose in a city the size of London, Sholokov might just as well retire to Siberia.

But Murphy was a good comrade. He returned to follow Sholokov and Rashad to the house on Sussex Place, did some investigating when he thought they were gone, and unwisely allowed himself to be followed back to his hotel on Russell Square.

Determined not to lose Murphy again, Sholokov took a room at the hotel, ordered up the KGB's tailor to bring some camouflage and armament, and sent Rashad—who tended to get underfoot and was (or seemed) inherently poor at conducting a surveillance—home to Sussex Place.

Never to return, as he found out later. The police had picked up all four members of the Palestinian hit-team. All he could do was hope that Rashad kept his mouth shut.

Sol Wedenfeld, Intelligence liaison officer at the Israeli embassy, drove Green down the M4 Motorway, heading into central London. He was a naturally undemonstrative man and had made little conversation with the agent after an initial greeting and summary of the day's events regarding Messrs. Murphy and Sholokov, compliments of a high-ranking official in the CID.

Green mulled over the information, wondering what Wedenfeld was holding back. He knew there was something on the man's mind, but decided to let him find his own time for revealing it—dark, dark secret that it must be.

"Where am I staying?" he asked as they joined the Great West Road in Chiswick.

"Hotel Russell. Same place Murphy put up last night. If Rashad, one of Sholokov's Palestinian playmates, had broken a few hours sooner the police would have Murphy in custody now."

"On what charge?"

"They'd think of something, then worry later about how to make it stick. Anyway, Murphy was gone by the time Rashad opened up, and Sholokov doubtlessly has him tagged. No reports on either man having been seen since then."

"How did Murphy leave the hotel, Sol?"

"Walked. He only had one small suitcase to carry. Probably caught a taxi a few blocks away so no one could connect him with the hotel. Or, if he was taking the underground, a station is just around the corner. Euston and King's Cross are also within walking distance."

"I see." Green fell silent, ruminating on what he should do next. Chiswick became Hammersmith became Fulham became South Kensington became Brompton became Westminster, the pavements filling with walkers on this warm May night, a cool breeze infrequently washing traffic fumes toward the south. And still Green sat with wrinkled brow as Wedenfeld negotiated the

Marble Arch roundabout.

He suddenly asked, "Did he see his daughter?"

"Who?"

"Murphy. He has a young daughter in the Cotswolds, near a place called Stow-on-the-Wold."

Wedenfeld frowned. "I don't have any information on that. Do you think he would risk going there?"

"Only if he's sure Sholokov isn't on his trail. I doubt if Murphy realizes the British police are also on to him. They may have already laid a trap for him there."

"Then we can stop worrying about him. The police won't let anything happen to him while he's in their custody." Yet a quiver of anxiety remained in Wedenfeld's voice, and Green again wondered whether he was going to tell him his problem.

It finally came out as Wedenfeld parked his car near the hotel.

"I wasn't intended as your special contact, Nathan. The Service doesn't ordinarily assign me to a high-visibility situation. For obvious reasons," he added needlessly. "But your original contact has been missing since this morning. We think she may have turned up something important and followed it through, then not had time to report. Or gotten herself in bad trouble."

"She?"

"Susan Meyer. You know her?"

The train pulled into Glasgow Central at exactly 3:45 p.m. and disgorged Scottish miners returning from a union demonstration in front of the House of Commons, Japanese youths bound for Ben Nevis and the plaque their countrymen had placed atop it, American engineers imported to help with the construction of oil platforms on Scotland's northwest coast, old English couples who—until their retirement—had never had an opportunity to see the beauty above the northern border, assorted salesmen either bringing or searching for good news—and three people who seemed to be together and yet not together, for they walked in each other's footsteps but always at a distance and with no sign or desire for recognition between them.

The man in front—tall, limber, and with a lupine walk that stretched his silent strides and gave his head a slight bobbing motion—directed his steps toward the Queen Street rail terminal half a mile away.

Behind him, a much shorter man tried to hold his own, his trunk-like legs scissoring twice as fast to keep up. Though his clothes looked expensive, he appeared oblivious to the gritty rain now falling.

The last figure in the loose-linked human chain was a young woman wearing jeans and a deep-blue slicker with an attached hood which she had drawn tight around her head, concealing her blond hair. She carried a large straw purse secured by a canvas belt and kept her head down as though trying to protect her make-up from the rain or watch her step on the slick, dark pavement.

Murphy entered the main concourse, stared up for a moment at the time-destination schedules listed across the top of one wall, and then proceeded to a platform at the far end of the station.

Sholokov made certain Murphy had boarded the waiting train, checked the departure time and platform number, and hurried back to the ticket office to purchase a ticket that would take him to the last stop on that line.

Susan Meyer, feeling conspicuous with only her purse in hand, went to a confectioner's stand and newsagent, bought a plastic carry-bag loudly proclaiming the world's debt to Robbie Burns, and stuffed it with an assortment of maps, magazines, candies, sandwiches, cigarettes, and a bottle of mineral water. She then walked to the end platform, flashed her Britrail pass which allowed her 21 days of unlimited travel, and boarded just behind Sholokov—whom she recognized from photographs Wend Ergatz had shown her immediately after Charon gave her the assignment. Her brief had been limited to feeding that stupid bastard Green with information. But if he wasn't around when she spoke to one of the maids who serviced Murphy's room at the Hotel Russell, if he failed to hear the maid say that Murphy threw a lot of travel pamphlets in his wastebasket and that they dealt particularly with Scotland and specifically with Glasgow, why, Mr. Green would simply have to forfeit the case to more capable hands.

The train, hours late because of a points failure up the line, finally lurched forward, beginning another exhausting journey to the Athens of the Highlands, Oban, on the road to the Western Isles.

CHAPTER SIXTEEN

Almost every night Percy Dalton walked from his small hotel on the Avenue de la Costa to St. Antoine Point where he could look across the bay to the gloriously bright lights of Monte Carlo, terraced like stacks of galaxies; look past Focignana Point to Larvotto Beach where the quality of the girls had pleasurably increased as the summer season drew nearer. The Casino in the foreground was an enticement to Paradise, a siren-call which he had unfailingly answered for the past two months.

He walked alone along the quay, passing Fort Antoine, and stood here with the wind in his face and the thunder of his heart beating in his ears. Monaco was a fantasy world, a place where dreams could be magically changed into reality. All you needed was one streak of luck on the wheel, a pair of supernaturally-charged dice, or a straight face above a string of nines.

Dalton had been endowed with none of those virtues. He was scraping the barrel and wondering about his future, realizing he could never return to England and never afford the cultural shock of America, regardless of the money to be made. He'd simply have to return to his old profession, hustle a job with a bank. Fluent in French, he was sure he could get what he wanted.

Sometimes he regretted having taken money which did not belong to him; but, like tonight, the feeling always passed when he stared at the lights of the city, lights which seemed to feed the money-trees of his fantasies. And the clean salty breeze off the Mediterranean helped clear his head, blow away the detritus of his anxieties, cleanse him of his guilt.

So what if his luck at the tables was incredibly bad. It would change. It had to. Nothing stayed the same. Purgatory didn't last forever; you ascended to Paradise after paying your dues. Everybody knew that, even the Italian gigolo, Massimo, whom he created to hide behind.

Yes, that's it! he thought. Go to church next Sunday. Pray, Percy. Lay your cards on the table, tell God you'll do anything he asks if only he spins the wheel for you. Sure, that's it. How else do all these goodie-goodies get ahead? They've got help, mate. There's that church on the Place St. Dévote, you can see it across the harbor from the Yacht Club. Go there—tonight. A place like that must be open 24 hours a day. No crap like at Anglican churches where they bar the doors at dusk.

He turned to leave, ready for redemption, and almost collided with the dark figure standing close behind him, a man buried in an unseasonably heavy coat and a hat pulled low over his eyes.

"*Comment s'appelez-vous?*" the man asked.

Dalton hesitated. Was that the usual manner of addressing a total stranger whom you had just met? Demanding his name?

"Je ne parle pas français." Let *that* satisfy the bugger.

"Is your name Percy Dalton?" The man's English was thickly accented. Balkan, Dalton decided. Definitely East European. How had he found him? Why was some Commie fucker even *looking* for him?

"Non—Massimo Colletti. Sono Italiano."

The sharp twangs of the 7.62mm Tokarev service pistol fitted with silencer were like guitar strings snapping, quieter than Percy Dalton's grunts of surprise as the slugs beat him against the parapet, punched a hole in his skull, toppled him backward and over the edge, into space, into the indelible, thirsty waters of the Mediterranean which swallowed him whole.

The train route from Glasgow to Oban is one of the most spectacular in the world. Ascending, it skirts Gare Loch, Loch Long, crosses the narrow isthmus separating Arrochar and Tarbet with the massive Ben Lomond to the southeast. Loch Lomond, the largest freshwater lake in Britain—24 miles long, 5 miles across at its widest point, and with a maximum depth of 623 feet—is followed along its northwest shore, then travels up Glen Falloch to Crianlarich where the track forks. The eastern branch leads north toward Fort William, passing through the desolate Moor of Rannoch, while the opposite branch leads west through Glen Lochy, touches the head of Loch Awe, and continues through the Pass of Brander, majestic Ben Cruachan to the right. The track finally dips down to the sea at the mouth of Loch Etive, opening a view to the mountains of Mull across the Firth of Lorn.

The names spelled magic for Murphy. He was anxious to get home—to forget the last two months, however futile that might prove to be. He knew there could be no rest; he'd committed himself beyond the point of return, spurning society's hypocritical niceties and therefore becoming prey as well as hunter. But that still did not disturb him. If he had had the chance to clear the slate he would not have taken it.

A scintillating blood-red ruby of anger commingling with remorse swelled inside him. He clenched his fists involuntarily. Thinking about what might have been made no sense, solved nothing, only tore a deeper gash in the fabric of his soul. And yet it had become such a part of him that he measured his present life according to how he could have shared it with his little Princess, the marvels of the world—like the scenery around him now—which they would have been enjoying together now had not..."

Night had fallen.

The light from a small bulb imbedded in the ceiling of the First Class compartment barely reached him; so he turned, flicking on a shaded reading lamp just above his head. He'd drawn the heavy canvas screens over the door and side panels; and now, with the cozy light behind him, he felt a security strangely unreal—as if he were already dead and buried, and a bomb beneath his seat would be meaningless.

Snapping open his suitcase, he removed a copy of *Newsweek*, relocked the suitcase, and began reading, darkness having obscured his pleasure in the rugged countryside through which the train was passing.

Yevgeny Sholokov looked at the dark, shrouded compartment, puzzled and impatient. He had no desire to storm it without the assurance that he could see his target once he got inside.

What was Murphy doing? The Russian knew he was inside, knew he was alone. If only there was some way of finding out whether he'd fallen asleep.

A young woman at the far end and an old drunk who belonged elsewhere but had the compartment next to hers were the only other passengers in this First Class car. Located between the locomotive and baggage car, it was isolated from the bulging Second Class section strung out behind, and especially suited what Sholokov had in mind.

A light went on in Murphy's compartment. Sholokov instantly retired to his own stall to check his hardware.

Three—or was it four?—hours had already passed. The train had pulled out of yet another tiny forsaken station not ten minutes before; and as they got closer to Oban—which Sholokov felt was Murphy's destination—more people would be moving around. Now was the perfect time to act if he was going to act. No more messing about. He had his instructions, the target was less than twenty feet away and apparently oblivious to his enemy's proximity, and Sholokov had his loaded Makarov, fresh from the Soviet embassy in London.

But I won't be using the gun first, Sholokov thought with a grim smile, opening his briefcase. No, I'm cleverer than that, Mr. Murphy. No mistakes this time.

Susan Meyer nervously lit another cigarette, then watched the smoke spiral out of the ventilator window. She had opened the window at Tyndrum, tiring of going to a door at every stop to see if Murphy had gotten off. The cool mountain air chilled her, but also kept her alert. She had not come this far to make a stupid mistake, fall asleep and let Murphy escape.

Escape? That hardly seemed the proper word, but was as good as any until she decided what she *would* do.

Now she wished she'd called Wedenfeld and told him what was happening. Maybe an opportunity would still show itself. If it didn't . . .

Murphy was a nice-looking man, handsome in a peculiar way, with the changeable face of an actor. She wondered what he did besides kill terrorists. Wedenfeld should have given her a solid briefing instead of treating her like his virgin kid sister. She hated that—not only because it pricked her female vanity, but because Israeli women had worked and fought beside their menfolk since 1948 when the state was formed. So why hold out on her?

Wend Ergatz would have told her more had he known more, but Tel Aviv obviously wanted to keep the affair quiet except to those with—how did the phrase go?— "the need to know." Which should have included her. She hadn't even been given a photograph of Murphy (if there was one). Instead, she had to rely on descriptions to recognize him—and on Sholokov whose photo she *had* seen and who could probably be expected somewhere nearby if his true ability as a stalker was at all close to his reputation.

Well, here she was, hot on the trail of a touted KGB agent and Murphy, perhaps the most wanted man in Europe if he once used the aliases Federico Basilia and Samuel Erinys. What was she going to do about it?

Sholokov could look after himself and only posed a problem insomuch as he might kill Murphy before she questioned him. Should she warn the American? The idea had occurred to her several times and seemed more acceptable on each occasion. What better way to gain the man's trust?

But what if he didn't take kindly to meddling women? What if he worried that—assuming he *was* Basilia—she might give away his secret?

The .25 Beretta in her purse gave Susan minimal security. She had never been much of a shot in the army, she disliked anticipating the use of a gun, and the small-caliber weapon had little stopping power unless one struck the heart or fired point-blank at the head.

She stared out the window, noting that a bit of the past day still clung to the heights. But even that would soon be gone.

The train had just left Dalmally, which meant (according to the map unfolded on her lap) Loch Awe would be coming up soon on her left, along with Kilchurn Castle. She wondered whether she'd be able to see it. No, probably too dark. And her compartment was on the wrong side of the train.

Well, that's easy enough to fix, she thought, stubbing her cigarette. All I have to do is stand in the corridor.

Before going out, she carefully peeked around the edge of the door to make certain Murphy wasn't thinking the same thing.

And saw the short, bulky figure of Sholokov moving toward her.

"He's not very happy," Green sighed, cradling the phone and leaning back against the headboard. "He wonders what the hell I'm doing sitting here in a fancy London hotel while she's out there somewhere, Jack the Ripper hard on her heels."

"You should have let me talk to him," Wedenfeld said from the other side of the room. He was rummaging through a refrigerated liquor cabinet, searching for a can of lager.

"Maybe I shouldn't have called him at all. Who knows who might be listening in?"

"You don't have to worry about that. No one knows what you're here for."

"Unless they saw us together."

"They could think we're two queers," Wedenfeld laughed.

"At least that would make the Russians happy. We'd be prime targets for blackmail."

"Screw 'em. Want a beer?"

"What are we going to do, Sol?"

"Watch the telly?"

"Susan *must* have found something. What was her assignment?"

Wedenfeld sat on the opposite edge of the bed and snapped off the tab on his can. "Act as personal liaison between you and Foreign Ministry Intelligence. Nothing else. She probably had a brainstorm and investigated." He shrugged. "It evidently paid off. She was given everything we got as soon as it came in, so what motivated her must have been from the reports."

"What—specifically?"

"I don't know. As I recall, the last tip gave us what Rashad told his inquisitors: that he and Sholokov—or Arpotin, as he was known to the Palestinians—followed Murphy to the Russell. Sholokov stayed, sending Rashad home to be caught by the police. By the time the Arab had sweat that information the two parties were gone. The airports, main bus and train terminals were covered but without results. So the police tried back-tracking, asking whether a J. M. Murphy or Mikhail Arpotin were aboard an earlier flight. The British still haven't received

Murphy's photo from America. They used his description instead, but no one appears to have seen him. Sholokov's photo brought no better results."

"The British had his photo? Then—"

"They got it from the French DST. Sholokov served two years in the Soviet embassy in Paris before being expelled in 1968 for undisclosed reasons. We understand the Russian was trying to corrupt local officials."

"If Susan was playing detective she would have come here first, asked questions of the staff."

"The police did that without picking up any leads."

"None at all?"

"A couple of months ago the hotel was plagued by an arsonist. The police were none too gentle in their investigation and the staff have, I understand, been resentful ever since. No one likes to be accused—even by insinuation—of a crime they did not commit."

"So?"

"So, Nathan, I wouldn't be surprised if a bellhop or clerk or maid withheld information from the police simply out of spite. But Miss Meyer may have charmed a clue out of one of them. We would have followed this up earlier," Wedenfeld said, anticipating Green's next question, "but we only began to worry about the girl when she failed to report from Heathrow, stating she was awaiting your arrival. By then it was too late. Now we'll have to wait for the day-shift to return."

"And we may be too late again," Green said morosely, trying to decide whether his anxiety about Susan's welfare stemmed from concern for a fellow agent or from something deeper: admiration for a woman whose courage reminded him of his dead wife.

Her hand dropped into the straw purse, gripping the small Beretta, the index finger caressing the trigger-guard.

But Sholokov stopped midway down the carriage (outside Murphy's compartment?) and drew something long and black from an inner jacket pocket. He then kneeled, glanced both ways, and put the black object against the compartment door. Holding it there with his heel as he leaned forward, he stuck his nose in the air, trying to reach an open ventilator window.

Susan sank back into her seat, her blue eyes wide with alarm.

What was she supposed to do? God, what *could* she do? Go out there? Sholokov would kill her. He probably had a gun with silencer; the old man next door wouldn't hear a thing; he'd kill her, kill Murphy, jump off at the next stop—Taynuilt, Connel Ferry, what did it matter, for godsake!—and be merrily on his way by the time the old man tripped over her corpse.

Oh, shit, Nathan, where are you, you stupid sod!

"Come to bed, Yiggy!" shouted Leah Charon, upset by her husband's late prowlings around the house and the ear-splitting clang of the phone, maddeningly insistent time after time after . . .

Charon came into their bedroom via the kitchen. He was outfitted in only his night-shirt, a glass of milk in one hand and a thick sandwich in the other.

"What, my flower?"

"In the name of all our holy—and don't try to sweet-talk me, Yigael Charon! When can a body get some rest? You should have been in bed . . . do you know what *time* it is, Yiggy?"

He placed his drink on the lamp-table and sat beside her on the bed, taking her hands. "Have we grown so old that we sleep the same hours as babes?"

"Something's wrong," she said, staring at him.

"I can remember nights when we had no desire to sleep. Remember, Leah?"

She tried to pull her hands away but he kept a firm hold on them. "This is no time to be vulgar, Yigael." And yet a familiar sparkle came back to her eyes, turning her once again into the beautiful young woman he'd first seen on the Haifa-bound refugee ship over thirty years before.

"Who is being vulgar? Who? We did not think it such a sin then, my flower."

"You are avoiding the question. Who was on the phone?"

He took a sip of milk, replacing the glass on its cardboard coaster. "Don't ask me that, Leah. You know I can't tell you."

"Your office? Don't they have families of their own? Why must they always bother you? Is there no one who can take responsibility except you?"

"It was not my office. Go back to sleep. I'll move the phone into the kitchen."

"No." It was now Leah who held tight to her husband. "You go into the kitchen and you forget your ulcer. The doctor said—"

"The doctor said I should snack more often to help dilute the acids in my stomach. I heard him, Leah."

"Is it about the man you have been looking for?"

He turned to her sharply. "How much do you know?"

"Very little. Don't be so serious, Yiggy, you frighten me. Some of the people you speak to on the phone have loud voices, that is all."

"You must not think about or remember what has been said. This is a serious matter—one I am particularly reluctant to discuss. But it has nothing to do with you or me personally," he lied, "so forget it."

"That's not fair. I'm your wife. Surely you trust me?"

"Of course I do. If it will help you sleep, I will say we are looking for a man."

"What did he do?"

"He is a good man," he went on, ignoring her, "who, because of a grave error on the part of our enemies, feels compelled to do some very bad things."

"Basilia—the man at Luqa Airport—he did nothing bad by saving those poor people."

Charon frowned, momentarily confused. He should have realized his wife was an acutely perceptive woman. He should have known, acted openly, saved himself this scene.

"I did not say it was Basilia."

"No, the papers said enough and your expression said the rest. Why do you want him?"

"I won't—I can't tell you that, Leah. Let it go."

"Who was the man from London?"

"Leah, you know better than to mess in these things. We've been married too long for you to interrogate me on what my job is."

"I know what your job is," she replied blandly. "But I am not at all certain that there is any purpose to it if all you can do is spend your time trying to find, as you rightly said, a 'good man.'" She paused. "I won't say anything more," and she turned over.

He stared at the back of her head for a moment, then moved to his own bed, glad that she had the good sense to get mad and sulk. He had no desire to tell her that her brother's daughter—their niece—was missing; had vanished (so Green presumed) while on the trail of the "good man" and the KGB agent.

Sholokov was known as an experienced assassin: callous, totally dedicated to the pursuit of a target, and brooking no interference. Nor would he now be burdened with Palestinian aides.

And as for Murphy . . . Who knew? If he was Basilia he could be just as cold and calculating as his stalker. He would have to be. Who could tell what he would do if confronted by a woman knowing more about him than was good for her?

Sholokov listened, but could hear only the clatter of the rails beneath. No one appeared at either end of the coach, the lighting was poor here, there was no reason to suspect anyone would be taking a particular interest in him during the time necessary for the small cylinder of chloropicrin gas to do its job.

Flattening the tube nozzle in his compartment, he had tested it under his door. It fitted perfectly. The gas would spew into Murphy's compartment and put him to sleep within minutes. Then Sholokov could enter, hold his breath until he opened the ventilator window—which he knew to be closed now—and kill the American as soon as the concentration of anesthetizing gas dissipated. Murphy wouldn't feel a thing.

After that it would be relatively simple to push the body out of a door. Dropping over a steep embankment, it might not be found for weeks—even months. Then Sholokov could pick up his next assignment.

He listened again. No, the train noises completely covered the faint hiss of gas from the spigot.

Once more leaning forward, he reached upward with his face, lifting it to the rush of cold night air coming through the open transom.

Only a minute more. Only a minute.

Green had not been content to let the matter rest until the morning. Despite the late hour, he asked Wedenfeld to get him the names of the hotel's staff, day and night shifts.

Wedenfeld, willing to humor the Shabak representative after the day's earlier disappointments, called his contact in the CID. "Fifteen minutes," he was told: the time it would take to get hold of someone who had the information.

Twenty minutes later Green was ringing the staff members not now on duty, saying he was a good friend of Miss Susan Meyer, that she had gone and was missing, and asking whether the person might have any information at all on where she might be.

Mrs. Bessie Hancock, head of the third floor maid service and the twelfth name on Green's list, seemed undisturbed by the late hour call; in fact, she was the first hotel employee who hadn't cursed at least once during the often abrupt conversations.

"Poor girl, I thought she might be getting herself in trouble."

"What do you mean?"

"Stop that, Monty!" she said to someone, then turned back to the phone. "Well, she wanted to know if I heard anything or seen anything that might tell her where Mr. Murphy had up an' gone. Said he was her brother. I knew right away something was wrong. Said her name was Myers—"

"Meyer?"

"That's what I said. But her brother's name was Murphy and she wasn't wearing a ring, so I knew she wasn't telling the entire truth about her relationship, I told Monty that right off. She seemed like a nice enough girl and he—Mr. Murphy—might have been her boyfriend, I thought. So I told her what I'd found."

Green motioned Wedenfeld nearer, gesturing for a pen. "You didn't give the police this information?"

"The coppers? I'd as soon lop off poor Monty's head! I told them nothing and I don't want to tell them nothing. You know what they did to me? You know what they tried to say about me? It would curdle your blood," she stated emphatically.

Green smiled, looking up at Wedenfeld. "I'm sure it would, Mrs. Hancock. Now could you tell me what you found, regarding Mr. Murphy's intentions?"

"You see, I usually leave the cleaning up to the girls. I kind of manage things, you know, make sure they do what's expected of them and check that the rooms have been properly tended before the guests return. Bernice was up with her sick baby all last night so she couldn't make it, and Jilly just up and quit the other day, so we was a bit short-handed, if you know what I mean. I had to pitch in with the linens and dusting and emptying trash. But I won't do the toilets and tubs. I draw the line on that. Ten years I did that and my hands are gone. Look at them! No, sir, I left that to the others. . . . Anyway, I was emptying trash in 323—Mr. Murphy's room—and saw these books, well, I guess you'd call them . . . little books, you know? He'd thrown them away. They had to do with Scotland."

"Scotland? Are you sure?"

"My sister lives up in Bishopbriggs, that's part o Glasgow. One of them papers of Mr. Murphy's was a ma of Glasgow and it caught my eye. I saved it, if you mus know."

"What else did you find, Mrs. Hancock?"

"Well, there was one of them rail guides—heavy boo with schedules and everything. And there was somethin about ferry services, MacBrayne or something like tha was the name of the company. That's all I found."

"Did you save anything besides the map of Glasgow' Anything that might help me?"

"No, that's all I kept."

"Was there any writing or any lines drawn on th map—anything specifying a destination perhaps?"

"Monty, get off! . . . No, I'm sure there wasn't. Th map's as good as new. That's why I wondered why Mr Murphy threw it out. It must have cost a pretty penny You won't be telling Mr. Winston, will you? He take none too kindly to us girls—"

"The manager? Of course not. You've been mos helpful, Mrs. Hancock, and I'm grateful."

"I hope you find her—Miss Myers, I mean. Monty an I have been worried ever since the coppers started askin all those questions about Mr. Murphy. He seemed friendly chap when I met him in the hall, but then yo never know nowadays."

"You and your husband need not worry. I'm sure tha Miss Meyer—"

"Husband?"

"Yes. Monty, isn't it?"

"Oh, heavens, no! I'm a widow! Monty is my pug!" And she burst out laughing.

He had spent ten minutes on the copy of *Newsweek*, finishing it. That was one of the drawbacks to a photographic-memory: the joy of reading did not exist unless you covered the rest of a page and went down it line by line: otherwise, the mind absorbing the contents of a page at a mere glance, you felt as though you'd already read the page and were wasting time.

Déja vu was a recurring symptom of the mnemonist's life. Everything he had read or seen or felt could be easily dredged from his brain. Existence became two jaded retinas screaming for the unusual, the unexpected, even the unwanted. Anything to change the routine of a sun always rising in the east, the biological demands of the body, the uniform habit of mind that collapsed human experience into a cubic area smaller than a squash. Curiosity could not solve the problem, either, for it was quickly satisfied. Only the eternally unanswerable questions remained: What is life? Why are we here? What should be the proper human destiny? Who made the Universe? Where did everything come from when there *was* no Universe, no atoms of hydrogen flying loose?

He shook his head fiercely. Thinking such thoughts always led him into a trap: If your reason for living is gone, why do you continue playing this foolish game? And then he would clench his teeth and spit out a string of curses reviling all life for leading him to this moment; excoriating both God and Satan: God because He gave and allowed to be taken away—and Satan because he took away but left the memory behind. There is no resurrection, no metempsychosis, no hope for the father who survives his offspring.

He threw the magazine on the seat opposite and

reached for a cigarette. It was foolhardy to think about the past. Wipe it away with the future. Wash it away with blood. Dilute your misery by sharing it with those who brought you to this reproachful state.

His hand was shaking as he brought out a box of matches. The compartment was too warm, much too warm. He felt nauseous, tired, dizzy. . . .

"Do you know what I want Santa Claus to bring me, Daddy?" his Princess had said, her tiny child's voice even tinier over long-distance telephone.

"No, darling, what do you want Santa Claus to bring?" He half-expected her to say a record-player, for she'd reached that age when music begins to exert a strong appeal for girls.

"A teddy-bear."

"A teddy-bear? No!"

"Yes! And a little one, too."

"Why a little teddy-bear, Princess?"

"So it won't be bigger than me, Daddy."

He had laughed, charmed by his daughter's innocence. Love rushed through him as though it were an emotion he'd never felt before.

"Wouldn't you rather have a Raggedy Ann?"

"No, a teddy-bear."

"Well, you'll just have to write Santa and ask him."

"You mean at the North Pole?"

"That's right, Princess. Or I could ask him. Santa and I are buddies and I'll be seeing him before Christmas. When I tell him what a good little girl you've been, I'm sure he'll bring you whatever you want."

"Would you ask him, Daddy, would you?"

Santa had come, of course, but Daddy's Princess had not been there to open the carefully wrapped little teddy sitting beneath the Christmas tree. She could not see the strings of brightly colored lights, the silver strands of tinsel icicles, the chocolate ornaments wrapped in glistening foil; she could not smell the foresty odor of the freshly-cut pine tree.

Because she was not there.

Because she was hundreds of miles away on a landing field near Baninah, Libya.

Because she had no eyes, no nose . . . no face. All that remained of his little Princess were ashes and a few charred bones.

Ashes to ashes . . . *blood of my blood* . . . dust to dust . . . *blood for blood* . . . in the certain belief that . . . *the Devil has beaten God* . . . from whom all blessings flow . . . *one by one, kill* . . . and so we consign the mortal . . . *Man's retribution is sure, God's problematic* . . . may the Lord have mercy on us all. . . .

Yes, the priest had shown enough guts to allow for the failings of her killers. "May the Lord have mercy on us all," he'd said; not "May the Lord have mercy on her soul," no, because she was already an angel, had been an innocent child murdered by troglodytes, bastards who crawled out of holes to wage war against people totally unconnected to their failed aspirations. Why? Because they knew they could get away with it; knew that Israel was a fortress set against them, and so aimed their AK-47s and grenade launchers and bazooka tubes at defenseless civilians from Europe and the Americas, convinced that the only retaliation would be stricter enforcement of passenger and luggage checks at airports. What a laugh! What an insane farce! How easy to intimidate democracies by blowing up their old women and children! . . .

His head nodded forward. He shouldn't be this sleepy
Eight hours of . . . rest . . . last night . . . should have
been . . . enough. . . .

He jerked the match out and struck it against the box
angry at his own lassitude. The match-head burst into
flame violently, oddly, burning green then quickly dying

Gas in the compartment. N_2O? CCl_3CHO? (Why
couldn't he smell it?) $CHCl_3$? CO? (But then the flame
would have been blue.) A bromoform? His college
chemistry text flashed page by page across his mind. . .

One day his Princess had said she wanted a puppy, but
he told her "No. Not until you're older."

"Why, Daddy?"

But he kept the reason—foolish, as it appeared later—
to himself. How could he tell a little girl about death,
about losing something very precious—forever? How
could he say he wanted to save her from that? Puppies
grow up and die. They don't live as long as we do. I don't
want you to experience grief, not now, not until you're
older.

Yet—was it *ever* easy? Old Ruff wouldn't necessarily
die of old age. He might contract an insidious, painful
disease and suffer for years unless he was put under.
Could his Princess accept that, learn to live with
omnipresent death? Would she understand why old Ruff
had to be gassed? . . .

Gas in the compartment.

He struggled to his feet, bracing himself with one hand
against the overhead luggage rack. With the other he
reached for the ventilator hatch.

Then he slumped back in his seat, unable to pull open
the window, knowing his strength had been sapped, that
his body only wanted to rest, that he was going to die. At

his stage of the game he was under no illusions as to what had happened. Arpotin was still around, still hovering in the shadows. He should have given the Hungarian more credit for his tenacity.

Who was the fellow working for? Of course, the Palestinian terrorists, the macho thugs who murdered—

NOOOOOO! . . .

She had been given a seat all her own on the jumbo jet, sitting between her grandparents' friends who were escorting her to London. With her strawberry-blonde hair and emerald eyes and little button nose and cheruby pink cheeks she must have dazzled everyone who saw her; for she was indeed a princess, regal, well-mannered, intelligent, and—perhaps more important than anything else—she possessed an astonishingly mature compassion for the feelings of other people. When the skyjackers commandeered the 747, he wondered how much she understood what was happening, whether the armed men had frightened her. But hadn't Daddy said on the phone, "Nothing's going to stop us from being together this Christmas, Princess, and that's a promise!"

A promise. . . .

He made one final surge, pushing his resisting arms upward, reaching, reaching . . .

Sholokov heard the dull thud of a body striking the floor of Murphy's compartment. A faint smile touched his lips as he knelt and turned off the gas.

Just as he thought: simple, effortless, sanitary. Murphy could be sitting behind a Degtyarev Pekhotnyy and it would be useless against a colorless, odorless, unexpected enemy. The Russian congratulated himself: using a poisonous gas might have killed or sickened other passengers, causing an uproar, so Sholokov insisted that his armorer furnish him with the knock-out gas. Only Murphy would die, and Sholokov would be the one who pinned him.

He picked up the gas cylinder, weighing it in his hand, wondering whether he should use it to kill Murphy. After all, it was disposable. His gun wasn't. And a bullet-hole was less likely to convince the police that Murphy had jumped or fallen from the moving train. No, this was the way it had to be done. Opening a crack in the door, he peered through—instantly recoiling from the eye staring back at him not six inches away. His blunt fingers wrapped around the grip of his holstered Makarov and jerked even as the door slid open, Murphy grabbing at the Russian's jacket.

The two men tumbled backward into the compartment, pulled by Murphy's sagging weight. Sholokov found his gun arm trapped between their bodies; while Murphy was still groggy from the soporific gas and acting purely by instinct.

Sholokov swung the metal cylinder at Murphy's head, but it slipped from his grasp, hitting and cracking the picture-window. Yet the movement served to break the man's hold on Sholokov, and the Russian staggered back, wrenching his Markarov free as he dropped into a seat.

Murphy lashed out with his foot, breaking his opponent's wrist and sending the weapon into the corridor. He kicked again, aiming for Sholokov's vulnerable head, but the blow was softened by a hastily thrown arm. His next kick, delivered with the experience of one trained in savate, would have collapsed Sholokov's windpipe had it landed, but the Russian assassin shifted away from its tight arc, then jabbed with the long hat-pin.

The sliver of steel entered Murphy's rear thigh muscle as he twisted his body to avoid it. The constriction of flesh around it jerked the pin from Sholokov's hand, and he was left weaponless.

Losing the needle in Murphy's leg was stupid; he knew that as soon as it happened. A fatal wound would be hard to administer with such a device, and impossible when the only approachable target-area was the man's leg. All Sholokov had done was anger the American, make his blood run quicker and his head clear faster.

He sprang to his feet, launching a head blow to Murphy's abdomen that sent both men crashing into a corner of the restricted space and winded Murphy.

Sholokov rained his fists against the man's face, though his right hand was ineffective with a broken wrist and his left hand was still bandaged. Nevertheless, he saw that Murphy was slipping badly, having apparently received a large enough dose of the chloropicrin to measurably slow his reflexes.

Then Murphy stiffened his leg into the dark-faced man standing above him, painfully compressing his genitals and driving him back, howling in agony. He could do no more. He felt as though he were fighting underwater, each blow sapping more energy with less results. Anesthetized by the gas, he had only a faint impression that his nose was broken and his lower lip split open, the acrid taste of blood in his mouth. Arpotin could still get his gun, and he knew he would be unable to stop him. And yet he had no choice but to try. In his imagination this particular scenario had not been dealt with, and so could not be realized. He wasn't ready to die—not yet. Not with unfinished business to tend.

But Sholokov, having crumbled to the floor, now had his hand on the Makarov. He swung the muzzle toward Murphy in warning.

His opponent, however, was in no condition to offer further struggle. Sitting limply against the corner seat with his hands resting beside his thighs, he was a study in exhaustion and vulnerability.

Sholokov pushed himself to his knees, sliding shut the door. A draft continued to race through the compartment, and he noticed that the ventilator window had been opened; he realized now how Murphy managed to remain conscious despite the dormitive vapor: fresh air had dissipated it, though evidently not before it had affected the American.

He rose to his feet, shuffling to the cracked viewing-window and bracing himself against it, his automatic trained on Murphy's head. The man's nose was bleeding profusely, blood dripping into his gashed mouth and onto his blue windcheater. He must kill him. Now. Before he regained his strength, his orientation. Whether Murphy really was Basilia did not matter. Orders were to kill him regardless. Yet Sholokov's pride wanted to know, needed to be certain *this* was the man who was the Alabet killer, the man sought—not one of the other four on the Israeli list.

He leaned forward, pressing the muzzle of the gun against Murphy's forehead.

"Basilia!"

The eyelids opened, then drooped half-way, and a weak hand gently touched the Makarov, pushing it aside.

Sholokov did not resist. The man had no more strength than a child now, fending off the gun as though he were in a drunken torpor.

"You—Basilia? You—Basilia? Yes?" Say it, you incompetent amateur!

Murphy jabbed the 6-inch hat-pin into Sholokov's left eye, burying it to its pearl hilt. Simultaneously he gripped the Russian's gun-hand, forcing it up as the man convulsively pulled the trigger—once, twice, blowing a hole in the roof and shattering the mirror between the two reading lamps.

Sholokov made no sound. A look of astonishment settled across his flat features; he pitifully dabbed at his ruined eyeball and then slumped to the floor, his limbs jerking mechanically. The gun in his fist exploded again, ripping off his kneecap. Having dropped into a coma, he did not react.

Murphy watched him for a few minutes, then realized the train was slowing to a halt. This would be Taynuilt. Usually flying to his island retreat, he was unfamiliar with these various stops, but he'd taken the time to research—and thus commit to memory—the train route to Oban. He was therefore able to accurately gauge the distance from Taynuilt to Connel Ferry, Connel Ferry to Oban, and consider the type of landscape between each station. The body must be disposed of where it would not be readily discovered. Forested areas were coming up on either side of the tracks. Deep ravines bordering the tracks would help—and could be expected along the line.

Of course, ditching the body would still leave the cabin's bullet-holes unexplained; but the one in the roof would probably go unnoticed for awhile, the pieces of mirror could be thrown out leaving an unexceptional hole in the wall, and the bullet that tore off Arpotin's patella had penetrated the bottom edge of the sliding door and would not draw immediate attention to itself. Once the body was out and the blood cleared away, perhaps the compartment's state might not look so bizarre to the casual observer. It all depended on how often the carriages were cleaned and reviewed. From the aspect of this carriage, Murphy decided he would have more than enough time to get out of harm's way before the police were brought in.

Ten minutes later, having hyperventilated with lungfuls of crisp mountain air, he checked the corridor. If anyone had heard the gunshots over the rattling of the old train, they must have attributed the reports to something else, for no one had come to investigate.

Murphy took two spools of toilet paper from the nearest latrine, wrapping one roll around Sholokov's damaged knee to prevent any more blood from leaking. Then, still wearing the gloves he'd taken from his suitcase, he quickly dragged the body to the door at the middle of the carriage and waited until that side of the train was on the outer rim of a curve.

He lifted the body in his arms and shoved it out. It seemed to hesitate a moment at the brink as though a spark of life remained to resist such rude treatment—then abruptly vanished, disappearing down a precipitous embankment that paralleled the tracks.

What a waste! Murphy thought, closing the door gently. Arpotin had no business in this affair. Why did Hungary export an assassin for the Palestinians to use in Britain against an American? What sense was there in such a diplomatically dangerous maneuver?

More to the point, what sense was there in worrying about things which did not matter? Cleaning up after Arpotin should be the first priority: removing bloodstains and bone fragments, discarding the gas cylinder and pistol, putting the compartment back in shape.

He turned, intent on erasing all evidence of the struggle, and found himself confronting a young woman in a blue slicker much like his own. She was smiling, but the small gun she aimed at him did not match her expression.

CHAPTER SEVENTEEN

"It's not going to be easy," Wedenfeld said, driving the short distance between Russell Square and St. Pancras Station. "You may be going at this in the wrong way. We have no positive information that Murphy or Sholokov or even Susan Meyer took a train to Glasgow."

"Of course not. But why hasn't Susan reported? We've got to follow this up for her sake."

Wedenfeld sighed as he turned onto the Euston Road. "The trail will already be cold, Nathan. Besides, I have others I could send for a routine investigation like this."

"It's not routine if Sholokov is involved." He paused, again checking the side-mirror to see if they had acquired a tail. "When do I arrive?"

"Your train leaves for Luton at 11:10. You arrive at 12:07. A taxi will be waiting to take you to the airport where you already have a seat on a charter-jet to Glasgow. You should be in Glasgow by two o'clock. What you intend doing there is a mystery to me, especially since hotels can be checked by phone and we have an import-export man in Edinburgh who could handle any leg-work."

"I can't just sit here," Green said, exasperated by his impotence and remembering General Charon's harsh words only a few hours before. "As soon as I get situated in Glasgow I'll phone and see if you have anything. Then I'll check the steamer offices. Mrs. Hancock recalled a schedule of ferry services found in Murphy's wastebasket. With any luck, our man is holing up on an island. A perfect trap."

Wedenfeld looked at Green and smiled wanly. "For him or you?"

"One move and I will shoot you in the head," she threatened.

The man did not reply, obviously shocked by her sudden appearance; but she felt his eyes appraising her, perhaps searching for a weakness, calculating the risks of grabbing for the Beretta.

She motioned toward the carriage door behind him. "Sholokov?"

This brought a faint reaction: his dark eyebrows rose slightly, gouging a furrow between them. Yet still he said nothing.

Susan Meyer had spent the last quarter of an hour debating whether or not she should investigate the three gunshots, though the problem of what to do could be settled merely by seeing who got off the train at Connel Ferry or Oban—Murphy or Sholokov.

Her curiosity, however, had concluded the debate and she finally ventured into the corridor just as a pair of legs disappeared down the short entranceway giving access to the center door. She followed, arriving in time to watch a man push a body off the train, and felt strangely relieved when she discovered it was Murphy who had survived.

"Was it Yevgeny Sholokov? Answer me!"

He reached out and gently pulled the Beretta from her grasp, checked the safety, and aimed the gun at her chest.

"BANG!" he yelled, and her eyes went wide. She licked her parched lips.

He handed the weapon back to her, grip first.

"Next time you'd be advised to flick off the safety," he said drolly. "Otherwise, a gun is good for little more than cracking nuts."

"I could have killed you! If—"

"I'd be dead, and *you* would have to push a body off the train and worry about it being found. But if you were going to shoot me you would have done it as I pushed this fellow past the door. I would have fallen after him, saving you time and energy. But you want me for something else. Whatever it is, might I recommend that we do it in my compartment? I have some cleaning to do before we reach Oban."

Susan stared disgustedly at her automatic, then dropped it into a pocket and followed Murphy. She was astounded by his casual attitude, his complete lack of interest in who she was or what she was doing here. Unexpected, it gave him an aura of subtle prescience which confused her. He should have been startled, suspicious, then cunning; instead, he appeared resigned, offering no explanation but giving no threat either. Maybe that would come later.

It shouldn't be happening this way, she told herself. She must phone Nathan Green and hold onto Murphy until he arrived. But how? The American barely acknowledged her existence—and seemed particularly unperturbed by her gun.

He was picking up shards of mirror when she entered his compartment, closing the door behind her. Hardly believing her own words, she asked, "Can I help?"

"Yes. Sit down and stay out of my way. When I finish, tell me if I've missed anything."

She sat, shivering at the evidence of a bloody battle in the room: cracked window, broken mirror, dark smear of blood across the floor, what looked like a bullet-hole in a wall.

"How did you kill Sholokov?"

"I simply defended myself against a man calling himself Mikhail Arpotin. How is not important."

"Arpotin is an alias. His real name is—or was—Yevgeny Sholokov."

"Who was he?"

"A KGB agent. Married, two sons, served in several embassy posts around Europe, was expelled from one of them. This past year he was posted somewhere in the Middle East, no one knows exactly where. He probably acted as a weapons instructor since he showed a disinclination for operational field-work. The Russians still considered him one of their finest hit-men, though. He had plenty of experience."

"Not enough," the man said, casting out the lozenge-shaped gas cylinder after wiping it of fingerprints.

"He was sent after a man named Basilia," Susan said, carefully watching his reaction. "Evidently he didn't find him."

Murphy dusted mirror slivers from the seat cushions and dropped them out the ventilator window.

"You must find this rather boring, Mr. . . . ."

"On the contrary, I'm fascinated. You tell me he is a Russian assassin, that he is seeking a man called Basilia. I

297

told you I killed Sholokov in self-defence, which would mean he attacked me. You, who seem to know so much about him, are here, having followed him all the way from . . . at least from Glasgow. With these facts in hand, you say Sholokov evidently didn't find Mr. Basilia. What do you make of that?"

"I . . ."

"My first impression is that you have concluded I am not Basilia—in spite of the fact Sholokov thought differently. My second impression is that you are cleverly playing stupid, hoping I will incriminate myself with some impromptu remark. And yet you realize that once I admit to being Basilia, I will have to kill you to protect my anonymity."

Susan's hand dropped into her slicker pocket. "*Are* you going to kill me?"

"No," he answered without hesitation.

"Why not?"

What could he say? If he intended killing her, that would be evidence of his identity. And that, had she not died, his Princess would have grown up to become a beautiful, golden-haired woman like the one before him now. No. There was nothing to say.

"Your employer should have sent a man," he said.

"And who do you think my employer is?"

"From your accent I would say the Israeli government—one of the intelligence services, possibly Mossad? Why you have chosen to address me if you were following Sholokov is so . . . perplexing that I must assume you were *not* following Sholokov at all, but were interested in me."

"Because your name is James Murphy," Susan answered simply. "Because you are suspected of being the Federico Basilia who rescued the skyjacked plane at Malta last April."

"How did Mossad reach that conclusion?"

"It is not a conclusion, Mr. Murphy, only a suspicion. I know nothing about how the Office discovered—or, I should say, uncovered—your name, nor on what basis it acted. My duty was not to contact you, but rather to serve as liaison for the man who would. What he intended doing with you was not part of my brief. But I can guess. You are not a viable target for assassination by the Israelis. You would probably be warned to"—how ludicrous it now sounded—"beware of Palestinian killer squads."

"Really?" Murphy said, amused.

"Sholokov and a network of Communist informants in Italy tracked Basilia to a town called Bellano, even though he'd already changed his name twice. But they missed him. . . . If you're Basilia then all of this is redundant."

"No, no, please go on," Murphy said, wiping the compartment floor with toilet tissues.

"I . . . quit the case at that point."

Murphy went out with the soiled tissues, returning a minute later. He surveyed the room. "We should be in Oban soon. How does the place look?"

"Okay to anyone but a forensic team."

"You enjoy building up my confidence, don't you?"

"What happens when we reach Oban? Are you just going to let me go?"

"Since your government has no reason to complicate my life by involving you in a case of justifiable homicide—"

"Me!"

"—I think I can trust you to keep silent about Mr. Sholokov. The police might take exceptional notice of an Israeli agent operating on British soil, following a law-abiding American tourist with her illegal hand-gun."

"But *you* killed him! That puffy nose of yours is evidence that—"

"I tried to protect myself. Then, frightened by the possible consequences of my lethal defense and half-crazy with worry, I disposed of the body. I acted in a state of shock. What court would convict an innocent American who had been ruthlessly hounded and assaulted by a mad-dog Russian killer? Even supposing I was jailed for a time, what good would accrue for the Israelis?"

"You are Basilia, aren't you?"

"If I am, you've successfully conveyed your warning. Your task is finished."

Calmed by the man's natural manner, Susan relaxed in her seat and fished out a cigarette from her jacket.

"It would help to know if *your* task is finished, Mr. Murphy. My government could be very forgiving if you simply chose to disappear. You have stirred a hornets' nest, causing us endless difficulties."

"Difficulties?" The man's tone was suddenly cold, and Susan looked up sharply, alarmed by the sarcasm and menace with which he imbued that one word. "What do you know of difficulties? Of a life ended before the body dies? Do you look for nuances in the shades of a sunset, praying you will see only the color of her hair and not the fire that consumed it? Can you imagine what the passage of time means to a man who survives only on memories? Did they teach you about that in spy-school, or were you only taught to kill and shadow and blackmail and put your emotions on ice from nine to five?"

What was he—? "Very eloquent, Mr. Murphy—but I'm not sure what you mean. If you could confide in me—tell me what made you do these things—perhaps I might be able to help. In spite of what you think, I'm not without feelings. And I'm alone. My contact has no idea where I am. Only you. Anything you said could be erased by killing me."

He gazed out the window at the rushing darkness, the sprinkling of lights at Connel slowly growing brighter. Soon they would be in Oban. The ferry would not be leaving until 3:15 p.m. the next day. He should have taken a plane. Riding the train was a mistake he sincerely regretted; though at the time he had thought it the simplest way of losing himself among holiday travelers. Instead, it proved a waste of time, providing this man Sholokov with a perfect opportunity to assassinate him.

"I wouldn't kill you. You've done me no wrong." And then, perhaps because her eyes seemed stained a darker blue by an empathetic compassion, he asked Susan, "Do you remember your childhood?"

Four hours after having seen him off at St. Pancras, Sol Wedenfeld received a call from Green.

"Where are you, Nathan?"

"The Britannia Hotel here in Glasgow. What do you have?"

Wedenfeld flipped through the notes on his office desk, mildly aware that he needed some sleep and it would not come until Green was satisfied. "Our target is not registered at any Glasgow hotel—at least in his own name. Nor has a James Murphy been a passenger on any flights out of Glasgow during the past fifteen hours, regular or chartered services. We couldn't raise anyone at Caledonian MacBrayne, and I doubt if you'll have much luck there. Too many tourists traveling at this time of year for one man to be noticed—especially when he doesn't want to be. For that matter, Murphy may have taken a coach—bus, you'd call it—to anywhere. You'd have to be very lucky to find someone who remembered him."

"Or Sholokov?"

"We don't know that Murphy didn't lose the Russian."

"Any news from your contact?" Green asked.

"Only a confirmation that London has been in touch with several Arab states on the subject of James Merton Murphy. We can expect the arrival of several hit-teams by tomorrow, all geared to track down Murphy."

"Are we going to counter?"

"Listen, old boy, do you think I'd tell you over the phone?"

"What about the Americans? Murphy's one of their nationals. Have they been alerted?"

Wedenfeld, aware that British Intelligence might be listening, was uncharacteristically emphatic. "Not to my knowledge. We are only getting second-grade information from the Foreign Ministry, Nathan, and it's often too old to be operational. Personally, I suspect the British want this mess cleaned up quickly and to the Arabs' liking. Washington would clog the gears by demanding an accounting of British perfidy. So I'm suggesting a course of diplomatic action in retaliation."

Green understood the code. "What is it?"

"We inform the CIA of Britain's action, present our supporting evidence, then sit back and watch the fireworks. It will be interesting to see how Whitehall extricates itself from the horns of this dilemma. By the way, Nathan . . . how do you like your hotel?"

Green said, "I love it. Beautiful place."

"Right. Keep in touch."

"Will do."

Ten minutes after Green rang off, two Glasgow detectives presented themselves at the Britannia Hotel, showed identification, and asked to see the registration book.

"Is there something wrong, officers?"

"We want to talk with one of the guests."

"Could I call to see if he's awake? This *is* rather an unusual hour . . ." Getting no response, the little man continued, "Which guest is it that you—"

"The chap in 28."

The clerk straightened his glasses, turning over the register and looking up. "Mr. Applebaum? Oh. I'm sorry, sir, but he checked out only a few minutes ago. Said his sister had suddenly taken a turn for the worse at the hospital."

The two detectives shared a glance, then returned their gaze to the clerk.

"Is that true?"

"What?"

"That he called his sister."

"I don't know if he called anyone."

"How'd he contact his sister—or how did she contact him to let him know she was sick? Don't you have a switchboard?"

"No. Only pay-phones—one on each floor."

"Where'd he say he was going?"

"He didn't. But he'd probably go to the hospital."

"Let's see his room, okay?"

There was nothing to see. Evidently Green hadn't even had time to unpack. The lavatory sink was dry. The ashtrays and wastebasket were empty. The telephone in the hall stared back at them mutely. Nothing left behind.

The British Foreign Secretary did not like the situation at all. Not at all. A few more incidents like this and the Labor Government would be picking up its teeth from the curb. Things were bad enough just trying to seal off classified data from the pinko Cabinet members who were unwisely included in the P.M.'s Wednesday suppers. Why did the burden always fall on him?

"How much do they know, John?"

His Under-Secretary—whom Scotland Yard contacted first because of the Secretary's famous dislike for nocturnal interruptions—slouched in the creaky leather chair across from his mentor. He was only slightly amused by the ridiculous figure the Foreign Secretary cut in his striped pajamas and red silk nightrobe, his porcine head topped by a tasseled night-cap straight from a Dickens novel.

"The monitored call to their embassy suggests they have a well-placed informant in the Ministry." He considered that enough of an explanation.

"And they know about our contacts to Beirut, Damascus, and the rest?"

"It would seem so, yes, sir. Their explicit threat to inform the Americans of our . . . activities in this affair alerted Special Branch and we were given a tape of the conversation. The Branch is convinced British prestige is somehow endangered."

"What do you think, John?" the Foreign Secretary

asked morosely. "Should we call it a day before the Yanks bomb Hastings?"

"I see no alternative, sir. The man sought by the yard—James Murphy?—has vanished. Last reported address at the Russell Hotel. The Israelis must have had some indication he went to Glasgow since they sent one of their agents there to locate him."

"Why? What would they want with Murphy?"

"I'm guessing, sir, but it seems he might be a rogue from their own intelligence organization."

"Not from his dossier."

"The Israelis are masters at building false identities for their foreign operatives. But as I said, it's only a guess, sir. They might want to take him back home before he causes more trouble—or silence him permanently."

"On British soil? Incredible, simply incredible! The nerve of the blighters!"

"You must also remember that we never sought confirmation from the Americans when the Israelis sent us Murphy's dossier and asked that we watch for him. The real James Murphy may have died two years ago. And . . ."

"Yes? Come out with it, John. What?"

"Well, sir, at the time we received the Israeli confidential bulletin on Murphy there was talk in the SIS about French Intelligence having received a similar document, though the wanted man was a Frenchman."

"The nerve! The bloody nerve of these—" But he stopped himself in time. No use in giving his protegé any ideas about the master's potentially debilitating prejudices. The last thing the Secretary wanted was to be labeled anti-Semitic.

"So what is your analysis?" he said in a calmer voice,

305

one usually reserved for his constituents.

"I have made none, sir. Nor can I. All we know is that Murphy is on the island, an Israeli agent named Nathan is after him, and a Russian assassin is lurking somewhere on the perimeter. Now we have to tell the Americans—which should untangle the mystery to some extent—if we are to save face. The Israelis don't owe us anything, and they would be glad to see us floundering in our own bile."

"Well phrased, John."

"Then I have your permission to relate to the Americans our investigative results from the past forty-eight hours?"

"Tell them anything," the Secretary said wearily. "And then find out what they do about it."

She sat in the tight back seat, crushed against him by the confines of the Mini, her arm casually slipped through his which balanced the suitcase on his knees. He stared directly ahead at the weaving ribbon of road.

Susan wondered what he was thinking.

They had been very lucky. He wanted to stay in Oban tonight and then charter a plane from South Ledaig, five miles away, to Glasgow; but when she told him how she managed to track him and that others would certainly be hot on the trail—her partner, for instance—once they spoke with Mrs. Hancock, he agreed there was only one course of action.

So they thumbed, taking the A85, a road which paralleled the tracks they had ridden less than an hour before.

After several cars passed without even slowing, Susan pulled back her hood, flouncing her mass of golden hair.

Two people with a suitcase were not good hitch-hiking prospects, but a pretty girl who happened to be accompanied by a man might interest a motorist. Or so he hoped.

The next car passed, slowed, jerked to a halt, and backed up. The round face revealed by the dashboard lights was encouraging: pleasant, middle-aged, and full of humor.

"Hello, my name's Hodgkins—Henry. We're heading Glasgow-way. If you two young people are going in that direction, I'd be glad for some company."

She'd been effusive in her thanks and they crowded into the rear seat, introducing themselves as Mr. and Mrs. Pone, Susan hoping her partner might be more loquacious, matching the garrulous Mr. Henry Hodgkins from Bishop Auckland—but he kept silent.

"My wife and I were up enjoying the salmon fishing," Hodgkins rambled. "Oh, pardon me, I forgot to introduce her. This is Adela, my wife—otherwise known as Hodgkins' Disease." He burst into thunderous laughter.

Adela Hodgkins did not share in his amusement, and Susan could tell she was against picking up strangers—especially blondes with prominent mammaries. With the resignation of one willing to take the bad with the good, however, she stoically accepted her husband's propensities and, after her initial frostiness, began to warm to the American couple riding with them.

"The wife wanted us to start back earlier, but I enjoy driving at night. These narrow winding roads give you an impression of dangerous speed." Hodgkins cackled maniacally. "Adela says I should do my racing around the house—then maybe the roof would be patched and the faucets fixed. Care to take the wheel awhile, Mr.

Pone? I guarantee it's quite a thrill."

"No, thanks," the man said.

"My husband suffers from night-blindness," Susan said.

"Nyctalopia," he murmured softly, and she looked up at him. His eyes were two pale sparks.

Oh God, oh God, she thought. I think he's *crying!* Why did I make him tell me? Why?

"What's that?"

"Connie was giving the medical term for night blindness. He has a fetish for explicitness in vocabulary, Mr. Hodgkins."

"Call me Henry."

"Henry. And I'm Sally."

"Hello, Sally."

"Hello, Henry."

"Your name is Connie, Mr. Pone?" Adela asked, purposely interrupting her husband's light banter. "What does that derive from, if I might ask?"

"Cornelius," Susan said. "But Connie thinks that sounds too stuffy."

"Cornelius. Connie. Why don't you shorten it to Corn?" Adela suddenly exploded into laughter, her head rolling backward and dangerously tipping her bee-hive hairdo. "Then you could call yourself Corn Pone! Hahahahahaheehee..."

"I do not imagine our guests find that particularly amusing," Henry said pointedly.

"As funny as Hodgkins' Disease," she snapped in retort.

"It *is* funny," Susan laughed. "Isn't it, darling?"

He winced as she elbowed him in the ribs. "Yes, Sally, pure scurrility."

"What'd you say, Connie?"

"There he goes with the big words." Susan sighed with mock resignation. "Stop it, darling, or our friends will think you're showing off."

"Are you a teacher, Connie?" Henry asked.

A pause; then, "I used to be."

"Oh? What did you teach?"

"The science of life."

"Biology," Susan put in.

"Did you hear that, Adela? A scientist in our Mini!"

"Don't be vulgar, Henry."

"Of course, biology is also the science of death, wouldn't you say, Connie? In that it studies transformations in living forms?"

"You sound like a man who has had some contact with the life sciences," Susan said,

"Actually, I'm headmaster of a public school in Auckland. The wife says I'm not pretentious enough in my position and act more like a lorry driver. True or false, Sally?"

"I'd hate to think what people thought *my* profession was just by judging my looks," Susan replied coyly, and they both laughed.

"You have a very personable wife, young fellow."

"Stop it, Henry, you're embarrassing the poor girl!"

"Nonsense! Do you two have any children?"

"Yes."—"No."

A lengthy pause during which Hodgkins looked at his wife and shrugged. "Which is it? Sally says yes, Connie says no. We have a stalemate. Cast your vote, Adela."

"I mean, we're *going* to have children. We don't have any as yet is what Connie meant. But in about seven months . . ."

Hodgkins cheered. "Huzzah, huzzah! Our congratulations!"

"You shouldn't be traveling like this, dear," Adela said with maternal concern.

"Oh, my doctor told us it would be okay as long as I didn't do anything strenuous, took my vitamins, and got plenty of rest. He said we should take a vacation before the baby came, since after it's born we'll be tied down for several years."

"A wise prognosis. 'Go while the going's good,' my father used to say. What are you hoping for—boy or girl?"

"Henry, you're not a detective," Adela scolded.

Susan looked at her partner and said, "A baby daughter."

"Good choice. And then a boy. A girl always likes to help mind her little brother. Do you have a name for the wee bairn?"

"Henry!"

"Oh, bloody . . . they know I'm only asking because I'm interested. Hush, woman!"

"Yes," the man said before Susan could reply, his voice deep and penetrating, seeming to emanate from his chest. "Her name will be Molly Jane."

CHAPTER EIGHTEEN

Oliver Mamgabwe had been tracking the wounded lion for nearly three hours, ever since sunup. A white poacher had taken a shot at it the evening before, failed to kill it, and was now at a hospital in Dungu, leaving behind his left arm and half his face.

Because any wounded predator endangered the peace of the tribal villages in and around Garamba National Park, a game warden had to track down the animal and kill it. The rough terrain made capture and treatment virtually impossible, for there were few roads, fewer trucks, one light spotter plane, and scanty funds to provide for the care and transportation of a 500-pound lion. It was simpler to kill the beast and be done with it.

An elder from the small village near the eastern fork of the Garamba River reported sighting the lion that morning; and as his park outpost was only half a mile away, Mamgabwe quickly responded, catching the animal's spoor four hundred feet upriver. The lion had stopped to drink and was still bleeding from its wound—not heavily, but enough to weaken it.

And there would be the pain, maddening an frustrating, turning the beast into a killing machin directed against the species that inflicted the woun Mamgabwe was not happy about facing this leonin wraith of vengeance with a bolt-action .30-06 Enfield, bu considered himself a good enough marksman to kill with the two shots he'd probably have time for. companion would have helped steady his nerves—bu he'd been alone at the outpost and no one from the villag wanted to help track a wounded lion.

He disdained the clouds of blue-black flies tha swarmed around his exposed neck and arms and face pushing on through the bush, always watchful for a sig that the beast might have stopped, heard his approac and hidden along the trail.

He came upon the jeep half an hour later.

Crossing a small stream in a wooded area, he happene to glance downstream. And saw the body.

Mamgabwe stood beside the black man's corpse reading the signs clearly. Not many animals could crush man's skull in their mouth. The tooth-marks on a flap o scalp lying nearby told him it was a lion. The dead ma had foolishly tried to run a foot-race with his pursuer hoping the lion would not cross the stream. But the stream was shallow and less than ten feet from bank to bank. Anyway, he never made it.

So what was a black man in khaki trousers and white shirt doing out here without a weapon? The condition o his boots showed that he hadn't been tramping through the woods very long, and he wasn't carrying any identification.

Mamgabwe back-tracked along the route the man had taken, soon coming to a clearing bordered on three sides by woods, the fourth side opening onto a broad savannah. In the distance a herd of gazelles grazed, undisturbed by the ugly tableau that now greeted the game warden.

At the edge of the woods from which he had emerged was a dusty jeep. The canvas top had been taken off. The sole occupant was in the rear seat, sitting upright. Only a jagged stump of muscular tissue, snapped arteries, and cervical vertebrae remained where the head should have been. What had survived of the man's white shirt—which was very little, for the left half of the chest had been torn away, revealing splintered ribs and a lung—was drenched in blood and seemed to have attracted every winged insect within miles.

Approaching, Mamgabwe saw a rifle in the man's lap. He extracted it from the clinging fingers and found that it had not been fired recently. Which meant one of two things: either the fellow was after big-game and had not found it until too late, or he simply had the job of protecting the jeep in case of attack—and had failed.

Since there was only one rifle—a .30 SAFN M49—Mamgabwe doubted whether this had been a hunting expedition. If it were, these two dead men would have been poachers; as such, they would liberally bury themselves in weaponry in case they came across some park wardens and had to fight their way out.

No, it appeared as though the lion had chanced upon an innocent party. Frightened, the driver perhaps tried to run it down; but the lion leapt directly into the jeep, landing on the rifleman and beheading him, talons anchored in his chest. The driver ran away and was killed as he tried to cross the stream.

Which left one question: Who was the passenger?

There had to be at least one passenger—excluding the

rifleman. Two black men do not ride around a national park in the heart of Africa unless they are: (1) poachers; (2) politicians; (3) game wardens; (4) revolutionaries; (5) eccentrics; or (6) madmen. Mamgabwe did not think these men were any of those, though they might well be working for one who was.

He found the third body lying two hundred yards from the jeep and in the direction of the open savannah. Thousands of hungry flies blackened the corpse, and it was not until Mamgabwe drove them off with his bushhat that he discovered the body belonged to a white man.

Two cameras were still looped around the torn neck: a Leica and a Miranda. The man might have been a nature photographer. Africa seemed full of them these days; their numbers increased in direct proportion to the decreasing wildlife population. A check at the nearest towns along the Kibali would certainly turn up his business here, since the jeep displayed the insignia of a state-run rental agency.

Searching through the man's pockets, Mamgabwe recovered a wallet, passport, a ring of five keys, an international immunization booklet, a tin of salt tablets, and a small spiral-bound notebook. Inside the notebook were lists of place-names, most of which the warden recognized immediately. The facing pages had corresponding notes of a rather bizarre nature. Isiro Airport, for example, was described in the following manner:

North hangar—shoot entrance w/zoom. Atom bomb on trolley. General Yamuto gesticulating. Workers run out. Cam lifts, pans landing-strip. Zoom on edge of jungle SE. Wilson in tree w/binocs. Cut to Kinshasa.

Atom bomb? General Yamuto? Mamgabwe had studied English at the mission school, but he could make no sense of this.

He flipped through the man's passport, comparing the photo to the dead man's face. Yes, definitely the same, even though one was dead.

Mamgabwe returned to the jeep and discovered it was in good working order, the keys in the ignition and enough gas in the tank to get him to Faradje. Evidently the three had stopped here so the white man could take his pictures. Then the lion attacked, killed the rifleman, the driver, and finally the white man. Why hadn't the white man . . . ? But the sequence of events was anyone's guess. The warden had enough to worry about. Should he keep after the lion or drive the bodies to Faradje before hyenas dragged them off?

The beast solved Mamgabwe's problem by breaking cover at that moment and rushing him.

Fortunately the warden was on the opposite side of the jeep and had time to unloose a shot before the lion sprang over the machine, jaws distended. He fired again as it swiveled back toward him. A head shot that stopped it cold.

He felt the sweat under his armpits, between his legs, across his brow. Funny how hot it had gotten. And so quickly.

Shouldering his rifle, he recovered the driver's body from the streambank and shoved it onto the rear seat; spent five minutes searching for the rifleman's head—finally finding it behind a tire; tramped through the tall grass to the insect-draped corpse of the American, Thomas George Shelleen.

Wearily unlooping the cameras and transferring them

to his own neck, Mamgabwe grasped the man's blood-stiffened shirtcollar and dragged the body toward the waiting jeep.

Several hours before Oliver Mamgabwe reached Faradje, a tall man and a strikingly beautiful blonde were boarding the *Peer Gynt* at Newcastle-on-Tyne's Commission Quay, bound for Bergen, Norway. Their passports had been checked and were in order. They were wished a good voyage and sent on their way, traveling unusually light. But then it was summer, wasn't it, even among the Norsemen?

The CIA station chief in London, informed of recent developments, was not particularly astonished by the selfish motivations of the Foreign Office—nor depressed by the fact that a lone American was defying the might of British Intelligence.

Though aware for some time that the Israelis were seeking James Murphy, the CIA had been unable to locate him. Why he was wanted did not appear in the Israeli request for help, but the timing of the request lent credence to the view that Murphy was the famed Federico Basilia, jokingly referred to in the Company as "Batman."

The station chief dutifully contacted Washington and was told that, since the British were prosecuting the search to their utmost ability, he should keep his operatives clear of the affair until such time as Murphy fell into police hands.

Nathan Green spent two days in and around Glasgow. Operating from a hotel in Kilmarnock, he made calls and visits to coach stations, train stations, ferry offices, and car rental agencies, always coming up empty-handed. The new photos Wedenfeld sent up hadn't been much help. No one remembered seeing Murphy, Sholokov, or Susan Meyer.

He read several newspapers each day for possible hints as to what might have happened to the triumvirate, and on the evening of the second day he was rewarded with a small front-page article in the *Glasgow Evening Times*, entitled "Murder in the Highlands."

Early that morning Oban police were summoned to a deep ravine several miles east of Connel Ferry. A Britrail lineman had spotted a body lying at the bottom and been quick to call for help. The victim was a white male approximately 40 years of age, dark-haired, dark-eyed. No identification on his person. He was evidently tossed from a moving train, though the medical examiner stated the cause of death as a sharp narrow object driven into the brain through the eye, causing cerebral hemorrhaging. The man had been dead for at least 36 hours. Police were conducting a search of the area further along the track, hoping for clues. The victim was found with a considerable amount of money in his pockets. No one as yet had been brought forward to help police with their enquiries.

In other words, Green thought wryly, no one has been arrested on suspicion of murdering Yevgeny Sholokov.

The next day he took a train back to London. Glasgow was a dead end; and Green decided that the sooner he faced Charon, the sooner he would know he'd have to look for another job.

The couple rented a car in Bergen and drove to Oslo. Once there, the man took a ferry to Copenhagen, then flew to Munich while the woman was en route to Stockholm by train.

Reaching Stockholm, Susan Meyer found a hotel and stayed one night before resuming her journey, catching a plane to Zurich the following morning.

Murphy, meanwhile, took a second plane to Milan, boarding an Alitalia flight for Geneva within minutes of arriving from Munich.

Susan rented a car in Zurich and drove to Geneva, meeting Murphy at an apartment he had rented two months earlier. It was on the Rue des Eaux Vives, overlooking Lake Geneva and its spectacular jet fountain. She loved it.

Murphy also seemed pleased, though he was not the sort of person who readily showed his emotions. He had disliked traveling on one passport, but now his apartment yielded two new ones which he'd kept hidden for an emergency. In spite of the fact he would have preferred retrieving his real passport from its grave in the garden of his cottage on Halaman Bay, he understood the obstacles: Scotland Yard detectives anxious for promotion, Israeli Intelligence agents, Palestinian hit-squads, and an amalgam of various foreign and domestic sleuths in need of quick answers. Oil speaks louder than justice, and the Arabs were probably slowing production until the Swiss or French or British or Germans or Americans or Italians finally expectorated the elusive Mr. Basilia—before their thirst for fossil fuel destroyed them.

Susan knew Murphy had come here for a reason, but didn't care to think too deeply about it. She liked the man, liked him more each day, and wasn't sure whether his appeal derived from a gentle forbearance or his stoic determination. He embodied many personalities, none of them easy to sort out or understand once one did.

She didn't want him to die.

Geneva, cosmopolitan, enchantingly civilized, home for many international relief and peace organizations, was also the base for several Palestinian groups bent on propagandizing their cause.

She didn't want him to die because she loved him. It was foolish and crazy and dangerous—but what the hell. Maybe she liked the way he tilted at windmills, or his romantic sense of honor and virtue—his medieval code of justice; or his sensitivity to the little things in life: his appreciation of the sky when few men looked up anymore, his passion for colors, his changeable moods like the ebb and flow of a great dark sea. If there existed any one reason why she loved him, she could not have said what it was.

Isn't life strange? she asked herself. I always wanted a man who could bend with the wind and not break. Instead I find a man who has been snapped in two but mended so strongly that now he leans *into* the wind, *becomes* that wind.

The worst part of their arrangement—the mutual agreement that, under the circumstances, they owed each other nothing and therefore had no reason to help or hinder their separate tasks, their separate destinies— was his trust in her. She disliked the responsibility he placed on her to keep silent; not that he invited complicity in his stratagems—though she was past caring about her professional responsibility since the man had no quarrel with Israel—but that he naively imagined she could allow him to go off and get himself killed despite the feelings she had for him.

A week had passed since their first meeting on the train to Oban. Susan spent her time sightseeing and wondering how she would explain her mysterious disappearance to the Office, knowing they must be looking for her. What excuse would be believed? Why hadn't she phoned Mossad Central in The Hague? What information did she collect on Murphy?

The man arose early each morning from his cot in the living room, made his breakfast (inevitably fried eggs on toast), then disappeared into his study. The bedroom he'd given her was next to it, but she never heard a sound from the study after he went in, locking the door behind him; nor was she ever permitted inside.

She guessed he was planning his next operation, pondering the variables, memorizing escape routes, calculating the risk of failure.

One night she tried to anger him, turn him from his course—with dismal results. A man who defends himself only with his wit is especially infuriating to a bitchy woman.

"Why do you keep bothering the Arabs? They're not all bad. Some of them are kind and understanding and would never think of injuring you."

"Must we go into this again?" he asked.

"And why not? Why should you waste your life? Haven't you spilled enough blood? Played judge and executioner long enough? From what you've told me, it seems you should let the terrorists drown in their own vomit."

"I said nothing of the sort. I *know* there are many Palestinians who have suffered the loss of their homes and farms, and yet they do not kill innocent people to gain attention for their problems. I mean them no harm. But the others must die."

"To prove what? Tell me. To prove what? That you can do it? That you're a big man with a gun? That's crazy!"

"The world is full of lunatics. The sane people are killed off first. Look, Susan, any fool knows our society is committing suicide. We're ready to dig our own graves rather than admit that some of our fellow human beings are innately evil, do not share our marvelous Christian spirit of leaving God's Will to God, and should be summarily executed whenever and wherever they are found—for the good of the lambs among whom the wolves lie."

"So you play the hunter and become just like the hunted. A joke!"

"I'm not a saint—I never claimed to be. But you should know better than I do that a policy of appeasement only prolongs the inevitable. How many Jews died believing the Nazis could not be as terrible as rumor said?"

"Killing Arabs won't bring her back," Susan cried, cornered by the mounting intensity of his argument.

"No," he replied in a curiously soft tone. "But it may save other innocent children. What is a man's worth to himself if the goodness in his life has died and yet he never attempts to rescue others from the same fate? Nothing. He has become a stone for his own grave, a walking monument to that blasphemous ideal saying men should possess the same unremitting forgiveness as God. We are *not* God, we are only *men*." Then, with a sudden change of mood, he yelled fiercely, "What do you expect from me? Mercy? Redemption? Though the dead survive?"

When she awoke the next morning she knew he was gone. She did not have to go into the kitchen and find an unused skillet or into the living room and see the low table clean of coffee cup and juice glass or try the study-door and discover it unlocked. She sensed all these things as though the apartment were speaking to her in sympathy.

She opened the door to the study and walked in.

A worn couch sat against one wall, a desk and chair facing it. The desk-top and drawers were empty. A metal wastebasket beside the desk was filled with ashes, accounting for the smoky odor in the room, despite both windows being wide open to the fresh May morning air. Besides that, there was nothing—

Then she saw the map tacked onto the wall behind the desk. He must have forgotten it in his rush to finish before she got up.

It was a large map. Of the Middle East.

Dressing quickly, Susan considered what she was about to do. Would he understand? And then forgive?

But Murphy wasn't a forgiving man. When she thought of his vindictiveness, she felt weak; he would never harm her, but he might easily lose all respect for her. They had an agreement. Only it was one-sided: she left him to his colored contact-lenses, nose-putty, cotton-wool, padded suits, hair dyes, fake moustaches, and assumed physical idiosyncracies if he . . . but he gave her nothing in return.

She packed her belongings in the suitcase he had left behind, called for taxi, and was out of the apartment by 9 a.m.

By 2:15 p.m. in Tel Aviv the news had been filtered

through upper-echelon ranks of Israeli Intelligence. An alert was put out to all domestic airports, and agents in Arab cities were contacted—when possible—and told to stay away from airports in case they were being followed: if Murphy was on his way there, Mossad did not want him caught because of Arab suspicions that an Israeli agent was meeting him.

By three o'clock, however, the external agents were released from the ban. A manifest revealed that the subject was aboard a TWA flight from Rome that would be arriving in two hours—at Ben-Gurion Airport....

Leonard Talmai drove his specially-equipped Volkswagen to a phone-booth on the northern outskirts of the city, taking a small stool into the booth with him. He dialed, spoke for two minutes, then returned to his car.

Ten minutes later he walked across the street to a black Fiat which had pulled alongside the curb, and climbed in beside a young Arab named Wadi Hassad, a dishwasher and an agent for the PLO intelligence organization, Rasd.

As the Fiat sped away, a car carrying two Shabak agents began a careful pursuit.

After driving north for three miles, the Fiat turned around, heading back toward Tel Aviv. It stopped beside the midget's VW and Talmai transferred to his own car.

The Shabak agents wondered whether they should grab Talmai and the Palestinian now. They certainly could not follow both men at once with only one car.

They decided to let Talmai go. He could be picked up at any time. The Arab was the man to track to his nest of spies.

Talmai must have sensed the danger. As the Shabak car drew abreast of his VW he veered into the road, his front bumper locking into the rear bumper of the other car, and he braked.

By then the Fiat was already out of sight, so the agents arrested Talmai. Not wanting to arrive empty-handed, they took him to Headquarters where he was grilled for three hours non-stop. But he merely repeated in his child-like voice that the Arab was a friend from Caesarea whom he'd met at a vegetable market two days previous. The man said he'd be in town today and gave a number to call so they could have a little chat. Talmai only knew his first name: Mohammed.

The interrogators sighed and shrugged and ordered more coffee. The idea of torturing information out of a midget really didn't appeal to them. But . . .

The old man was checked again for weapons—as were the other passengers on the TWA flight—when he arrived at Ben-Gurion Airport. He passed the metal-detector test and a light frisking, and was told to join the line of passengers walking toward Passport Control. There would be no problem, the guard said. You're an American, aren't you? Ever been to Brooklyn? That's where *I'm* from.

The old man was indeed an American—no mistake about it. Few men of other nationalities would be caught dead in a flashy blue-and-white checkered casual suit, yellow shirt, white tie, and white loafers. His socks were green with a Scottish thistle embroidered on the sides.

Yet he did not seem like the usual retiree, straight from his concrete Miami condominium. The tanned skin set off his brilliant white hair, giving him the appearance of a patriarch, a noble Indian chieftain who was forced to wear the hand-me-downs of several white men who all had bad taste. He had a quiet dignity about him and took no offense at the body search, though everyone who watched felt ashamed for his having to undergo such an indignity. The poor old guffer. And with a bum leg too.

He reached Passport Control, was questioned briefly about his reason for coming to Israel and how long he intended visiting, then had his passport stamped and went to collect his baggage.

As he pulled his large gray-vinyl suitcase from the moving luggage ramp he felt a slight pressure around his upper right arm.

"Mr. Vincent Azrael?"

He turned half-way to look at a uniformed airport guard. The man was smiling pleasantly, his face full of concern for the senescent traveler.

"Yes, I am he," he answered, his voice quavering.

"You wished to bring a certain walking-cane into the country. There seems to be—"

"That is quite correct, young man. I asked the airline authorities in Rome whether it would be permissible to bring my cane with me—even though it's a sword-cane. You see, I was partially crippled while flying in the Dominican Republic. Of course, that was before your time. But I need the old stick to help me get around. Can't walk far without it. And I've had it for many years, so it holds sentimental value for me—as well as providing a bit of protection. I'm not as young as I used to be. I was told I could bring it if I didn't carry it on me. If I put it with the baggage."

"I understand, sir. But naturally Israel is worried when a foreigner tries to import a deadly weapon into the country. I'm sure you will be allowed to keep your cane with you, but there are certain formalities to be attended to first. Permit papers to be signed, for example. Could you come this way, please?"

Mr. Azrael followed the guard to a small, windowless room on the first floor of the terminal building. The only furniture were three metal folding-chairs and a desk, behind which sat a steely-haired man reading several typewritten pages. He instantly set them face-down on the desk and rose with his arm outstretched as the two men entered.

"Mr. Azrael?"

"Yes, yes, my name is Vincent Azrael."

General Charon nodded to the guard. "Lock the door, would you, Nathan? Just so we won't be disturbed. Sit down, please."

Green locked the one door into the room and leaned against it as Charon and the old man sat. His features betrayed nothing of what he was thinking.

"Now, shall we get down to business?" Charon said. "Exactly what are you planning to do here, Mr. Thomas George Shelleen?"

CHAPTER NINETEEN

Wadi Hassad radioed the information to his colleagues in Lebanon using a mobile transmitter installed in his car. He knew the message would be intercepted by Israeli Intelligence and his position triangulated, so he had to keep moving or risk capture.

The Palestinian also knew there was no need for a reply. When his superiors received the news, they would be prepared. Hassad's job ended as soon as he completed the transmission.

The lime-green walls absorbed the light from two overhead fluorescent strips, giving the room a dingy appearance.

The old man said nothing, staring at Charon in puzzlement.

"The charade is over Mr. Shelleen. I suggest you tell us the whole story. We may be able to help you."

"Oh, really! Might I ask who you think I am?"

"Thomas Shelleen, born 1946. Occupation: actor-stuntman-producer. Married Annabelle Criar in 1966.

Divorced. One child: a daughter, died in December of last year," Charon recited tediously.

The old man chuckled, then broke into a wheezing cough. When he had regained control of himself, he said, "Forgive me. Until ten years ago I worked as a postal official—never got enough fresh air. Ruined my lungs. Then I was told I was too old and would have to leave."

"Very interesting—but patently false."

"Do you want to see my passport?"

"Which one?" Green asked sarcastically, speaking for the first time since they'd entered the room. "Basilia, Derna, Erinys, Murphy, Azrael? ... and there are obviously others. All but the correct one. What we can't understand is how the real Murphy figures in this. Mind telling us?"

"Gentlemen, you have me flabbergasted. Really you do. I have no idea whatsoever—"

"Come, come," Charon remonstrated, sitting forcefully back in his chair and looking disgusted. "We've been expecting you, Mr. Shelleen. Miss Meyer called us, you see, told us you might be on your way to one of the Middle Eastern states. Not having been briefed on Mr. Murphy, of course, she thought you *were* the James Murphy we, the British police, and almost every West European intelligence service have been seeking. But her description and a rendition of things you told her convinced us you were actually Thomas Shelleen. Naturally, you couldn't be expected to travel under that name. So, knowing you have a predilection for connotative names, our enquiries concerned airline manifests."

The old man began coughing again. "Could I have some water, please?"

Charon nodded to Green and the latter exited.

"The man who just left, Mr. Shelleen—he lost his wife to terrorists five years ago. They shot her in the head because she tried to stop them from harming another plane passenger. He understands how you feel. Would you rather speak to him—alone?"

"This must be a joke. Tell me. It's a joke, isn't it? You can't be *serious*."

"As I was saying, we checked manifests and came up with the peculiar name of Vincent Azrael."

"If I was a younger man I'd bust you in the chops!"

"The burlesque is over. You're an incredible actor, Mr. Shelleen, quite incredible, though picking such a name for yourself was an amateurish stunt. We would have screened passengers individually in any case, but you made it simple for us. You forgot that we Israelis are surrounded by Mohammedans and are, through expediency, familiar with their religion. Every schoolboy knows that Azrael is the Islamic Angel of Death."

"How *peculiar!*"

"All we have to do is take your fingerprints and send them to Washington. You served in the U.S. Marine Corps, so we should be able to make a match quite easily. And then once we wash out your hair, remove the tinted contacts, and wait for your sun-lotion tan to fade away, we can compare you to one of your publicity shots. Or fly out someone who knows you to make a positive ID. Any way you look at it, Mr. Shelleen, we have you cold."

Green entered with a glass of water which he handed to the old man. He glanced at Charon who shook his head.

Charon said, "Doubtlessly you are wondering what we plan to do with you. As far as the state of Israel is concerned, you have entered the country illegally and are therefore subject to immediate deportation to the United States. Since we have a fair inkling of your purpose in coming here and know you intend no harm toward Israel or its people, I'm sure it will be quite unnecessary to detain you for more than a day or two—or until such time as you can be remanded to the custody of a representative of your State Department. What happens to you then is not our concern, though I suspect you will be convicted of several passport violations and imprisoned."

"At least you'll be safe," Green said.

"Safe?"

"From the malevolent powers that are looking for you, Mr. Shelleen. There are more Sholokovs waiting for you out there, more Hani Rabats. No one could escape them forever. But you can trust us to keep your identity and presence here a secret. Nevertheless, you will be in some danger. Somehow the Russians learned about our list of five names and—"

"Five names?"

"We can go into that later. It's a long story and not yet finished. You haven't told us how the real James Murphy figures in this. Is he an accomplice? He must be. You'd better get word to him to come back into the real world before it's too late. He might not find a Susan Meyer to rescue him from the evil of his ways."

"Susan," the man whispered. Years vanished from his face, his sunken chest expanded, his shoulders squared, and he stared directly into Yigael Charon's eyes, startling the Shabak chief by their chameleonic change, their sudden alertness and cunning.

"Could I see her, please?"

And that was all he would say until she arrived on an El

Al flight at 2:23 the next morning—by which time his destiny had taken another strange path.

The PLO had specific contingency plans for just such an occasion. Admittedly, they were formulated on the expectation that one or more of the top leaders from the 40-member Central Council might fall into Israeli hands and need swift rescue; but they could be applied in reverse with (the Palestinians hoped) the same efficacy. It helped to know, too, that the Israelis were unable to resist a bargain in their favor, and the terrorists fully intended to make the bait as sweet as possible.

Not wanting to take the blame for any unexpected consequences of their plot, the chiefs of Yasser Arafat's Al Fatah passed on the information they had received from Wadi Hassad. The PFLP was more than glad to accept the unstated assignment, over-riding the objections of splinter groups like the Popular Democratic Front for the Liberation of Palestine, the Popular Front-General Command, a reconstituted Black September, and the Palestinian Special Branch—as well as grumblings from al-Saiqa and the Arab Liberation Front.

Special units based in Europe were called to duty and given the mission's code-word: Arachne.

Two pairs of killers had soon booked reservations on an SAS flight from Stockholm to Paris. In Milan, a pair of terrorists were on their way along the A8, heading out of the city and toward Malpensa Airport 29 miles northwest. While in London, six Israeli youths who had qualified for the International Young Scientists' Convention and now rode a special mini-bus, gawking and pleading with their driver and guard to let them out so they could meet somebody, for goshsakes, were being discreetly tailed by a pair of Arabs in a dark BMW. The Arabs spent most of their time as students at the University of London and were unlikely killers. The two AKM-S assault rifles resting on the floor of the passenger side, however, made their apparent innocence less convincing.

The Premier called an emergency meeting of his military staff and intelligence chiefs for 1:00 a.m. Middle East Time. It was a short-notice summons, but because bad news always travels fast, there were no absentees.

Getting straight to business—as was his manner—the Premier said, "We have a serious problem, gentlemen. At seven o'clock tonight in London, two Arab terrorists shot out the tires of a bus carrying our six representatives to a student scientists' convention. The young people had been touring the city. Their guard—a security officer from our embassy—was killed, as well as the English driver. The children have been taken hostage and are being held in St. Paul's Cathedral. I understand the bus had parked near there when the attack came."

"What are the British doing about it, Mr. Premier?" one of the generals asked angrily.

"They have sealed off the area and are trying to negotiate for the release of the children. They have also called in their Special Air Service Regiment, or a part thereof, to handle the possibility of making an armed rescue; though it seems the hostages are bottled up in a spiral staircase inside the dome and will be hard to reach. The SAS Regiment won't act until it receives directions from us—sharing the responsibility, you might say, or the blame—so I've asked that a man from GIR Unit 269 be sent to oversee any rescue attempt and offer his suggestions. Has that been done?"

Arcus Voight, head of the Special Flying Squad, replied, "It has, Mr. Premier. I sent one of our top men to London as soon as I received your orders. He was under loan to Shabak, but General Charon graciously agreed to release him."

"He has completed his assignment with us," Charon said simply.

"Ah. Well, just so you have a good man on the job. The British are aware that they carry the responsibility for freeing the hostages, but I don't want them claiming we gave them bad ideas."

He paused to wipe his glasses, then picked up a sheet of paper.

"Two hours ago an Alitalia 737 bound for Lisbon was struck by an explosive missile as it took off from Milan's Malpensa Airport. The plane crashed back to earth. Twenty-eight of the 105 passengers and crew died, according to my most recent information. Italian military authorities think an armor-piercing bazooka rocket did the damage."

"Anyone caught?"

"The police put up roadblocks as quickly as they could. The army is out. They're confident . . . but nothing yet."

The Premier studied the dejected faces around him, then proceeded. "Also tonight, a Scandinavian Airways flight from Stockholm to Paris underwent an attempted hijacking. It failed, fortunately. You've been following that incident, Arcus. Why don't you tell us what happened?"

Voight, a tall, balding man 55 years old, spoke with a clipped German accent. "The skyjackers were poorly prepared for their operation—as though it had been thrown together at the last minute. Only one gun was smuggled aboard—how, I do not yet know. The plane was nearing the German coast when the armed skyjacker walked forward to the cockpit, drawing his pistol. A stewardess noticed the weapon and threw the contents of a coffee decanter into the man's face, blinding him. His companions surrendered."

"What about them, Arcus?"

"Not much to tell. They were traveling on false passports—three Moroccans and a Tunisian. Morocco and Tunisia do not elicit as much interest from immigration authorities as, say, Syria or Libya. No positive ID on any of them, but I wouldn't be surprised if they are carrying around Beirut laundry-marks."

The room was silent for a moment as the group gauged the importance of these various terrorist acts in relation to the security of Israel.

"And the London killers. Who are they and what do they want?" Badon of Military Intelligence asked. "They must have stated their demands by now."

"As a matter of fact, they haven't," the Premier replied. "Instead, they told the British to contact us. We would know what they want."

"What!"

"At exactly midnight I received a call at the Red House from the Egyptian Foreign Minister who, as you know, has been in Jerusalem for the past week trying to convince us to evacuate all Jews from the West Bank. The point is, he phoned to say his government had just received a message from the Flop and could I see him immediately.

"I didn't have to. A few minutes later my Chief of Staff

called, conveying the contents of an intercepted radio transmission between Beirut and Cairo. Soon I was speaking to Yigael here. His men had tapped the Egyptian Minister's phone and heard something astounding, something that confirmed the earlier calls and indicated Cairo's innocence in this matter.

"Gentlemen, the three incidents tonight are meant as a warning of much wider disorders unless we do as we are told."

Shouts of anger rang out as the audacity of the challenge registered among the assembled military and intelligence chiefs.

"Wait!" The Premier held up his arms for attention. "The PFLP murderers ask for very little. They want only one man."

"Who is so important to them? Do they want you, Mr. Premier?" Badon demanded.

"An American. The man who rescued the passengers at Luqa, the man who exterminated the terrorists at Alabet, the man they refer to as James Murphy—since the traitor Leonard Talmai was caught before learning the man's true identity and giving it to them. The man whom we are presently holding at Nathanya."

"Why do they want him?" asked the commander of the Israeli Air Force.

"I think that should be obvious, Shalom. Revenge. The Palestinians were unable to kill him in Europe and they fear they will never have another chance now that he is within Israel's borders. It is a question of honor to them. His mere existence is a stain on their vaunted invincibility—not to mention his effect on their morale."

"More so than Mossad's specialists?"

"Yes—because he is just as much a fanatic as the Arabs. He can operate at any time in any place, having little fear for his own life and no worry about political repercussions should he be caught. He is the ultimate killing machine: intelligent, highly-motivated, imaginative, and unconstrained by government policy."

"You make the American sound like a psychopathic genius," Charon said with obvious distaste.

"But what are we going to do? If he is an American, giving him up will be a matter for Washington to decide. Can you imagine the American public's response if we were to unilaterally turn over one of their own to those butchers?"

"Do we have a choice, Shalom?" Charon asked. "What about the hostages?"

"We can mount a counter-terrorist offensive," Voight enthused. "Frighten them off!"

"Let us constrain ourselves, my friends. We need to approach this calmly," the Premier said.

"How much time do we have?"

"Until six this morning—less than five hours from now," he added, hoping to inspire some quick and worthwhile suggestions. "At that time we must start our man on his way to Benghazi. We've been allowed three hours to get him there. If he is late or not sent, the six children in London will die and more commercial planes will be shot out of the air. One can also assume that more planes will be hijacked."

"The Americans must be held responsible," Badon insisted.

"No."

"But Mr. Premier—"

"No. Not so. The Americans do not know we have Mr.

Shelleen. They have not yet been contacted as to his future disposal. Yigael's office was still arranging a request for positive identification when all these things happened. I told him to drop it and destroy any and all evidence connected with Shelleen's presence here. If the Americans know anything, they think we have Mr. Murphy. Even supposing they also monitored the radio transmission between Beirut and Cairo tonight, they will still believe we have James Murphy—because that is what the Arabs believe."

"Shelleen, Murphy . . . what does it matter? They are *both* Americans."

"True, Yigael. However, the terrorists seem inclined to the view that this affair should be kept strictly between them and us. I cannot think they fear bad publicity or the weight of world opinion, so I must suppose it again revolves around the nature of their egotism. To admit before the world that they must resort to child-kidnappings, skyjackings, and the mid-air destruction of civilian aircraft in order to blackmail a government into giving up one man who has operated in Europe without any protection except that with which he provides himself . . . well," he said, catching his breath, "that is not saying much for their expertise."

"They have plenty of expertise," Beitel growled. "The Palestinian groups wiped out many of our diplomats and agents during the early '70s. They did it expertly. Not always, but usually they escaped to kill another day. Why they missed Shelleen is a matter of bad luck, spotty communications, poor alliances with KGB men—"

"—and Shelleen's uncanny knack for disguises. Admit it. Shabak has followed his career for over two months. We've researched his background, and we know who we are dealing with. The American *created* his luck," Charon said.

The Premier sighed. "I wish we could discuss his disposal rather than his virtues, gentlemen. We do not—"

The Assistant Director of Mossad entered the Situations Room and handed a slip of paper to his superior, then quietly exited. Yitzhak Beitel read the message and handed it to the Premier, who had grown agitated at the interruption.

"What is it now?"

"More bad news." The Premier read aloud: "'Special charter DC-10, operated by Dallas Airtaxi Service and carrying 232 passengers and crew on a return flight from Barcelona to Dallas, was diverted at 00:45 and, based on reports by the co-pilot, is heading southwest for Libya.'"

"Think it's a coincidence?"

"No. . . . No, I don't."

The men resumed their prayerful attitude, conscious only that they should be saying something. But that would mean an acceptance of responsibility.

It was with relief then that they heard Yigael Charon say, "He has to go."

"What's that?"

"The American—Shelleen. We have a policy of never bowing to terrorist demands, but we must also face facts. No one need know we gave him up. We are not necessarily setting a precedent. And we can argue for guarantees for the hostages."

"If we traded him, what would we think of ourselves afterward?"

"I say we have no choice. He means nothing to us."

"He's a fellow human being," Voight argued.

"So are the Arabs."

"You know what I mean. He is on *our* side."

"He's a mad killer, rabid with revenge. No loss to anyone. Remember, Mr. Premier, that if word ever leaked that you chose the life of one American assassin over the lives of hundreds of innocent travelers—of six Israeli children!—you would be dragged through the streets by your own people!"

"Let's not get melodramatic, Shalom. I understand our dilemma—without your pomp and circumstance." He paused. "Perhaps we should take a vote."

"A vote is meaningless," Beitel countered. "Your vote can over-rule the majority, so counting hands is purposeless, Mr. Premier."

The Premier folded his arms across his narrow chest and leaned forward as if suffering from cramps. It was true: he did not want the responsibility. He hated his obsession with guilt, aware it proceeded from a certainty that, no matter what he did, someone would die.

"Very well," he said at last. "Very well. I will see the Egyptian Foreign Minister and ask that he put me in direct contact with a PLO representative—or whoever the hell is running this thing. Then I will make arrangements for the release of the hostages and transference of Mr. Shelleen to Libya. And may God help us all."

As soon as Susan Meyer landed, she was picked up by Charon and two bodyguards. The Shabak chief and his niece sat in the rear seat of his limousine during the drive, discussing the case. But it was only when Susan noticed she was not being taken home to Tel Aviv that Charon finally revealed their destination.

"Nathanya? Why, uncle?"

"Your Mr. Shelleen is staying there. I thought you might like to see him."

"At this hour? No . . . I couldn't face him. He must hate me for what I did. No, take me home."

"I'm afraid you have no choice, Susan." His eyes wandered across the coastal road, settling on the silvery surface of the Mediterranean and the black outlines of distant patrol boats. But all he could see was that it wasn't going to be easy. . . .

"Do you love him, Susan?"

"Why? What . . .?" Her eyes echoed her fears in the darkness.

"Certain . . . events have transpired, Susan," he began. . . .

He was asleep when she entered the room.

The furnishings were not as bad as she had expected. There were curtains to cover the bars on the windows, a vase of daffodils sat on the sill, a refrigerator occupied one corner and a television occupied another. The bed was large, with a cushion mattress and reading-lamp clipped to the mahogany headboard. A narrow door beside it evidently led to the lavatory.

All in all, this was a luxurious jail-cell for a condemned man.

The man lay on his side, fully-clothed, his legs scissor-like across the bed. His breathing was steady, rhythmic. She touched the flap of his ear with a finger, and he reacted by nodding and smacking his lips.

What a little boy! she thought. So vulnerable. Sleeping so soundly—probably the first time in weeks, knowing he is surrounded and protected by . . . friends? At least not enemies.

She didn't think she could do it.

She must.

She couldn't.

She had to.

She couldn't.

She nervously looked back at the door. It was closed—locked by now. Uncle Yiggie wanted to give her the pleasure (no, no, not the right word, not now, too late) of speaking with Tom Shelleen in private.

She couldn't.

She had to.

She couldn't.

She drew the gun from her purse. As an agent of the state security force, she had been issued the pistol when she boarded the El Al flight from Geneva. Just in case.

God must know. Must understand. I can't let them torture him, spoon out his eyes, crack—

She clenched her teeth. Don't think about it. She set the muzzle against his temple.

As she pulled the trigger, his eyelids blinked open.

He jerked her down onto the bed and clapped a hand over her mouth as she began screaming.

"Stupid woman! You'll wake the whole house!" he whispered in her ear, relaxing his hold.

"You weren't asleep?" she asked incredulously, speaking in gasps.

"How can I sleep? There seems to be a parade of tanks past my window every ten minutes."

She sat up. "I'm sorry."

"That you screamed? Every Mata Hari is allowed at least one good yell a day." He ran a hand through his hair. The white hadn't been completely washed out, but it did not hamper his youthful good looks. "Think nothing of it."

"If you're going to patronize me, I'll leave."

"Why are you so feisty? Oh. Four o'clock. No wonder. As I remember, you're usually asleep by this time."

"If you expect me to blush . . ." She bit her lip, turning away.

"Okay, what's the matter?"

"Dammit, why don't you hit me? Tell me what a lying tramp I am for betraying you? Why?"

"Would it matter? Look at me, Susan. Come on, look at me. Do you think I expected to get away with this bag of bones in one tidy bundle? You merely hastened what was bound to happen. Anyway, you must have had your reasons."

"You're a fool, Thomas Shelleen."

"And you are a bigger fool, Susan Meyer. That's the second time you tried to shoot me without first flicking off the safety. Don't you ever learn?"

"I . . ." Now was the time to tell him—now, before he was so sure he'd escaped the jaws of death.

"Yes?"

She related the story Charon had told her, coldly enunciating the terrorist atrocities, the blackmail, the Premier's decision, the Palestinians' response.

"You will first be flown to Cairo where a PLO representative will come aboard to verify your presence. Then your plane will be escorted to the Libyan border. In their eagerness to get you, the terrorists have agreed to make certain concessions guaranteeing the safety and release of the hostages. We don't want any tricks anymore than they do."

"That's good. My death will mean something."

"You will stand on the airfield between the hijacked jet

nd the plane you arrived in. If you are in full view of the
errorists, the passengers will be allowed to transfer to
our plane, and it will take off as soon as they are all
board."

"And the six children in London?"

"Will be released when the PLO man sees you in
Cairo."

"But my death won't stop terrorism."

"Israel will have carried out its part of a defined
agreement, securing the lives of hundreds of innocent
people. We do not expect your death to end the war,
merely end one battle in a draw."

She hesitated, and so he asked, "Is that all?"

"My . . . superior wishes to know if you have any . . .
final requests. You can be given cyanide tablets that
fit like caps over your teeth. One hard bite and . . .
and . . ."

"Stop it, Susan," and his hand gently framed the back
of her head, pulling her body against his where she
sobbed into the pillow.

"Forget it," he said, stroking her golden hair. It tickled
his arms, blown into feathery strands by a warm breeze
through the open windows, fine cobwebs that tangled in
his fingers. He wanted to know her very much, know who
she was, what she thought. It suddenly occurred to him
that they could have fallen in love and had children. But
the idea seemed ridiculous now. As always, nothing
mattered until it was too late to appreciate the things that
should—or might—have mattered in one's life. Passing
signposts in the dark: and you never knew whether they
were billboards or route indicators until they were too far
behind to make any difference.

"It's okay, it's all right," he crooned, and he knew they

were the same words Molly used when he became depressed by his ex-wife's death in a hunting accident near the Reindeer Lake cabin. Annabelle had won it as part of her property settlement; she'd always loved that cabin and he cleverly worked it into his suit for custody of Molly. So in the end they both got what they wanted most....

Annabelle had taken one of her husky boy-friends duck-hunting close to the cabin. The lummox didn't know a fart's worth about shotguns. He blasted a wooden decoy, Annabelle scolded him, and he playfully rebuked her by blowing off her face. Accidentally, of course. He hadn't understood that a double-barreled shotgun has an individual shell for each barrel and they can be fired separately or in tandem. The fool. . . .

Susan was sitting up, daubing at her eyes with a corner of the bed-spread. She kept her back to him.

"I'm sorry."

"Stop apologizing. You're like the British. Sorry this, sorry that. Always so polite. They sound like Mandarins on an ant farm."

She burst into convulsive laughter at this ridiculous image, visualizing the excruciatingly polite Chinese trying to make headway among the diminutive inhabitants without squashing them flat.

"Feel better?"

She nodded. How long did they have? Less than two hours. Less than . . .

"Make . . . love to me."

"Susan—"

"God," she laughed nervously, "I'm not even sure of your real name!"

"Flash Gordon."

She turned on the bed, facing him. He could see a smile on her face—contradicting the smudged mascara. "Make love to me, Flash. Or is it Mr. Gordon?"

"Some other time."

"There is no other time. For us." She looked as though she were about to cry again. "Kiss me."

"Can't. I'm due on the planet Mongo in five seconds."

"Then kiss me until then."

"My wife wouldn't approve. See this ring?"

But he did kiss her; and somehow the loneliness of these past six months seemed less dense. He even thought he sensed a light behind the lead shielding he'd molded around his heart: a dim, flickering light full of promise, of hope, of love.

Only it was moving away.

He roughly pushed her from the bed. "Get out!"

"What? I don't—"

"Get out! Leave a condemned man to his dying thoughts!"

Susan got to her feet, smoothing her dress, and stared down at him for a moment.

"I should have killed you on the train. I should—" She covered her mouth, horrified.

"Wait," he said as she reached the door. "I have something for you." He held up her purse which she had forgotten on the bed. "It's in here. Now go."

She rode back to Tel Aviv in Charon's car, answering her uncle's questions tersely. Not until she'd locked the door of her apartment behind her did she break down in a fit of tears. It wasn't like her. She'd been taught control. Total control.

And then she found the pocket watch he had slipped into her purse. She snapped open the case and found herself looking at a young girl with reddish-blonde hair, laughing emerald eyes, and a slightly quixotic smile—just like her father's. A man who was about to die a second time. A second . . .

Susan ran to the phone.

CHAPTER TWENTY

The Israelis used a Hercules C-130 military transport plane to ferry their prisoner to Benghazi. Landing in Cairo nearly two hours later than expected, the plane was inspected by three PLO representatives. Cocky and antagonistic, they were surprised by the scale of the four-engined plane and its auditorium-sized hold. It was made to look even larger by the presence of only sixteen people inside: four crewmen, a military policeman, two doctors, four nurses, three flight attendants to take over from those on the skyjacked charter, a government negotiator who spoke Arabic, and a tall, lanky man who sat silently on a bench near the front of the hold.

"Is that him?" the PLO man demanded, jabbing a stubby finger at the seated man.

The Israeli negotiator, Moshe Teirav, stiffly turned away, muttering—in Arabic and for the obvious benefit of the Palestinians—"Did you expect him to have horns and a third eye?" He despised the PLO and had no orders to be civil to any of its members—which made him a hard negotiator.

The Arab walked over to the man who, though seated, appeared quite tall. *"Qui etes-vous?"* he asked, for he spoke no English but had been informed that Murphy knew French.

"Un homme."

"Un American?"

"Oui."

"Comment s'appelez-vous?"

"James Murphy."

The Arab looked closely at the man, frequently referring to a description in his hand. He spoke briefly with his comrades, then turned and spat at the man's feet.

With that, the three Palestinians departed, promising they would contact their superiors; and that, with suitable guarantees of their freedom from arrest, the London kidnappers would be instructed to release their hostages. The Benghazi skyjackers would also be contacted and told the plane was on its way but would be two hours late.

"Too bad we're not carrying bombs instead of Murphy," the diplomat groused, watching the trio climb into a long, black limousine and be chauffeured away.

The MP shrugged. He had not been told much about Murphy—only that the man was voluntarily offering himself in exchange for the hostages, but that it must appear as though he were a prisoner of the Israelis. Why the PLO wanted him was not the MP's business, but it was clear the fellow meant something special to the terrorist organization.

As for Murphy, he retained his seat by the window. To those traveling with him he looked like a very sick man. Both doctors on the flight offered him sedatives, believing he suffered from air-sickness; but Moshe Teirav pulled them aside, asking how *they* would feel if they were about to be delivered unto the enemy. Not too cheerful, surely. Leave the poor man in peace. He doesn't have much time.

Because the Libyans believed they had something to hide among their sand dunes, Roman ruins, and oil derricks, the C-130 paralleled the coastline on the trip to Benghazi. But after landing, the crew was told the plane would be refueled, new flying instructions issued, and the transport must proceed to Sabhah, a desert city nearly 500 miles to the southwest and over 300 miles inland. The hijacked jet was waiting there.

Though the Israelis felt proud that the Libyans feared a sea-mounted rescue of the hostages, they were uneasy about being buried so deep within Libya's borders—where anything could happen. They had no choice but to go on, however, trap or no trap.

As the huge transport taxied for take-off, new orders came from the Control Tower: Do not attempt to leave. The charter flight is on the diagonal runway. Taxi to a position approximately 500 yards from the end of this runway. The transfer will be made there as agreed. Two impartial Libyan officials will certify that nothing goes wrong due to a misunderstanding.

Teirav snickered. *Impartial* Libyans! He thought they were extinct. And the Palestinians—playing games as usual, trying to upset the Israelis, knock them off balance.

The Lockheed Tristar shimmered in the afternoon heat, ghostly behind the furnace drafts rising off the tarmac. As the C-130 drew nearer, Murphy unbuckled his seatbelt and walked to the toilet.

The Cabinet Committee for Security and Foreign Affairs once again assembled in the Red House, the Premier's office at the Israeli Army's GHQ in Tel Aviv.

"The plane has landed safely at Benghazi," the Premier said, cradling the phone.

"How soon will we know the results?" Badon asked.

"Our surveillance ship will know the instant the plane lifts off. The crew was given a two-word code hinging on success or failure, and it won't matter who monitors the transmission. The code word will then be relayed to us here."

"What if it is neither success nor failure?"

"Explain yourself."

"Suppose, for instance, the bastards hand over only half of the hostages."

"Then they can trust us to make heavy reprisal raids on every *fedayeen* camp within range of our bombers."

"Poor boy," Charon muttered. But no one heard him. Politics is an exacting game. You either play all-out to win or you're a born loser; and you certainly don't allow one man to mean more than the joy of winning. So even if someone had heard Charon's remark, it would have meant nothing to them.

The man stepped out of the huge rear bay of the C-130, squinting against the fearsome brightness of the afternoon sun. In spite of the heat he wore a bulky navy-blue topcoat. Sweat dripped from his loose-hanging arms, blinded his stinging eyes, stained his crotch. Yet he had been adamant about wearing the coat, and everyone assumed it was to hide his shivering.

Teirav came up behind him, laying a hand on his shoulder. "I can walk you half the way there. They'll allow it, Murphy."

"No," the man answered in Hebrew. "I can make it on my own."

"How do you feel?"

"Frightened. . . . How fast does it work?"

"Seconds. Bite down, grind your teeth, swallow. Those bastards won't know what happened to you. You'll be beyond them."

"And my body?"

Teirav stared at his polished shoes. A large, black ant was crawling up the sole. What could he say? Knowing the Arabs, pieces of Murphy's corpse would be selling tomorrow as souvenirs in Benghazi's Fondouk.

"We will do our best to recover it. They want you dead, but they have no use for your body," the negotiator lied.

"I would like to be buried beside my wife, if possible."

"I will do all I can, Murphy. Ah. Here come the Libyans."

The two men were in full dress-uniform, bars and medals littering their chests. Beneath the peaked caps two stony faces stared grimly, first at Murphy, then at Teirav, then back to Murphy.

"Which of you is James Murphy?" one of them asked in Arabic.

"He is," Teirav said. "But he does not know Arabic. Could you speak in English or French or"—the negotiator smiled icily—"Hebrew?"

"Very well. English. I am Lieutenant Kaddoumi. This is Lieutenant Tachumet. We are here to verify that both sides have agreed upon the same rules for transfer of the prisoners. Shall I state them for your benefit?"

"Please."

Kaddoumi rocked back on his heels as he had seen British officers do when they wished to be imperious, and said, "Murphy will walk midway between the two planes. As you can see, we have set a barrel to mark the spot where he must stop. He must stay there while the passengers and crew of the American plane transfer to your craft. If he does not, the Palestinians will fire indiscriminately at the passengers—and I assure you they are well-armed.

"If Murphy stays beside the barrel until all passengers are aboard your plane, you will be permitted to leave. In fact, it is my understanding that you *must* leave."

"Yes," Teirav agreed. "Our government does not believe it would be in the best interests of the hostages to witness the death of their rescuer."

Murphy swayed alarmingly, and Teirav was forced to brace him with an arm around his shoulders. "What will happen to the American jet?"

It was Kaddoumi who now smiled. "I am told it will become part of Palestine's new air force. You need not trouble yourself about that."

"I'm not."

"Then that is all? You understand the conditions for the release of the passengers and crew? They are as you and the Palestinians agreed? Is it not so?"

"Yes, yes, we understand. Let's get on with it. Are you all right, Murphy?"

"What's wrong with him?" Kaddoumi asked suspiciously. "Has he been drugged?"

"He's no more anxious to be a martyr than you would be."

Kaddoumi's lips twisted as if he were about to speak. But he thought better of it and merely gestured Murphy toward the distant black barrel, isolated on the smoking strip of tarmac.

"The American Ambassador is on the line, sir."

The Premier nodded to his aide and picked up the phone apprehensively. Those Security Council members who still remained with him, waiting for final word on the hostages, were tight-lipped, but he knew what they were thinking: somehow the Americans had found out what was going on.

"Yes, Mr. Ambassador? Yes, this is he. . . . What? Are you certain? . . . When was this? . . . Yes, I understand. In fact, you couldn't reach him because he is sitting here beside me. . . . No, no, that is quite all right. The matter has been brought to my attention and I have asked that I be kept posted on any new developments. . . . What? . . . Well, I believe we have the same interest in this man as you do. He is an irritating element in current negotiations with the Arab states. . . . Yes, I think we must go on what we have, and those are . . . Geneva? . . . Of course I will tell him. Thank you very much, Mr. Ambassador. Can my family expect you and Hilary for supper next week? Tuesday? . . . That would be fine. Shalom."

The Premier took out a large blue-and-white handkerchief and patted his balding head.

"Well?" Mossad's Beitel asked.

"The ambassador was trying to reach you. Something to do with the Americans we were looking for."

"Yes?"

"Our Mr. Murphy was traced as far as Geneva."

"You mean Shelleen."

"No—Murphy. There's more. Three days ago the

353

American embassy in Kinshasa received the personal effects of a Thomas George Shelleen. He'd been killed by a rogue lion in the interior a week before."

"What!"

"Evidently it *was* Shelleen. Since a body doesn't preserve very well so near the Equator, it was buried in the nearest village. Probably half-eaten already."

"Then Murphy must be . . ."

"Murphy. Did you have any inkling of this, Yigael?"

Charon opened his eyes, only partially aware he was being addressed. "What? Yes, what?"

"A hard night, Yigael? You seem to find this meeting exceedingly routine. I was asking whether you had reason to believe Murphy was not Shelleen or . . . I mean, Shelleen was not Murphy. That is . . . quite confusing, wouldn't you say?"

Charon *had* just passed through a miserable night. He hadn't even had time to phone Leah and tell her he would not be home. That duty fell to his private secretary—which doubtlessly put unnecessary thoughts in Leah's head.

"The man we first knew as Murphy is actually Thomas Shelleen, Mr. Premier."

"But you never did get his fingerprints from the Americans."

"They were not needed. One of my operatives collected film clips of Shelleen. There is no disputing the man's identity. If a body was found in Zaire then it belongs to Murphy."

"Are you sure, though? Can you be absolutely sure?"

"Absolutely? Enough to stake my reputation on it," Charon said. "We have to assume, of course, that Murphy and Shelleen knew each other. We know they were both living in San Francisco during the first half of 1972, and that Mrs. Shelleen was attending classes at the same college where Murphy taught. We also have sufficient reason to believe that when Murphy arrived in London last November he met Shelleen who was there doing promotional work for a new film.

"By a sad coincidence, Shelleen lost his daughter to a terrorist atrocity the following December—even as Murphy's wife died when a bomb exploded on a plane she was taking back to San Francisco the previous April. The two men must have commiserated with each other, and Shelleen convinced his friend they should do something about getting back at the Palestinian killers.

"Since Shelleen needed a fool-proof cover but could not be two places at once, he traded identities with Murphy. Murphy was instructed as to what would be needed and went off to Africa in March to scout shooting-locations for a motion picture, using a doctored passport in Shelleen's name. Shelleen had already left his co-producer in mid-February, telling him he was on his way. Obviously he didn't go to Africa but spent his time in Europe, seeking out contacts who could—for a price—furnish him with weapons and false documents, and mailing postcards Murphy had written to his daughter beforehand. In other words, the two men were covering for each other, though neither could have guessed that we would finally pick out their names by concentrating on a particular motivation for the Luqa-Alabet affairs.

"So in March we have both men out of contact but in circulation. Then April arrives and the skyjacking over Malta. Shelleen is there like a shot. He has spent the previous month preparing for just such an opportunity. With his large resources he can buy the materials necessary for his planned operation. And he is a consummate actor, a talent much needed in this line of work. With a combination of luck, daring, and a natural aptitude for killing fostered by his burning desire for revenge, he succeeds. . . . You know the rest."

"And Murphy?" the Premier asked.

"He was told to keep out of the way and file delaying reports to Shelleen's co-producer until such time as he heard of Shelleen's capture or death—or he was contacted. Unfortunately, he appears to have run aground on his own peculiar destiny."

The Premier glanced at his watch. "Well, gentlemen . . . soon we should be hearing the results." He immediately knew the words sounded false, trite, and in bad taste. More was at stake than the final score of a tiring game. Much more.

No one looked at the celebratory bottles of champagne on the side-table.

The C-130 slowly lifted off the runway with its heavy burden, then swung northwest, its four prop-jets biting at the air in a mad effort to put the Libyan coastline far behind as fast as possible.

After twenty miles the escort of four MiG-21s dropped away, obviously perplexed. They had intended shadowing the transport to the latitude of the Egyptian border; now that the plane showed its determination to fly indefinitely in the wrong direction, however, they saw no reason to indulge its aberration.

When informed the MiGs were leaving, the crowded passengers inside the Hercules transport gave a thunderous cheer, at last releasing their pent-up emotions. A carnival atmosphere prevailed, women clutching strange men and dancing, men pounding each other on the back and exchanging business cards, children racing around the enormous hold—until a crewman told everyone to please sit down "unless you want this bird to take a swim."

Only the fifteen original passengers now aboard the plane realized the exact nature of what they had left behind. And their smiles were half-hearted.

The man stood with his back to the oil barrel, his eyes glued to the open door of the DC-10 and the metal ramp that led up to it. Several times he thought he saw movement inside, but he was given no indication that he should approach.

They're making me wait on purpose. They want me to collapse from the heat before they come near. They're afraid of me. And for good reason.

The plane he arrived in had taken off hours ago. It seemed like hours, but he couldn't say for sure. The Israelis told him not to wear a wrist-watch, so he had no way of knowing what time it was. But the sun had moved, he knew that much. His shadow grew steadily longer across the tarmac.

At least the passengers from the charter were safe and on their way home. That meant everything. And presumably the kids in London had been released. His life was going to have some meaning now, no matter what else might happen. He wasn't going to die as he had feared—sick and useless, old before his time, a zombie with no place else to go.

The heat oppressed him. The heavy coat absorbed it, contained it, threatened to liquefy him.

I have to move, he thought. If I don't move now it will

be too late. I won't be able to move. And then the pain will start again, the memories of what life used to be like and what it has become. No. I must move.

He took a step and felt the ache of weary muscles, heard the creak of joints almost soldered tight by the merciless sun.

How long until the sun goes down? Three—four hours? Three—four minutes?

He suddenly found himself walking towards the DC-10, his legs unsteady but recognizing their duty.

When he was 100 yards from the plane, two figures appeared at the top of the ramp. Both were holding automatic rifles—evidently furnished by the Libyans since the Palestinians couldn't possibly have smuggled them aboard, even in Barcelona. The skyjackers seemed genuinely surprised to see him, though he knew they must have been watching him all this time.

"Stop!" one of them called. "Take off the coat!"

The man shrugged it from his shoulders, letting it drop to the ground. The coat was much too confining for his barrel-shaped chest; and even if the terrorists only wanted to see the pattern of their bullets on his white shirt, he was glad to be rid of it.

"Come on!" they shouted. They were laughing now, and two more terrorists had joined them. They waved and called and laughed and acted quite happy to be having Murphy as a guest.

He was now within 50 yards of the DC-10, staggering but still moving, painfully closing the distance.

The field had cleared. The Libyans who were supposed to escort him had disappeared long ago; the flat terminal buildings had apparently melted into the ground; no other planes were arriving or leaving. He heard only the slap of his feet on the sweating tarmac. And a bird somewhere? He couldn't tell. A phone began ringing in his left ear but there was no one home. No one to answer it.

Forty yards and he stumbled to the right, falling on one knee and shearing off a layer of skin as the light cotton trousers tore open.

The terrorists were silent now, watching him like four hungry hawks watch a young rabbit which has lost its way back to the warren.

No, not yet, he thought, picking himself up. His chest felt like a mighty anchor embedded in mud. He could struggle with it until he was blue in the face, but it moved only when it was ready.

His eyes were again stinging and he wiped them with his sleeve—only to stumble again as the weight of his arm seemed to pull him to the right, closer to the wing's shadow.

"Here! Here!" One of the terrorists had shouldered his rifle.

The man looked apologetically in their direction and started once more towards the glowing ramp; but a fresh wave of nausea erupted inside him, dizziness blocked his coordination, and he tumbled onto his back, his legs twitching like those of an overturned tortoise.

Not yet, God, not yet!

The Arabs were laughing again as he pushed himself to his knees and started crawling, his injured knee leaving a trail of blood that dried instantly. One terrorist took several steps down the ramp so he could keep an eye on the man.

"This way! You go the wrong way!" they screamed in delight. "Come back, Terrible One!"

He was in the shadow at last—the cool, dark shadow where wing joined fuselage, where truth and reality become as one, and death . . .

Now. I cannot go any further. I do not want to die. I have reached the end-all and the be-all. I am the end.

His tired arms gave way and he slipped forward, scraping skin from his forehead, nose, and chin as he sank on his belly.

Over, over, damn you! Look at them! The killers! You have your revenge in hand!

The man rolled over, raising his head with great effort and dropping both hands on his chest in a prayerful attitude.

The four terrorists had descended from the plane. They approached him with guns ready, remembering now Murphy's fearsome reputation as a death merchant. He might be acting, after all, and their leaders had not taken such pains with this operation to have it fail when so close to success.

Two of the Palestinians hung back as their comrades reached the stricken man, drawing knives.

He smiled up at them, at the bright fanatical eyes, the angry malice curling their young lips.

"*L'chayim*," he said. And with a forefinger pressed the indented button riding on his sternum beneath the shirt.

Thirty pounds of metal-encased plastic explosives hidden underneath his shirt, wrapped in coils around his body, instantaneously shredded the man's body and the two nearest Arabs. Shrapnel tore into the aluminum-alloy wing and belly tanks of the plane, and hundreds of gallons of aviation fuel gushed forth, igniting.

The two other terrorists had been blown backward by the initial explosion. One was already dying from a piece of metal that had ripped open his throat. His partner scrambled to his feet and attempted to escape.

It was useless. The fuel spread too quickly, catching him in its flames, setting his clothes afire, starving his lungs of oxygen. He tried to scream; but he only crackled, his body twisting horribly, flailing, blackening, bursting in pink pustules like a garden of roses, his flesh carbonizing, back arching as fire licked at bare vertebrae, then toppling forward and remaining motionless, shrinking and steaming as super-heated water hissed out of it.

By the time the airport's rescue-units arrived, nothing existed worth saving. They wisely let the fire burn itself out—which made cleaning up afterward that much easier.

And then, as it always does, everything went on as usual.

CHAPTER TWENTY-ONE

The Israeli Cabinet Committee for Security and Foreign Affairs was pleased with its success. The hostages in London and Benghazi had been released, only one casualty—the expected one—darkened the record, and this whole business of the mysterious assassin who provoked Middle East tensions could be forgotten. There were plenty of other disagreements between Arab and Jew to keep the cauldron bubbling.

The Americans, strangely enough, learned about "Murphy's" death through the KGB. One of their double agents happened to mention the incident during a debriefing session with his CIA control.

Two months earlier the KGB Directorate for Western Europe suddenly issued instructions that the search for James Murphy was to be dropped. The double-agent, sent to Tripoli to organize a penetration of the Egyptian Executive Branch by Libyan Intelligence, mentioned the matter to his Arab liaison officer and asked if the Palestinians had finally located their man.

Yes, he was told. Sent by the Israelis, Murphy died in

Benghazi a week previous, though not before taking several of the PFLP's top men with him. Nevertheless, he was finished—as were the other four men whom the Israelis suspected of being Federico Basilia and Samuel Erinys: Dalton (shot in Monte Carlo by the KGB), Shelleen (dead in Africa—killed by a lion, if an esteemed comrade in the House of Representatives was to be believed), the Frenchman Usil (strangled in a West German sanitarium by a member of the Baader-Meinhof gang), and Andersson (shot by a PFLP hit-team in Innsbruck where he had taken up his old engineering profession).

Of course, the double-agent told his control, the Israelis may have concocted the list merely to throw everyone off the scent of their Mossad agents, but that was unlikely. The CIA agreed. All evidence pointed to Murphy as being Basilia.

Rather than embarrass their ally, the Americans simply closed the book on the Basilia case. The President was satisfied that Israel did what it had to do; and he was especially pleased to learn that Murphy's young daughter in London had found an anonymous benefactor who placed in trusteeship exactly $500,000 for her maintenance, education, and stake in the future. The Israelis were exceptionally generous—but then they had cause to be. Murphy not only pried loose hundreds of hostages but also helped eliminate some of Israel's most implacable enemies.

Israeli self-congratulations faded quickly as the job of securing the country against internal and external threats again preoccupied the intelligence forces, and the man who buried himself deepest in his work was General Yigael Charon.

Once upon a time Charon had envisioned a beautiful mating of Nathan Green and Susan Meyer which would produce superlative offspring. Nathan, commando hero, and Susan, Special Intelligence agent. Of course, she must quit the service and . . .

At least she agreed to see Nathan one last time. He wanted to apologize for something, he told Charon. Beautiful girl, Charon commented. Green said nothing, but there was a glimmer in his eyes which Charon had not seen there before. Charming, he said.

But he knew it would never work out. Besides being a crude effort at selective breeding, the plan was based on the assumption Nathan and Susan would fall in love; but in fact they hated each other. He felt like a foolish old man for ever considering the idea; yet, because he was Susan's closest living relative (except for Leah) and therefore could be expected to feel responsible for her future, he had, like a parent, wanted her to marry someone equal to her in intelligence and ambition. Love, however, rarely thought that necessary to happiness.

Anyway, Susan *was* quitting the service—and emigrating. She said she'd had enough dirt on her hands, that they would never wash clean.

"You sound like Lady Macbeth," he had replied.

"Perhaps, uncle. I know I *feel* like her. I guess I just wasn't cut out for all this cloak-and-dagger stuff. And I want a life of my own, something more than what the Office allows me."

At first he argued. But after going home and having Leah give him a good verbal thrashing for being so damned self-centered, he threw his influence behind Susan's efforts to escape from her job and leave Israel for parts unknown.

Charons even ordered two sets of forged documents for her protection, a going-away present....

RELEASE REPORT—HADDASAH HOSPITAL, JERUSALEM
 Patient: Zacalny, Emil Klaus
 Date of birth: August 29, 1940; Vienna, Austria
 Nationality: Israeli
 Admission date: April 5th last
 Diagnosis: Metastatic carcinoma—orig. pylorus
 Prognosis: Terminal
 Attending physician: Alexander Coteman

Emil Zacalny admitted himself to this hospital last April, complaining of rectal bleeding and tenderness. A diagnosis was soon arrived at, and cobalt radiation treatments began, the disease having proved surgically inoperable. Chemotherapy began in May but with little hope of cure. The disease was only partially arrested. Upon being apprised of our inability to do more than ease his pain, he requested that he be allowed to stay at the hospital until such time as his illness proved fatal. This wish was granted, Mr. Zacalny having donated his body to medical research.

On June 6th last I received an early morning call from Mr. Zacalny. He requested that he be released for two days, after which he would return to the hospital. I assured him he was free to leave at any time.

Since then neither I nor the hospital staff have heard from this patient, and I believe it inconceivable that he could have survived his illness so long. Still, there have been no reports of his death from the Bureau of Registration. I must therefore conclude that, in the absence of a medical miracle, Mr. Zacalny has either been lost or committed suicide in some desolated area, or he has traveled to another country and died there.

I think it only proper that the police be made aware of Mr. Zacalny's disappearance, for his own sake as well as the hospital's.

The police were amused by the phrase "lost or committed suicide in some desolated area." It indicated a naivete common to the laity: i.e., those who were unconnected with police work.

Nonetheless, they made enquiries of the few people who had known Zacalny, discovering he had no family (his wife having died childless several years before) and that everyone thought he was still at Haddasah Hospital.

A routine check was made with Immigration authorities. According to their records, Emil Zacalny had not left Israel.

The handful of people who might have helped the police in their search never came forward. Being or having recently been in the employ of Israel's security services, they were bound by an oath of secrecy.

The body of Emil Zacalny was never found; and not encouraged in their search, the police filed the matter away as one of those unsolved mysteries which might— given time—solve itself.

"I'm sorry," he said.
"What for?"
"For everything that happened, for not always being

honest with you. But ... it's part of my nature to conceal."

"Conceal what?"

"Must you always be so argumentative?"

"I don't want to argue. I want to know what we're going to do next."

"I don't know."

There was a long pause. Then she said, "You once told me I shouldn't apologize so much. You said—"

"I remember, Susan."

"Sarah. Get the name right, darling. I'll be living with it for some time. Do you like it?"

"As much as any."

"You don't like it. What's wrong with it?"

"*Nothing's* wrong with it. It's a pretty name."

"Sarah Serein. Why Serein? Why did you pick that name?"

"Can't you—"

"What does it *mean?*"

"Serein is a fine rain from a cloudless sky. It seemed to fit my mood at the time."

"You know, you can be very poetic when you want to be."

"It's not pretentiousness, if that's what you're implying."

"I implied no such thing!" she protested. "God, I wonder how we're ever going to learn to live together."

"We've done all right for the last four months."

"Two months. You were off ... working the first two. Uncle finally told me."

"I stand corrected. I did penance for not expiring."

"Stop being so formal, Mr. Serein."

"I humbly apologize, Mrs. Serein."

They were quiet while the stewardess brought their supper trays, then filled their coffee cups.

"How long until we land?"

"About two and a half hours."

"Do you think we'll like New Zealand?"

He smiled grimly. "I'm sure. As long as it likes us."

"I love you."

"Whuu . . . ?" He was startled, and looked around to see if anyone had heard her, for she certainly hadn't delivered her words *sotto voce*.

"It's true. When I first met you I felt an empathy. No pity, no sympathy really. Just love."

"You didn't even know me."

"Well, now's the time for the three of us to get acquainted."

He stared at her. She always liked that because it gave her a chance to stare back into those humorous green eyes—like two Caribbean pools reflecting the changing sky.

"What?"

"I'm pregnant, Tom."